D1266863

THE GALACTIC GOURMET

BOOKS BY JAMES WHITE

The Secret Visitor (1957)
Second Ending (1962)
Deadly Litter (1964)
Escape Orbit (1965)
The Watch Below (1966)
All Judgement Fled (1968)
The Aliens among Us (1969)
Tomorrow is Too Far (1971)
Dark Inferno (1972)
The Dream Millennium (1974)
Monsters and Medics (1977)
Underkill (1979)
Future Past (1982)
The Silent Stars Go By (1991)

THE SECTOR GENERAL SERIES

Hospital Station (1962)
Star Surgeon (1963)
Major Operation (1971)
Ambulance Ship (1979)
Sector General (1983)
Star Healer (1985)
Code Blue—Emergency (1987)
The Genocidal Healer (1992)
The Galactic Gourmet (Tor, 1996)
Final Diagnosis (forthcoming from Tor, 1997)

THE GALACTIC GOURMET

A SECTOR GENERAL NOVEL

JAMES WHITE

TOR®

A TOM DOHERTY ASSOCIATES BOOK
NEW YORK

THE GALACTIC GOURMET

Copyright © 1996 by James White

This book is printed on acid-free paper.

A Tor Book
Published by Tom Doherty Associates, Inc.
175 Fifth Avenue
New York, N.Y. 10010

Edited by Teresa Nielsen Hayden

Tor Books on the World Wide Web:
http://www.tor.com

Tor® is a registered trademark of Tom Doherty Associates, Inc.

Design by Nancy Resnick

Library of Congress Cataloging-in-Publication Data

White, James.
        The galactic gourmet / by James White.
            p.   cm.
        "A Tom Doherty Associates book."
        ISBN 0-312-86167-2
        I. Title.
    PR6073.H494G35   1996
    823'.914—dc20   96-1406
                                        CIP

First Edition: August 1996

Printed in the United States of America

0   9   8   7   6   5   4   3   2   1

FOR PETER
MY ONCE AND FUTURE SON

THE GALACTIC GOURMET

CHAPTER 1

Gurronsevas had long been accustomed to being accorded the
outward forms of respect by persons nominally his superior,
and usually it was because of his enormous physical strength and
body mass, rather than his less obvious attributes of high intelligence and unrivalled professional experience. Being invited to view
the final approach from the courier vessel's tiny control deck was
a courtesy rarely extended to a ship's passenger even when, as in
his own case, he was the only one. But he wished heartily that the
Captain had shown less politeness and more consideration by allowing him to complete the voyage in *Tennochlan*'s uncluttered and
much roomier cargo hold.

He watched in polite silence and mounting awe, his physical
discomfort forgotten, as the gigantic, complex structure that was
Sector Twelve General Hospital grew larger until the forward view-
screen was entirely filled by the breathtaking sight of dazzling, regimented lines of approach beacons, dock floodlighting, and the external ports and ward-viewing galleries that were ablaze with every
color and intensity of light that the occupants considered normal.

Beside him Captain Mallan showed its teeth briefly and made
the untranslatable, barking sound which among Earth-humans sig-

nified humor. It said, "Enjoy the view while you can. The people who work here rarely get the chance to see the outside of their world."

The other officers on the flight deck maintained the silence of subordinates and, there being nothing of importance that he wished to say, Gurronsevas joined them.

Suddenly the image disappeared to be replaced by a picture of a pale-green Illensan chlorine-breather whose outlines were partially concealed by the yellow fog inside its protective envelope. It was seated at a communications console, and the flat, translated voice still retained some of the hissing and moaning quality of the original word-sounds as it spoke.

"Reception," it said quickly. "Identify yourselves, please. State whether patient, visitor, or staff, and give species. If there is an emergency condition please give patient clinical details first, then the physiological classifications of the others so we can arrange suitable accommodation, life-support, and proper type and periodicity of meals."

"Meals," said the Captain, looking at Gurronsevas and showing its teeth again. It pressed the transmit stud and said briskly, "No medical emergency on board. I am Major Mallan, commanding Monitor Corps scoutship *Tennochlan,* courier flight from Retlin on Nidia. Crew of four, all Earth-human DBDG classification plus one passenger, Gurronsevas, a Tralthan FGLI joining the hospital staff. All are warm-blooded oxygen-breathers and this one, myself, would certainly appreciate a change from ship rations . . ."

"Wait," said Reception, who plainly was not disposed to waste time discussing the subject of Earth-human food, the ingestion of which would have been instantly lethal to an Illensan. The image of the hospital structure returned to the screen, looking closer and even more impressive, but only for a moment.

"Please follow the red-yellow-red beacons to the vacant Class Three docking cradle adjoining Lock Twenty-three," it went on briskly. "Monitor Corps officers will report to Colonel Skempton. Gurronsevas will be met by Lieutenant Timmins on arrival."

Was this another courtesy, Gurronsevas wondered, from a

being who might or might not consider itself his superior? Somehow he doubted it. The being in Reception had not been impressed by his name, yet they must have heard of him even amidst the poisonous yellow fog of chlorine-breathing Illensa. But there had been no mention of the famous or the renowned or the great Gurronsevas, whose name and unique ability was admired and debated by the cultured members of every warm-blooded, oxygen-breathing species in the Federation, and whose unique contribution to and presence on any one of their home worlds would have been a matter for planetary pride. There had merely been the brief statement that Gurronsevas would be met.

A lesser being than himself might have felt uncertain, or even insulted.

The entity Timmins turned out to be an Earth-human DBDG whose dark-green uniform coveralls, although clean and well-pressed, were so well-worn that the insignia of rank were all but invisible. Its head fur was the color of dull copper, it showed its teeth readily in the non-aggressive grimace its species called a smile, and its manner was brisk and moderately respectful.

"Welcome on board, sir," it said when the introductions had been performed. "Technically, Sector General is too small to be a planet and too large to be a star-going vessel, but a ship is how the purists like to refer to it when we are not calling it something much more derogatory. As soon as convenient I had planned to show you to your quarters and explain the equipment and functioning. As Head of Maintenance your environmental control systems are a part of my responsibility, but Major O'Mara would like to see you in his office sooner than that. Allowing for traffic density in the intervening corridors, and a delay while changing to lightweight protective envelopes for the short-cut through the level of the chlorine-breathing PVSJs, it should take about twenty minutes. On the way you can have the usual but usually inadequate briefing given to a new arrival.

"With your permission, sir," he added, "I'll lead the way and talk as we walk."

As Gurronsevas followed Timmins out of the lock antechamber and along the boarding tube and into the hospital proper, the Lieutenant apologized in advance in case he was imparting information already known to him, and explained that Sector General was the largest, most technologically advanced and professionally respected multi-environment hospital ever to come into being. Many planetary cultures had contributed to its building, fabricating sections and transporting them over a period of nearly two decades to the assembly area in Galactic Sector Twelve. It was supplied and maintained by the Monitor Corps, the Federation's executive and law-enforcement arm, but it was not and never would be a military establishment. In its three hundred and eighty-four levels could be reproduced the environments of all of the life-forms known to the Galactic Federation, a physiological spectrum ranging from the ultra-frigid methane life-forms through the more normal oxygen- and chlorine-breathing types to the more exotic beings who lived by the direct conversion of hard radiation.

Gurronsevas missed a few of the Lieutenant's words because he was being forced to concentrate a large proportion of his attention on avoiding injury or embarrassment by colliding with or walking on entities larger or smaller than himself. He was travelling inside a combination white-walled, three-dimensional maze, and a noisy and overcrowded extra-terrestrial menagerie, and soon he would be expected to find his own way through it.

Two crab-like Melfan ELNTs and an Illensan PVSJ chittered and hissed their displeasure at him as he stopped awkwardly in the middle of an intersection to let them pass. In so doing he jostled a tiny, red-furred Nidian who barked a reproof at him. But the simple translator that he had been given on *Tennochlan* was programmed only for Earth-human/Tralthan speech, so that he did not know what exactly anyone within earshot was whistling, cheeping, growling or moaning at him.

". . . Theoretically the staff member possessing the greater medical seniority has right of way," Timmins was saying, "and you will soon learn to identify the different ranks from the color markings on the arm-bands that everyone wears. As yet you have no arm-band, so your rank is uncertain . . . Quickly, please, move flat against the wall!"

A great hissing and clanking juggernaut that was nearly half the width of the corridor was bearing down on them. It was the mobile protective armor used by SNLU medics, who normally breathed superheated steam, and whose pressure and gravity requirements were many times greater than that of the—to them, lethal—environment of the oxygen-breathing levels. In a situation like this, Timmins said with a brief show of teeth, it was better to ignore differences in rank, allow the instinct for self-preservation to take over, and get out of the way fast.

"You are adapting to the situation here very well, sir," the Lieutenant went on. "I have known first-time visitors to the hospital who went into a panic reaction, they ran and hid themselves or froze into fear paralysis, when confronted with so many different life-forms in such a short space of time. I think you will do well."

"Thank you," said Gurronsevas. Normally he would not have volunteered personal information to another person on first acquaintance, but the Earth-human and its compliment had pleased him. He went on, "But the experience is not entirely strange to me, Lieutenant. It is similar to the situation during a multi-species convention, although there the delegates were not usually so well-mannered."

"Really?" said Timmins, and laughed. "But if I were you I would reserve judgment on their manners, at least until after you are issued with your multi-channel translator. You don't know what some of them have been calling you. We're within a few minutes of the Psychology Department now."

On this level, Gurronsevas noted, the corridors were much less crowded but, strangely, their progress was less rapid. For some reason the Earth-human was slowing his previously fast walking pace.

"Before you go in," said Timmins suddenly, in the manner of

one who has come to a decision, "it might be a good idea if you knew something about the entity you are about to meet, Major O'Mara."

"It might prove helpful," Gurronsevas agreed.

"He is the hospital's Chief Psychologist," Timmins went on. "What I believe your species calls a Healer of the Mind. As such he is responsible for the smooth and efficient operation of the ten-thousand-odd, sometimes *very* odd, members of the medical and maintenance staff . . ."

Taking into consideration the very high levels of species toleration and professional respect among its personnel, the Lieutenant explained, and in spite of the careful psychological screening they all had to undergo before being accepted for service in a multi-environment hospital, there were still situations when serious inter-species and interpersonal friction could occur. Potentially dangerous situations could occur through simple ignorance or misunderstanding or, more seriously, an entity could develop a xenophobic neurosis towards a patient or colleague which might affect its professional competence or mental stability. It was O'Mara and his department's duty to detect and eradicate such problems or, as a last resort, to remove the potentially troublesome individual from the hospital. There were times when this constant watch for signs of wrong, unhealthy or intolerant thinking, which the Major and his staff performed with such dedication, made them the most disliked beings in the hospital.

". . . For administrative reasons," Timmins continued, "O'Mara bears the rank of Major in the Monitor Corps. There are many officers and medical staff here who are nominally his senior, but keeping so many different and potentially antagonistic life-forms working together in harmony is a big job whose limits, like those of O'Mara's authority, are difficult to define."

"I have long understood," said Gurronsevas, "the difference between rank and authority."

"That's good," said Timmins, pointing at the large door they were approaching. "This is the Department of Other-Species Psychology. After you, sir."

He found himself in a large outer office containing four desk consoles ranged on each side of a broad, clear stretch of floor leading to an inner door. Only three of the desks were occupied—by a Tarlan, a Sommaradvan, and another Monitor Corps officer of the same rank and species as Timmins. The Tarlan and Sommaradvan remained bent over their work, but each curled an eye inquisitively in his direction, and the other officer looked at him Earth-human fashion with both its eyes. Placing his six feet as gently as possible against the floor so as to minimize undue noise and vibration, a politeness he practiced among lower-gravity entities in confined surroundings, he moved further into the room.

He remained silent because in these circumstances he did not consider it proper to speak to any subordinate person until he had first spoken to their superior.

Timmins said briskly, "Gurronsevas, newly arrived on *Tennochlan,* to see the Major."

The other officer smiled and said, "He is waiting for you, Gurronsevas. Please go in. Alone."

The inner door slid open and Timmins said quietly, "Good luck, sir."

CHAPTER 2

The inner office of the Chief Psychologist was larger than the outer one, Gurronsevas saw, and if anything it resembled a well-appointed torture chamber from his native Traltha's pre-civilized past. Ranged around the walls and encroaching towards the center of the floor, and in two cases hanging from the ceiling, was a weird and wonderful assortment of furniture that was designed to enable the different species with business in the office to sit, lie, curl up, or hang at ease. As a member of a species who preferred to work, eat, sleep and do everything else standing on its six feet (except on occasions when eye-level other-species social intercourse was necessary), Gurronsevas found these office accessories of marginal interest. That was why he moved without hesitation to stand in the clear area of floor before the rotatable desk console at which sat this entity of indeterminate authority, O'Mara.

Gurronsevas directed all of his eyes towards O'Mara but remained silent. The Major knew who he was so it was unnecessary to introduce himself, and he wanted it to be established from the beginning, at the risk of committing a minor act of insubordination or impoliteness, that he was a person of strong will who would not be forced into making unnecessary conversation.

The Major appeared to be old (as Earth-humans counted their years), although the head-fur and hairy crescents shading its eyes were grey rather than white. Its facial features and the two hands resting on top of the desk remained motionless while it was returning his gaze. The silence lengthened until suddenly it nodded its head. When it spoke it did not use either his name or its own.

There had been a brief and silent contest of wills, but Gurronsevas was not sure who had won it.

"I must begin by welcoming you to Sector General," said O'Mara, and not once did he allow the flaps of skin that protected and lubricated its eyes to drop. "We both realize that these words are nothing more than a polite formality because your presence here was not requested by the hospital, nor is it as the result of unusually high medical or technical aptitude. You are here because someone in Federation Medical Administration had a rush of brains to the head and sent you, leaving us to discover whether or not the idea is viable. Is that a fair summation of the situation?"

"No," said Gurronsevas. "I was not sent, I volunteered."

"A technicality," said O'Mara, "and possibly an aberration on your part. Why did you want to come here? And please don't repeat the material in your original submission. It is long, detailed, most impressive, and probably accurate; but very often the facts contained in documents of this kind are shaded in favor of the applicant. Not that I am suggesting that deliberate falsification has taken place, just that an element of fiction is present. You have no previous hospital experience?"

"You know I haven't," Gurronsevas replied, resisting an urge to stamp his feet in irritation. "I do not consider that a bar to the performance of my duties."

O'Mara nodded. "But tell me, in as few words as possible: did you want to work here?"

"I do not work," said Gurronsevas, raising and lowering two of his feet with enough force to make the floor-mounted furniture in the room vibrate. "I am neither an artisan nor a technician. I am an artist."

"Please forgive me," said O'Mara in a voice which seemed to be totally devoid of contrition. "Why have you decided to favor this particular hospital with your artistry?"

"Because it represents a challenge to me," he replied fiercely. "Perhaps the ultimate challenge, because Sector General is the biggest and best. That is not a clumsy attempt at flattering you or your hospital; it is a widely-known fact."

O'Mara inclined its head slightly and said, "It is a fact known to each and every member of the hospital staff. And I'm pleased that you have not tried to use flattery on me, clumsy or otherwise, because it doesn't work. Neither can I conceive of any circumstances where I would use it on another entity—although I have been known, on a very few occasions, to stoop to politeness. Do we understand each other? —And this time you may take a few more words to answer the questions," it went on before Gurronsevas could reply. "What is there about this medical madhouse that attracted you, why did you decide to come, and what kind of influence do you have that you were able to swing it? Were you unhappy with your previous establishment or superiors, or they with you?"

"Of course not!" said Gurronsevas. "It was the Cromingan-Shesk in Retlin on Nidia, the largest and most highly-acclaimed multi-species hotel and restaurant in the Federation. They treated me very well there, and had that not been so there were several other establishments that vied with each other to obtain my services. I was quite happy there until about a year ago, when I spoke with the Monitor Corps ranking officer on Nidia Base, Fleet Commander Roonardth, a Kelgian."

Gurronsevas paused, remembering the ridiculously short and simple conversation that had brought his former life of contentment and boredom to an end.

"Go on," said O'Mara quietly.

"Roonardth wished to compliment me in person," Gurronsevas went on, "and it was a personage of sufficient importance for me to be called to its table so that it could do so. Kelgians are, as

you know, very forthright beings who are psychologically incapable of lying or even of being polite. During the conversation that
ensued it said that it had just consumed the finest meal of Crelletin
vine-shoots in its life, rendered even more enjoyable because of its
recent stay in Sector General where it had been taken after an un-
specified but clearly life-threatening accident in space. Roonardth
had no complaints about the medical services, but said that when
it criticized the meals being served, it was told by an Earth-human
DBDG nurse of a conspiracy aimed at poisoning long-stay patients
whose convalescence was overlong, but that it was nevertheless for-
tunate in that it did not have to eat in the staff dining hall.

"The Fleet Commander said that no doubt the remark was an
example of what Earth-humans called humor," he went on, "but it
also suggested that if someone like Gurronsevas (if there were anyone else like Gurronsevas) were to take charge of Sector General's
commissariat, then patient recuperation and staff morale would be
greatly enhanced. It was a high compliment that gave me much
pleasure. But later I began thinking about it and feeling dissatisfied
with a style of life which, I realized, had become pointless and boring. When Roonardth next came in to dine, I excelled myself so as
to have the opportunity of speaking to it again, and I asked if the
Fleet Commander's earlier suggestion had been a serious one.

"It was," Gurronsevas ended, "and Roonardth had the rank
and sufficient influence with the department responsible for maintaining the hospital to have me sent, after a wait of a year, to Sector General."

"Yes," said O'Mara. "Roonardth carried enough clout. I assume that you spent the waiting time familiarizing yourself with the
layout and organization of the hospital? And, like any eager little
newcomer, you are anxious to make a good impression on everyone as quickly as possible, and have already made plans to that effect?"

Gurronsevas' first thought was to point out to the diminutive
Earth-human that, possessing as he did more than five times the

other's body mass, he could scarcely be described as 'little.' Then he decided that O'Mara must have used the word deliberately in an attempt to unsettle him, and answered simply, "Yes."

The Major regarded him in silence for a moment, then it nodded and briefly showed its teeth. "In that case, what are your immediate intentions?"

"As soon as possible," said Gurronsevas, trying to control his enthusiasm, "I shall call a meeting of all hospital food technicians and associated medical personnel, with the purpose of introducing myself to those few who may not already know of of me by reputation . . ."

O'Mara was holding up one hand. It said, "*All* food technicians? Even the chlorine-breathers, and the ultra-low temperature and other exotic life-forms?"

"Of course," Gurronsevas replied. "But I would not make any major changes in the exotics' diets . . ."

"Thank God for that," said O'Mara.

". . . Without first making a careful study of the probable effects and obtaining the medical and technical advice of those with prior experience. But in time I intend to increase the present range of my culinary expertise, extensive though it already is, to include the dietary requirements of species other than the warm-blooded oxygen-breathers. I am now, after all, the hospital's Chief Dietitian."

O'Mara was moving its head from side to side in a gesture, Gurronsevas had learned, that indicated non-verbal negation. Impatiently he wondered what objection this unpleasant entity had to him doing his job.

"I'll tell you exactly what you are," said O'Mara, "and what you will do. You are a potentially dangerous contradiction. As a newcomer to the hospital without prior technical or medical training you should be classified as a trainee. Instead you have arrived as the head of a department whose ramifications are completely unknown to you. Two points in your favor are that you are aware of your ignorance; and, unlike our trainees, you have wide experience of other-species social contact. Nevertheless, you will soon be faced with and have to adapt to physiological types not normally found in the dining rooms of the ultra-exclusive Hotel Cromingan-Shesk. Since you appear to have a high opinion of your own importance and I, on rare occasions, am capable of exercising tact, I have avoided using the words *will* or *must do*, even though they are more appropriate in this case. No, don't interrupt.

"While you are learning the ropes," O'Mara continued, "please remember that, in spite of the influence you may have with the high-ranking gourmets of the Monitor Corps, you are here on probation, the period of which can be shortened in three ways. One, you may find the work too much for you and decide to resign. Two, I decide that the work is too much for you and kick you out. Three, and this is an improbability that comes within the category of wish-fulfillment, you display such a high level of aptitude that we are forced to confirm your position and request that you stay.

"Before you do or plan anything," it went on, "familiarize yourself with the hospital. Take all the time you need—within reason—to settle in. Before making any dietary changes have them vetted by the Diagnostician-in-Charge of the relevant department for possibly harmful medical effects. Should you encounter any psychological problems of your own I will, of course, try to assist you—provided you can satisfy me that you are not able to solve them yourself. If you have any other problems or questions while settling in, call on Lieutenant Timmins for help. You will find, if you have not already done so, that he is a polite and helpful person and one of the few people in this place who, unlike myself, seem able to suffer fools gladly.

"When I have more time to spare," it continued, "we will discuss the boring administrative details. Your salary, entitlement to paid leave and reduced transportation charges to your home world or chosen place of vacation, and supplies of free protective clothing and equipment. With or without the clothing you should wear a trainee's arm- or leg-band so that—"

"Enough!" said Gurronsevas loudly, making no attempt to

hide his feeling of outrage. "I require no salary. By the exercise of my unique talents I have already amassed more wealth than I could hope to spend during the rest of my life, no matter how profligate I should become. And I remind you again that I am a specialist renowned throughout the Federation and *not* a trainee, so I shall wear no trainee's badge or—"

"As you wish," said O'Mara quietly. "Is there anything else you wish to say to me? No? Then I expect you have other things to do less wasteful of your time and mine."

The Chief Psychologist glanced pointedly at its wrist chronometer, then tapped briefly on its console. When its communicator lit up it said quietly, "Braithwaite, I will see Senior Physician Cresk-Sar now."

Gurronsevas returned to the outer office seething with anger and making no attempt to place his feet quietly on the floor. The Nidian Senior waiting to see O'Mara took hasty evasive action while all the eyes of the department's staff remained firmly on their work displays, even though small items of equipment resting on the console desks were vibrating noisily with every foot-fall. He stopped only when he reached the waiting Timmins.

"That is a most infuriating entity," he said angrily. "As a Healer of the Mind it is incredibly lacking in sympathy or sensitivity, and, although I am not in that profession, I would say that it causes more psychological distress than it cures."

Timmins was shaking its head slowly. It said, "You are quite wrong, sir. The Major is fond of saying that his job here is to shrink heads, not swell them. If the meaning of that particular Earth-human phrase is unclear to you I will explain it later. He is a very good psychologist, the best that any mentally distressed or traumatized entity could wish for, but he also likes to project the image of a thoroughly nasty and sarcastic person to those friends and colleagues about whom he has no cause for professional concern. If he were ever to show you sympathy and concern, and to act towards you as a patient rather than a colleague, you would be in real trouble."

"I—I'm not sure that I understand," said Gurronsevas.

"In fact, sir," said the Lieutenant, smiling again, "you showed commendable restraint. The inner office is supposed to be sound-proofed and we heard your voice raised only once. Many of the others try to slam the door on the way out."

"Lieutenant," said Gurronsevas, "it is a sliding door."

"Even so," said Timmins.

CHAPTER 3

The compartment was much smaller than his former quarters in Retlin, but a beautiful and almost three-dimensional picture of Tralthan mountain scenery that covered one wall gave it a feeling of spaciousness, while the colors used to decorate the other walls and ceiling were identical to those he had left. A small but adequate body-immersion pit, terraced on one side for ease of entry, was recessed into the floor under the picture wall. There was a gravity control unit so that he could increase the compartment's G-level for exercise or relaxation, since the standard gravity pull used inside the hospital was just over half Tralthan normal. A console with communicator and large view-screen was set into one corner, and the two containers (one large and one small) that had come with him on *Tennochlan* were already waiting inside the entrance.

"This is unexpected and very pleasant, Lieutenant Timmins," said Gurronsevas. "My thanks for your efforts in making it so."

Timmins smiled and made a dismissive gesture with one hand, then used it to point at the communications console.

"The operation is standard," it said, "and there are a large number of medical training and information channels available, including one covering the detailed geography of the hospital which you will find helpful, with a recall provision for study purposes if required. To understand them you will need to use your multichannel translator pack; that's it lying on top of your console. Unfortunately, the entertainment channels are, well . . . I know the Earth-human material is old and not very good, and the other-species staff have similar complaints. There is a rumor, never officially denied by O'Mara, that the Senior Physician in charge of training, Cresk-Sar, has deliberately arranged this to encourage more study during leisure periods."

"I understand," said Gurronsevas, "and sympathize."

Timmins smiled again and said, "You have concealed storage spaces here and here, and recessed attachment points for any pictures or wall hangings you may have. They work like this. Would you like help unpacking and arranging your personal effects?"

"Since I have very few, that will not be necessary," Gurronsevas replied, and pointed. "But as quickly as possible I would like that larger container to be stored under moderate refrigeration where I can have ready access to it. The contents will be required for my work."

The expression on Timmins' soft, yellow-pink features was probably one of curiosity, which Gurronsevas did not intend to satisfy as yet, then it said, "There is a cold-storage facility at the other end of your corridor. We don't need to waste time going for a gravity sled; it isn't very heavy."

A few minutes later Gurronsevas's precious container was in a cool, safe place, and Timmins went on, "Would you like to rest now, sir? Or tour part of the hospital, or maybe visit our dining hall for warm-blooded oxygen-breathers?"

"None of those," Gurronsevas replied. "I will return to my quarters and familiarize myself with the hospital layout. Then I would like to find my way to the dining hall, alone. Sooner rather than later I must learn to—how does your species put it?—stand on my own six feet."

"Understood, sir," said Timmins. "You have my personal comm code. Call me if you need help."

"My thanks, Lieutenant," said Gurronsevas. "I will need help—but hopefully not too often."

Timmins raised one hand and left without speaking.

Next day Gurronsevas was able to find his way to the correct level without having to ask anyone for directions, but this was because, during the final stages of the journey, he followed two Melfan student nurses who were discussing the necessity for hurrying their next meal to avoid being late for a lecture. He was sure, however, that he would be able to find the place again without passive guidance.

In the four principal languages spoken throughout the Federation—Tralthan, Orligian, Earth-human and Illensan—and as a spoken identification for translation by the other user species, the sign above the wide, doorless entrance announced MAIN DINING HALL, SPECIES CLASSIFICATIONS DBDG, DBLF, DBPK, DCNF, EGCL, ELNT, FGLI AND FROB. SPECIES GKNM & GLNO AT OWN RISK. Gurronsevas moved inside and stopped, paralyzed as much by the sight of so many other species together in one place as by the muted roar of their barking, grunting, growling, cheeping and whistling conversations.

Gurronsevas did not know how long he stood staring across that vast expanse of highly polished floor with its regimented islands of eating benches and seating grouped together by size to accommodate the incredible variety of beings using them. It was far beyond anything in his previous experience. He identified members of the Kelgian, Ian, Melfan, Nidian, Orligian, Dwerlan, Etlan, Earth-human, and his own Tralthan species, plus others that were completely new to him. Many of them were occupying tables and using eating utensils that had been designed for entirely different life-forms, seemingly for the purpose of conversing with other-species friends.

There were beings terrifying in their obvious physical strength, others so horrifying and repugnant that they belonged in the realms of nightmare, and one, a large, insectile creature with three sets of beautiful iridescent wings, had a body so fragile that the sight of it among the others aroused immediate feelings of concern. There were very few vacant spaces at any of the tables.

It was obvious that space was at a premium in Sector General and, whenever it was physiologically possible, the beings who worked together were expected to dine together—although not, Gurronsevas sincerely hoped, on the same food.

He was wondering if it was possible to prepare a meal that every warm-blooded, oxygen-breathing species would find instantly palatable, and thinking that that would be the ultimate challenge for the Great Gurronsevas, when he was struck two soft double-blows from behind.

"Don't block the entrance, stupid!" said a silver-furred Kelgian in the unmannerly manner of its race as it pushed past him. On his other flank its companion added, "Stand dreaming there much longer and you'll starve to death."

As he moved further into the hall, Gurronsevas realized suddenly that he felt hungry, but even stronger was his feeling of curiosity regarding the beautiful, outsized insect life-form hovering and eating above a nearby table that was furnished for Melfan ELNTs. Beside and below it there was a vacant place.

It was indeed an insect, he saw as he came up to its table, an enormous, incredibly fragile flying insect that was tiny in comparison with most of the other beings in the hall. From its tubular exoskeletal body there projected six pencil-thin legs, four even more delicately formed manipulators, and three sets of wide, iridescent wings that were beating slowly as it hovered a short distance above the table as it wove a long, stringy substance (which Gurronsevas immediately recognized as Earth spaghetti) into a cable before conveying it delicately to its mouth.

At close range, he thought, the delicate creature was even more beautiful. For a moment its hovering flight became less stable and a series of trills and clicks issued from an unidentified body orifice like a musical backing to the translated words.

"Why thank you, friend," it said. "I am Prilicla. You must be Gurronsevas."

"You must be telepathic," said Gurronsevas in surprise.

"No, friend Gurronsevas," said Prilicla, "I am a Cinrusskin. Our race possesses a faculty which enables us to sense emotional radiation, but it is empathy rather than telepathy. You were radiating feelings characteristic of a mind that is undergoing a completely new experience, but with the unease which usually accompanies such feelings overlaid by intense curiosity. Other trace emotions are present which support the principal indications. These combined with the foreknowledge that a Tralthan was expected to arrive shortly to take charge of Dietetics enabled me to make no more than an accurate guess."

"I am nevertheless impressed," said Gurronsevas. The warmth and friendliness emanating from the little being was almost palpable. "May I join you?"

"Stranger, you are too damned polite," a large Orligian from the other side of the vacant place broke in loudly. It was elderly, its bristling grey fur concealed most of the straps of its equipment harness, and it was seated not very comfortably on the edge of the table's Melfan support cradle, all of which may have contributed to its own lack of politeness. "I am Yaroch-Kar. Just grab the seat before somebody else does. In this place you'll find that the polite people are always badly undernourished."

Further along the table an Earth-human made the sound Gurronsevas had learned to identify as laughter, and in a softer voice the Orligian went on. "The mechanism for food selection and delivery is standard. Just key in your physiological classification and the menu display will list the food available. We have a lot of Tralthans here so there is a good selection, even though the quality and taste are matters for argument."

Gurronsevas did not reply. He was modifying his earlier opinion regarding this impolite Orligian. The being had tried to be helpful. It was still trying.

"With newcomers like yourself," it went on, "it sometimes happens that the meals being consumed by your fellow diners, perhaps even the diners themselves, are visually distressing to the point where the appetite is affected. If such is the case with you, just keep one eye on your platter and close the others. Nobody here will be offended. And if you really are the person who is to be responsible for the quality, or lack of it, of hospital catering, life would be easier for you if you kept that knowledge to yourself for as long as possible."

"My deepest thanks for the information and good advice," said Gurronsevas. "Regrettably, I may not be able to take all of it."

"You are being too polite again," said the Orligian, and returned its attention to its platter.

As he moved closer to the table, being careful to straddle and not risk deforming the Melfan chair by allowing his underside to rest on it, the trilling, clicking speech of Prilicla came again.

"I feel your hunger as well as your curiosity about my method of eating," it said, "so please assuage one while I satisfy the other . . ."

Prilicla might not be telepathic, Gurronsevas thought as he keyed in his choice, but with an empathic faculty of such sensitivity the difference was negligible.

". . . I find that eating while in flight aids the digestion," it went on, answering the first unasked question, "and, should it be too hot for fast consumption, the wing downdraft helps cool the soup of my Earth-human friends. The stringy material that I am weaving and eating is, of course, the Earth staple called spaghetti, which is very popular with the DBDGs on the maintenance staff. It is produced synthetically, as you know, and has a bland taste that is offset by a sauce which, when present in too large a quantity, sometimes splashes my features or those persons seated too close to me. Is there anything else you would like to know, friend Gurronsevas?"

"Professionally, I find this most interesting," he said, forgetting in his excitement to use the mouth not engaged in eating. "Do you eat any other varieties of non-Cinrusskin food? Or do you know of anyone else in the hospital who eats other-species food? Is there anyone at this table who does?"

Yaroch-Kar put down its eating tools and said, "Diagnosticians do it sometimes, when they have a particularly strong other-species Educator tape riding them and they aren't sure who they are. Apart from that a few have done it as a dare, or for a covert departmental initiation. I mean, imagine an Orligian like me eating, say, a helping of Melfan greeps and having to chase them around the bowl. I, personally, am very glad the practice isn't widespread."

Gurronsevas could not believe what he was hearing. "You mean *live* food is served here?"

"I exaggerate, but only a little," said Yaroch-Kar. "The greep dish is mobile rather than alive; otherwise it is the same near-tasteless synthesized stodge we all eat. The material is treated with nontoxic chemicals which allow each piece of food to be given a small electrical charge. Half of them are charged positively and the other half negatively, then the pieces are mixed just inside the serving outlet. For the few moments before the charges neutralize each other, the effect is visually realistic and quite disgusting."

"Fascinating," said Gurronsevas, thinking that this Yaroch-Kar was unusually knowledgeable where hospital cuisine was concerned. Perhaps it thought of itself as a gourmet, and he was anxious to continue the conversation. He went on, "At the Cromingan-Shesk we had to import live greeps, usually crottled, which made them a rare and expensive delicacy. But isn't it theoretically possible to produce a meal that would be metabolically suited to, and attract and satisfy the appetites of all warm-blooded oxygen-breathers? A dish that would combine the visual appearance and taste sensations of, say, the Kelgian crelletin vine-shoots, Melfan swamp nuts, and greeps, of course, Orligian skarkshi, Nallajim bird-seed, Earth-human steak, and spaghetti, too, and our own . . . Is something wrong?"

With the exception of the hovering Prilicla the other entities at the table were making loud, untranslatable noises. It was the Earth-human who replied.

"Wrong?" it said. "The very idea is driving us to the point of imminent regurgitation."

Prilicla made a short, trilling sound which did not translate, then went on, "I can detect no feelings of emotional or digestive distress, friend Gurronsevas. They are exaggerating their verbal responses for humorous effect. Do not concern yourself."

"I understand," said Gurronsevas, returning all attention to the Cinrusskin. "Does weaving the spaghetti strands into a cable also aid your digestion?"

"No, friend Gurronsevas," Prilicla replied. "It is done for my own amusement."

"When I was very young," Yaroch-Kar joined in, "which was a long time ago, I can remember being verbally chastised for playing with my food."

"I, too, have a similar memory," said Prilicla. "But now that I have grown up to be big and strong, I can do as I please."

For a moment Gurronsevas stared in astonishment at the thin, egg-shell body, spidery limbs and incredibly fragile wings then he, too, joined the others in making the untranslatable sounds that were his own Tralthan equivalent of laughter.

CHAPTER 4

A lengthy period of wakeful thinking, so concentrated that he had no clear idea of the elapsed time, was interrupted by the insistent sound and flashing light of his door signal. It was Lieutenant Timmins.

"Please excuse the interruption, sir," it said briskly. "I trust you slept well. Is there anywhere special you would like to visit or people you want to meet? The catering computer, the food synthesizer banks, the ward diet kitchens or the food technicians responsible for . . ."

Gurronsevas held up two of his upper limbs, loosely crossed in the non-verbal request for silence, a Tralthan gesture which Timmins must have understood because he stopped talking at once.

"For the present," said Gurronsevas, "none of those things. I know that you must have other duties, Lieutenant. So long as they permit it, I would prefer to have no close personal contact or conversation with anyone but yourself."

"I have other duties, naturally," said Timmins, "but I also have an assistant who tries very hard to make me feel redundant. For the next two days, and thereafter at mutually convenient times, I will be at your disposal. What would you like to do first?"

It was plain that Timmins was becoming impatient, but Gurronsevas did not move. He said, "At the risk of sounding repetitious and tedious, hopefully for the last time, I must remind you of my former position on Nidia. The Cromingan-Shesk was a very large, multi-species hotel and its kitchens, of which I had overall charge, were complex, technically advanced and, as you would expect, subject to periodic and most inconvenient malfunctions. I was able to reduce the number of these foul-ups by acquainting myself with the basic operation of the invisible support structures, the various other-species food reception systems, processors, ovens, and ancillary equipment, right down to the proper use of the smallest cutting implement and spoon. As well, I made myself familiar with the work of the sub-cooks, the waiters, those responsible for table decoration, the maintenance technicians, and so on down to the lowliest member of the cleaning staff. I made it my business to know enough to tell, if or when a fault occurred, whether I was being given a reason for it or an excuse.

"Before I try to give instructions to anyone in my department," he went on, "I want to know the geographical extent of my new responsibilities and the practical problems that are likely to occur, so that the gulf of ignorance between my subordinates and myself will be as narrow as possible. My learning process should begin at once."

Timmins' mouth had opened while Gurronsevas had been speaking, but the configuration of its lips seemed wrong for a smile, and finally it said, "You will have to travel extensively through the maintenance tunnel network. In places it can be dirty, unpleasant and dangerous. Are you sure that is what you want?"

"Quite sure," said Gurronsevas.

"Then we can talk as we walk," said the Lieutenant. "But it would be better, at least in the beginning, if I talked and you listened. There is a personnel access hatch in the wall at the end of your corridor . . ."

According to Timmins, the maps of the hospital's maintenance tunnels and substations, which Gurronsevas had studied so assiduously before his arrival, had been produced for the information of interested non-specialists—the drawings were too simple, too pretty, and years out of date. As soon as they entered the maintenance access door he was confronted by a flight of descending stairs which should not have existed.

"They're strong enough to support your weight," said Timmins, "but take them slowly. Or if you prefer we can use another access point where there is a ramp. Some Tralthans find stairs difficult . . ."

"I used them in the hotel," Gurronsevas broke in. "Just don't ask me to climb ladders."

"I won't," said the Lieutenant. "But you go first. It isn't politeness; just that I don't want to risk a quarter of a ton of Tralthan falling on me. How is your eyesight?"

"Very good," said Gurronsevas.

"But is it good enough," Timmins persisted, "to clearly identify the subtle shadings and dilutions of color brought about by changes in the ambient lighting? Are you claustrophobic?"

Trying to hide his impatience, Gurronsevas said, "I am able to tell by sight alone the degree of freshness, to within a few hours, of a wide range of commonly consumed fruit and vegetables. I am not claustrophobic."

"Good enough," said Timmins. With a hint of apology in its voice it went on, "But look above and around you. All of the interconnecting corridors, tunnels, service bays and alcove shelters are just like this. The walls and ceilings are covered with cable looms and piping, all of which is color-coded. This enables my maintenance people to tell at a glance, like you and the fresh vegetables, which are power cables and which are the less dangerous communication lines, or which pipes carry oxygen, chlorine, methane, or organic effluvia. The danger of contamination of wards and staff accommodation by other-species' atmospheres is always present, and such a local environmental catastrophe should not be allowed to happen because some partially-sighted entity connected up the wrong set of pipes.

"Normally," it went on, "I would not have to ask about visual acuity or claustrophobia because O'Mara's psychological screening would reject anyone with those defects before they were accepted for training. But your psych file was not open to me because you are not a trainee . . . That alcove just ahead on the right. Get in, quickly!"

For the past few seconds Gurronsevas had been aware of a high-pitched, wailing sound of steadily increasing volume. He felt Timmins' small, soft hands pushing at his lower flank in a manner which in another Tralthan would have been considered an intimacy, but it was simply urging him to move more quickly into the alcove before squeezing in beside him.

A gravity sled, piled so high with unidentifiable stores and equipment that there seemed to be only inches to spare between the load and the corridor walls, wailed past them. Above the sound of the warning siren the Earth-human driver shouted, "Morning, Lieutenant." Timmins raised a hand but did not speak because by then the other entity was beyond conversational range.

Now he knew the reason for the alcoves.

"It would save time if we used a gravity sled instead of walking," said Gurronsevas. "I was accustomed to driving in Retlin city center, where the traffic was quite horrendous, and was considered competent."

Timmins shook its head and said, "Not good enough. If you intend spending a lot of time in the service tunnels, I will arrange specialized driving instruction, in an empty cargo bay with collapsible practice-walls so that you won't damage the hospital's structure or yourself. But the chief reason for not using a sled right now is that it would move too fast for you to be able to see or learn anything useful about where we were going."

"I understand," he said.

"Good," said the Lieutenant. "But now, a little test. Based on what little you have learned and your observations so far, what can you tell me about the stretch of tunnel we have just entered?"

Very many years had passed since Gurronsevas had attended

school, but then as now he had always tried hard to impress his teachers. He said, "For a few seconds I was aware of muted rumbling and shuffling sounds and muffled other-species voices, too many and too faint for translation, coming from the ceiling. This leads me to assume that we are passing under one of the main corridors. There is a faint smell that I cannot identify which I think in greater strength would be unpleasant. I also note that, while the color coding which identifies the overhead power and communication cables, as well as the piping which carries the water and oxygen-nitrogen mixture used by warm-blooded oxygen-breathers has remained consistent, several large-diameter pipes coded for water have also appeared, and a few narrower runs with a color coding about which you have not told me. I have a question."

"One good answer," said Timmins, smiling, "deserves another. Ask."

"There were no identifying markings on any of the mechanisms and equipment we have passed," said Gurronsevas. "Are you and your maintenance staff required to recognize by sight and memorize the function of all these mechanisms?"

"God, no . . . !" Timmins began, when the siren of an approaching vehicle driven by a silver-furred Kelgian who did not speak forced them to take refuge in the nearest alcove. When they emerged, it continued, "Not even a Diagnostician has *that* good a memory. On your right is a red-blue-white–coded cabinet, that one with three of the large-diameter water pipes entering it. On the outer face is a large inspection panel with a small, hinged lid set into it. Pull back the lid and press the button inside."

Gurronsevas did so and was surprised when a new voice began speaking to them. He could not recognize the original language but the words came clearly through his translator.

"I am a standby pump for the purpose of topping-up the environmental fluid in the Chalder main ward. This supply contains trace elements favored by its AUGL water-breathers which, although not toxic, make it unsuitable as a drinking water supply for other warm-blooded species. Functioning is automatic. The large inspection panel is opened by inserting your general-purpose key into the slot marked with a red circle and turning it, as indicated by the arrow, through ninety degrees. For component repair or replacement consult Maintenance Instructions Tape Three, Section One Thirty-two. Do not forget to close the panel before you leave.

"I am a standby pump for . . ." it was repeating when Gurronsevas closed the lid, silencing it.

"A verbal label," he said admiringly, "understandable by everyone with a translator. I should have realized."

Timmins smiled and said, "We are moving into the Illensan levels. The smell and the new color code you spotted indicate the presence of chlorine. But before we go any farther we need protective suits, so turn into the next opening on the left. In there, at least, you won't have to worry about traffic."

The place was a multi-species suit store, he saw at once, and the transparent doors of the cabinets ranged around the walls revealed their contents while verbal labels gave any special fitting instructions on request. Timmins lifted out a suit for itself and donned it quickly before directing Gurronsevas towards one of the Tralthan cabinets.

"With your six legs you may find getting into that thing tricky at first," it said, "so I'll help you. The garment is a combination of lightweight environmental protection and general purpose coveralls. On mine there is a head-hood which can be sealed should there be an emergency involving other-species contamination such as a major seal malfunction at an oxygen and chlorine interface, or between the Telfan hot level and anywhere else. Yours contains a short-duration air supply, cooling and drying elements to control perspiration and guard against heat prostration, and an emergency beacon to summon help should you get into trouble.

"Don't use the beacon unless you cannot get to a communicator and have a serious emergency," the Lieutenant went on, "or until you are sure that you cannot solve the problem yourself. If a full rescue team with medical support turns out and finds that you are only lost or lonely, harsh words will be spoken."

"Harsh words," said Gurronsevas, "would be deserved."

Timmins smiled and continued, "The suits also give protection against dirt, and cuts and abrasions from metal projections. Unlike the medical levels and your kitchens at the Cromingan-Shesk, we do not need to work in super-clean conditions. Static charges build up in the equipment which attracts dust, and with the lubricants used everywhere it makes for a very dirty combination that is difficult to remove, particularly for entities who are covered with fur. The protective coveralls are a uniform color, Monitor Corps green, with the exception of the transparent suits used by Kelgians who need their fur to be visible for non-verbal communication. Before dressing, medical or departmental insignia of rank are transferred to the outside of the garment. Now check your head seal. Is the general fit comfortable?"

"Quite comfortable, thank you," Gurronsevas replied. "But I have a question prompted by the AUGL water pump that spoke to me. The problem of improving the taste of food used by water-breathers is one I had not considered until now. As soon as I have gained some knowledge of the maintenance levels' geography and food distribution network, I would like to discuss the problem with the Chalder patients. Can you arrange that?"

"That is a medical matter," said Timmins slowly. "It would be better if you asked permission and found out the most convenient visiting times from Nurse Hredlichli, who is in charge of the AUGL ward."

"Then I shall do that," said Gurronsevas. "But you sound hesitant. Am I likely to encounter some difficulty?"

"Charge Nurse Hredlichli," the Lieutenant replied, "has the reputation of being only slightly less obnoxious than O'Mara. But now, before I take you to see the main synthesizer unit under the dining hall, attach this trainee's band to one of your fore-limbs in a position where it will be easily seen."

This was the second time he had been told to wear the demeaning badge of a trainee, Gurronsevas thought, but the angry response he had given the impolite Chief Psychologist would scarcely do for this friendly and well-mannered Lieutenant. He was still searching his mind for reasons—or were they, perhaps, excuses?—for refusing the band when Timmins spoke again.

It said, "I myself, and soon everyone else in the hospital, will know that you are not a trainee but a specialist with considerable seniority. However, on the maintenance levels people are always in a hurry and accidents happen easily. You have seen how some of us drive, and there are many other situations where you would be at risk. Isn't it simple good sense to let those with experience know that you have none, so that allowances can be made? After all, the hospital needs a Chief Dietitian more than it needs another patient."

For a long moment Gurronsevas argued silently with himself, feeling shame because he could not be sure whether he was using his intelligence or giving in to moral cowardice.

"Well, if it is a matter of my continued survival," he said reluctantly, "all right."

CHAPTER 5

Gurronsevas was feeling very proud of himself. He had met and spoken with all the members of his staff individually—and, when required, at length. His principal assistant, a Nidian called Sarnyagh-Sa, had required careful handling because it had been expecting to inherit the retiring Chief Dietitian's position, but it was able, responsible, a little unresponsive to new ideas as yet, but showed long-term promise. Without ingratiation or implied diminution of his own authority or responsibility, Gurronsevas asked for the help of everyone. His intention was to be approachable by all levels of staff, provided the approach was not a waste of his time. He hoped that relations within other-species Catering would be pleasant and professional, but noted that the degree of the former would be strictly dependent upon the quality of the latter. The general response had been good, although a few of them had thought it strange that the Great Gurronsevas had worn maintenance coveralls during their interviews.

And after just five days of exploring the food supply maintenance tunnels with Timmins and just three half-days of anti-gravity sled driving instruction, the Lieutenant had told him that he need no longer travel on foot or with company. On the sixth day he had driven an unloaded sled from the synthesizer complex under Level Eighteen to the short-term storage facility on Thirty-one, using only the service tunnels and without having to request a navigational fix, in just twenty-four standard minutes without hitting anyone or anything—at least, not hard enough for a written report to be necessary.

Timmins had told him that he was doing exceptionally well for a beginner, and now Gurronsevas was trying hard not to allow his feelings of pride and pleasure to be destroyed by the ill-mannered, acid-tongued, chlorine-breathing Illensan he currently faced.

"When we need one of you people quickly," said Charge Nurse Hredlichli, "it seems that the maintenance sub-species suddenly becomes extinct; and when we don't want you, you clutter up the place. What is it you want?"

Since the Cromingan-Shesk had not catered for chlorine-breathers, it was the first time he had seen one of the PVSJ classification at close range. The Illensan's spiny, membranous body resembled a haphazard collection of oily, unhealthy vegetation that was partially obscured by the yellow mist of chlorine inside the entity's protective envelope, and Gurronsevas found himself wishing that the fog had been denser. Hredlichli was drifting motionless in the water-filled Nurses' Station in front of a patient-monitor screen. He had not been able to locate its eyes amid the tangle of head-fronds, but presumably the Charge Nurse was looking at him.

"I am Chief Dietitian Gurronsevas, Charge Nurse, not a maintenance technician," he said, making a great effort to be polite. "With your help I would like to interview one or more of your patients regarding the ward food supply, with a view to making improvements. Could you suggest the name of one that I can talk to without interrupting its medical treatment?"

"I could *not* suggest a name," said Hredlichli, "because our patients do not give them. On Chalderescol a person's name is known only to close members of its family and is otherwise given only to its intended life-mate. Here they are known by their medical file-names. AUGL One-Thirteen is convalescent and unlikely to be seriously stressed by a lot of stupid questions, so you may talk to it. Nurse Towan!"

A voice from the communicator, faintly distorted by the intervening watery medium, said, "Yes, Charge Nurse."

"When you finish changing One-Twenty-Two's dressings," said Hredlichli, "please ask One-Thirteen to come to the Nurses' Station. It has a visitor." To Gurronsevas it went on, "In case you don't know, a Chalder won't fit in here without wrecking the place. Wait outside."

The ward was probably smaller than it looked, Gurronsevas thought as he awaited the arrival of AUGL-113, but size and distance were hard to judge in this dim, green world where the difference between the shadowy inhabitants, their medical equipment, and the decorative vegetation designed to make them feel at home was difficult to define. Timmins had told him that some of the plants were living rather than artificial, a species that gave off a water-borne aromatic which the patients found pleasant, and that it was Maintenance Department's responsibility to see that the foliage stayed healthy no matter what happened to the patients. Sometimes it was difficult to know when the Lieutenant was being serious. It had also told him that the natives of the ocean world of Chalderescol embarrassed easily and were the most visually fearsome beings that he was ever likely to meet.

That, Gurronsevas thought as he watched the enormous, tentacled, torpedo shape that was speeding silently towards him, he could believe.

The creature was like an enormous armored fish with a heavy, knife-edged tail, a seemingly haphazard arrangement of stubby fins, and, around its waist, a thick ring of tentacles projecting through some of the only openings visible in its organic armor. The tentacles lay flat against its body while it was moving forward, but they were long enough to reach forward past the thick, blunt wedge of its head. As it swam closer and began to circle him, one of its tiny, lidless eyes regarded him. It drifted to a halt and its waist tentacles fanned forward to hang in a great, undulating circle around it. Suddenly the mouth opened to reveal a vast, pink cavern edged with the largest, whitest, sharpest teeth Gurronsevas had ever seen.

"Are, are you my visitor?" it asked shyly.

Gurronsevas hesitated, wondering whether or not he should introduce himself. A member of a culture which did not use names other than among family or loved ones might feel embarrassment if he should use his. He should have remembered to ask the Charge Nurse about that.

"Yes," he said finally. "If you have nothing more important to do and will allow it, I would like to talk to you about Chalder food."

"With pleasure," said AUGL-113. "It is an interesting topic that causes much argument but rarely leads to violence."

"About hospital food," said Gurronsevas.

"Oh," said the Chalder.

He did not have to be a Cinrusskin empath to sense the deep criticism implied by that single word. He said quickly, "It is my intention, in fact I have accepted it as a personal and professional challenge, to improve the quality, taste and presentation of the synthetic food provided by the hospital to its many life-forms. Before any improvement is possible I must know in what way or ways the present synthesized diets, which to me seem little more than near-tasteless organic fuel, fall short of the ideal. The work has just begun, and you are the first patient to be interviewed."

The cavernous mouth closed slowly then opened again. The patient said, "A laudable ambition, but surely unattainable? I must remember your phrase, *tasteless organic fuel*. Using it to a host on Chalder would be the ultimate culinary insult, because there we take our food seriously, and often in excess. What can I tell you?"

"Practically everything," said Gurronsevas gratefully, "because my ignorance regarding Chalder food is total. What edible animal and vegetable varieties are there? How are they prepared, presented and served? On the majority of worlds the methods of presentation stimulates the taste sensors and adds much to the enjoyment. Is it so on Chalderescol? What spices, sauces or condiments are used? And the concept of a culinary spectrum which is comprised of only cold dishes is completely new to me . . ."

"Being ocean-dwelling water-breathers," One-Thirteen broke in gently, "our people were late in discovering fire."

"Of course, I'm stupid not to have . . ." Gurronsevas began when the voice of Hredlichli interrupted both of them.

"Whether or not you are stupid is not for me to say," it called from the entrance to the Nurses' Station. "At least, not out loud. It is time for our mid-day meal and the patients are hungry and, with the exception of the one you are talking to, are on special diets and require nursing assistance during feeding. So make yourself useful: draw One-Thirteen's rations and let the poor thing eat while you talk."

He followed Hredlichli into the Nurses' Station, thinking how strange it was that the unpleasant Charge Nurse was telling him to do exactly what he himself would have wished to do. But before he could follow the thought to its incredible conclusion—that Hredlichli might not be as unpleasant as it seemed—the food delivery chute started spitting out large, brown-and-grey mottled globes into a waiting carrying net. When the net was full he towed it out to One-Thirteen.

"Keep your distance and push them at it one at a time," Hredlichli called after him. "You don't want to become part of the meal."

Two Kelgian nurses, their fur rippling in dimly-lit silver waves inside their transparent protective suits, and a water-breathing Creppelian octopoid who needed no protection, passed him on their way in.

"What are they, eggs?" Gurronsevas asked as he pushed them one by one towards the patient's open and waiting mouth. One-Thirteen's jaws closed much too quickly for him to be able to see whether the material was soft and surrounded by a hard, uneven shell, or solid all the way through. His curiosity remained unsatisfied until the last of the objects had disappeared into the vast jaws and the patient's mouth was again free for speech.

"Are you getting enough to eat?" he said. "Relative to your body mass, the meal portions appear, well, meager."

"My tardiness in replying," the patient replied, "should not be taken as an impoliteness. On Chalderescol the ingestion of food is an important and pleasurable activity, and to converse while eating is considered to be an implied criticism of one's host for allowing a guest to become bored with what is being provided. Even here, where the food is open to serious criticism, the habit of good manners remains."

"I understand," said Gurronsevas.

"To answer your questions," Patient One-Thirteen went on, "the food objects resemble but are not eggs, although they have a hard, edible outer shell enclosing a quantity of concentrated nutritious fibre, synthetic, of course, which expands to many times its original volume when exposed to our digestive juices, thus giving a feeling of physical repletion. As a species we Chalders have an educated palate, and well do we know that hunger makes the most effective sauce, but the taste of these food objects is artificial and unsubtle and . . . to describe them more fully my language would of necessity become impolite."

"Again I understand," said Gurronsevas. "But can you describe the differences in appearance and consistency, as well as the taste, between the natural and synthetic varieties? You will not offend me by using impolite language to describe foul-tasting or badly-prepared food because I have been doing so to my kitchen staff for a great many years . . ."

Patient One-Thirteen began by saying that it did not want to sound ungrateful to the hospital because the treatment it had received had, after all, saved its life. Medical and surgical wonders had been performed in the crowded and claustrophobic, to an AUGL, confines of the ward, and to complain about the food being unappetizing seemed petty under the circumstances. But on its home world there was space in which to eat, and to exercise, and to sharpen the taste sensors with expectancy and uncertainty by having to chase certain varieties of food which were not easily caught.

On the ocean world of Chalderescol, in spite of the civilizing influences of many centuries, the Chalders still felt a physiological as well as an aesthetic need to chase their food rather than have it served dead and, so far as their instincts were concerned, in the early stages of decomposition on a platter. To remain physically healthy they needed to exercise their jaws and teeth and massive, armored bodies, and the time of maximum effort and enjoyment, except for the brief period every year when they were able to procreate, was when they were eating.

The hospital food was hard-shelled enough and undoubtedly nutritious, but the contents were a soft, tasteless, disgusting pap that resembled the partially pre-digested and newly-dead material given to toothless AUGL infants. Unless immobilized by serious illness or injury, an adult Chalder was forced to concentrate its mind on other and more pleasant things if it was to avoid nausea while eating the vile stuff.

Gurronsevas listened attentively to AUGL-113's every word, occasionally asking for clarification or offering suggestions, but always remembering to make due allowance for creative exaggeration on the part of a patient who was obviously pleased at having someone new at whom it could complain. But the constant discussion of food in its many unpalatable forms, to a Chalder, was reminding Gurronsevas that it had been four hours since he himself had dined.

"If I may interrupt you to summarize the problem," said Gurronsevas when the other began repeating itself with only minor variations. "First, there is the shape and consistency of the food, which is inadequate in that it exercises only the jaws and teeth. Second, the taste is unsatisfactory because it is artificially produced with chemical additives and, to the discriminating palate of the Chalder, any such substitution is immediately detectable. And third, the water-borne odors which the real food animals emit when they are being chased are not present.

"In my recent study of similar problems as they relate to other life-forms in the hospital," Gurronsevas went on, "I have discovered that the ward menu is under the control of the clinical dietitian, who acts under the direction of the physician-in-charge, rather than being the responsibility of the food technicians. Rightly, the primary concern of the physician concerned is to prescribe food that supports the clinical needs of its patient and is an extension of its medical treatment, so that the taste and odor have a low order of priority—if, indeed, they are considered at all. But it is my belief that they should be considered, and seriously, if only for the psychologically beneficial effects on convalescent patients like yourself who should be encouraged to eat and exercise.

"Regrettably," he went on, enthusiasm for his subject dulling the pangs of personal hunger, "there is little I can do about taste and texture, at least not until I have had consultations with your physician-in-charge and the relevant food synthesists. But as a general rule most varieties of food can be made to seem more appetizing by varying its manner of presentation. An interesting combination of colors, for example, or an imaginative shaping and arrangement of food on the platter so that there is a visual appeal as well as . . ."

Gurronsevas broke off in mid-sentence, remembering that patient AUGL-113 did not use a platter and that the principal visual attraction of the food would be its ability to go scuttling all over the dining area. But his embarrassment was short-lived because Hredlichli had emerged from the nurses' station and was swimming quickly towards them.

"I must interrupt this excessively long and, to me, less than interesting conversation," said the Charge Nurse as it drifted to a halt between the patient and himself. "Senior Physician Edanelt is due to make its evening rounds. Please return to your sleeping frame, One-Thirteen. And Dietitian Gurronsevas, if you wish to continue the discussion you will have to wait until Edanelt has completed its ward rounds. Shall I contact you then?"

"Thank you, no," he replied. "Patient One-Thirteen has given me some very useful information. I am grateful to both of you, and hopefully I shall not need to return until I have been able to make a positive improvement in the AUGL ward diet."

"I will believe that," said Charge Nurse Hredlichli, "when I see it."

CHAPTER 6

When Gurronsevas had asked for the use of a large, enclosed volume of water that was not so deep that there would be the risk of his air-breathing helpers drowning, but extensive enough so that the experiments could be carried out without the test objects colliding too often with the retaining walls, he had not expected anything quite as large as this, and for a moment surprise rendered him speechless.

Bright but well-concealed lighting combined with some inspired landscaping had given the recreation level the illusion of tremendous spaciousness. The overall effect was of a small, tropical terrain beach enclosed on two sides by low cliffs containing several large and small cave mouths which were the concealed access tunnels to several diving boards, all of which were constantly in use, that projected at various heights from the soft, artificial rockface. The beach was open to the sea, which seemed to stretch to a distant horizon rendered indistinct by heat haze. Overhead the sky was blue and cloudless. The bay was deep blue, shading to turquoise where it met the shelving beach, and the wave-making machinery had been turned off for the duration of the experiment so that the water lapped gently onto soft, golden sand that was pleasantly warm underfoot.

Only the artificial sun, whose light had an orange tinge that Gurronsevas found strange, and the varieties of alien greenery fringing the cliff-tops kept it from looking like a tropical bay anywhere on his home planet.

"Newcomers are always impressed," said Lieutenant Timmins proudly, "by their first sight of our recreation facility for warm-blooded oxygen-breathers. At least one-third of the medical staff are off-duty at any given time and most of them like to spend a few hours here. Sometimes the place is so crowded you can hardly see the beach or ocean for bodies. But space is at a premium in Sector General, and the people who work together are expected to play together as well.

"Psychologically," Timmins went on, still speaking in the manner of a proud parent of what must have been Maintenance Department's favorite brainchild, "the most effective part of the environment is the one you don't even see. The whole area is maintained at just under one-half standard gravity, and a half-G pull means that the people who feel tired can relax more comfortably and the ones who are feeling lively can feel livelier still. Unfortunately it lacks privacy, but there are so many different life-forms enjoying their leisure in so many strange ways that your experiments are likely to pass unnoticed.

"Do we start now or wait for Thornnastor?"

"Now, please," said Gurronsevas, and began helping Timmins and its two Melfan assistants to transfer their equipment into the large, brightly-colored raft that was waiting in the shallows.

Only once did Gurronsevas pause when his communicator came briefly to life with the message that Diagnostician Thornnastor had been unavoidably delayed and would not be able to join them as planned, but it was sending Pathologist Murchison in its place. Judging by its sudden change of facial expression, the news pleased Timmins very much.

But they were all too busy making adjustments to the propulsion system of one of their test objects—the only one which so far had not blown itself to soggy pieces or otherwise proved a failure—to notice the pathologist's arrival until it had swum out to the raft, pulled itself on board and spoken to them.

"Thornnastor had no time to brief me," Murchison said. "What is that thing? And what am I doing here, apart from watching fully grown and presumably mentally adult beings playing in the water like children?"

It was a tall Earth-human DBDG, Gurronsevas saw, with the flabby and top-heavy aspect common to many females of that species. Long yellow head-fur darkened by water clung to its neck and shoulders and, Earth being one of the few cultures containing beings who still observed a nudity taboo, it wore two ridiculously narrow strips of fabric around its chest and pelvis. Even though the words implied criticism its manner seemed pleasant. Before replying he reminded himself that Murchison was Thornnastor's principal assistant and the life-mate of another Diagnostician, Conway, and that he should not be too quick to take offense in case none had been intended.

"It might look that way, ma'am," Timmins said before Gurronsevas could speak, "and I must admit that this isn't the most unpleasant project I have ever been given. But there are serious, technical, and medical-support reasons for what we are doing here."

"For playing with a toy boat?" asked Murchison.

"Technically, ma'am, it isn't a boat," said the Lieutenant, smiling. It lifted the test object out of the water so that the pathologist could see it more clearly. "It is a prototype submersible vehicle with a flattened ovoid configuration that is designed to remain in a state of stable equilibrium at whatever depth it is placed, after which it is supposed to alter its position and depth randomly and at speed.

"The propulsion system," Timmins went on, "is a thin-walled plastic cylinder of compressed gas which fits into this cylindrical opening in the stern, just here. Smaller depressions around the circumference and on the top and underside house smaller capsules of compressed gas which are used for changing attitude. The walls of these steering capsules are water soluble and of varying thickness so that they need differing periods, anything from five to seventy-five seconds, to melt and release the gas. This means that the changes in direction will be random and the vehicle consequently very difficult to catch, at least until the propellant gas runs out which, in this test specimen, will be in two minutes. We are about to do another test run, ma'am. You should find it interesting."

"I can't wait," said Murchison.

Timmins and the two Melfan technicians lifted the test vehicle onto the raft and climbed on board. Their combined weight made the raft tip alarmingly. Murchison stepped backwards quickly to give them space to work, arms outstretched to maintain its balance, and Gurronsevas remained in the water. He was tall enough for his feet to touch the bottom while his cranial breathing passages remained in air. Two of his eyes he positioned under the surface to watch for any underwater swimmers who might be about to encroach on the test area, and with the other two he watched until the vehicle was refuelled and ready.

"This time we'll place it at a depth of one-half meter," Gurronsevas said, "because I want to closely observe its behavior from the moment the main propulsion unit's seal dissolves until the first steering capsule bursts. Hold it as level as possible, let go simultaneously and withdraw slowly so that you will not create turbulence which might cause an attitude change before thrust is applied. Is this understood by everyone?"

"It was understood," said one of the Melfans so quietly that it was plain that the remark was not intended to be overheard, "the first time you explained it."

Gurronsevas decided to be diplomatically deaf.

Murchison had not spoken directly to Gurronsevas since its arrival; and since Timmins had been eagerly passing on all of the necessary information, there was no reason other than mere politeness for him to speak to the pathologist. He was beginning to have serious doubts about the feasibility of the whole project, and to say less now would reduce any subsequent embarrassment caused by an apology for wasting the other's time. In any case, the pathologist was lying flat on the raft with its face and both eyes directed at the launch preparations.

Gurronsevas noted with growing impatience that most of Timmins' attention was being directed at Pathologist Murchison. He reminded himself that the Earth-human DBDG classification belonged to a species which (unlike the vast majority of other life-forms within the Federation, who were intensely active only for short periods in the year) was capable of sexual arousal and activity throughout its adult life. There were some who envied them this ability, but privately Gurronsevas considered it a disadvantage which all too often reduced the quality of their mentation. But again, this was a good time to maintain diplomatic silence.

The next test began well, with the thin, bubbling jet of compressed gas driving the vehicle forward in a not quite straight line at a slowly increasing velocity and constant depth. The Chalder's prey was amphibious so that it was normal for it to release air while fleeing. When the first lateral thrust came with its smaller and briefer explosion of bubbles, the vehicle made a wide curve that was bringing it back towards the raft. Another gas capsule melted and burst on the same side and the circle tightened until suddenly the vehicle broke the surface and began spinning and skidding uncontrollably over the water as the propulsion unit reinforced the spin set up by the two lateral jets. The others burst at random without effect and a moment later the vehicle came to rest, still spinning slowly, with its topside breaking the surface.

One of the Melfans retrieved it and a technical argument started regarding the inherent instability of the flattened ovoid configuration. Gurronsevas was too angry and disappointed to join in, but not so Murchison.

"This is not my specialty," said the pathologist, "but when I used to play with my big brother's toy boats as a child, they were fitted with keels which gave them directional stability even when the wind changed. When we grew older and progressed to speed-boats and submarines we had radio-controlled rudders and diving vanes to maintain or change direction or depth. Couldn't something similar be used here?"

Timmins and the Melfans stopped talking but did not reply. They were all looking at Gurronsevas. Plainly he could remain silent no longer.

"No," he said. "Not unless the radio receiver and actuating devices could be fabricated from materials that were non-metallic, non-toxic and edible."

"*Edible?*" said Murchison. In a quieter voice it went on, "So that's why I was sent here. Until now I didn't know that Thorny had a sense of humor. Please go on."

"In its final form," said Gurronsevas, doing so, "the entire vehicle would have to be edible, or at least non-toxic to the Chalder life-form, and that would include the water-soluble gas containers for propulsion and steering. The problem with the addition of a keel, which would also have to be edible and not sharp-edged enough to risk injury to the patient's mouth, is that the structure would change the visual appearance of the vehicle so that it no longer resembled the Chalders' natural and greatly preferred food source, which is a streamlined, hard-shelled, aquatic animal of the size and configuration of our test object. A weak and convalescent Chalder patient might not consider it worth the effort to chase unfamiliar food.

"You will understand," Gurronsevas continued, "that the confined space of the AUGL ward causes physical as well as physiological effects which unnecessarily lengthen the period of convalescence. The patients become lazy, listless, almost debilitated by their inability to exercise properly. I should explain that the physiology of the AUGLs is such that—"

"I am familiar with the physiology of the Chalders, among others," said Murchison.

For a moment Gurronsevas radiated embarrassment so strongly that he was surprised the water around him did not steam.

He said, "My apologies, Pathologist Murchison. This Chalder knowledge is very new to me, and very exciting, and in my excitement I stupidly assumed a similar level of ignorance in others. I had no wish to offend you."

"You didn't," said the pathologist. "I was just trying to stop your wasting time on an unnecessary explanation. But I have no knowledge or professional interest in the non-intelligent life-forms on Chalderescol, including the food animal you are trying to copy. How does the real one propel itself and take evasive action and manage to retain directional stability?"

Feeling greatly relieved, Gurronsevas said quickly, "On each side the animal has a set of eight laterally-mounted paddles. Their frequency of beat and angle of attack against the water can be varied so as to make the animal rise, dive, or—by going into reverse beat on one side—make a sudden change in direction. The paddle structure is a translucent framework supporting a transparent membrane which, when the creature is fleeing, is beating so fast as to be virtually invisible. When there is a change in direction, minor turbulence is created which is visually similar to the bubbles produced by the test object's attitude jets.

"Regrettably," he added, "the model looks but does not behave like the real thing. It is hopelessly unstable."

"That it is," said Murchison. For several minutes it remained silent, staring thoughtfully at the test object in the water while Timmins stared just as intently at the pathologist and the two Melfan technicians talked quietly to each other. Suddenly it spoke.

"We need a keel of some kind," it said in a quiet but excited voice, "but one which will not alter the object's appearance. The original life-form uses paddles which are translucent and move too quickly to be seen. Why don't we use an invisible keel?"

Without giving anyone a chance to reply it went on, "We should be able to make it from a shaped and hardened transparent gel possessing the same refractive index as water. It would have to be edible, naturally, and be weak enough structurally not to damage the patient's teeth or digestive tract. Some of the constituents I have in mind—well, the taste would range from neutral to down-right awful, but we can work on that until—"

"You can produce this edible stabilizer?" Gurronsevas broke in, incredulity making him forget good manners. "Your department has done so before?"

"No," said Murchison. "We have never been asked to do so before. It will be a difficult but not impossible biochemical problem to devise an edible and Chalder–non-toxic material of the required consistency. The shaping of the material into a keel and its attachment to the vehicle will be covered by your food synthesizer programming."

"Meanwhile," Timmins joined in, "we can start fitting non-edible and visible keels to the test vehicle to see which size and shape works best. Kledath, Dremon, lift it onto the raft. We've got work to do."

Murchison rolled off the raft so as to give the others more space to work. It lay floating on its back beside Gurronsevas, completely relaxed, with eyes closed and only its face above the surface.

"I think you have solved this problem, Pathologist Murchison," he said, "and I am most grateful."

"We aim to please," the pathologist said. Its mouth opened slightly in a smile and the eyes remained closed. "Have you other problems?"

"Not exactly," said Gurronsevas. "I have thoughts and questions and ideas, not yet fully formulated, which are likely to develop into problems. Right now my ignorance about some aspects of my future work here is close to total and, well, I would welcome suggestions."

The pathologist opened one eye briefly to look at him, then said, "Right now I can think of nothing better to do than listen and make suggestions."

On the raft the three technicians were concentrating all of their attention on the test vehicle, so much so that Timmins had stopped casting sidelong glances at Murchison. They had attached a long, narrow keel and the Lieutenant was suggesting that they add a similar dorsal fin so as to equalize water resistance on the top and undersides. With the expected increase in longitudinal stability, which would reduce the earlier tendency to sideslip and go into a spin every time it changed direction, the lateral thrusters would need to be strengthened so as to sharpen the turning angles.

The conversation could not have been more technical, Gurronsevas thought as he directed all of his eyes towards Murchison, if they had been designing a spaceship.

"Thanks to your suggestion," he said, "our test object should act as well as look like the food animal it is meant to be. That is important because there is much more to food than its outward appearance. There are also taste, smell, consistency, visual presentation, and contrasting or complementing sauces which, I hope to demonstrate in time, are vital accompaniments to the often bland edible material that the hospital synthesizers provide. In the case of our Chalder we have been able to reproduce the consistency with the hard shell that encloses the soft contents, and the presentation, which is the mobility of a dish that is apparently trying to escape being eaten. But that is all."

"Go on," said Murchison, opening both of its eyes.

"In the present instance," said Gurronsevas, "the difficulty of adding a conventional sauce to a dish that is moving rapidly underwater is well-nigh insurmountable. The thick-shelled, immobile eggs currently being fed to AUGL patients, in spite of the artificial taste additives they contain, are most unappetizing. To an Earthhuman like yourself an analogy would be that they taste like cold mashed potato sandwiches . . ."

"My department was consulted about those artificial taste additives," Murchison broke in, "to make sure there would be no harmful side-effects. The taste concentration can easily be increased if that is what you want."

"It isn't," said Gurronsevas firmly. "The diner, I mean the patient, is aware of the artificial taste and finds it objectionable. I had it in mind to reduce the taste components in the material rather than increase them, it being more difficult for the sensorium to detect artificialty in trace quantities than in heavy concentrations. My plan, or rather my hope, is to mask the diluted artificial taste with a sauce that requires no physical ingredients. Instead I will rely on the best condiment of all, hunger, reinforced by the excitement of the chase and the uncertainty of capturing the meal. Intellectually the Chalder will know that it is being fooled, but subconsciously it might not care."

"Nice, very nice," said Murchison approvingly. "I'm pretty sure that will work. But you are missing a bet."

"A, a bet?"

"Sorry, an Earth-human expression," it said, and went on, "When a land animal is being hunted it usually emits a special body odor, a glandular secretion indicative of its fear and increased level of physical activity, and the same may hold true here. Synthesized fear pheromones—in this case, in the form of a fast-dispersing water-borne scent—could be released into the propulsion system, again in trace quantities so as to hide the fact that they are artificial."

"Pathologist, I am most grateful," Gurronsevas said excitedly. "If your department can provide me with this substance, then the solution to my Chalder problem is complete. Can you do so, and how soon?"

"We can't," Murchison said, shaking its head. "At least, not yet. We will have to investigate the physiology and endocrinology of a food animal about which the medical library may not be fully informed. And if a secretion of the type we are postulating exists, it would take a few days to analyze and reproduce the molecular structure and test the synthetic variety for possibly harmful side-effects. Until then, Gurronsevas, save your thanks."

For a long moment he stared at the pathologist as closely as Timmins had done earlier, although not for the same reason, at the ridiculous, wobbling bulges on its upper thorax and the disproportionately small, Earth-human head which in this case held a mind that could never be described as tiny. He was about to thank it again when there was an interruption from Timmins.

"It's ready to launch, sir," said the Lieutenant. "Same depth as last time?"

"Thank you, yes," said Gurronsevas.

Once again the test vehicle was lowered carefully into the water and held in position below the surface. Timmins said, "This time I've loaded attitude thrusters on the port side only so that, if the new stabilizers work and the thing achieves some distance, it will circle back to us. On the synthesized production version the changes of depth and direction will be random and . . . Bloody hell!"

A large, brightly-colored ball, inflated to near-solidity, had landed with a loud thump on the raft where it had bounced twice before rolling into the water beside them. Instinctively one of the Melfan technicians raised a pincer to push it away.

"Leave it and hold still!" said the Lieutenant sharply. "Don't disturb the water. The jet seals are melting and we're committed to a launch . . . There she goes."

The vehicle began to move forward, slowly at first but steadily picking up speed, and this time in a perfectly straight line. When the first lateral thrust came it changed direction sharply and proceeded on the new course without sideslipping or apparent loss of speed. There was another abrupt change in direction, and another, both achieved cleanly and without loss of stability, and it was curving back towards them. A few seconds later, its compressed air capsules exhausted, it coasted to a stop beside the raft.

"It needs fine tuning," said Timmins, pulling its lips into the widest Earth-human smile Gurronsevas had ever seen, "but that was a definite improvement."

"Yes indeed," said Gurronsevas, who could not smile but wished that he could. "Pathologist Murchison and yourself, and technicians Kledath and Dremon deserve the highest—"

He broke off because suddenly the immobile domed head of a fellow Tralthan was rising from the water beside them, followed by a waving tentacle wearing the arm band of a trainee nurse.

"Please," it said, "can we have our ball back?"

CHAPTER 7

Present for the trial of the first batch of the new food samples were, in descending order of rank, Senior Physician Edanelt, who had overall medical responsibility for the AUGL ward, Pathologist Murchison, Gurronsevas himself, Lieutenant Timmins, Charge Nurse Hredlichli, and the rest of the ward's nursing staff. They were all packed so tightly into the Nurses' Station that there was barely room for the food, which had been wrapped separately in five plastic envelopes to protect the thruster seals against premature contact with water. Patient AUGL-113 was drifting about thirty meters from the station's entrance, its ribbon tentacles curling and uncurling slowly with impatience.

The normal meal of hard-shelled, artificial eggs had been served and the remains cleared away, and 113 had been told to expect a surprise, possibly a pleasant surprise.

At Gurronsevas' signal, Timmins moved closer to help him strip off the plastic cover. In addition to the stabilizers, which were all but invisible as well as being not too bad to eat, the upper and lower surfaces of the self-propelled edible packages had been colored so that they closely resembled the grey-and-brown mottled shell of a young but fully-grown specimen of the original food animal. Murchison's researches into the body markings, behavior, and glandular excretions under stress had been necessarily brief, but thorough.

Within a few seconds the main thruster seal melted and a thin stream of compressed air bubbled out. Gurronsevas and the Lieutenant held the package steady and then, to help it overcome the inertia and initial water resistance, gave it a firm push in the direction of 113.

The Chalder's mouth opened wide, whether in surprise or anticipation they could not be sure, then its tremendous jaws crashed shut. But its prey had changed direction suddenly, climbing to pass over 113's massive head and continuing into the tepid, green depths of the other end of the ward. The patient turned ponderously end for end and went after it. Distorted by the intervening water there came the sound of massive teeth closing on emptiness, followed by a noise like a discordant gong being struck as 113 collided with the resting-frame of an immobilized fellow patient, before it managed to catch the food-shell.

The regular chewing and crunching sounds that followed were diminishing when Timmins and Gurronsevas launched the second one.

This time the chase was short-lived because the first random change of direction sent the food straight into 113's mouth. The third package was able to evade capture until its compressed air supply ran out and it drifted dead in the water, but by then 113 was far too excited to notice or care about this strange behavioral anomaly. Number four it lost altogether.

That was because its erratic course took it too close to the resting-frame of the tethered patient AUGL-126, who snapped it out of the water as it was passing and devoured it within seconds. A heated dispute ensued between 113 and 126, with accusations of theft being countered with those of selfishness, which was ended by the release of the fifth and last food-shell.

It must have been that the convalescent 113 was tiring, Gurronsevas thought, because the chase was a long one and its movements seemed to lack coordination. Several times it collided heavily with the resting-frames lining both sides of the ward, or tore away masses of the decorative and aromatic vegetation that was loosely attached to the walls and ceiling. But its fellow patients seemed not to mind and either shouted encouragement or tried to take a bite out of the food-shell as it went past.

"It's wrecking my ward!" said Hredlichli angrily. "Stop it, stop it at once!"

"I think most of the damage is superficial, Charge Nurse," said Timmins, but it did not sound very sure of itself. "I'll send you a repair squad first shift tomorrow."

Patient 113, having caused the fifth food-shell to completely disappear, was returning to the Nurses' Station. It swam slowly past two resting-frames whose structures were visibly deformed and between drifting tangles of artificial vegetation until it was just outside the entrance. Its great, pink cavern of a mouth opened wide.

"More, please," it said.

"Sorry, no more," said Senior Physician Edanelt, speaking for the first time since its arrival in the ward. "You have been taking part in an experiment conducted by Chief Dietitian Gurronsevas, an experiment which in my opinion requires further modification. Perhaps there will be more tomorrow or soon after."

As 113 turned to leave, Hredlichli said quickly, "Nurses, check the condition of your patients at once and report back if this, this *experiment* has caused any clinical deterioration. Then try to tidy up the mess as best you can." It turned to the Senior Physician and went on, "I don't think the experiment should be modified, Doctor. I think it should be forgotten like a bad dream. My ward can't take another such . . ."

The Charge Nurse broke off because Edanelt had raised a forelimb and was clicking a pincer together slowly in the Melfan sign that it wanted attention.

"The demonstration has been interesting and on the whole

successful," it said, "although the present devastation in the ward might suggest otherwise. The unnecessarily slow rate of recovery with Chalder patients has a psychological basis, as we know. Post-operatively they tend to become listless, bored, lazy and uncaring about their future. This new food package, which should be served only to mobile, convalescent patients, promises to change that. Judging by the reaction of One-Thirteen and future convalescent patients I would expect the boring nature of mealtimes to be relieved, considerably, by this constant reminder of the pleasures of chasing and eating the real food that awaits them on their home world. The patients under clinical restraint, observing their mobile brethren, will try to reach the convalescent stage as quickly as possible.

"You are all to be complimented," it went on, looking at the four of them in turn, "but especially the Chief Dietitian for its imaginative solution to what has been until now a serious problem among recuperating Chalders. I have, however, two suggestions to make."

Edanelt paused and they waited in silence. The Melfan was an unusually polite entity considering its high medical rank, but to a mere Pathologist, a Lieutenant of Maintenance, a Charge Nurse and even a Chief Dietitian, the suggestions of a Senior Physician rumored soon to be elevated to Diagnostician were indistinguishable from orders.

"Gurronsevas," it went on, "I would like Timmins and yourself to redesign the mobile Chalder meal with a view to reducing its velocity and maneuverability. The physical effort involved in catching the food, however enjoyable it is for the diner and exciting for the watchers, could place the patient in danger of a relapse. Also, a less agile food package would greatly reduce the risk of structural damage to the ward equipment and decoration."

It turned towards Hredlichli and continued, "That risk could be further reduced by the right psychological approach on the part of your nurses and yourself. Nothing too authoritarian, you understand, because the Chalders are a sensitive species in spite of their imposing physical appearance. Just a gentle reminder that we are friends who are trying to cure them as quickly as possible so that they can go home. And suggest that at home they would not display such unruly eating manners in the dwelling of a friend. I feel sure this approach will greatly reduce the risk of structural damage. That should make you feel happier, Charge Nurse."

"Yes, doctor," said Hredlichli in a very unhappy voice.

"It will certainly make the maintenance department happier," said Timmins. "We will begin work on the modifications at once."

"Thank you," said Edanelt, and returned its attention to Gurronsevas. "But I can't help wondering which problem our very unpredictable Chief Dietitian will address next."

For a moment Gurronsevas was silent. On the Station's communicator the nurses were reporting on the condition of their patients who, they said, were displaying excitement but no other symptoms that would arouse clinical concern. The Senior's words, he realized, had not been a mere politeness. It was honestly curious and awaiting his answer.

"I am undecided, Doctor Edanelt," he said, "because I still lack dietary experience in many areas. For that reason I began with this minor and isolated problem involving a small number of Chalders, rather than modifying the meals served to a species which is more numerous within the hospital, and which would object massively if the changes were not to their liking. I plan to concentrate initially on the dietary needs of individuals. The first tests will be conducted on volunteers, but later it may be necessary to conduct them covertly without the knowledge of the target subjects. I would not want to attempt any major changes with the larger species' groups until I have more knowledge of medical and technical problems involved."

"Ghu-Burbi be thanked," said Hredlichli.

"That seems like a sensible plan," Edanelt said. "Who is to be your next subject?"

"A staff member this time," Gurronsevas replied. "I had several entities in mind but, under the circumstances, and out of consideration for its co-operation in providing facilities for today's test, *and* as a well-deserved favor in return for the severe emotional distress caused by the damage to its ward, I think Charge Nurse Hredlichli is the obvious choice."

"But, but you're not even a chlorine-breather!" Hredlichli burst out. "You'll *poison* me!"

Edanelt's crab-like, Melfan body began shaking gently and it was making noises which did not translate. Gurronsevas said, "True, but I have responsibility for the food requirements of everyone in the hospital, regardless of species, and I would be failing in my duty if I restricted my professional activities to warm-blooded oxygen-breathers. Besides, Pathologist Murchison has extensive experience with the PVSJ classification as well as having an Illensan chlorine-breather attached to its department, and they have both promised advice and assistance. They would not allow me to release any edible variants that were unsafe. If you are willing to volunteer, Charge Nurse, I can promise that you will be in no danger."

"The Charge Nurse will be pleased to volunteer," said Edanelt, its body still shaking gently. "Hredlichli, the culinary reputation of Gurronsevas throughout the Federation is such that you should feel greatly honored."

"I feel," said Hredlichli helplessly, "that I have just contracted a life-threatening disease."

CHAPTER 8

On Gurronsevas' second visit to the Department of Other-Species Psychology he found the same three entities busy at their desk consoles, but in the intervening time he had discovered who as well as what they were. The Earth-human in Monitor-green uniform was Lieutenant Braithwaite, O'Mara's principal assistant; the Sommaradvan, Cha Thrat, was an advanced trainee; and Lioren, the Tarlan, was a specialist in the uncertain area where other-species religions and psychology overlapped. This time he did not address himself to the entity possessing the highest rank, as was his custom, because all three of them might be able to help him.

"I am Chief Dietitian Gurronsevas," he said quietly. "If it is possible I would like to obtain information and assistance with a matter requiring a high degree of confidentiality."

"We remember you, Gurronsevas," said Lieutenant Braithwaite, looking up. "But you have called at the wrong time. Major O'Mara is attending the monthly meeting of Diagnosticians. Can I help you, or will you make an appointment?"

"I have called at the right time," said Gurronsevas. "It is about the Chief Psychologist that I wish to consult you, all of you, in confidence."

There came the strange, negative sound of three entities ceasing to work. Braithwaite said, "Please go on."

"Thank you," Gurronsevas said, moving closer and lowering his voice. "Since I joined the hospital I have not seen the Chief Psychologist visit the main dining hall. Is O'Mara in the habit of dining alone?"

"Correct," said Braithwaite, and smiled. "The Major rarely dines socially or in public. It is his contention that doing so might give the staff the idea that he is only human after all, with all the usual human faults and weaknesses, and that might be prejudicial to discipline."

"I do not understand," said Gurronsevas, after a moment's thought. "Is there an emotional problem involved, a crisis of identity perhaps? If the Chief Psychologist does not wish to be thought of as human, to which other species does it believe itself to belong? This information, if it is not privileged and you are willing to divulge it, would greatly assist me in the preparation of suitable meals. I am assuming that the solitary eating habit is to conceal the fact that it does not eat Earth-human food."

Cha Thrat and Lioren were making quiet sounds which did not translate and Braithwaite's smile had widened. It said, "The Chief Psychologist is not psychologically disturbed. I'm afraid my remark—about him not wanting to appear human—suffered in translation, and misled you. But what is it that you want to know, and how exactly can we help you? You give the impression that it has something to do with the Major's food intake."

"It has," said Gurronsevas. "Specifically, I would like all the information you can give me regarding its food preferences, the ordering frequency of favorite dishes, and any critical remarks the subject has made or may make about them in future.

"It is surprisingly difficult," he went on quickly, "to gather this kind of information without attracting attention to myself and arousing comment regarding a project that should remain secret until its completion. Many entities within the hospital dine alone, either out of personal preference or because urgent professional duties make the journey to and from the dining hall too wasteful of their time. Any record of the food ordered by them is erased once the order is filled and dispatched, there being no necessity to store such information, and the only way of discovering the dishes chosen would be to intercept the original order or breach the delivery vehicle, neither of which could be done covertly. It would be much simpler if you were to give me the necessary information."

"Unless the food chosen indicates depraved tastes, whatever that may mean in this medical madhouse," said Lioren, speaking for the first time, "information on food preferences can scarcely be classified as a privileged communication. I see no reason for withholding such information, but why not ask the Major for it directly? Why the need for secrecy?"

Surely the need is obvious, Gurronsevas thought. Patiently he said, "As you already know, I am charged with the responsibility for improving food presentation and taste, since the quality and composition of the synthetic materials used is standard and nutritionally at optimum levels. But the introduction of changes in appearance and taste, many of them quite subtle, to large numbers of diners, has one serious disadvantage. The changes would give rise to widespread discussion and argument regarding personal preferences rather than the reasoned and detailed criticism that would be of value to me.

"Naturally," he went on, "the testing of single members of selected species, as I have been doing with the AUGL patient One-Thirteen and Charge Nurse Hredlichli, produces useful data. But even with this method time can be wasted, albeit sometimes pleasantly, in debating culinary side-issues. I have decided, therefore, that for the best results the subject should be unaware of the test until after its conclusion."

For a moment Lieutenant Braithwaite stared at him, its mouth open but neither speaking nor smiling, and Cha Thrat had joined in its silence. It was Lioren who spoke first.

"As a person," it said quietly, "the Chief Psychologist is not well-beloved by anyone I know, but it is greatly respected by all. We would not wish to join in a plot to poison it."

"Could it be," said Braithwaite, finding its voice again, "that the pressure of responsibility and the enormity of its task has caused our Chief Dietician to develop a death wish?"

"The problem lies in my specialty," said Gurronsevas sharply, "not yours."

"Sorry," Braithwaite said, "my question was not meant to be taken seriously. But you risk offending a very powerful and short-tempered entity who is unlikely to conceal any mistakes if they occur. Maybe you should think about that before you begin."

"I have thought about it," said Gurronsevas. "If there is confidentiality, the risk is acceptable."

"Then we will give you what help we can," the Lieutenant replied, "but it may not be much . . ."

The arrival of O'Mara's meals was witnessed every day by one or more of the outer office staff, and the contents were enclosed in a sealed and insulated delivery float with a transparent cover. They were able to identify the meals going in and to draw conclusions from the uneaten remains coming out. Occasionally they were able to hear O'Mara criticizing a meal loudly enough for his remarks to be heard through the office door. The criticism usually included an identification of the dish that had been particularly offensive.

". . . So you can see," Braithwaite ended apologetically, "that any information that we can give you will be incomplete."

"But helpful," said Gurronsevas. "Especially if you will agree to keep me informed regarding the Chief Psychologist's words and reactions during and subsequent to the consumption of its meals. For the reasons already explained, I would be most grateful if your observation were of a covert nature and any behavioral changes, no matter how small, associated with the menu modifications I shall be making, were relayed to me without delay."

"How long is the project likely to last?" asked Braithwaite. "A month? Indefinitely?"

"Oh, no," he replied firmly. "There are over sixty different food-consuming life-forms in the hospital requiring my attention. Ten, or at most fifteen days."

"Very well," said the Lieutenant, nodding. "The observation of minor changes in personality or behavior, which can sometimes be an early indication of a major psychological problem developing, is what we in this department are trained to do. Is there anything else we can do for you?"

"Thank you, no," said Gurronsevas.

As he was turning to leave, Lioren said, "Speaking of personality changes, we are hearing rumors about Charge Nurse Hredlichli. Over the past few days it has been behaving very oddly, showing sympathy and consideration for its junior ward staff and showing early signs of becoming almost a likable personality. Had your PVSJ menu changes anything to do with that, Chief Dietitian?"

They were all making the quiet, untranslatable sounds which indicated that the question was not a serious one. Gurronsevas laughed softly in return.

"I hope so," he said. "But I cannot guarantee a similar result with Major O'Mara."

With the small part of his mind that was not concentrating on collision avoidance in the busy corridors between Psychology and the level housing Food Synthesis Control, Gurronsevas thought about Hredlichli. He had spent much more time than he had intended on the PVSJ exercise, but that was because the chlorine-breather had wanted to talk more than eat, and he knew that, however pleasantly, much of the time had been wasted. But in a few hours' time Hredlichli and himself would be ending this phase of professional contact, and he was almost sorry.

He was not surprised to see Murchison and Timmins already there when he arrived. The pathologist waved a hand at him and said that it had deserted its department for the rest of the day because this was where the action was. The words sounded like a shameful admission of professional negligence and irresponsibility, but he had learned not to take everything the pathologist said seriously.

Because of Gurronsevas' anxiety in case anything went wrong, Timmins had been asked to advise on the Maintenance Department support regarding the final program changes that were going into the synthesizer serving the PVSJ dining compartment, and hence was too busy to notice his arrival or even the presence of Murchison. Food Technicians Dremon and Kledath were making it clear by the impatient ruffling of their fur that they did not require advice.

Murchison moved closer to him and said briskly, "We completed our analysis of the sample of protective film used on that item of furniture in the exercise lounge adjoining the chlorine-breathers' dining area. The material has already been passed as safe, and it still is, but the film applied to that particular exerciser contained a small quantity of foreign matter that was probably introduced accidentally during manufacture. When exposed to the ambient chlorine atmosphere over a long period the material dissolves out, releasing trace quantities of a gas which, although completely foreign to their environment and metabolism, is harmless to chlorine-breathers even in high concentrations. The Illensan in Pathology describes the odor as appetizing. That was a nice piece of observation and deduction on your part."

"Thank you," said Gurronsevas. "But most of the credit should go to Hredlichli. It was the Charge Nurse who pointed out to me in the first place that a number of its colleagues who used that piece of equipment before meals—apparently Illensans suffer digestive upsets if they exercise after meals—insisted that it helped them work up an appetite. When one is pointed in the right direction it is much easier to reach one's destination."

"You are too modest," said Murchison. "But what are you planning to do next, and to whom?"

Gurronsevas was thinking that this was the first time in his life that he had ever been accused of modesty, when Timmins, whose head had been bent over the control console display, turned to say, "I can't wait to hear the answer to that question, too."

They were all watching him. Even the Kelgians were silent, their fur standing up in tight motionless tufts of curiosity. Gurronsevas knew that he would have to speak very carefully if he was to tell them what but not who.

"The PVSJ was a challenging but almost theoretical exercise for me," he said, "in that it involved the preparation and presentation of edible materials which I myself could not taste and which would have been instantly lethal had I tried. My next project will be more challenging but less dangerous to all concerned because, although the taste and presentation may be personally obnoxious, the food will not poison me or any other warm-blooded oxygen-breather.

"The test subject this time will be an Earth-human DBDG," he went on, "a member of the species which makes up more than one-fifth of the hospital's medical and maintenance staff and whose food preferences, as I know from my long experience in the Cromingan-Shesk, are very difficult to satisfy. Subsequently I hope to deal with the Kelgian, Melfan and Nallajim species, although not necessarily in that order."

The Kelgians' fur was eddying about their bodies with a motion too irregular for Gurronsevas to read their feelings with accuracy. Murchison was smiling and Timmins said quickly, "I would be pleased to volunteer, sir."

"Lieutenant," said the pathologist firmly. "Join the end of the line."

He was about to tell them that he no longer needed Earth-human volunteers when the lab communicator lit up with the image of Hredlichli. He saw at once that the Charge Nurse was calling from its private quarters because its features were clearly visible rather than being softened by a pressure envelope.

"Chief Dietitian," it said, "I would greatly appreciate having another progress report on your latest attempt to synthesize gree in yursil jelly, to which I was looking forward with great eagerness. The sample has not reached me. What happened to it?"

Food Technician Liresschi happened to it, thought Gurronsevas.

Aloud, he said, "Progress has been very good since we talked yesterday. In fact, I have finalized for synthesis five additions to the PVSJ menu: two main courses, and the three other complementary or contrasting sauces that we devised for use with existing dishes. By main meal time tomorrow your Illensan friends will be able to test the results. But be sure to remind them that all of the dishes have been synthesized and that the characteristic, lifeless taste of synthesized food about which you have complained is disguised, not removed, by the new material.

"One of the ingredients in the fryelli sauce does not occur naturally on your home world," he went on, "but Pathology assures me that it is metabolically harmless to you. Its appeal lies in the appetite-enhancing effect of the odor and appearance. The sauce itself is tasteless, but you will have difficulty in believing that anything that looks and smells so pleasant to you does not also taste good.

"Where the gree is concerned," he continued, "the changes are minor and for the most part visual. The surface of the translucent yursil jelly contains small, irregular convolutions which, when the diner is leaning forward to eat or talk, make it appear that the embedded synthetic gree beetles are in motion and therefore still alive. The weight of visible evidence overwhelms the diner's taste sensors so that—"

"No doubt it looks and tastes wonderful," Hredlichli broke in. "But what happened to the sample?"

Choosing his words carefully, Gurronsevas said, "Because it was due shortly to go into production, I sent it to you by way of Food Technician Liresschi for synthesis scanning and additional taste evaluation. Liresschi gave the sample full approval, but said that there were subtleties of taste that required repeated sampling before it was entirely satisfied. Regrettably, there was insufficient sample remaining for it to be worth passing on to you. But I shall be pleased to send you another—"

"But, but you said that the sample would be enough for four helpings!"

"Yes," said Gurronsevas.

"Food Technician Liresschi is a culinary barbarian," said Hredlichli angrily, "and a greedy slob!"

"Yes," said Gurronsevas again.

The charge nurse made a sound which did not translate, but before it could go on Gurronsevas said quickly, "I want to thank you for the help you have given me during our long talks together. Because of them, significant improvements have been made in the present Illensan menu, and in time more will follow. This project has therefore achieved its initial purpose and now I must begin another involving the dietary requirements of a different life-form. Again, Hredlichli, my thanks."

For what seemed like a long time Hredlichli did not reply, and Gurronsevas wondered whether his words had been lacking sensitivity. Over the years the Illensans had earned the highest professional respect but not the liking of their other-species medical colleagues, due largely to the difficulty of making easy social contact with them or having those opportunities to air their mutual non-medical thoughts, opinions and complaints which the oxygen-breathing species took for granted. Rightly or wrongly, they felt themselves to be a small, underprivileged, chlorine-breathing minority to whom nobody listened, so that individually and as a group their dispositions had suffered. There had been a marked change in Hredlichli's manner towards him during his work on the Illensan menu improvements, but whether that was due to him winning the Charge Nurse's heart through its stomach, or that the other had at last found someone who found what it had to say of value, or simply that it had made an other-species friend, Gurronsevas did not know.

He wished suddenly that one of the Psychology staff, Padre Lioren preferably, had been there to tell him what he had said wrong, and how best to unsay it. Then suddenly Hredlichli spoke.

"I may have a compliment as well as a complaint for you," it said hesitantly, "but I am not sure because, until recently, our ignorance regarding the eating habits and formalities of warm-blooded oxygen-breathers was complete."

Gurronsevas maintained a polite silence, and Hredlichli went on, "I have been discussing our work together with my Illensan friends and they are as pleased as I am about your menu changes. We have questioned the non-medical library computer and discovered that on Earth, which is one of the many worlds where the preparation and presentation of food has evolved into a major art form, there is a custom originating among a racial group called the French which appeals to us. At the end of a particularly pleasant meal the diners ask what they call the *Chef du Cuisine* to join them so that they can express their appreciation in person.

"We were hoping," the Charge Nurse ended, "that you will visit us in the Illensan dining-room during main meal tomorrow so that we can do the same."

For a moment Gurronsevas was unable to speak. Finally he said, "I am aware of that Earth custom and I am, indeed, greatly complimented. But . . ."

"You will be in no danger, Gurronsevas," Hredlichli said reassuringly. "Wear whatever type of environmental protection you choose. Only your presence will be required. We do not expect you to eat anything."

CHAPTER 9

When there were over ten thousand members of the medical and maintenance staff plus a few thousand patients that he would ultimately have to please, it was neither sensible, efficient nor even fair that he concentrate all his efforts towards the satisfaction of one being, even though it was probably the most influential entity in the hospital. The O'Mara project, Gurronsevas had decided, must be allowed to progress concurrently with those of others which were likely to present fewer problems.

The decision had been influenced by his spies from the Psychology Department who, after five days during which he had engaged in some subtle tinkering with the Chief Psychologist's food intake, had reported no discernable change in Major O'Mara's temper, behavior following meals, or manner towards subordinates or anyone else.

During one of their daily meetings in the dining hall, Cha Thrat suggested that the Major might be one of those rare people with the ability to ignore their sensoria while engaged in serious professional mentation during meals, and was therefore unaware of the changes. Braithwaite agreed, saying that it had smelled the difference the Chief Dietitian had made to O'Mara's meals, and that it would gladly offer itself as a more appreciative and responsive subject. Gurronsevas had replied by saying that data obtained from an objective and even hostile source was more valuable than that from an appreciative volunteer.

"However," he ended, "as there was no strong negative response from O'Mara, I have assumed that the changes are acceptable and have already introduced my Earth-human menu changes into the main dining hall's synthesizer. You, Lieutenant, and probably every other Earth-human in the hospital, will let me know what they think."

"We will," said Braithwaite, smiling as it called up the menu. "Which meals?"

"I need decent food, too," said Cha Thrat, "as much and as often as Earth-human DBDGs."

"I am aware of that," Gurronsevas replied, "and the hospital's single Sommaradvan DCNF has not been forgotten. But your species joined the Federation comparatively recently and, during my time at the Cromingan-Shesk, we did not have the opportunity of catering for Sommaradvans. Data on your eating habits and preferences is therefore scarce. If you wish to discuss them with me now I would gladly listen, if only to take my mind off the taste of this unappetizing mush that resembles only visually a truncated creggilon in uxt syrup. But my own favorite other-species dish is the Nallajim strill millipede, a beautifully-marked crawler with black and green hair about so long, and served live, of course, in an edible cage of cruulan pastry."

"Please," said Braithwaite, "I am about to eat."

"I, too," Cha Thrat said, "am suffering increasing abdominal discomfort. In a moment I shall probably turn myself inside out."

"Suffering is good for the soul, Cha Thrat," Padre Lioren joined in, "and if you do that we will find out whether or not you've got one."

Gurronsevas was trying to devise a reply that was both culinary and theological when a Hudlar wearing the insignia of a junior intern approached the table and vibrated its speaking membrane.

"Chief Dietitian Gurronsevas?" it said shyly, and waited.

The Hudlars had the thickest and most impervious skin of any Federation species, Gurronsevas knew from long experience, and the most sensitive feelings. He said, "Doctor, may I help you?"

"You may be able to help me, and my FROB colleagues," it said. "But is this an inconvenient time for you? Our problem is serious but non-urgent."

Gurronsevas said, "I have a few minutes to spare before leaving for Loading Bay Twelve. If you need more time than that we can talk as we walk. What is the problem, Doctor?"

While they had been speaking, all of Gurronsevas' eyes had been on the creature who, although not much greater in size, had a body mass at least four times that of his own. It had six tentacular limbs which served both as locomotor and manipulatory appendages and, like many immensely strong beings forced to live among entities many times weaker than itself, it was careful and gentle in its movements.

The FROB physiological classification, Gurronsevas reminded himself, had evolved on a heavy-gravity world with an ultra-dense atmosphere that resembled nothing so much as a thick, high-pressure soup. It was covered by a body tegument, transparent where it enclosed the eyes, that was as tough as flexible armor plating. As well as protecting them against the savage external pressure of their native environment, it enabled them to work comfortably in any atmospheric pressure down to and including the vacuum of space. Their skin was completely without seam or body orifice, the speaking membrane served also as its sound sensor, and they did not breathe. Food was ingested through organs of absorption that covered both flanks and the wastes were eliminated by a similar mechanism on the underside, both systems under voluntary control. When off-planet their food had to be sprayed on at frequent intervals because they were an energy-hungry species.

The most common problem with Hudlars was periodic starvation. When their minds were concentrating on their duties or an
interesting conversation, and often while they were hurrying to the
dining hall sprayers, they collapsed helplessly onto a ward or corridor floor whenever their food ran out, and they could not be re-
vived until they were repainted. If the coating of food was applied
without delay, there were no ill-effects, so the condition was considered to be a nuisance rather than a medical emergency. To reduce the incidence of Hudlars collapsing from malnutrition at the
wrong times and places, every oxygen-breathing ward in the hospital stocked a supply of Hudlar paint for use in these non-
emergencies. But this one's organs of absorption were thickly covered by nutrient paint, Gurronsevas saw, so its problem could not
be food.

It is always wrong, Gurronsevas told himself as soon as the
Hudlar began to speak, *to jump to conclusions.*

"Sir," it said, "everyone is talking about the alterations you
have made to the Chalder, Illensan and Earth-human menus. I, we
Hudlars, that is, would not want you to think that we are compli-
menting you simply for the purpose of influencing your future actions, because the compliment is deserved whether or not you . . .
Oh, are you leaving for Bay Twelve now? I, too, have business there.
Shall I walk in front of you, Chief Dietitian? We would make better time because the other entities using the corridors will try to
avoid colliding with a Hudlar, regardless of any differences in medical rank."

"Thank you, Doctor," said Gurronsevas. "But I'm not sure
that I can do anything for you. Hudlars are, well, Hudlars. My experience of serving patrons of your species was similar to what
happens here, except that a light screen was placed around their
dining area to protect nearby patrons from misdirected nutrient.
The food tanks were taken from stores, and the only function of
my kitchen staff was to ensure that the spraying equipment was
arranged on a suitably decorated floater. What changes had you in
mind, Doctor?"

Five minutes later they were moving along the corridor leading to the null-G drop-shaft that would take them close to Bay
Twelve, and still the other had not spoken. Gurronsevas did not
know whether it was disappointment or shyness that was keeping
the intern's speech membrane silent.

Finally, it said, "I don't know, sir. Probably I am wasting your
time and trying your patience. The food we are given is perfectly
suited to our nutritional needs and cannot be faulted, but it is utterly tasteless and unexciting when it enters our absorption organs.
I do not wish to criticize the Hospital or yourself because all Hudlar food supplied by the home planet tastes like this because, as you
will already know, it must be dried and all constituents likely to
cause spoilage removed before it is emulsified prior to suspension
in the nutrient paint. Attempts at synthesizing Hudlar food have
been unsuccessful, and most unpalatable."

It was Gurronsevas turn to remain silent. He sympathized
with the Hudlar, but he had asked a question and he was not going
to ask it again.

"I don't know what if any changes are possible," the intern
went on. "All Hudlars working away from our home planet use the
paint and are resigned to its use. But if only we could look forward
to the pleasure rather than the utter boredom of eating, we would
not, I feel sure, collapse so often in inconvenient places."

It had a point, Gurronsevas thought.

They were moving through the entrance to the control center
of Bay Twelve, through the transparent canopy he could see the
open cargo locks of the unloading dock and the hold of the recently
arrived freighter. The first sealed containers, brightly color-coded
to indicate origin and contents, were being withdrawn by the tractor beam operators. To facilitate the transfer both the bay and the
ship's cargo hold were airless and gravity-free. The final placement
of the containers was the responsibility of a swarm of cargo handlers of different species wearing red-and-yellow protective suits.
The whole process, Gurronsevas thought, resembled nothing so
much as a crowd of chidlren playing with outsized building blocks.

"Doctor," he said, "how and why does the nutrient paint differ in taste from the food on your home world?"

The Hudlar tried very hard to tell him how and why in great detail, and the picture of the other's planetary environment that emerged was intriguing and just short of incredible. As a child student Gurronsevas had been exposed to the basic information about Hudlar during the lessons on the Geography of Federation Planets. But now he was beginning to appreciate and understand it as would a native. The word-picture had holes in it, however, because the Hudlar was pausing from time to time, often in mid-sentence, as if its attention was not entirely on what it was saying. When Gurronsevas followed the direction of its gaze the reason became clear.

"That vessel has a Hudlar crew," he said, pointing at the open cargo lock and the figures who were busy positioning containers for withdrawal. "Are you acquainted with someone on board?"

"Yes," said the intern. "We grew up together. A friend of the family who is presently in female mode and who is to become my life-mate."

"I see," said Gurronsevas carefully. The mechanism of Hudlar reproduction was a subject he had not felt a need to study, and he did not want to become embroiled in the emotional problems of a lovelorn Hudlar.

"If I understand you correctly," said Gurronsevas, ignoring the change of subject, "the atmospheric broth that you absorbed on your home world consisted of tiny pieces of living animal and vegetable tissue which, because of the violent and continuous storms which sweep your planet, remains permanently in suspension in the lower reaches of your gas envelope. The toxic material that is also present is identified by the taste sensors in your organs of absorption and, because it produces a stinging or burning sensation, it is either rejected or neutralized. The intensity of your overall taste sensations are in direct proportion to the degree of toxicity. Is it the absence of these unpleasant taste sensations that is your principal complaint?"

"Correct, sir," said the Hudlar promptly. "The occasional bad taste is, or would be, a reminder of home and normality."

Gurronsevas thought for a moment, then said, "I well understand the concept of combining sweet with sour, or the astringent with the bland to improve the taste sensation. But frankly, I do not think the Hospital would allow me to introduce toxic material deliberately into a species' menu, especially if it would quickly render the remainder of the food supply inedible."

The Hudlar had no features to reflect its feelings, but the hard muscles supporting its speaking membrane had begun to sag. Gurronsevas went on, "However, I am willing to look at the problem. How can I obtain samples of this mildly toxic material? Must you send to Hudlar for it?"

"No, sir," said the intern quickly, its speaking membrane once again stretched stiffly in excitement. "A large volume of Hudlar atmosphere came aboard the freighter while it was loading on the home world. There is a pocket of it on the recreation deck. It will be pretty stale by now, but the non-edible material you need will be present in quantity. And if you would be interested in a tour of the ship while you gathered specimens, I would be pleased to arrange it."

Gurronsevas was remembering the Hudlar medic's childhood friend who was in female mode somewhere within the freighter. He thought, *I'm sure you would.*

CHAPTER 10

The Hudlar medic needed magnetic wrist pads, a sealed air-bag communicator to enclose its speaking membrane, but no other environmental protection of any kind, so that it dressed very quickly and was ready long before Gurronsevas; but, being a Hudlar, there was no other way for its eagerness to show.

As soon as Gurronsevas had learned of the arrival of a Hudlar freighter at Bay Twelve, he had decided to spend some time studying the unloading operation. It was a matter of professional curiosity. He wanted to observe and if necessary question all aspects of the hospital's food supply, storage, distribution and processing systems even though, as the Chief Dietitian with a specialist catering staff, he might never have need of the information. But he had followed this rule on taking up all new appointments and he had no wish to change the habit of a lifetime.

A few minutes later they were emerging into the temporary vacuum of the vast unloading dock, accompanied by repeated warnings not to get in the cargo-handlers' way or between the tractor-beam projectors and the incoming containers that were being moved and stacked with seemingly reckless speed. With the Hudlar taking the lead and staying close to the floor plating, and as they were about to enter the lock itself, an impatient voice on Gurronsevas' communicator ordered a three-minute hold on unloading operations to allow two members of the hospital staff to traverse the lock in the wrong direction. The voice, whose species of origin was unknown, sounded authoritative but impatient.

Another Hudlar detached itself from the cargo-handling team and joined them. It was polite and friendly, and became even more so when the intern explained Gurronsevas' position at Sector General and his professional interest in improving the quality of Hudlar tanked food. There were no objections to two members of the hospital staff touring the ship, it said, provided one of the crew accompanied them. It immediately volunteered itself for the duty and led the way towards the nearby personnel lock.

Like Chalder Patient One-Thirteen, Hudlars did not give or use their names in the presence of anyone who was not a member of the family or a close friend, and this one had not even revealed its rank, duties or identity number so that Gurronsevas did not know what it was. Judging by its assured manner of speech while it was discussing the mechanics of its race's food ingestion, it was possible that the other was the ship's medical officer.

Whether or not it was the friend in female mode that the intern had come to visit was also unknown. Hudlars were said to be very undemonstrative beings, at least in public.

"Is the gravity setting and external pressure comfortable for you?" asked the second Hudlar as they moved into the crew quarters. It was looking at Gurronsevas's protective envelope, whose flexible sections were pressed tightly against his body. Hudlars could live and work for long periods in airless and weightless conditions, but whenever possible they preferred the home comforts of high pressure and heavy gravity.

"Quite comfortable," Gurronsevas replied. "In fact, these conditions more closely approximate those on my home planet than the standard Earth-G maintained in the hospital. But I shall not unseal my suit, if you don't mind. Your air is rich enough in oxygen not to be lethal, but there are other constituents, some of them still appear to be alive, which might cause me respiratory distress."

"We do not mind," said the second Hudlar. "And you will find more of those constituents on the recreation deck, which is the best place to withdraw your non-edible samples. Is there anywhere else you would like to visit?"

"Everywhere," said Gurronsevas. "But especially the dining area and kitchens."

"You do not surprise me, Chief Dietitian," said the Hudlar, making an untranslatable sound. "Are you familiar with the layout of these vessels?"

"Only as a passenger," he replied.

"As a passenger," the second Hudlar went on, "you will already know that the majority of the Federation's starships are built by Nidia, Earth and your heavy-gravity Traltha because those three cultures produce the most dependable vessels. Even though the control systems, life-support and crew accommodation are built to suit the user species, Tralthan ships are the most favored by both the commercial operators and the Monitor Corps itself . . ."

"Who say," Gurronsevas joined in proudly, "that even the Tralthan earth-moving machinery is put together by watch-makers."

The Hudlar paused for a moment, then it said, "Correct. But I have no wish to give offense by presuming a low level of general knowledge. Only to say that this is a robust ship, built to Hudlar specifications on Traltha, so you can relax and throw your not in-considerable weight around safe in the knowledge that our equip-ment and fittings are not susceptible to accidental damage."

"No offense was taken," said Gurronsevas. Appreciatively he stamped his six heavy feet in turn with a force that would have se-riously dented Sector General's flooring. "Thank you."

As he followed them towards the control deck, he thought that the lighting was a little dimmer than that of his native Traltha, and made worse by some kind of colloidal suspension in the air that formed a grey film on his visor which he had to wipe clean every few minutes. Apparently the two Hudlars were not troubled by it.

Gurronsevas showed a polite interest in the equipment and displays on the control deck, but lingered at the screen which showed the unloading operation as viewed from the freighter. The Hudlar crew-member explained that the food material for the synthesizers in the warm-blooded, oxygen-breathing section, which was not susceptible to damage or chemical change through rough handling, was the first to be off-loaded. The Illensan material and their own tanks of compressed Hudlar nutrient required more handling before transfer to their respective storage facilities by the hands and gravity floats of specialist cargo teams, rather than being thrown about by tractor beam operators. The internal transfer teams, who operated without spacesuits, would join the other handlers as soon as the freighter's hold and the airless loading bay were returned to normal atmospheric pressure. This was happening as they watched, but given the size of the combined volume of the receiving dock and freight hold, the process was necessarily a slow one, and so would leave just enough time for the less fragile stores to be unloaded.

"The ship carries enough of all three types of cargo to keep the hospital supplied for one-quarter of a standard year," the Hudlar went on. "Supplying food for the more exotic life-forms, like that TLTU Diagnostician you have who breathes superheated steam and eats the Maker alone knows what, or the radiation-eating Telfi VTXMs is not our responsibility. Nor, I hope, is it yours."

"It isn't," said Gurronsevas, and added silently, "at least not yet."

If anything, he thought, the ship's dining area resembled an other-species communal shower. It was capable of accommodating up to twenty diners at a time although there were only five crew-members waiting to enter when Gurronsevas and his escort joined them. He was advised to remain outside and to observe the proceedings through a direct vision panel in the corridor rather than suffer the inconvenience of a protective suit and helmet plastered with Hudlar food. His two guides, whose well-covered organs of absorption showed that they had dined recently, remained with him.

The others hurried inside and the last one in switched on the facility.

Immediately the food sprayers set at close intervals into the walls and ceiling began pumping in nutrient at high pressure until a thick fog of the stuff filled the room. Then fans concealed around in walls came to life, whipping the dense atmosphere into a room-sized storm and keeping the food particles airborne.

"The food is identical with that used in the hospital and on all Hudlar ships and space accommodations," the Hudlar medic explained, "but the violent air movement closely resembles the continual storm conditions found on our world and makes it feel, if not taste, more homely. The recreation deck is even more home-like as you will see, but foodless and, for you, much less messy."

The recreation deck was empty because the rest of the crew were either dining or off-loading cargo. Lighting that was more subdued than that of the corridor outside made it just possible for him to see the details of exercise equipment, unlit reading and entertainment screens and hard, irregular masses of what might have been sculptures. There was no soft furniture or bedding because the Hudlars were too hard-skinned to require soft padding on which to relax. A tightly-stretched, circular membrane set into the ceiling was emitting whistling and moaning noises which he was told was relaxing Hudlar music, but it was fighting a losing battle against the howling and buffeting sounds of the artificial gale that was blowing around the room.

So strong were some of the gusts at times that they threatened to blow him off his six widely braced Tralthan feet.

"Small objects are striking my suit and visor," said Gurron-sevas. "Some of them appear to be alive."

"They are wind-borne stinging and burrowing insects native to our home world," said the Hudlar medic. "The tiny amounts of toxic material secreted by their stings affects our absorption organs briefly before being neutralized. To a species like your own, who have a well-developed sense of smell, the insects perform a function analogous to that of a sharp-tasting, aromatic vegetation. How many specimens will you require?"

"A few of each species, if there is more than one," Gurronsevas replied. "Preferably living insects with their stings and poison sacs intact. Is this possible?"

"Of course," said the medic. "Just open your specimen flask and reseal it when enough of them have been blown inside . . ."

He had been toying with the idea of sectioning off an area of the hospital's main dining room for the exclusive use of Hudlars, and of introducing wind machines and a small swarm of native insects so as to make their dining environment more enjoyable, but now it would have to be discarded. The insects blowing against his suit were trying with great persistence to bite and sting him through the fabric, and the thought of the havoc they could create among the hospital's unprotected diners should they escape from the Hudlar enclosure was too frightful to contemplate. He decided that the nutrient sprayers were a simple and well-tried method of feeding even though the food itself tasted like nothing on Hudlar.

While they were continuing to describe the sensations caused by native insects attacking the outer layers of their absorption organs, Gurronsevas noticed that a slight, intermittent tremor was affecting their limbs. He knew that the condition was not due to lack of food because both had recently been sprayed and, if it was a medical problem, then the intern would have made some mention of it. But was there another possibility?

Apart from the other-species and therefore sexually neutral presence of himself, they had been alone together in the empty recreation deck for nearly two hours. Gurronsevas did not know whether or not their species required privacy for what they might be intending to do, but he had no intention of waiting to find out.

"I am grateful to both of you," he said quickly. "Your information has been interesting and may prove helpful in solving your problem, although at present I do not know how. But I must not impose on your kindness any longer and will leave you without delay.

"Please," he went on as the Hudlar medic began moving towards the entrance, "I have a very good sense of direction so there is no need to accompany me."

There was a moment's silence as he turned to go, then the intern said, "Thank you."

"You show great consideration," said its friend.

Since joining Sector General the operation of Federation standard airlock controls had become a matter of routine, as had the checks on his protective envelope before changing environments. When the outer seal opened, his helmet indicators showed enough air in his tanks to last for half an hour. His thruster fuel was running low, too, but that was unimportant because he could make a weightless jump to the cargo lock and use thrust only for any minor course corrections.

During his visit the ship's vast freight hold had been almost emptied, but when he switched on his communicator there was the same continuous flow of instructions to cargo handlers and tractor beamers. The composition of the freight streaming through the cargo lock had changed to double-layer, 200-pack bales of Hudlar sprayers interspersed with strings of the bright yellow-and-green tanks containing the poisonous, high-pressure, chlorine-based sludge required for the Illensan food synthesizers. As the seal closed behind him, Gurronsevas positioned his six feet carefully on the wall, waited until there was a break in the rapidly-flowing stream of freight going past, and jumped towards the cargo lock.

At once he knew that he had made two very serious mistakes.

For the past two hours Gurronsevas and his leg muscles had been accustoming themselves to the three Gs of the Hudlar ship rather than the nil-G of the loading bay, so he had used too much power in his jump. He was off-course and spinning slowly and moving much too fast . . .

"What the blazes are you *doing?*" said an angry voice in his earpiece. "Get back onto the deck!"

. . . And he had forgotten to tell the tractor-beamers, who

could not see his jumping-off position because of the restricted view through the cargo lock, of his intention to return to the hospital. Quickly, he used his thrusters, but misjudged again and found himself tumbling towards one of the Illensan tanks.

"Beamer Three," said the voice again, "pull that damn Tralthan out of there!"

Gurronsevas felt the sudden, invisible tug of the tractor beam, but it was off-center so that it pulled only on his forebody and sharply increased his rate of spin.

"Can't," said another voice. "It's still using thrusters. Stop moving, dammit, so's I can focus on you!"

He had no intention of stopping. Behind him an Illensan food tank, touched briefly by the tractor beam, was rushing towards him. He used the thrusters at full power, not caring which direction he took so long as it would avoid a collision with that hurtling chlorine bomb. An instant later he crashed into a 200-unit bale of Hudlar sprayers.

In spite of the gravity-free state of the freight hold, the mass and inertia of a spinning Tralthan body was considerable. So was that of the food sprayers, several of which burst open in a great, soft explosion of nutrient paint that drove the others apart and into the path of the Illensan tank. The jagged edge of a broken sprayer must have ruptured it because there was another and greater pressure explosion and, as the constituents of the Hudlar and Illensan food reacted chemically with each other, a rapidly expanding cloud of yellow-brown, hissing and boiling gas began drifting towards the open cargo lock.

"Cut all tractors to the ship," said a voice urgently. "We can't see through this muck . . . !"

The steady procession of freight items that were still moving past him into the opaque cloud around the cargo lock and continuing through it—but not all of them. Some were striking the rim and bursting open with enough force to knock subsequent items off-course. The sounds of collisions and pressure explosions were continuous and the toxic cloud was growing rapidly, shooting out fat, yellow-brown filaments and threatening to engulf the entire freight hold within minutes.

Hudlars could survive the environments of most of the Federation planets as well as the vacuum of space, but contact with chlorine was instantly lethal to them.

Somewhere a siren came suddenly to life, its short, urgent blasts reinforcing a new voice that was repeating, "Contamination alarm, major oxygen-chlorine incident Loading Bay Twelve. Decontamination squads Two through Five to Bay Twelve at once . . ."

"Urgent to all Hudlar cargo handlers," the first, authoritive voice returned. "Evacuate your hold immediately and take cover in—"

"Duty officer, *Trivennleth,*" a new voice broke in. "We cannot get them all inside in time. Less than a quarter will reach safety. Propose pulling free with airlocks open, changing attitude ninety degrees using maximum leteral thrust port-side bow rather than main drive to minimize structural damage to the hospital—"

"Do it, *Trivennleth!*" the first voice replied. "All cargo bay personnel, reseal your suits and grab hold of something solid. Massive decompression imminent . . ."

Above the braying of the siren, Gurronsevas could hear a great metallic creaking and groaning from around the cargo lock as the freighter's lateral bow thrusters applied lateral pressure to push the interface surfaces apart. Suddenly there was the high-pitched whistle of escaping air that sucked away the obscuring clouds momentarily, revealing a dark, widening crescent where the airlock seals on one side had been pulled apart, then he felt himself being sucked towards the opening with the other loose pieces of cargo.

For an instant it seemed that every tank and sprayer in the vicinity was hitting him and splashing his suit with nutrient, then suddenly he was outside and the objects were drifting away from him.

If he had been wearing a heavy-duty suit, Gurronsevas knew that he would not have survived. But the lightweight protective envelope had been flexible enough to remain undamaged, although the same could not be said for its wearer. His left flank and outer surfaces of his medial and hind limb on that side felt like one great, livid bruise, and he had the feeling that it would feel worse before it felt better.

To take his mind off his discomfort, Gurronsevas moved his eyes to the few remaining areas of his helmet that were not obscured by paint so that he could watch what was happening while he awaited rescue.

The projecting structure of Bay Twelve's cargo lock had suffered a minor deformation when the freighter had twisted itself free, but the seal was still open and projecting a misty cone of escaping air mixed with pieces of unsecured cargo which were colliding and bursting against each other. *Trivennleth* had turned through ninety degrees and was lying parallel with the hospital's outer hull. By comparison the freighter's hold was only a fraction of the volume of the unloading bay and must have been airless by now, because its lock showed no signs either of mist or escaping cargo.

Its duty officer had acted decisively and well, Gurronsevas thought, and wondered why the Captain had not taken charge during the emergency. He was considering the possibility that the commanding officer had been the person he had left sharing the recreation deck with the Hudlar intern when he became aware that a voice in his headset was talking about him.

". . . And where is that stupid Tralthan?" it was saying angrily. "*Trivennleth*'s crew are safe in vacuum, no casualties. The same with our oxy-breathing handlers. Senior Dietitian Gurronsevas, come in please. If you're still alive, respond dammit . . . !"

It was then that Gurronsevas discovered that his suit had not escaped entirely without damage. The communicator's Transmit light would not come on.

Not only was his air running dangerously low, nobody would be able to hear his calls for help.

CHAPTER 11

It was completely incredible, Gurronsevas told himself angrily, that the Federation's foremost exponent of the art of multi-species cuisine was going to end his life asphyxiating inside a spacesuit smothered in Hudlar nutrient. No matter how subtly worded the manner of his death might be, as the final entry in a professionally distinguished life it was unfair, unsuitable and undignified. He could only guess at the kind of farewell message some of his less serious-minded colleagues would inscribe on his Pillar of Memory. But as yet he felt far too angry and embarrassed to be really fearful.

Surely there must be some means of signalling his predicament other than by radio. But the voices in his receiver—which, unlike the stupid transmitter, was working perfectly—were saying otherwise.

"Gurronsevas, come in please," said one of them. "If you can hear me but cannot respond, release your distress flare . . . Still no reply, sir."

"You're forgetting that it's a hospital suit," a second voice said, "for interior use only. It doesn't carry flares. And Gurronsevas had no reason to draw one because it wasn't expecting to leave the bloody hospital! But it is wearing a short-duration thruster pack.

You know what a Tralthan looks like so *look* for it. This one has a thruster pack and will be moving independently with respect to the general drift of cargo and trying to return to the cargo lock, if it is conscious and uninjured, that is."

"Or still alive."

"Yes."

Gurronsevas tried to ignore the pessimistic turn the conversation was taking and concentrated instead on the helpful advice it contained. The endless metal landscape of the hospital structure, the blunt, torpedo shape of the Hudlar freighter, and the cloud of dispersing cargo, some of it still steaming and spraying out a thick mist of chlorine or nutrient paint, was wheeling grandly around him. As the first voice had suggested, he should begin by moving independently of the material surrounding him. But first he would have to use the thrusters to kill his spin.

Because of his minimal experience of maneuvering with a thruster pack, it required several minutes as well as a considerable waste of fuel, which the indicators showed to be already dangerously low, before he was able to neutralize his spin. He estimated that at best he had only enough thrust to move himself, slowly, for a few minutes and a distance of a few hundred yards, and that his terminal velocity would fall far short of that needed to break free of the expanding cloud of cargo debris, much less bring him back to the unloading bay before his air ran out.

The voices in his headset were agreeing with him, but otherwise they were not being helpful.

". . . And we checked the suit register, sir," one of them was saying. "It shows the recent withdrawal of one Tralthan-style protective suit with a three-hour air supply and a standard thruster pack, just under two and three-quarter hours ago. If Gurronsevas used the thrusters during its visit to the Hudlar ship and remained sealed while doing so, it might not be able to move far or breathe for very much longer. A search and rescue team is suiting up, but where do we tell them to look for it?"

"Suppose it uses its remaining thrust to spin rapidly," said another, "that would enable us to get a visual fix on a rapidly rotating body of roughly Tralthan mass and—"

"I don't know, sir," the first voice replied. "Some of those cargo items are large and have mass and momentum in proportion. If Gurronsevas was unlucky enough to be caught between two colliding masses, it might no longer bear much resemblance to a Tralthan."

"Mount a tractor-beam on the outer hull," said the first voice quickly. "Use it in conjunction with the rescue team who will spread themselves out to search the cargo cloud in one sweep. If they spot anything that looks like our wanderer, you pull it in."

"Tractor mounts aren't exactly portable, sir," said the other voice. "We'll need time to clamp it in position and realign the—"

"I know, I know. Just do it as fast as you can."

Through the few clear patches in his helmet, Gurronsevas saw that he had stabilized himself with respect to the hospital because the cargo lock of the unloading bay, reduced by distance to a small, brightly-lit square, was no longer moving past him. Already tiny, Earth-human figures were moving equipment, presumably the tractor beam installation, through the lock and onto the hull. A few seconds later the first members of the rescue team came shooting out in powered suits to scatter towards their assigned search areas.

None of them were heading directly towards him, and Gurronsevas himself was headed for trouble.

The cargo debris was still expanding and dispersing all around him and the nebular fog of nutrient and chlorine was fading to a thick mist, except for one area nearby where a Hudlar food container had collided with something that had broken off its sprayer nozzle and sent it spinning. The container was discharging its contents in a thin, high-pressure jet as it spun so that it was encircled by a continuous expanding spiral of nutrient. Gurronsevas was too close and moving too fast to evade the bright, insubstantial rings of vapor with his thrusters, and could only wrap his arms around his head to protect the remaining clear areas of the helmet.

Just before he reached the bright, insubstantial barrier, Gurronsevas could almost believe that he was approaching and penetrating the orbiting equatorial dust of some vast, ringed planet, and he thought that the ending of his life was accompanied by some unusual and interesting experiences. He was pleased when he passed through without any further deterioration in helmet visibility.

Beyond the rings he saw another object about fifty yards ahead, a large, seemingly undamaged bale of Hudlar nutrient drifting without spin and motionless with respect to himself. It was not, therefore, a threat.

The rescue team was being widely deployed, but none of the voices reported sighting him, and he could see only one of them through the fog. He was wondering if he should wave his arms in an attempt to attract that single Earth-human's attention when he caught sight again of the spinning food sprayer that was producing the rings.

Perhaps, Gurronsevas thought with a faint stirring of hope, he would have time for many more interesting experiences before his life came to an end.

The undamaged bale of Hudlar food tanks was drifting nearby. He used the suit thrusters to close with it. In spite of his shortage of air and the need for urgency, he used minimum power so that the contact would be gentle enough not to set the bale spinning or damage the food tanks that lay like a large, tightly-packed carpet of eggs that was moving up to meet him.

He landed gently and, moving with great care, positioned himself as close to the center of the layer of tanks as his ungainly physiology would permit. Because the cargo had been orbitally loaded in weightless conditions and the hyperspace jump to Sector General had also been gravity-free, the two-layer bale was held in one piece by a tightly-stretched open net rather than a solid container. Gurronsevas was able to look between the long, tightly-packed cylinders to the opposite face of the bale, and beyond it to the hospital's outer hull.

Looking through the opening between the group of tanks closest to his helmet, Gurronsevas attached himself to the bale and used his suit thrusters to send it into a slow, controlled roll. When the brightly-lit cargo lock of Bay Twelve came into view, he checked the roll and with gentle applications of side thrust then centered the target in this crude sight and waited for a moment to be sure that it would stay there. Then he forced himself to think.

Gurronsevas estimated that there were one hundred food tanks in the layer around him, all of their nozzles pointing vertically upwards. A central group of about twenty of them were covered by his body and were therefore useless for his purpose, but the outlying tanks could be emptied without him being covered with nutrient. Very carefully he extended all his arms, selected two pairs of tanks that were equidistant from his central position, opened the nozzles for a maximum delivery jet rather than a spray, and switched all four on simultaneously.

He felt a very gentle pressure as the tanks emptied their contents rapidly into space. But the inertia of the cargo bale and his own large body had to be overcome, and it was too great for there to be any noticeable reduction in his velocity away from the hospital. He opened the valves on all of the tanks he could reach and was soon surrounded by spurting, inverted cones of nutrient paint. It was very important that his strange vehicle's center of thrust did not deviate from its intended direction of flight, so every few seconds he sighted through the tiny spaces between the tanks to ensure that the brightly-lit and now slowly expanding opening into Bay Twelve had not moved aside. Whenever it showed a tendency to drift, he corrected with his suit thrusters.

According to the helmet indicators, his thrust power had been exhausted minutes earlier. He assumed that the inaccuracy had been designed into them so that they read empty when there was, in fact, a small safety reserve remaining. Fervently he hoped that the same design philosophy had been used on his air tank indicators.

His difficulty in breathing, the pounding in his head and the increasing pain in his chest were probably psychosomatic, he told himself, and caused principally by foreknowledge. But he did not believe himself.

He was moving away from the expanding cloud of cargo debris and Lock Twelve was growing larger ahead. The rescue team members were continuing to send in negative reports. Surely, thought Gurronsevas, someone should have spotted him by now. Then suddenly they all did.

"Rescue Four, it looks as if one of the Hudlar bales sustained freak collision damage that ruptured the tanks on one side. It is moving in a direction opposite to the rest of the cargo and could be a personnel hazard . . ."

"Five here. Freak collision hell! Our missing Tralthan is riding on that thing. Oh man, that is one nice trick. But it's going in too fast . . ."

"Rescue team, can any of you intercept?"

"Rescue One. No, not before it hits. We're all moving in the wrong direction. Hull tractor beam, can you soft land it?"

"Negative, One. We won't be operational for another ten minutes."

"Then forget it and clear the area in case it lands on top of you."

"I don't think so, One. We've computed its trajectory and think it will make it through the airlock. That Tralthan knows how to . . ."

"Rescue One. All internal tractor beamers switch to pressor mode. Catch it as it comes in. Decontamination and medical teams stand by . . ."

His heartbeat was becoming so rapid and thunderous that it was difficult to hear the rest of the conversation and, in spite of the blurring of his vision, he could see the bright opening into Bay Twelve rushing closer. The nutrient tanks propelling him were emptying themselves, but unevenly so that his bale was beginning a slow, lateral roll that was moving him towards the edge of the lock opening.

For an instant Gurronsevas thought that he would pass through safely, but a corner of his vehicle struck the coaming and the whole bale disintegrated into its component tanks. Miraculously, he had escaped injury, but suddenly he was in the middle of about two hundred full and empty food tanks, all of them tumbling at high speed towards the inner wall of the unloading bay. Then he felt as if he had been punched all over his body as the immaterial rod of a pressor beam brought him to an abrupt halt, leaving the tanks to crash and burst against the inner wall. Those that were not already empty emptied themselves rapidly in all directions.

One of them struck his chest as it spun past, not violently enough to cause pain, but suddenly his communicator transmit light came on. All it had needed was a solid thump.

"Don't leave it hanging up there, dammit," said an authoritative voice. "Pull it into the personnel lock. Duty medic, stand by . . ."

"Gurronsevas," he said with great difficulty. "I need air, not medical attention, urgently."

"You're talking to us . . . good!" came the reply. "Hang on, we'll have you hooked up to a new tank in a few minutes."

Gurronsevas spent what seemed like a long time in the lock chamber having his protective garment cleaned of any possible chlorine contamination and removed, but his irritation was tempered by the fact that while the process was going on he was able to breathe again without difficulty, and think. The duty medic, a very officious Nidian, could not believe that he had escaped serious injury and wanted to transfer him to an observation ward, but that Gurronsevas would not allow. He compromised by allowing it to use its portable scanner on every square inch of his body.

He had plenty of time to listen to the voices in his headset describing many interesting events that he was unable to see. They spoke of small, unpressurized vehicles being dispatched to examine and retrieve the dispersing cargo for the purpose of salvage or later safe disposal, of *Trivennleth* redocking and of the temporary, fast-setting sealant that was being applied to the warped freight lock and the preparations for unloading its remaining cargo.

They did not mention Gurronsevas's daring self-rescue again, he noted with some disappointment. Perhaps they were too busy.

When the Nidian doctor finally released him, Gurronsevas asked directions to Bay Twelve's operations center because there were words that he must say to the people there. The staff, who were mostly Earth-human, looked up at him as he entered. None of them spoke, nor did anyone smile. Placing his feet quietly against the floor to demonstrate politeness and the fact that he was at a psychological disadvantage, he walked across to the being who was occupying the supervisor's position.

"I wish to express my sincere gratitude for the part you and your subordinates played in my rescue," said Gurronsevas formally. "And for any small way in which I may have contributed to your cargo accident, I tender my apologies."

"Any *small* way . . . !" began the supervisor. Then it shook its head and went on, "You saved your own life, Gurronsevas. And that idea of using the nutrient as a propulsion unit was, well, unique."

When it became plain that the Earth-human was not going to say anything else, Gurronsevas said, "Shortly after I joined the hospital I was told by an entity I shall not name, and whom I considered to be a culinary barbarian, that food is just fuel. I had not realized that it might be speaking the literal truth."

The supervisor smiled, but only for an instant, and the expressions of the others did not change. Gurronsevas did not need to be a Cinrusskin empath to know that he was not highly regarded by these people just then. But if they would not respond to a pleasantry, they could not refuse a polite request.

He went on, "I have in mind to make some important changes to the food supply of the Hudlars, among others. To make them it is possible that I shall require the permission and cooperation of the hospital's Chief Administrator. May I use your communicator? I want to talk to Colonel Skempton."

The supervisor swung its chair around to look through the observation window, a wall-sized sheet of transparent material as clear as air in the small areas where it was not covered with nutrient paint, at the team working on the damaged airlock, and at the littered and paint-splattered loading bay before turning back to face Gurronsevas.

"I feel sure," it said, "that Colonel Skempton will want to talk to you."

CHAPTER 12

It soon became clear that the loading bay supervisor was not familiar with the workings of the Chief Administrator's mind, because he was unable to talk to Colonel Skempton in spite of three attempts to do so. When Gurronsevas tried a fourth time, he was informed by a subordinate that the whole Gurronsevas problem had been passed to the Chief Psychologist who had been given Colonel Skempton's recommendations for its solution, and it was Major O'Mara that Gurronsevas should speak to, without delay.

The atmosphere in the Psychology Department's outer office reminded him of a gathering in the Room of Dying around the remains of a respected friend, but neither Braithwaite, Lioren nor Cha Thrat had a chance to speak to him because Major O'Mara did not keep him waiting.

"Chief Dietitian Gurronsevas," O'Mara began without preamble, "you do not appear to realize the gravity of your position. Or are you about to tell me that you are innocent, and that you are right and everyone else wrong?"

"Of course not," said Gurronsevas. "I admit to bearing some responsibility for the accident, but only because I was in precisely the wrong place at the wrong time and in circumstances where an accident was likely to occur. I cannot be held entirely responsible for it because, as you must agree, unless an entity is given complete control over a situation it cannot be held completely responsible for what happens. I had little control and, therefore, much reduced responsibility."

For a long moment O'Mara stared up at him in silence. The crescents of fur above its eyes were drawn downwards into thick, grey lines and its lips were tightly pressed together so that respiration was taking place, quite audibly, through its nasal passages. Finally it spoke.

"Regarding the matter of responsibility," it said, "I require clarification. Shortly after the accident I was contacted by a Hudlar who said that it shares responsibility for the accident with you. What have you to say about that?"

Gurronsevas hesitated. If the Hudlar medic was to become involved with the loading bay accident as well as a possible misdemeanor on the freighter, it might lose its internship at the hospital. The intern had been a well-mannered being, helpful with its suggestions regarding the Hudlar food problems and, no doubt, professionally competent or it would not have been accepted for training in Sector General.

"The Hudlar is mistaken," he said firmly. "It had business on board and accompanied me into *Trivennleth,* acting as my guide and advisor regarding some food problems. It wanted to escort me back again, but I insisted that I could return alone. Since I am Chief Dietitian and it a junior intern it had no choice but to comply. In this matter the Hudlar is blameless."

"I understand," said O'Mara. It made an untranslatable sound and added, "But you should also understand that I am not greatly impressed by acts of unselfishness or nobility of character. Very well, Gurronsevas, no official notice will be taken of your Hudlar intern's earlier words to me, but only because, in this instance, a trouble shared will not be a trouble halved. Have you anything else to say in your own defense?"

"No," said Gurronsevas, "because there is nothing else that I have done wrong."

"Is that what you think?" said the Major.

Gurronsevas ignored the question because he had already answered it. Instead he said, "There is another matter. For the continuance of my dietary improvements I require material which is not presently available in the hospital. But I am uncertain whether obtaining these supplies, which will have to be transported from many different worlds and will therefore incur considerable expense, is a simple matter of requisitioning them or one that will require special permission from the hospital authorities. If the latter, then it is only simple politeness that I ask the Chief Administrator in person. But for some reason Colonel Skempton refuses to talk to me or even . . ."

O'Mara was holding up a hand. It said, "One reason is that I advised him against seeing you, at least until the emotional dust settles. But there are others. You did cause that mess in Bay Twelve. Not deliberately, of course, and a major contamination, depressurization and structural damage to the cargo lock and *Trivennleth's* hold is expensive in maintenance time as well as the cost of—"

"This is shameful!" Gurronsevas burst out. "If, through some miscarriage of the law and deformation of Monitor Corps' regulations, I am to be held responsible for this damage, then I shall pay for it. I am not poor, but if I do not have sufficient funds, then deductions can be made from my salary until the cost is repaid in full."

"If you had the life span of a Groalterri," said O'Mara, "that might be possible. But it isn't, and in any case, you will not be asked to pay for the damage. It has been decided that the tractor-beamers have become so fast and proficient in their work that they may have grown a little over-confident, and their safety procedures are being tightened. Between the Corps budget and *Trivennleth's* insurance brokers, the financial aspect will be taken care of and need not concern you. But there is another price that you are already paying and I'm not sure if you can afford it. You are losing your reserves of good will.

"During your visit to *Trivennleth* and subsequent unscheduled EVA," O'Mara went on, without allowing him time to speak, "less catastrophic events were taking place in the AUGL ward. The convalescent Chalders became overexcited while chasing their self-propelled lunch and, according to Charge Nurse Hredlichli, all but wrecked the ward. Specifically, eleven sections of internal wall plating were seriously deformed and four Chalder sleeping frames were damaged beyond repair, fortunately without ill effects to the patients occupying them at the time.

"I know that Hredlichli is obligated to you," the Major went on, "because of improvements you made in the Illensan menu, but at present I would not say that it considers itself to be your friend. The same situation exists with Lieutenant Timmins, who is responsible for repairing the damage not only to the Chalder ward but minor sub-structures in Bay Twelve.

"But it is Colonel Skempton that you should worry about, and avoid meeting, because he wants you fired from the hospital and returned to your previous planet of origin. Forthwith."

For a moment Gurronsevas could not speak. It was as if his immobile, domed cranium were a dormant volcanic mountain about to split open under the double pressures of shame and fury over the fate that had allowed such a cruel injustice to be perpetrated on a being as professionally accomplished, and with so much to offer this establishment, as himself. But it was the feeling of shame which predominated, and so he forced himself to speak the only words that could be spoken in this situation.

Gurronsevas turned to leave, making no attempt to muffle the sound of his feet, and said, "I shall tender my resignation, effective immediately."

"I have found," said O'Mara in a voice that was quiet but somehow managed to halt Gurronsevas in mid-turn, "that words like forthwith and immediately are used very loosely. Consider.

"A ship bound for Traltha or Nidia or wherever else you decide to go," the Chief Psychologist went on, "may not call at Sector General for several weeks; or, if you choose to go to an obscure

Tralthan colony-world infrequently visited by commercial or Monitor Corps vessels, for much longer than that. The delay would enable you to complete any current projects before you have to leave. This would benefit the hospital, provided you do not involve it in any more near-catastrophes. And you personally would benefit because the longer you spend here the less likely it will seem to outsiders, including your colleagues in the multi-species hotel business, that your separation from Sector General was involuntary and your professional reputation would suffer minimum damage.

"Insofar as it is possible for a Tralthan," O'Mara continued, showing its teeth briefly, "try to keep a low profile. Do nothing to attract Colonel Skempton's attention, nor annoy anyone else in authority, and you will find that your departure will be something less than immediate."

"But eventually," said Gurronsevas, making a statement rather than a question, "I will have to go."

"The Colonel insisted that you leave the hospital soonest," it said, "and I promised that you would. Had I not done so you would have been confined to quarters."

The Chief Psychologist sat back in its chair, giving a clear, non-verbal indication that the interview was at an end. Gurronsevas remained where he was.

"I understand," he said. "And I would like to say that you have shown sensitivity and concern for my feelings in this situation. Your reaction is, well, surprising and confusing, because I could not imagine an entity with your reputation acting in such a sympathetic fashion . . ."

He broke off in embarrassment, aware that the attempt to express his gratitude was verging on the insulting. O'Mara sat forward in its chair again.

"Let me dispel some of your confusion," it said. "I am, of course, aware of your covert tinkering with my menu, and have been from the beginning. And no, the outer office staff did not betray you. You forget that I am a psychologist, and the type of continuous, non-verbal signals they were emitting was impossible to hide from me. And you betrayed yourself by significantly improving the taste of meals which were formerly so tasteless that I could safely engage my mind with more important matters while eating. But not any more. Valuable time is wasted wondering what new culinary surprise lies in ambush, or speculating afterwards on precisely how you achieved a particular taste. Not all of your changes were for the better, and I have sent you a list of my reactions to all of them together with suggestions for further modifications."

"That is most kind of you, sir," said Gurronsevas.

"I am not being kind," said O'Mara sharply. "Nor sympathetic, nor do I possess any of the other qualities you are trying to attribute to me. I have no reason to be grateful to a being who is merely doing its job. Is there anything else you want to say to me before you leave?"

"No," said Gurronsevas.

He could hear the movable furniture and O'Mara's desk ornaments rattling as he stamped out of the office.

"What happened?" said Cha Thrat when the door had closed behind him. From the way they were staring at him, it was obvious that the Sommaradvan was speaking for Lioren and Braithwaite as well.

Anger and embarrassment made it difficult for Gurronsevas to keep his voice at a conversational level as he replied, "I am to leave the hospital, not immediately but soon. Until then I am to do my job, as O'Mara calls it, without attracting attention to myself. I'm afraid the Major knows that you cooperated with me in making the menu changes. It was pleased with them but not grateful. Will any of you suffer because of the conspiracy?"

Braithwaite shook its head. "If O'Mara had wanted us to suffer, we'd have known about it by now. But try to look on the bright side, Gurronsevas, and do as he says. After all, the Major seems to approve of some of the things you are doing and wants you to continue doing them. If he had been displeased, well, you would not have been leaving soon but on the first ship going anywhere. You don't know what will happen."

"I know," said Gurronsevas miserably, "that Colonel Skempton wants to get rid of me."

"Perhaps," said Lioren gently, "you could covertly introduce substances into the Colonel's meals which would eliminate the problem by—"

"Padre!" said Braithwaite.

"I did not mean substances of lethal toxicity," Lioren went on, "but taste-enhancers similar to those used on Major O'Mara. There is a saying current among Earth-human DBDGs that the way to a man's heart lies through its stomach."

"Surely," said Cha Thrat, "a questionable and risky surgical procedure."

"I'll explain it to you later, Cha Thrat," said Braithwaite, smiling. "Lioren, psychologically that is sound advice, but Skempton is unlikely to be influenced as easily by Gurronsevas's cooking. His psych file says he is a vegetarian, which means that—"

"Now that I don't understand," Cha Thrat broke in again. "Why should a member of the DBDG classification, which is omnivorous, elect to become a herbivore? Especially when the basic food material is synthetic anyway. Is it some kind of religious requirement?"

"Perhaps," Lioren replied, "it has beliefs similar to the Ull, who say that to eat the flesh of another creature, sentient or otherwise, is to preserve its soul within the eater. But the Colonel has never consulted me on religious matters so I am unable to speak with certainty."

"Cooking for herbivores," said Gurronsevas, "has never been a problem for me."

Braithwaite nodded and Cha Thrat remained silent. Both of them were looking at the padre, all of whose eyes were directed steadily at Gurronsevas.

"May I also remind you," said Lioren quietly, "that this is a very large establishment housing many thousands of entities who, because of the nature of the work they do and their feelings and motivations regarding it, tend to have very short memories where the occasional interpersonal conflicts are concerned. If people held grudges in a place like this the level of mental health would be very low, and the type of person who would hold a grudge is excluded by the psychological screening.

"It may be that other events will transpire," it went on, "although hopefully not with as much potentiality for disaster as your own recent adventure, which will turn Colonel Skempton's attention in other directions and reduce its present hostility towards you. You are to leave the hospital soon, you say, but as a measure of time that period is flexible and your departure might not be permanent. To God or fate or whatever random operation of the laws of chance that you may or may not believe in, all things are possible."

Lioren paused for a moment, then added, "My advice is to follow the Major's advice and concentrate on the work that you are uniquely qualified to perform, and do not give up hope."

The advice was sound if ridiculously overoptimistic, Gurronsevas thought. But when he left them he was walking quietly and he did not know why he was feeling better.

CHAPTER 13

The feeling of optimism lasted for only a few hours, and during the first three days of maintaining a low profile he grew increasingly depressed, uncertain and lonely. His visits to his food synthesizer staff and Pathology became infrequent and brief because the people in both places kept looking at him when they thought his attention was elsewhere, but whether it was with sympathy or morbid curiosity he did not know. Apart from those few occasions he remained in his quarters, refused to answer the communicator and ate only from the food dispenser, which did not help lift his depression one little bit.

In the middle of the fourth day someone began tapping politely but with extraordinary persistence on his door. It was Padre Lioren.

"We have not seen you in the dining hall recently," it said before he could speak. "You could be overdoing the low profile instruction, Gurronsevas, because a complete absence will often attract more attention than a normal presence. In any case, most other species, myself included, have difficulty telling Tralthans apart without reading their IDs. I am on my way to the dining hall now. Would you like to join me?"

"My room," said Gurronsevas, embarrassment making him irritable, "is far from your normal path between the Psychology Department and the dining hall."

"True," said Lioren. "Perhaps I was making another call on this level, or I could be telling a therapeutic untruth. Which it is you will never know."

Without knowing why, Gurronsevas said, "All right, I'll come."

If more than the usual number of entities were watching him, he did not know about it because he kept his four eyes directed on Lioren, Braithwaite, Cha Thrat and his platter, and none of the conversations at nearby tables were about him. When he joined the others Gurronsevas wondered aloud how they had been able to obtain O'Mara's permission to leave their office unattended, and Braithwaite told him that it was an unwritten law of the hospital that nobody became mentally disturbed while the Psychology Department was out to lunch. Gurronsevas suspected that to be another therapeutic untruth, and decided that they were trying to humor him.

But very quickly the conversation became serious.

"We hear that you haven't been spending much time at the food synthesizers these past few days," said Lieutenant Braithwaite suddenly, "and there have been no recent menu changes. Was this by choice or is your work being hampered by others? O'Mara wants to know."

Surrounded as he was by three psychologists, he decided that it would be pointless not to tell the truth.

"Both," said Gurronsevas. "I had an aversion to meeting people, and my work was hampered, not by others but by a shortage of necessary supplies. I had intended seeking Skempton's assistance in providing them, because they are not on the normal list of provisions and may be expensive to bring here, but I am forbidden to speak to the Colonel."

"I see," said Braithwaite. After a moment's thought it went on, "In this medical madhouse we order up so much weird and wonderful stuff, equipment and medication and such, that procurement isn't normally a problem for any head of department. . . . Are you on friendly terms with Thornnastor."

"Thornnastor has always behaved politely towards me," said Gurronsevas. "But I fail to see the relevance of the Diagnostician-in-Charge of Pathology in this matter."

"Of course you don't," said Lioren, "at least not yet. But if you were to explain your difficulty to Thornnastor, it should be possible to circumvent the Colonel. Skempton's principal assistant is the Chief of Procurement, Creon-Emesh. It and Thornnastor have been close friends for many years, so much so that it would be difficult for either to refuse a favor asked by the other."

"I understand," said Gurronsevas. "When two members of a species engage in such a long-term emotional and sexual relationship, they think and feel as one . . ."

He broke off because Braithwaite and Cha Thrat seemed to be having respiration difficulties. Before he could express his concern, Lioren said, "They have been playing bominyat together, many say to planetary championship level, at every opportunity for more than a decade. Creon-Emesh is a Nidian, so the relationship is not, therefore, physical."

"My deepest apologies to both entities," said Gurronsevas in confusion. "But if Creon-Emesh is the Colonel's assistant, would it not tell—"

"It would not," said Braithwaite firmly. "It may be that I am divulging privileged information from Creon-Emesh's psych file . . ."

"I would say there was no doubt about it," said Lioren.

". . . when I tell you that the Chief of Procurement is an intelligent, able and ambitious entity who does not believe in bothering its superior with trifles, or even serious problems which it is capable of solving itself. In short, it is one of those rare and valued assistants who is constantly trying to make its superior redundant. It has respect but no strong affection for Skempton, and it will be aware of the Colonel's present antipathy towards you, so if you were to make the request in confidence and word it so that Creon-Emesh was faced with a challenge in the bominyat tradition . . ."

"With a mind as devious as that," said Cha Thrat, "the Lieutenant should play bominyat."

". . . you might get your supplies," Braithwaite continued, ignoring the interruption, "without the Colonel knowing anything about it. Or would you prefer me to make the suggestion to Creon-Emesh?"

"No," said Gurronsevas. "In my time I, too, have played bominyat, but only at inter-city level, so Creon-Emesh and I will have that in common. I am most grateful, both for the suggestion and your offer of help, but I would prefer to do it myself."

"If you are a bominyatti, too," said Braithwaite, raising a hand to acknowledge and dismiss his thanks, "you have nothing to worry about. But enough of these games of devious diplomacy and calculated manipulation of obligations. What menu surprises are you planning for us?"

The off-duty accommodation of Creon-Emesh was spacious, for a Nidian, but tiny and claustrophobic so far as the majority of other species were concerned. The ceiling was so low that, even with his knee-joints bent to maximum flexion and his arms tightly folded, Gurronsevas's head scraped the ceiling and his body threatened to dislodge the pieces of decorative vegetation hanging from the walls or demolish the ridiculously fragile furniture. An area on one side of the room had been cleared and the ceiling raised for the convenience of a more massive visitor, Thornnastor presumably, and he moved to it with relief.

"You are not here just to play bominyat," said Creon-Emesh before Gurronsevas could speak, "so that can wait. Thorny keeps telling me that my place resembles a Tralthan rodent's nest, so if you say anything polite about it I would not believe you. Please do not waste playing time. What is it exactly that you want of me?"

Gurronsevas tried not to take offense. The Nidians as a species,

it was said by their many critics, were not particularly strong or intelligent or in possession of effective natural weapons that had enabled them to become dominant on their home planet; they had
got there purely through their sheer, bad-tempered impatience
to evolve. But he felt it necessary to display a modicum of good
manners.

"Nevertheless," he said, "I am obliged to you for agreeing to
this meeting, especially as it is taking place when you are supposed
to be off-duty."

"Off-duty, on-duty, hah!" said the Nidian impatiently, nodding towards a display screen which was showing columns of figures rather than one of the entertainment channels. "It is the curse
of the truly dedicated not to know the difference. But if what I hear
about you is true, you have the same problem. What exactly is it
that you want from me?"

"Information on ordering procedures, assistance and your
discretion," said Gurronsevas. The other's bluntness of speech
seemed to be contagious.

"Explain," said Creon-Emesh.

But not too contagious, Gurronsevas thought. This was a situation which would need more than a few words of explanation. He
said, "When I came to Sector General I carried few personal effects
because, as you well know, Tralthans do not wear clothing and
scorn the use of body ornaments. Instead I brought with me a
quantity of herbs, spices and condiments native to Traltha, Earth,
Nidia and the other worlds who practice the cooking of food with
imagination rather than as a means of eliminating any harmful
bacteria it might contain. Material from this personal store has
been used to modify the standard meals of a few test subjects, and
now I wish to incorporate them, as well as a number of other improvements I have planned, in the main dining hall menus. When
I am forced to leave the hospital I would like to be remembered for
something other than the accident in Bay Twelve, or wrecking the
Chalder ward or—"

"Yes, yes, I sympathize," Creon-Emesh broke in. "But what do you want me to do?"

"The material is used in very small quantities so far as individual meals are concerned," Gurronsevas went on, "but if they are to be made available to everyone, which was my intention from the beginning, the small supply brought with me from Nidia will be exhausted within a week."

"Then order what you need," said Creon-Emesh. "You have a budget."

"Yes, a generous one," said Gurronsevas unhappily, "but regrettably insufficient. That is why I wanted to speak to Colonel Skempton, to have it increased. The supplies I need originate on a score of different planets, and the transportation costs alone would greatly exceed it."

Creon-Emesh gave a sudden, sharp bark and said, "You are too innocent for your own good, Gurronsevas, and plainly you have been too busy to discuss this problem with anyone in Procurement. But your only concern lies with the preparation of food rather than how it reaches us. Had you not become a foul stench in Skempton's nose, the Colonel would have educated you in our ways, as I am about to do. So listen carefully.

"You already know," it went on quickly, "that the Monitor Corps is responsible for the supply and maintenance of Sector General. For this it uses a very small part of the Federation's overall budget that finances the service as a whole. Supply includes providing us with species-specialized surgical instruments and equipment, medication, other-species atmospheres and, of course, food mass to top-up the synthesizer reservoirs as well as the Hudlar and Illensan food tanks which are more convenient to import. The Monitors also bring us patients who are beyond the clinical capabilities of the Federation planetary hospitals and are referred here for treatment, or the casualties of space accidents, or newly-discovered life-forms who are damaged or diseased or otherwise in need of medical care. Because the Corps vessels are not designed specifically for the large-scale transport of freight, they charter ships like *Trivenn-*

leth to do the work. It is therefore possible, with a little creative accounting within your budget allowance, to purchase supplies from any part of the explored Galaxy and have the transport charges set against the Corps' overall supply and maintenance budget, which is much too large for them to worry about what you are doing. Do you understand what I'm telling you?"

It was as if the artificial gravity grids in the floor had failed and he was about to float into the air, so great was the weight that had been lifted from him. But before Gurronsevas could find the words to express his understanding and his gratitude, Creon-Emesh spoke again.

"Naturally, the maintenance aspect does not concern you," it said, and barked softly, "although recently you have been the cause of quite a lot of structural repairs being carried out. You have a list of your requirements?"

"Thank you, yes," Gurronsevas stammered. "The principal items have been committed to memory. But will what you are doing for me cause you to smell as badly to Skempton as I do, or otherwise affect your chances of career advancement? And are you sure all this can be hidden from the Colonel?"

"To answer you in order," said Creon-Emesh impatiently, "no, no and no. We cannot hide anything from the Colonel, the system we use precludes it. Skempton will be able to see everything we do but, as it has been said many times, life is too short to waste time checking every requisition order which, on average, number several thousand per day. He leaves that to trusted but obviously untrustworthy subordinates like myself. So long as the identification codes, routing instructions and quantities ordered are not abnormal they will be accepted without question. If any of the items are likely to arouse Supply Department's suspicions, I'll tell you to think again.

"And remember," it went on, "ordering in quantity is preferable to periodic reordering of small amounts, which would increase the chances of what you are doing being detected. What are your principal needs?"

He tried to thank it again, but the other seemed to be interested only in his needs which, because of the little Nidian's continued lack of objection, were becoming more ambitious and daring by the moment. But Gurronsevas's enthusiasm was checked when Creon-Emesh barked suddenly and held up both of its tiny hands.

"No," it said firmly. "You cannot have morning-gathered Orligian crelgi leaves. Gurronsevas, be reasonable."

"I am reasonable," he replied. "The leaves have a subtle taste-enhancing effect which has crossed the species barrier, and are widely used by cooks of many warm-blooded, oxygen-breathing races. I am also disappointed."

"You are also forgetful," said the Nidian. "They would arrive here three days minimum after picking, because that is the fastest they could be hyper-jumped here. Our Orligian procurement office would have no trouble supplying them, but a jump like that is ordered only for urgently-required medication or to carry a critically ill patient. An emergency jump from Orligian to Sector General with a crate of herbal plants would most certainly attract the Colonel's attention, so it must be no to that one. Accept the leaves dry-frozen by normal freight delivery and I'll say yes."

Gurronsevas thought for a moment, then said, "There is an alternative called, on Earth, nutmeg. The taste difference is too subtle to be detected by anything but the most educated of palates, and it travels well. I have added it to the edible mud shell of the magma-flashed Corellian struul dishes to enhance the otherwise bland taste of the fish. And on Nidia the sauce I used with your braised criggleyut contained a sprinkling of nutmeg seasoning to bring out the—"

"You intend to add criggleyut to our menu?" Creon-Emesh broke in excitedly. "It has been a favorite of mine since my adult fur grew."

"At the earliest opportunity," Gurronsevas replied, and added, "About fifty pounds of it would be adequate for my Nidian and other-species' requirements."

Creon-Emesh shook its head. "You haven't been listening to me, Gurronsevas. Without mentioning it to you I have been trebling and quadrupling the amounts you have been ordering because you are not asking for enough. Small quantities attract attention. The unloading bay personnel might think that anything that small must be urgently required medication wrongly coded, rather than food, and open it to check, which would bring you to Skempton's attention. With a taste-enhancer that has so much other-species popularity and a long shelf life, I suggest a minimum order of five tons."

"But it is used in minute quantities," he protested. "Five tons of nutmeg would last us a hundred years!"

"In a hundred years," said Creon-Emesh, "the hospital will still be here, I expect, and its inhabitants will still be stuffing their eating orifices with food. Is there anything else? I want time for a game before you go."

CHAPTER 14

Visiting the hospital's Pathology Department reminded Gurronsevas of Nidia and his daily trips to the multi-species butcher's to buy fresh meat for the Cromingan-Shesk's carnivore-omnivore menu. Here he was not allowed to serve the whole or partially dismembered carcasses on show because they had once harbored intelligence and the hospital's regulations on that point were strict. No real meat, fresh or unfrozen, must ever be used.

Thornnastor, the multiply absent-minded Diagnostician-in-Charge, rarely spoke to him but the words of Pathologist Murchison and the rest of the department's staff were helpful, friendly, and, as now, even complimentary.

"Good morning," said Murchison, looking up from its scanner examination of an organic something which he could not identify. "You surprised us yet again. My hus . . . I mean, Diagnostician Conway says thanks for whatever you did to the synthi-steaks, as do I and, I'm sure, a great many other Earth-humans. Very nice work, Gurronsevas."

As Diagnostician-in-Charge of Surgery, Conway was second only to Thornnastor among the medical hierarchy, and it was also

Murchison's life-mate. In his present situation the gratitude of important beings could only be helpful.

Greatly pleased, Gurronsevas said self-deprecatingly, "The changes were minor and mostly of presentation, a small matter of culinary psychology, nothing more."

"Your Diagnostician's Alternative menu," said Thornnastor, turning an eye towards him and speaking directly to Gurronsevas for the first time in three days, "is not a small matter."

Gurronsevas agreed. To his mind all of the hospital's Diagnosticians and Senior Physicians with other-species teaching duties had been little more than culinary cripples who were handicapped to a greater or lesser degree by the alien Educator tape donors who shared their minds, often imposing on them their own alien viewpoints, emotional responses and, inevitably, food preferences.

The Educator tape system was necessary to the hospital's operation, Gurronsevas had learned, because no doctor, no matter how brilliant or able, could hold in its mind all of the physiological and pathological data necessary for the treatment of such a large number of other-species patients. With the tapes, however, the impossible became a matter of simple if sometimes unpleasant routine. A doctor with an other-species patient to treat was impressed with the mind-recording of a medical authority of that species until treatment was completed, after which the tape was erased. The reason for this was that the entire mentality of the donor entities were transferred and, even though they had no actual presence, and the host doctor knew this to be so, a non-material personality who had been tops in its field did not easily assume a subordinate position, and often gave the impression that it was the donor rather than the host who was in charge. Only Seniors and Diagnosticians of proven mental stability, and engaged in permanent teaching duties or ongoing research projects, were allowed to retain their tapes over long periods, but there was a price to pay.

Psychological problems were none of Gurronsevas's concern, even though he might have solved one of them. He was slowly extending his Diagnostician's Alternative menu and soon he would be able to cater for every life-form on the senior medical staff. Beings like Thornnastor, who possessed the appetite for food normal to a Tralthan of its body-mass, would no longer be seen seated at their dining benches, with eyes averted from the platter, in a vain attempt to conceal the contents from its other-species alter ego, whose revulsion would be communicated to the host mind. Now a tape-ridden diner could simply indicate the dish it required and request a visual presentation that would keep the donor entity happy, and the incidence of senior medical personnel going into periods of involuntary starvation would soon be a thing of the past. Even the acid-tongued Chief Psychologist O'Mara, Gurronsevas had been told, had been faintly complimentary about those particular changes.

But the person who was acknowledged to be the Federation's foremost practitioner in the art of other-species cooking should use self-depreciation in moderation.

"I agree that it was not a small matter," he said to Thornnastor. "It was a simple but quite brilliant idea on my part, one of many still to come."

Thornnastor made the low, moaning sound that one Tralthan uses to another to express concern and warning, and Murchison verbalized the non-verbal message. It said, "Be careful, Gurronsevas. After that *Trivennleth* incident you should not risk attracting attention to yourself."

"I am grateful for your concern, Pathologist," he said, "but I am supported by the belief that nothing very unpleasant can happen to an entity who, like myself, is working only for the general good."

Murchison laughed quietly and said, "Unless this is a social visit, which would be a unique occurrence, what problems are troubling you today?"

Gurronsevas paused for a moment to organize his thoughts, then said, "I have two problems. For the first I require your advice regarding my proposed changes in the Hudlar nutrient paint . . ."

Briefly he described his visit to *Trivennleth* and the idea that had come to him during the continuous, insect-laden artificial gale that blew around the ship's recreation deck. He produced his specimen flask and indicated a few of the insects that were still trying to bite or sting their way through its transparent walls. According to the Hudlars, the effect of these stingers on their organs of absorption was pleasant, stimulating, non-harmful and analogous to being in the thick, soupy fresh air of their home world.

"Even though it would greatly please the Hudlars on the staff," Gurronsevas went on, "I know that introducing a swarm of their native insects into the FROB section is inappropriate. Instead my intention, subject to Pathology Department's approval and cooperation, is not to release the insects but to have the contents of their poison sacs analyzed and the toxic material, less than a fraction of one percent by volume, added to the nutrient paint. If it can be produced in the form of a fine grit, a simple modification of the sprayer nozzle will allow minute amounts to be released into the food spray at intervals so that it would affect their absorption organs with the same random distribution as the original insect bites . . ."

"I cannot believe this," Thornnastor broke in, turning all four eyes in Gurronsevas's direction. "Have you forgotten that this is a hospital, where we are supposed to be curing people, rather than trying to poison them? Are you intending deliberately to introduce toxic material into the Hudlar food supply, and you want us to assist you?"

"That is perhaps an overly dramatic simplification, sir," Gurronsevas replied, "but yes."

Murchison was shaking its head from side to side, but its teeth were showing. Neither of them spoke.

"I am not myself a doctor," Gurronsevas went on, "but all of the medically-trained Hudlars with whom I have discussed the idea agree that the introduction of toxic material into their food in trace quantities would increase their eating pleasure, and they feel quite certain that there would be no harmful effects. I am inclined to distrust feelings of certainty when they involve subjective pleasures, remembering the long-term effects of chewing Orligian blue-hemp, smoking Earth tobacco or drinking fermented Dwerlan scrant, all pleasurable and supposedly harmless pastimes. That is why I am asking for your help to find out whether or not this alteration to the Hudlar menu is harmful.

"But if it is harmless," he went on excitedly, giving them no chance to speak, "just think of the result. No more Hudlars collapsing from malnutrition because their food is so tasteless that they forgot to eat it. Instead they would not forget because they would be looking forward with anticipation to their next spraying. And if the change proved successful here, there is no reason why it should not be introduced on ships and space construction sites wherever Hudlars are working off-planet. It would also, although I assure you that this is not an important consideration with me, be yet another culinary triumph for The Great Gurronsevas which would resound throughout the Federation. I would, of course, give all due credit to your department for the advice and assistance given . . ."

"I understand," Thornnastor broke in. "But if the changes you propose prove harmless, they would be important enough for me to discuss them at the next meeting of Diagnosticians where, regrettably, Colonel Skempton will be present. Do you wish to risk attracting its attention?"

"No," Gurronsevas replied firmly. A moment later he went on, "But I am having difficulty with the idea that a menu change, perhaps one that will turn out to have beneficial and far-reaching effects for the entire off-planet Hudlar population, should be withheld because of my own moral cowardice."

Thornnastor returned three of its eyes and part of its attention to the examination table before it replied, "Leave your specimens with Pathologist Murchison," it said. "You mentioned a second problem?"

"Yes," said Gurronsevas, turning to leave. "The problem is technical rather than medical, a matter of flash-heating a new dish to an ultra-high temperature for a precisely calculated duration so that the edible crust is hard-baked while the filling remains cold. It requires only another lengthy visit to the maintenance levels, which are already well-known to me, to familiarize myself with the food distribution and heat exchange systems adjoining the fusion reactor. No toxic additives are involved, no changes or risk to existing structures and equipment, the procedure I have in mind is perfectly safe and nothing whatever can go wrong."

"I believe you," said Pathologist Murchison as it took the specimen flask from him, "but why do I feel so uneasy?"

Eight days later he was remembering Murchison's words and his own stupid feeling of certainty while Major O'Mara was trying, with considerable psychosomatic success, to remove the thick, Tralthan skin from his back with a verbal flaying. And Gurronsevas's attempts to explain and excuse served only to make the Chief Psychologist angrier.

"... I don't *care* if it was a simple technical operation performed routinely by maintenance technicians every two weeks," said O'Mara quietly, in a strange voice that seemed to increase in fury as it decreased in volume, "or that the maintenance manual says that component failures of this kind are common and there was no cause for alarm because of the back-up system. This time *you* were there, which is usually reason enough for a catastrophe. And instead of a faulty cleaning cylinder blocking an emergency coolant supply pipe and needing retrieval, the sensors reported a quantity of unidentified ash which should not have been there. Suspecting that the ash indicated a major contamination, the entire reactor was closed down and the hospital went on standby . . ."

"The ash is harmless," Gurronsevas said, "a simple organic mixture of . . ."

"*We* know it's harmless," the Chief Psychologist broke in. "You've already told me that, and what you were trying to do with it. But Maintenance doesn't know, yet, and are investigating very carefully what they think might be a unique and possibly life-threatening situation. I estimate a minimum of two hours before they discover the truth and report it to Colonel Skempton who will want to see me. About you."

O'Mara paused for a moment, and when it went on it seemed that the anger in its voice was being diluted with sympathy as it said, "By that time I will be able to tell him with certainty that you have left the hospital."

"But, but Sir," he protested, "this is unjust. The component failure was an accident, my involvement was peripheral and the offense venial. And two hours! The time limit is unreasonable. There are instructions that I must give my food synthesizer staff and . . ."

"Neither of us has time to waste debating the concepts of justice and reasonable behavior," said O'Mara quietly, "nor will you have time for personal farewells. Lioren is waiting to help you clear your accommodation of personal effects and to conduct you to the ship without delay . . ."

"Where is it going?"

". . . which will, if or when its primary mission is accomplished," O'Mara went on, ignoring the question but answering it anyway, "either return you here to face your fate or leave you on a world of your choice, always provided you don't do something stupid to irritate its captain. Whatever you find to do, please try to stay out of trouble. Good luck, Gurronsevas. And go. Now."

CHAPTER 15

Unlike O'Mara, it was possible to reason with Lioren, at least to the extent of convincing it that the time saved in clearing his quarters should be added to that needed to leave proper instructions to his food technicians. Much time was wasted even so, because his people spent more of it regretting his departure and wishing him well than listening to his orders, so much so that he was feeling quite embarrassed when his time ran out and he had to leave the hospital.

He did not, however, have to travel very far.

"I—I don't understand," Gurronsevas protested. "This is a ship. A small, powered-down, empty ship, judging by the silence, the poor lighting, and this isn't passenger accommodation. Where am I? What am I supposed to do here?"

"As you can now see," Lioren said, switching on lights as it spoke, "you are on the casualty deck of the special ambulance ship *Rhabwar*, and you are to wait, patiently and very quietly, for its departure. While you are doing that the small number of people who know your whereabouts will be able to say, with the minimum of moral discomfort, that you are no longer in the hospital because, technically, this will be the truth.

"Being a Tralthan," it went on, "you are accustomed to sleeping on your feet and will be physically comfortable here. Do not try
to explore. Apart from this level, the ship was designed for operation by Earth-humans or other beings of similar or lesser body
mass. Its officers and medical team will behave much more pleasantly towards you if you do not damage the structure and equipment.

"The casualty deck's food dispenser is there," it went on, pointing, "and the nursing station console, which is over there, will enable you to call up all the information you could possibly need
about *Rhabwar.* Study it well before departure. You can call up the
training and education channels if you are bored, but do not use
the communicator because officially you are not here. Do nothing
to attract attention. Don't leave the ship, however briefly, or show
yourself in the boarding tube or access corridor. I will visit you as
often as possible."

"Please," said Gurronsevas. "Am I some kind of stowaway?
Does the crew know I'm here? And how long must I wait?"

Lioren paused inside the lock chamber. It said, "I have no information regarding your shipboard status. *Rhabwar*'s medical
team knows you are here, but the ship's officers do not, so you must
not reveal your presence to them until after the first hyperspace
jump. I don't know how long you will have to wait. Five days, according to one rumor I've heard, perhaps longer. The people concerned are having trouble making up their minds. If I find out for
certain, I'll tell you at once."

Lioren disappeared into the boarding tube before Gurronsevas could think of another question.

He waited for a moment until the confusion in his mind had
settled into curiosity and, moving carefully and placing his feet on
nothing less solid than the deck, began investigating his surroundings.

Each one of the compartment's walls was pierced by a large
direct-vision panel. One showed a featureless expanse of metal
which was probably the hospital's outer hull, another a section of

the docking cradle, and the other two looked out across the dazzling, white plains of *Rhabwar*'s delta wings. From the wall areas around and between the viewports projected equipment whose purpose would have been a total mystery to him even if it had been properly illuminated. In the center of the floor and ceiling were the circular openings to the communications well that gave access to the decks forward and aft. It was fitted with a multi-species ladder but was too narrow for a Tralthan.

The console that Lioren had indicated was surrounded by a mass of what appeared to be inactive medical monitoring equipment. He was still feeling too confused and ignorant to think constructively, so he called up the hospital's main library, keying for a Tralthan printed translation with spoken backup, and asked for the available information on the ambulance ship *Rhabwar*.

The console screen lit with a message that was repeated from the speaker unit in a condescending voice. "Information is available on this subject without restriction," it said. "Please specify precise requirements or choose from the following options: Ship design philosophy. Structural layout. Engineering and medical systems, sub-systems and equipment. Operating power reserves and mission duration. Crew and medical personnel specialties. Medical log of previous missions. Non-technical summary."

Gurronsevas felt like an uneducated child as he chose the last item on the menu. But as the screen and the speaker began to present their information, his feelings changed rapidly to those of surprise and wonder because the summary began with a history lesson, an illustrated discussion on the formation and evolution of what had become the present Galactic Federation, from a philosophical viewpoint that was completely new to him.

On the screen there appeared, small but diamond-sharp, a three-dimensional representation of the galactic double spiral, with its major stellar features and the edge of a neighboring galaxy, shown at distances that were not to scale. As he listened, a short, bright line of yellow light appeared near the rim, then another and another—the links between Earth and the early Earth-seeded colonies, and the systems of Orligia and Nidia, which were the first extra-terrestrial cultures to be contacted. Another cluster of yellow lines appeared showing the worlds colonized or contacted by Traltha.

Several decades were to pass before the worlds available to the Orligians, Nidians, Tralthans and Earth-humans were made available to each other. In those days, the precise, emotionless voice explained, intelligent life-forms still tended to be suspicious and distrustful of each other—in one case, the early contacts between Orligia and Earth, to the point of declaring the first and so far only interstellar war. But time as well as distance was being compressed in the summary.

The tracery of gold lines grew more rapidly as contact, then commerce, was established with the highly advanced and stable cultures of Kelgia, Illensa, Hudlar, Melf and their associated colonies. Visually it was not an orderly progression. The lines darted inwards to the galactic center, doubled back to the rim, see-sawed between zenith and nadir, and even made a jump across inter-galactic space to link up with the Ian worlds—although in that instance it had been the Ians who had done the initial traveling. When finally the lines connected the member worlds of the Galactic Federation, the result was an untidy yellow scribble resembling a cross between a DNA molecule and a child's drawing of a bramble bush.

Provided the exact coordinates of the destination world were known, it was as easy to travel through subspace to a neighboring solar system as to one at the other side of the Galaxy. But one first had to find an inhabited planet before its coordinates could be logged, and that was proving to be no easy task.

Very, very slowly a few of the blank areas in the star charts were being mapped and surveyed, but with disappointing results. When the Monitor Corps scoutships discovered a star with planets, it was a rare find—even rarer when the planets included one that harbored life. And if one of the native life-forms was intelligent, jubilation—tempered with a natural concern over what might become a threat to the Pax Galactica—swept the worlds of the Federation. It was then that the Cultural Contact specialists of the Monitor Corps were sent to perform the tricky, time-consuming and often dangerous job of establishing contact in depth.

On the screen appeared a succession of tabulations giving details of the survey operations mounted, the number of ships and personnel involved and a cost figure that had too many digits to be credible. The voice went on, "During the past twenty years they have initiated First Contact procedures on three occasions, all of which resulted in the species concerned being accepted into the Federation. Within the same time period, Sector Twelve General Hospital became fully operational and also initiated First Contacts which resulted in seven new species joining the Federation.

It might have been Gurronsevas's imagination, but there seemed to be a hint of pride creeping into the library computer's condescending voice as it continued, "In every case this was accomplished, not by a slow, patient buildup and widening of communications until the exchange of complex philosophical and sociological concepts became possible, but by rescuing and giving medical assistance to a sick or space-wrecked alien.

"In giving this assistance the hospital demonstrated the Federation's goodwill towards newly-discovered intelligent species more simply and directly than by any time-consuming exchange of concepts.

"As a result there has recently been a change of emphasis in First Contact policy. . . ."

Just as there was only one known way of traveling in hyperspace, there was only one method of sending a distress signal if an accident or malfunction stranded a vessel in normal space between the stars. Tight-beam subspace radio was not a dependable means of interstellar communication, subject as it was to interference and distortion by the radiation from intervening stellar bodies, as well as requiring inordinate amounts of a vessel's power that a distressed ship was unlikely to have available. But a distress beacon did not have to carry intelligence. It was simply a nuclear-powered device which broadcast a location signal, a subspace scream for help which ran up and down the communications frequencies until, in a matter of days or hours, it died.

Because all Federation vessels were required to file course and passenger details before departure, the position of a distress beacon was usually a good indication of the physiological type of the species that had run into trouble, and an ambulance ship with a matching crew and life-support equipment was sent from the ship's home planet. But there had been instances, far more than were realized, when the disasters had involved beings unknown to the Federation in urgent need of help which the would-be rescuers were powerless to give.

It was only when the rescue ship concerned was large and powerful enough to extend its hyperspace envelope to include the distressed vessel, or when the casualties could be extricated safely and a suitable life-support provided them within the Federation ship, were they transported to Sector General. The result was that many hitherto unknown life-forms, beings of high intelligence and advanced technology, were lost except as interesting specimens for dissection and study.

Another factor that had to be considered was that, whenever possible, the Federation preferred to make contact with a star-travelling race. Species who were intelligent but planet-bound might give rise to additional problems because there was no certainty whether full contact would help or hinder their future development, give them a technological leg-up or a crushing inferiority complex, when the great, alien starships began dropping out of their skies.

For a long time an answer to these problems had been sought and, in recent years, one had been found.

It had been decided to design and equip one vessel that would respond only to those distress beacons whose positions did not agree with the flight plans filed by Federation starships, a very special ambulance ship that would answer the cries for help of life-forms hitherto unknown to the Federation.

Gradually, as Gurronsevas concentrated more and more deeply on the displays, it seemed that his mind and the darkened casualty deck around him were becoming filled with pictures of devastated ships and drifting masses of space wreckage, and populated with the dead or barely living debris they contained. Sometimes the organic wreckage had to be extricated with great care because it belonged to a species new to the Federation, and beings who were in great pain and mental confusion from their injuries could react violently against the strange and terrifying monsters who were trying to rescue them. But there had been other times when the distressed ship had been undamaged and it was the crew who were urgently in need of assistance. Then it was *Rhabwar*'s commanding officer, a specialist in other-species technology, who had to find a way into the vessel and solve its alien and life-threatening engineering puzzles before the injured or diseased crew-members, who again might react violently at their rescuers' approach, could be treated.

The log was filled with such instances.

There was a full description of *Rhabwar*'s response to the distress signal from a ship of the Blind Ones and their sighted and incredibly violent mind-partners, the Protectors of the Unborn. And there was the vast gestalt creature of unknown name and origin whose miles-long colonizing vessel had been wrecked in interstellar space and a large-scale military as well as major surgical operation had been required to put the scattered pieces together and transport them to their target world. And there had been the Dwerlans and the Ians and the Duwetz, and many others.

Gurronsevas did not know enough about medicine to understand all of the clinical details, but that no longer mattered. So deeply engrossed did he become in the information and incredible events that were unfolding on the screen that, had the food dispenser been less conveniently placed to the console, he would not have bothered to eat. He was beginning to worry about the dangers he might have to face during *Rhabwar*'s next mission, but in a way he felt almost sorry that he lacked the qualifications to take an active part in it, especially when the ship personnel list revealed that he was already well-acquainted with two members of the medical team, Prilicla and Murchison.

On the screen the wreckage of alien starships and their other-species casualties disappeared to be replaced by a schematic drawing of the ship, and the voice began describing the ship's deck layout, crew and casualty accommodations, and principal systems, while the relevant areas were graphically highlighted. Gurronsevas tapped hold because the information being presented was becoming just so much meaningless light and noise. He had lost track of time. He was tired and hungry and his mind was too full of strange and wonderful information for sleep. Perhaps it was sheer fatigue that was causing his mind to throw up such fanciful ideas, but as he recalled some of the things that had been said and done to him by the Chief Psychologist and others, and in particular the things that should have been done and had not, his thoughts were making him feel afraid, uncertain, even more confused—and almost hopeful.

Rhabwar was indeed a very special ambulance ship. Soon it would depart on one of its very unusual and probably dangerous missions for which it had been designed. But what was a disgraced Chief Dietitian doing on board, unless O'Mara was trying to give him another chance?

CHAPTER 16

The next four days passed very quickly and without the slightest feeling of boredom, and it was only when complete body and brain fatigue forced him to leave the console that he moved to his concealed resting place behind a set of casualty bed-screens to try, not always successfully, to switch off his mind. Then on the fifth day he was awakened by the lighting being switched on and a voice saying loudly, "Chief Dietitian, this is Lioren. Waken quickly, please. Where are you?"

Gurronsevas' mind was too confused by suddenly interrupted sleep for him to reply, but by lowering the concealing bed-screen he answered the question and signaled his returning consciousness.

There was a sharpness in Lioren's tone that Gurronsevas had not heard before as it said, "Have you returned to the hospital or talked to anyone, however briefly, since we last spoke?"

"No," said Gurronsevas.

"Then you don't know what has been happening during the past two days?" it asked, making the question sound like an accusation. "Nothing at all?"

"No," said Gurronsevas again.

Lioren was silent for a moment, then in a friendlier voice it said, "I believe you. If you remained on *Rhabwar* and know nothing, hopefully you may not be at fault."

Gurronsevas disliked the implication that he might have lied. He tried to keep his anger in check as he said, "I have spent all of the time studying, doing exactly as I've been told, for a change, and thinking about my possible future position here. It is about that, if it could spare a few minutes, that I would like to speak to O'Mara. Now please tell me what you are talking about?"

The other hesitated again, in the way of a person who is trying to impart bad news as gently as possible, then said, "I have two pieces of information for you. The first is inexact and may turn out to be unpleasant for you. The second is very unpleasant for you unless you can assure me that you had nothing to do with the situation. I prefer to tell you the less unpleasant news first.

"It is about *Rhabwar*'s next mission," said Lioren. "This is little more than a rumor, you understand, because the mission is being discussed at a very high level by people who rarely gossip. A large number of expensive hyperspace signals have been exchanged about it. Contact with a newly-discovered intelligent species is involved, but there is doubt regarding the ambulance ship's ability to handle the situation. *Rhabwar*'s medical team thinks they can help and the cultural contact people insist it is their job. I think the final decision has been taken but implimentation was delayed because of the epidemic."

"What epidemic?"

Lioren hesitated, then said, "If you have not gone into the hospital or contacted anyone there you would, of course, know nothing. Your ignorance also increases the possibility that you have no responsibility for the situation."

"What situation?" said Gurronsevas, in a voice so loud with exasperation that it must have reached to the other end of the boarding tube. "What epidemic? And what have I to do with it?"

"Nothing, I hope," said Lioren. "But stop shouting and I'll tell you about it."

According to Lioren an unidentified epidemic had swept

through the hospital's staff and patients three days earlier. Only the warm-blooded oxygen-breathing species had been affected, although not all of them. Hudlars, Nallajims and a few others had escaped, including, for some unknown reason, several members of these species who had succumbed but who, as individuals, appeared to have immunity or were lucky enough not to have been exposed. The symptoms were nausea increasing in severity over the first two days, after which the patients were unable to take food by mouth and had to be fed intravenously. More serious was the fact that over the same period there was a gradual loss of the ability to communicate coherently or coordinate limb and digital movements. It was too soon to say that the IV feeding was successful in all cases; there were too many staff members affected who were too sick to investigate either their own or their patients' clinical condition properly, but there were indications that the symptoms of nausea and brain dysfunction were receding among those who were being fed intravenously.

"... But we can't keep every warm-blooded oxygen-breather who is affected, close on four hundred of them, on IV feed indefinitely," Lioren went on, "Even with them working round the clock, there aren't enough other-species medical staff to handle it. So far there have been no fatalities, but with ordinary patients still requiring treatment or surgery, we are being forced to use trainees and junior medics who are operating beyond their level of competence. Deaths are just a matter of time. We don't have the people for a proper investigation because the investigators are being affected too, in spite of the same-species barrier nursing precautions.

"Some of the senior medical staff escaped," Lioren continued. "Diagnostician Conway told me that in its case this might have been because it was concentrating on a Nallajim project at the time and its Educator tape was making it difficult to eat anything that did not look like birdseed. But if that is a factor in its immunity and if there is a correlation between the food eaten or not eaten and the onset of symptoms ..."

"Are you suggesting *food poisoning?*" Gurronsevas broke in, trying to control his anger. "That is insulting, outrageous and impossible!"

"... Given the widespread and concurrent onset of nausea symptoms, the obvious diagnosis would be food poisoning," Lioren went on, ignoring the interruption but answering the question. "The bulk material used for food synthesis is thoroughly tested for quality and purity before shipping, and sealed for transit in a manner that precludes chemical or radiation contamination. The many new taste enhancers recently introduced by you are subject to the same rigorous safety regulations but, because of their number and variety, it is more likely that toxic or infective contamination gained entry through this channel. And I agree, any form of toxicity finding its way into the hospital's food supply system is highly unlikely, but not impossible."

"Nothing is impossible," said Gurronsevas angrily. "But this is so close to it that ..."

"I don't wish to sound callous," Lioren broke in, "but if this outbreak is due to contaminated food, your professional embarrassment will be great, and even greater will be the relief of the medical staff because it would mean that they are faced with a medical problem that requires simple treatment. But if it is not food poisoning, and the nausea is a secondary symptom of a condition affecting the brains of several different intelligent life-forms, then we have a much more serious problem. It means that there is a hitherto unknown pathogen loose in the hospital that is capable of crossing the species barrier. Even a non-medical person like yourself knows that that, too, is impossible. But on Cromsag I learned the hard lesson that no possibility should be discounted."

Gurronsevas did know. From the time when he had made his first journey off-planet he had been told that there was no risk of him contracting other-species' diseases or infections. A pathogen that had evolved on one world could not affect any living thing that had evolved on another, a fact that greatly simplified the practice of multi-species medicine and surgery. But he had heard it said that the Federation medical authorities were constantly on the lookout for the exception that proved the rule. Regarding Cromsag, he had no idea what had befallen the Padre there, and he felt sure that this was not the time to ask.

"It is most urgent," Lioren went on, "that the food poisoning possibility be confirmed or eliminated as quickly as possible. The normal procedures for pathological investigation and analysis are too slow and uncertain right now. The investigators are too busy treating patients, or are patients themselves, or they have discounted the food-poisoning theory because it is too unlikely for them to waste time on it. But you will know what to look for and where. Food is your area of expertise, Chief Dietitian."

"But, but this is inexcusable," Gurronsevas said angrily. "It is a personal affront. Never before have I been associated with an establishment or a food service operation so lax in its standards of food hygiene that patrons were poisoned wholesale!"

"It may not be food poisoning," Lioren reminded him firmly. "That is what you and I have to find out."

"Very well," said Gurronsevas. He took a deep breath and sought for inner calm before going on, "I would like to have the patients questioned regarding the exact composition of the suspect meals, the time that the meal was eaten, if any unusual taste or consistency was detected, and whether the patient visited any particular section of the hospital or engaged in any activity that was common to all of them and which might have brought it into contact with a source of infection other than the food. Then I want to check on the operation of the main dining hall and subsidiary food computers and call up a breakdown of the menu demand and synthesizer output for the times when the infection is thought to have occurred. I would like to obtain this information at once."

"I can tell you exactly how one patient behaved," said Lioren quietly. "But Gurronsevas, please remember that the food poisoning idea is mine alone. Officially you are not in the hospital and, if you are innocent in this matter, it would be wrong to make you reveal yourself."

"If the symptoms in all cases are uniform," said Gurronsevas, feeling in no mood for another semi-apology, "an interview with one patient may be enough. Who and what was it?"

"The patient is Lieutenant Braithwaite," said Lioren. "About twenty minutes after we returned from the dining hall . . ."

"You *dined* together?" Gurronsevas broke in sharply. "This is exactly the kind of information I need. Can you remember which dishes you, or it, ordered? Tell me everything you can remember about the meal. Every detail."

Lioren thought for a moment, then said, "Fortunately, perhaps, my selection was from the Tarlan menu, a single course of shemmutara with faas curds. You can see that I am not adventurous where food is concerned. I did not look closely at Braithwaite's meal, or the codes it used while ordering, because the sight of most kinds of Earth food causes me internal uneasiness. We took only the main courses because it had a meeting with O'Mara directly after lunch. But I did notice that its platter contained a small, flat slab of synthetic meat, the stuff Earth-humans call steak, with several round, slightly toasted, yellow vegetables, and two other kinds of vegetation that looked like a heap of tiny green spheres and some pallid, round grey domes that looked particularly disgusting. There was a small dab of brownish-yellow, semi-solid material, possibly a condiment of some kind, at the edge of the plate. And, yes, a thick, brown liquid had been poured over the steak . . ."

Gurronsevas wondered what Lioren would have noticed if it had been looking closely. He said, "Did Braithwaite make any comment about the food, during or after eating the meal?"

"Yes," said Lioren, "but there was nothing unusual about that. A few other beings, not Earth-humans, had ordered the same meal and commented on it in my hearing. Some of the warm-blooded oxy-breathers here are in the habit of crossing the species divide in search of new taste sensations, and the practice has increased since your menu changes were incorporated. This is highly complimentary to yourself, or has been until . . ."

"Just tell me what Braithwaite said," Gurronsevas broke in. "Everything."

"I am trying to remember," said Lioren, with a Tarlan gesture that might have signified irritation. "Oh, yes. Braithwaite said that the meal had a peculiar, gritty taste, and that this was strange because it had ordered the same course on previous occasions without noticing anything odd about it. It also said that you were continually experimenting with the menu, that the latest change was probably an acquired taste, but if so, it was not masochistic enough to want to acquire it. The remainder of the meal was eaten quickly and silently because it did not want to be late for the meeting.

"On the way back to the department," Lioren continued, "it complained of feeling what it called queasy, and self-diagnosed the trouble as a digestive upset caused by it eating too fast. The meeting a short time later, comprising O'Mara, Braithwaite and Cha Thrat, was concerned with the psych profiles of the latest group of trainees. Because department business was being discussed rather than a personal interview, the connecting door had not been closed. I heard but did not see all that ensued. Cha Thrat filled in the visual details later."

Lioren made a series of small, untranslatable sounds, then cleared its breathing passages noisily and went on, "My apologies, Gurronsevas, this is not a laughing matter. Braithwaite began complaining of growing nausea, but answered Cha Thrat's sympathetic questions about its condition with loud abuse, calling O'Mara and Cha Thrat names that are not in polite usage, after which it became creatively if unintentionally insubordinate towards the Major, and ended by regurgitating onto the printouts covering the desktop. Soon afterwards Braithwaite began to lose both coherency of speech and muscular coordination in its limbs, and O'Mara had it transferred to a ward for clinical investigation. By that time the wards were filling up with similar cases.

"That was forty-three hours ago. Even though all of the patients affected have shown an almost complete remission of symptoms, since then the Major has been spending as much time as possible with Braithwaite, trying to establish whether its assistant's abnormal behavior was due to a new pathogen that has invaded and attacked the brain functions of those affected, which is the theory favored by the senior medical staff, or a side effect of food-poisoning which is the solution preferred by myself.

"If I am wrong it is better that you stay out of sight and, hopefully, beyond reach of the infection," Lioren ended. "If I am right, then the Chief Psychologist will not be pleased with you."

Nobody here is pleased with the Great Gurronsevas, he thought. *At least, they do not stay pleased for long.* He tried to fight against the wave of anger and disappointment that was sweeping over his mind by concentrating on what for him could only be a minor culinary puzzle.

"I will need to access the food service program," he said briskly. "But do not concern yourself, it will not require giving my identity."

Lioren's description had enabled him to identify the suspect meal, and given a close estimate of the time that the infection—if that was what it was—had occurred. The number of all meals selected were listed and stored on a daily basis so as to indicate current demand and to facilitate re-ordering and withdrawal of the non-synthetic material from stores. Diners' choices were subject to psychological factors—personal recommendations of an item by one's friends, the latest eating fad, a new entry on the menu that everyone wanted to try—which ensured that the total number of any given meal ordered would vary from day to day. But he knew the day and the suspect course, and now the number he was looking for was being displayed. He was tapping in the list of ingredients and requesting their full biochemical analyses when suddenly Lioren moved closer to the display screen.

"Any progress?" it said, in the voice of one who already knew and did not like the answer.

"Yes and no," he replied, moving an eye towards Lioren. "I am fairly sure that the suspect meal has been identified, and of the number of times it was served, but the . . ."

"You can be absolutely sure," said Lioren. "I know the total ward admission figure for the outbreak. It agrees exactly with yours. This does not look good for you, Gurronsevas."

"I know, I know," he said, pointing angrily at the display. "But look at that. The meal ingredients are innocent, uncomplicated and completely innocuous, and prepared according to my instructions. After processing and shaping in the synthesizer only three non-synthetic ingredients were added. These were trace quantities of the Orligian and Earth herbs chrysse and Merne Lake salt in the sauce and a light, overall dusting of nutmeg. None of them could have caused food poisoning. Could toxic material have been introduced externally, perhaps by a seepage of waste contaminants from adjoining piping . . . ? I must speak directly and at once to my first assistant."

"You must not call anyone within the hospital . . ." Lioren began, but Gurronsevas ignored it.

"Main Synthesizer, Senior Food Technician Sarnyagh," said the Nidian whose features appeared on-screen. If its expression was surprised, irritated, or worried at seeing him, Gurronsevas was unable to tell under the facial fur. Inevitably it said, "Sir, I thought you had left the hospital."

"I have," said Gurronsevas impatiently. "Please be quiet, and listen . . ."

As soon as he had finished speaking, Sarnyagh said impatiently, "Sir, that was the first question asked after the trouble developed. We called in our entire staff and spent the next two shifts answering it, even though Maintenance assured us that the layout and design of the associated plumbing made such cross-contamination impossible. We also checked the food synthesizer banks and enhancer storage, all of which tested pure. Have you any other ideas, sir?"

"No," said Gurronsevas, breaking contact. His earlier anxiety was fast approaching desperation, but there was a vague idea stirring at the back of his mind that was refusing to come out into the light, a tiny itch left by something the food technician might have said. To Lioren he went on, "If the fault isn't in the delivery system then it must be in the meal, which it isn't. Maybe I should make a closer study of the ingredients, even though they have been in use for centuries on and off their planets of origin. I will need the non-medical reference library."

There was a bewildering mass of information available on food herbs even in the comparatively small general library possessed by Sector General, and finding the three he wanted required a careful search through background material which, even with computer assistance, was very slow. He learned much interesting but useless information about the part played in the Kelgian local economy by their exports of Merne Lake salt, but the only associated fatalities had occurred during the dawn of their history when warring natives had drowned in it while it was still a body of water. It was the same with the Orligian chrysse polyps, and the references to Earth nutmeg were many but lacking in useful detail, until he came on one very old entry that might have been included as an afterthought.

Suddenly the itch at the back of his mind came out to a place where he could scratch it. His kitchen staff had been under pressure from the medical hierarchy. In the middle of a sudden emergency, a small change might be made, forgotten, or be considered too minor to be mentioned to a superior. Suddenly Gurronsevas stamped all of his feet, heavily and one at a time.

When the loose equipment on the casualty deck had stopped rattling, Lioren said, "Gurronsevas, what is happening? What is wrong with you?"

"What is happening," he replied, tapping the communicator keys as if each one was a mortal enemy, "is that I am trying to recall that miscenegenated apology for a food technician, Sarnyagh. What is wrong with me is that I want to commit violent bloody murder on another supposedly sapient being!"

"Surely not!" said Lioren in a shocked voice. "Please calm yourself. I feel, and I am sure that you will agree, that you may be overreacting verbally to a situation that in all likelihood might not require physical violence to resolve . . ."

It broke off as Sarnyagh's image reappeared. In a voice that was composed of equal parts of deference and impatience, the food technician said, "Sir. Was there something you had forgotten to ask me?"

Gurronsevas sought for inner calm, then said, "I refer you to my original instructions regarding the composition and presentation of Menu Item Eleven Twenty-one, Earth-human DBDG species, and additionally suitable for use by and available on request to physiological classifications DBLF, DCNF, DBPK, EGCL, ELNT, FGLI and GLNO. Compare the original composition with that of the meals actually served following taste enhancement and display both. Explain why an unauthorized change was made."

And if no change had been made, Gurronsevas was about to be very seriously embarrassed. But he felt sure that he would not be.

Sarnyagh looked down at its console and tapped briefly. Two short columns of data appeared as a bright overlay across its furry chest, with two of the quantity figures highlighted.

"Ah, yes, now I remember," said Sarnyagh. "It was a small change, or rather a correction of an error which it seemed that you yourself had made. If you can remember, sir, your menu instructions for this ingredient specified point zero eight five of the dish's total food mass which was, with respect, a ridiculously small quantity for something that is listed as an edible vegetation, so I assumed that the amount that you had intended was eight point five. Was I mistaken? Too cautious, perhaps?"

"You were mistaken," said Gurronsevas, striving not to scream abuse at it and to keep his voice at a conversational level, "and not cautious enough. Couldn't you tell by the *taste* that something was wrong?"

Sarnyagh hesitated, obviously suspecting that it might be in trouble and trying in advance to talk its way out of it, then said quickly, "I regret, sir, that I have neither your vast culinary experience nor your unrivalled ability to taste and evaluate a wide variety of other-species dishes. My preference is for the simple home cooking of Nidia and an occasional venture onto the Kelgian cold menu. The few times I tried it, I found Earth food to be lumpy, with too many color contrasts and aesthetically repugnant, so I would not have known whether it tasted right or wrong. Even though the change was minor and I would have asked your permission before making it had you been available, it was not made without careful consideration.

"Before making the change," Sarnyagh went on, "I checked with the medical computer to make sure that the item was not listed as toxic, which it was not. Also, the kitchen supply which you had brought with you from the Cromingan-Shesk had been running low. When I ordered a top-up I discovered that Stores had recently received several tons of the stuff. At the rate of use you had specified there was enough to keep us supplied for centuries. That was when I decided that you had made a mistake and corrected it. Have you any further instructions, sir?"

The reason for the overstocking had been purely administrative and of questionable legality, Gurronsevas remembered. It had been a means of ordering in bulk so that the material would be covered by the virtually inexhaustible supply funding of the Monitor Corps rather than his own department's relatively low budget. But he could not mention that without word of the transgression reaching Skempton through official channels; he did not want that to happen even if, as seemed likely, the Colonel already knew of it unofficially. No blame should attach itself to the Head of Procurement, Creon-Emesh, who had been most helpful to him. And Sarnyagh had done a neat job of passing most of the responsibility for its mistake back to Gurronsevas, and the food technician was going to get away with it.

He was reminded of the times in his own youth when he had learned the hard way that one's seniors had been placed above him because they knew more, not less, than their ambitious subordinates.

"My instructions," said Gurronsevas coldly, "are to reverse your unauthorized change and restore Eleven Twenty-one DBDG to its original composition. Do it at once. I am very displeased with you, Sarnyagh, but any disciplinary action that is needed must wait until . . ."

"But, sir!" Sarnyagh broke in. "This is unfair, petty. Because I made a harmless change on my own initiative and you think, wrongly I assure you, that it is a threat to your authority you are going to . . . Sir, there is much more important and urgent work to be done here. Following recent instructions of Diagnosticians Thornnastor and Conway we are in the process of physically check-ing through our entire food preparation and delivery system for possible entry points for contamination. Impossible, I know, but there has been a major outbreak of what they think might be food poisoning and . . ."

"That particular problem," said Gurronsevas firmly, "has been solved. Just do as I say."

When Sarnyagh's image disappeared, he went on to Lioren, "Perhaps I will not murder it, after all. But if you could tell me how to inflict some non-lethal injuries requiring a lengthy and uncom-fortable period of recuperation, I would be grateful."

"I hope you are joking," said Lioren uncertainly. "But is the problem really solved? And how?"

"I am joking," he replied. "And yes, your epidemic of so-called food poisoning is over. I'll tell you about it quickly so that you can contact Diagnostician Conway at once. It was a simple matter of . . ."

"No, Gurronsevas," Lioren interrupted gently. "This is your specialty. Conway is one of the few people who knows you are here. You will save time by telling it yourself."

A few minutes later, Diagnostician Conway was staring in-tently at him from the screen as he began to describe the unautho-rized change that had been made in DBDG Menu Eleven Twenty-one.

He went on, "It occurred because of my then ignorance, which has been rectified within the past few minutes, regarding a little-known side effect of the Earth herb, nutmeg, which is a taste enhancer that I like to use with this particular dish. Although it is no longer listed as a toxic substance, probably because its unpleasant gastric side effects when taken in quantity made it unpopular as a drug, in the distant past nutmeg was known as a mild hallucinogen. That was many centuries ago, when the use of mind-damaging drugs was common in several cultures. The quantity used in meal DBDG Eleven Twenty-one was one hundred times the specified amount. The Earth-human DBDGs and other species, taking it for the first time in these quantities, would be likely to suffer from progressively increasing hallucinations, lack of physical and mental coordination and nausea of the type that has been described to me.

"The error is being rectified as we speak," Gurronsevas added, "and the DBDG food service operation will be fully restored within the next two hours. The symptoms will fade rapidly and, according to the historical reference, the recovery of non-habitual users, your patients, will be complete within a few days. I am certain that your emergency is over."

For a moment Diagnostician Conway was silent except for the sound made by a long, slow exhalation of breath. Its recessed eyes swiveled to look past Gurronsevas at Lioren and the casualty deck behind them, then it smiled and said, "So you were right after all, Padre Lioren, and we were frightening ourselves needlessly over a widespread but basically simple digestive upset. And you, Gurronsevas, have solved our problem within a few minutes without even being here. That was nice work, Chief Dietitian. But what do you suggest we do with the food technician responsible?"

"Nothing," said Gurronsevas. "I have always accepted responsibility for the professional conduct, including the few mistakes, of my subordinates. Sarnyagh will be disciplined if and when I return."

Behind him Lioren made a quiet, untranslatable sound. Conway nodded and said, "I understand. But your return may not be for some time. Now that the epidemic scare is over, we will be launching *Rhabwar* within the hour."

CHAPTER 17

Following Lioren's lengthy farewell, and even lengthier exhortations against exercising his initiative too freely and the necessity for making friends, Gurronsevas had so much to think about that only a few minutes seemed to pass before there came another, expected interruption. It was the sound of movement forward, suggesting that several people were entering the ship through the crew access lock, and one of them was moving aft along the central well on the way to the Power Room. Simultaneously, another group entered the other end of the boarding tube and approached rapidly. From the babble of other-species word sounds he estimated that there were four different voices, but they were speaking too quietly for his translator to separate them. Quickly he dimmed the lighting, raised the bed-screen and concealed himself behind it.

As they entered the casualty deck the lighting came on at full intensity, the voices fell silent and there was the loud, unmistakable hiss and thump of the airlock closing.

The lengthening silence was broken by a voice speaking quietly in the musical trills and clickings of its native Cinrusskin speech, so that the translated words were unnecessary for the identification of the speaker.

"I sense your presence close by, my friend," said Prilicla. "At present and until the hyperspace insertion is complete, the casualty deck will not be in sound or vision contact with Control. You are among friends, Gurronsevas, so please lower that screen and show yourself."

There was a moment's silence while he stared at the four of them and they at him, then the Kelgian member of the medical team said, "Gurronsevas! You are *that* Gurronsevas? I thought you had left the hospital."

Murchison laughed softly and said, "You were right, Charge Nurse, it had."

"Friend Gurronsevas," said Prilicla as it fluttered gracefully into the air to hover above his head. "You already know Pathologist Murchison and myself, and we were not surprised by your presence because O'Mara told us that you were already on board, and why. Doctor Danalta and, as you can see from the agitated state of its fur, Charge Nurse Naydrad did not expect you, and may have seen you only at a distance. But in a ship of this size there are no distances, so we will have no choice but to become very close acquaintances and, I believe, friends."

A large mound of dull green, wrinkled jelly wobbled closer, extruded a single eye, ear and mouth and said, "We have seen each other on several occasions but, as a polymorph, there were personal or clinical reasons why I was looking like something else at the time. You do not show the surprise, even aversion, that many entities display when meeting me for the first time. I am very pleased to make your closer acquaintance."

"And I yours, Doctor Danalta," said Gurronsevas. "Your name and work are familiar to me because to, ah, pass my waiting time here I ran the log of recent missions, including the part you played in many of them. Even though the medical details were beyond me it was fascinating viewing. Towards the end I did not want to pass the time in any other way."

Prilicla settled slowly to the deck, its incredibly fragile, iridescent body quivering, but with the slow, gentle tremor that indicated pleasant emotional radiation in the area. It said, "The Chief Dietitian is too polite to mention it, but friend Gurronsevas has feelings of the most intense curiosity. Since the rest of us are fairly normal life-forms I must assume that its curiosity is regarding you, friend Danalta. Would you like to satisfy it?"

"Of course it would," said Naydrad, rippling its back fur disdainfully. "Our medical superblob likes nothing better than impressing strangers."

And it was also used to dealing with the other's impoliteness, Gurronsevas saw, because it quickly extruded a three-digited, Kelgian fore-limb and made a gesture with it which disturbed Naydrad's fur even more and said, "I would be happy to do so. But what is it about me that particularly interests you, Chief Dietitian?"

As they continued talking, the view from the direct vision panels around them showed that *Rhabwar* was edging its way through the sprawling, three-dimensional maze of the hospital's outer structures and the traffic markers. Once it was in clear space, Gurronsevas had learned, thrust would be applied which would take it out to the prescribed Jump distance where the hospital's more delicate items of equipment would not be affected by *Rhabwar*'s entry into an artificial universe that the ship had created for itself. But the time was passing very quickly and pleasantly because Danalta liked talking about itself and, unusually with such people, knew how to make the subject interesting.

Danalta's physiological classification was TOBS. It belonged to a species that had evolved on a planet with a highly eccentric orbit which produced climatic changes so violent that an incredible degree of physical adaptability was necessary for survival. The species had become dominant on its world and developed intelligence and a civilization, not by competing in the evolution of natural weapons but by refining and perfecting their adaptive capability. When faced by natural enemies or life-threatening events they had the four options of flight, protective mimicry, the assumption of a shape frightening to the attacker, or encasing themselves in a dense, hard shell. The species was basically amoebic but with the ability to extrude any limbs, sense organs or protective tegument necessary to any environment or situation in which it might find itself.

". . . In pre-sapient times the speed and accuracy of the mimicry was all-important," Danalta went on, and without a pause in its conversation it took the shape of a scaled-down Tralthan who was a perfect miniature of Gurronsevas himself, then more life-sized replicas of Naydrad and Murchison. "To avert a threat by natural predators, rapid reproduction of the would-be attacker's actions and behavior patterns were an important part of the process. This meant that we also had to develop the faculty of receptive empathy so that we could know how the other being expected us to look and act although, needless to say, it lacks the range and sensitivity of Doctor Prilicla's empathic faculty.

"With such physical and psychological protection available," it continued, "our species has become impervious to bodily damage other than by physical annihilation or the application of ultrahigh temperatures, which are threats posed by modern technology rather than natural enemies. While we have no trouble mimicking an infant in every detail we still, regrettably, die of old age."

"Fascinating," said Gurronsevas. "But surely, with this natural protection available, your species has no great need for doctors?"

"You are right," Danalta replied, "there is no need for the healing arts on my world, and I am not a doctor. But to a mimic of my capabilities, and at this point I must say that they are considered much greater than average among my people, an establishment like Sector General represents a tremendous challenge. Because of the work I am able to do on *Rhabwar* and among the ward patients, my friends insist on giving me that title.

"Do you have another question, Chief Dietitian?"

Gurronsevas felt himself warming towards this utterly strange being who, like himself, had come here solely because of the professional challenge.

While he was still trying to frame his simple question, which to a species as weird as Danalta's might give offense in a politely roundabout fashion, he felt a sudden dizziness. *Rhabwar* had reached Jump distance and entered hyperspace, a fact confirmed by the direct vision ports which were showing only a flickering greyness.

Prilicla said gently, "Gurronsevas, your hesitancy suggests that the question you wish to ask may be an indelicate one dealing, perhaps, with the subject of reproduction? Please remember that Danalta is a receptive empath, as am I. We are not telepaths. We *feel* that you have another question. We do not know what it is, only that you feel the answer to be important."

"Yes, it is important to me," Gurronsevas admitted, then went on, "Doctor Danalta, what do you eat?"

Pathologist Murchison leaned its head back and laughed, Charge Nurse Naydrad's silvery fur was rolling in slow, uneven waves from nose to tail, and Prilicla's body was reacting to what Gurronsevas now knew to be a sudden burst of pleasant emotional radiation. Only Danalta's body was still and its words serious.

"I am afraid that I will prove a grave disappointment to you, Chief Dietitian," it said, "because my species does not possess the sense of taste. Apart from the ultra-hard metals, I can and do eat anything and everything regardless of consistency or appearance. In moments of deep mental concentration I have been known to dissolve a hole in the deck plating on which I am resting, and in the past this has caused great annoyance to the ship's officers."

"I know the feeling well," said Gurronsevas.

While the others were displaying amusement in their varying fashions, he was remembering Lioren's final words to him. Gurronsevas was on probation, the Padre had warned him, and there were things he must try to do and not to do. Obviously he must make no attempt to tinker with the ship's food synthesizer. Above all, he must remember that he was on a small ship carrying a very small crew of specialists, and he must try very hard to make friends rather than enemies of them. Since the medical team had come aboard he had been trying to do that, by negating his own importance and displaying a friendly and admiring curiosity about Danalta and, in time, the others. Surprisingly, it had not required a great effort on his part, but now he was wondering whether he had overdone the uncharacteristic charm and they secretly thought of him as being shallow and insincere, or was it simply that they were trying as hard to be friendly as he was. He was also wondering if he would have as much success making friends with *Rhabwar*'s non-medical officers.

As if on thought-cue the internal comm screen lit up to show the Monitor-green–uniformed head and shoulders of an Earth-human.

"Casualty Deck, this is the Captain," it said sharply. "I overheard your last few minutes' conversation. Doctor Prilicla, what is that, that walking Tralthan disaster area doing on my ship?"

Even though Control was at long range for the Cinrusskin's empathic faculty, the Captain's emotional radiation was causing the empath some minor distress. Without hesitation Prilicla said, "For the period of the present mission, friend Gurronsevas has been co-opted to the medical team as a non-clinical advisor. Its expertise could prove helpful in what lies ahead. Please do not be concerned about possible effects on the structure of the ship, friend Fletcher. The Chief Dietitian will be accommodated on the casualty deck, it requires no special life-support and it will not risk damaging your light-gravity furniture and equipment by going forward, unless at your express invitation."

There was a moment's silence, but Gurronsevas was too startled and confused by Prilicla's words to be able to fill it with a question.

He had often heard it said that the little empath was not averse to bending the truth, a fact which Prilicla itself freely admitted, if by so doing it could improve the quality of emotional radiation in the area. An emotion-sensitive felt everything that those around it were feeling with the same degree of intensity, but the suggestion that Gurronsevas could advise *Rhabwar*'s medical team on anything during the forthcoming mission was utterly ridiculous. Doubtless the lie would improve the Captain's emotional radiation, Gurronsevas thought, but the effect would be temporary.

"I feel your curiosity, friend Fletcher," said Prilicla, no longer trembling as the Captain's anger diminished to irritation, "and I intend to satisfy it as soon as possible."

"Very well, Doctor," said the Captain, then went on briskly, "We are presently in hyperspace cruising mode, estimating the Wemar system in just under four standard days and the ship is running itself. A few minutes before boarding I was given the coordinates of the target system and the preliminary briefing tape, which there has been no opportunity to scan, and told that we would be fully briefed on arrival. Now would be a convenient time to run the tape so that we non-medics can be let into the secret of what we are supposed to be doing there."

"I don't know anything about it, either," said Naydrad, its fur spiking in irritation. "At least, nothing but a rumor that three weeks of top-level discussions were needed to decide whether or not *Rhabwar* could do the job. And when they did finally make up their minds, they keyed my alarm for a full emergency turn-out when I was right in the middle of . . ."

"Friend Naydrad," Prilicla broke in gently, "it is often the case that the time taken to reach a decision has to be deducted from that needed to carry it out. The rumor was not entirely accurate. I took part in those discussions but, in spite of our unrivaled reputation for pulling sick or damaged life-forms out of trouble, I was not sure that *Rhabwar* is capable of performing this mission. Many of the hospital's military and medical authorities agreed with me; the Chief Psychologist and a few others did not. The only reason for the secrecy was to avoid hurting the feelings of *Rhabwar*'s crew by publicly displaying their lack of confidence in us.

"And the questions that I feel you all wanting so badly to ask," it went on, "should wait until we have viewed the Wemar material.

"When you are ready, friend Fletcher."

CHAPTER 18

A t the time of its discovery three months earlier, it was not thought that the world, which its dominant intelligent species called Wemar, would cause the cultural-contact specialists of the Monitor Corps any serious problems. It was an environmentally distressed world with subsistence level living standards for the tiny remnant of its surviving population that verged on uninhabitability. In its recent history—from the orbital studies of industrial archeological remains the date was estimated at a little over four centuries earlier—the native culture had been technologically advanced to the level of maintaining orbiting space satellites, and there were traces of a non-permanent base on the system's closest and uninhabitable planet.

Because of their background of recently lost space technology, two important assumptions had been made. One was that the Wem would not be frightened by the idea of a galaxy inhabited by other intelligent beings and, even though they might be surprised and uneasy at the sudden arrival of a starship in orbit around their world, they would not be completely against the idea of making friendly contact with other-species visitors. The second assumption was that when contact had been widened and their natural fears al-

layed, they would agree to accept the offers of material and technical support which they so desperately needed.

Both assumptions proved wrong. When two-way translation-
communication devices were soft-landed in the few inhabited
areas—sound and vision communications were a part of their lost
technology—the natives exchanged only a few angry words before
ordering the strangers to leave Wemar and its system before smash-
ing all of the off-world devices. Evidently they had grown to fear
all forms of technology as well as the people who used it. Only
one small, isolated group had shown some trace of reluctance at
breaking off contact but they, too, destroyed the translator-
communicators that had been sent to them.

Plainly the Wem were a proud species who would not accept
the kind of help that the off-worlders were so anxious to give them.

Rather than risk the situation degenerating further, the commanding officer of the orbiting Monitor preliminary contact ship
obeyed the first order by ceasing to send down any more communication devices, and ignored the second, safe in the knowledge that
the planet-bound Wem could do nothing against the orbiting vessel which continued its close observation of the surface. Shortly afterwards, Wemar had been declared a disaster area, and *Rhabwar*
had been sent to assess the medical problems and, if possible, suggest a solution.

It had never been the Federation's policy to do nothing while
another intelligent species tried to commit suicide.

Rhabwar emerged from hyperspace some ten planetary diameters
from Wemar. From that distance it appeared to be like any other
normal, life-bearing world, with wisps and blankets of cloud and
the fat, white spirals of cyclonic weather systems softening and
breaking up its continental outlines and polar ice fields. It was only
when they had closed to within one diameter that the abnormal details became plain.

In spite of the generous scattering of rain-bearing clouds, it was only in a narrow band around the equator that the surface veg-etation showed any traces of normal growth. Above and below the green belt and into the north and south temperate zones the col-oration became increasingly tinged with yellow and brown until it merged into the tundra fringing the polar ice-fields. There were no large tracts of desert visible on those areas, it was simply that the once-thick forests and rolling grasslands of the past had withered and died or burned in what must have been great country-sized conflagrations due to naturally occurring lightning strikes, and the new growth was still fighting its way through the ashes of the old.

They were still watching but not enjoying the view when the casualty deck's communicator lit with the image of the Captain.

"Doctor Prilicla," said Fletcher, "we have a signal from Cap-tain Williamson on *Tremaar*. He says that it is operationally un-necessary for *Rhabwar* to dock with his ship, but he would like to speak with you at once."

The commanding officer of a Monitor Corps survey and pre-liminary contact vessel would hold a lot more rank than the Cap-tain of an ambulance ship, Gurronsevas thought, and clearly this one intended to use it.

"Senior Physician Prilicla," Williamson said without pream-ble, "I have no wish to give personal offense, but I am not pleased to see you here. The reason is that I am not happy with a mission philosophy based on near desperation and the assumption that if your presence here does not do any harm then it might do some good. From your briefing you already know that the situation here has gone sour and there are no signs of it improving. We are main-taining constant visual and surface sensor surveillance, but we have no direct communication with anyone on the surface. There is one small group of Wem who may be less proud and stubborn, or sim-ply more intelligent than the others, who gave the impression that a few of their number thought they might be able to benefit from our offers of help. But they, too, stopped speaking to us and smashed our translators. Personally, I believe there is still a possibility that, provided we do nothing further to offend them, this group might resume contact and, if it is handled carefully, enable us to reopen communications with the other, less amenable groups who in time will accept the large-scale disaster relief they need so badly."

Williamson took a deep breath and went on, "Regardless of your good intentions, *Rhabwar* blundering uninvited into this situation could end this tenuous future hope. And if you were to set down in an equatorial region, where the political power and the remains of their offensive technology are concentrated, it could also result in damage to your ship and casualties among your personnel. The efforts of a small medical team are not going to significantly affect the situation here, except possibly for the worse. . . ."

While the other Captain was speaking, Gurronsevas studied its manner and minor changes of facial expression. It was an Earth-human who in many ways resembled Chief Psychologist O'Mara. The hairy crescents above the eyes and the head fur showing below the uniform cap were an identical shade of metallic grey, the eyes never looked away nor did they blink, and its words carried the self-assurance that went with the habit of command. In manner, however, Williamson was much more polite than O'Mara.

The preliminary briefing had suggested that the medical team could expect some arguments from the authorities on-site, Gurronsevas thought worriedly, but this sounded like a very serious difference of opinion indeed. He wondered what a shy and timid emotion-sensitive like Prilicla could do against such strong opposition.

". . . Regrettably," Williamson continued, "I cannot order you back to Sector General because, theoretically, you have operational authority at the scene of any disaster, and this could quickly become a disaster on the largest scale. But the Wem are a proud race with a degenerating culture which, as often happens in situations like this, still retains much of its weapons technology. We do not want to risk another Cromsaggar Incident here. For the safety of your crew and to avoid the physical and non-physical trauma that a failure with casualties would bring to any empathic entity who was responsible, I would strongly advise you to return to Sector General without delay.

"Please give my advice serious consideration, Senior Physician Prilicla," it ended, "and let me know your intentions as soon as possible."

Prilicla was maintaining a stable hover in front of the communicator's vision pick-up and giving no indication of being intimidated, Gurronsevas saw, or perhaps it had only one form of response to another thinking being regardless of the other's high rank or bad manners. It said, "Captain, I am grateful for your concern over the safety of my crew, and for your understanding of the emotional distress I personally would suffer in the event of them sustaining injuries. Knowing this, you must also know that I belong to the most physically fragile, timid and abjectly cowardly species in the Federation, the members of which will go to great extremes to avoid physical pain or emotional discomfort for ourselves or those around us which, for an empath, is the same thing. Friend Williamson, it is a law of nature, an evolutionary imperative, that I take no unnecessary risks."

Williamson gave an impatient shake of its head and said, "You are the senior medical officer on *Rhabwar*, the ambulance ship that has more high-risk rescue missions to its credit than any other vessel in the Monitor Corps. You may argue that at the time those risks were necessary and unavoidable, even by a being to whom cowardice is a way of life. But with respect, Senior Physician, the risks you would take on Wemar are unnecessary, avoidable and stupid."

Prilicla showed no physical reaction to the other's harsh words and, Gurronsevas realized suddenly, the reason must be that *Tremaar* was orbiting many thousands of miles away and far too distant for even an empath of Prilicla's hyper-sensitivity to detect Williamson's emotional radiation. Gently, it said, "My immediate intention is to assess for myself the situation in the north temperate zone, where the technology level and living conditions are primitive and, hopefully, the Wem minds are more flexible, before deciding whether or not to land and/or subsequently abort the mission."

Captain Williamson exhaled audibly but did not speak.

"If or when we land," Prilicla went on, "I would be grateful if you would maintain orbital surveillance of the area so as to warn us of any hostile action that the Equatorials might be mounting against us. *Rhabwar*'s meteor shield will protect the ship against anything the Wem can throw at us, but I have no intention of starting a war, even a defensive war, and will lift off and go elsewhere before that can happen. I would also be pleased to have any new information not contained in our preliminary briefing. I would appreciate having that information as soon as is convenient.

"Our primary interest is in areas where there is little or no weapons technology," Prilicla continued, "and subsistence-level conditions with, if possible, a higher than average infant population. We are assuming that Wem parents resemble other civilized beings in that they would be willing to subordinate their racial pride and anger at outside interference if by so doing they could alleviate the hunger of their children. And if the proper approach can be made and the parents can be influenced into accepting our help, it would be advisable to minimize their embarrassment by not being too obvious regarding the food supply operation."

For a moment Williamson turned its head to give a quiet instruction to someone off-screen, then it returned its attention to Prilicla and said, "We both know that once you land in the disaster area, and in this case that means anywhere on this whole damn planet, you have the rank. Very well, your immediate requirement is for continuous intelligence updating, protective surveillance from orbit, and covert supply drops at night if or when necessary. You've got it. Anything else?"

"Thank you no, friend Williamson," said Prilicla.

The other began shaking its head slowly from side to side, then it said, "I was told that trying to make you change your mind would be like fighting cobwebs—a maximum expenditure of energy with minimum results. I have said all that I can to dissuade you.

It was good advice, Senior Physician, even though I cannot force you to take it, but . . . be very careful down there, friend."

Before Prilicla could reply, Williamson's face disappeared to be replaced by that of Captain Fletcher, who said briskly, "*Tremaar* is already sending the update you requested. Their communications officer tells me that it includes some nice close-ups of adult and young Wem, the disposition of their defenses and some ideas about their social structure and behavior, which are mostly guesswork, but that last bit is unofficial. I'll run the new material on your repeater screen as soon as we have it all. Meanwhile, *Rhabwar* is closing Wemar under cruising thrust and we are estimating low-orbit insertion in thirty-two hours and two minutes."

"Thank you, friend Fletcher," the empath replied. "That will give us plenty of time to review the new information before landing."

"Or time to change our minds about landing," said Naydrad.

Murchison laughed quietly and said, "I don't think so, that would be too sensible."

A few minutes later the main screen began displaying the new material and, during the discussion that followed, Gurronsevas quickly discovered what it was like to be an unseen observer.

Surprisingly it was the non-medic Fletcher who began by saying that, with all due respect, his opposite number on *Tremaar* had been deliberately exaggerating the threat posed by the Wem heavy weaponry which, they had seen for themselves, was very old, badly corroded, and showed no signs of recent use, while the emplacements and connecting system of defensive pits were overgrown or reduced by natural erosion. The long-range weapons were of the chemically-powered type firing solid or exploding projectiles, but in Fletcher's opinion they would be a greater danger to the users than their targets. Because the vision pickups sent down could not be directed inside a Wem dwelling or sub-surface arsenal without them being immediately seen and destroyed, it was possible that the Wem had concealed stocks of portable weapons but this, too, was unlikely.

"My reason for believing this," Fletcher went on, "is based on our covert observations of the young Wem. Like most youngsters, they play at being hunters or warriors, using the toy spears or bows and arrows that are the harmless, scaled-down weapons of the adults. But not one of them has been seen pointing a pretend weapon and shouting 'Bang!' which, incidentally, seems to be the same word-sound in every species' language, so it is unlikely that chemically powered weapons are used widely by their parents. As well, the population of the Wem fortified villages we've seen have shrunk so much that their defenses can no longer be fully manned. My feeling is that the early fortifications were built to repel raiders in search of meat. But now the surviving Wem are so widely scattered, and their numbers and those of their food animals so reduced, they are no longer capable of mounting a long-range raid because they would probably starve before reaching the target village.

"I think Captain Williamson was trying to scare us off before we could take a close look at the situation," Fletcher ended. "It is my feeling that the Wem do not pose a physical threat. What I don't understand is why, even though these people are facing imminent starvation, they are so choosy about their food."

"Thank you, friend Fletcher," said Prilicla. "Your words leave us feeling greatly reassured. And we are asking ourselves the same question. Friend Danalta, I feel you wanting to speak."

The green, organic mound that was currently the shape-changer quivered, added a loose, shapeless mouth to its single eye and ear, and said, "I have observed that hunger can make a civilized people behave in a most uncivilized fashion, especially when their dietary spectrum is limited. Fortunately, my own species was able to survive and evolve intelligence by eating anything and everything that wasn't trying to eat us. But can we decide whether this is a matter of tradition, some form of early religious conditioning? Or is it due to a basic physiological need?"

"No Wem burial places have been discovered," said Fletcher. "The outward sign of remembering or honoring the dead can indicate a belief in the afterlife. We can't be certain, naturally, but our present information suggests that the Wem are not religious."

"Thank you, Doctor," said Murchison. It moved to the console, tapped for RECALL and HOLD when the screen displayed the first of many close-up pictures of the natives, and went on, "The Wem life-form belongs to physiological classification DHCG. For the non-medics among us, that is a warm-blooded, oxygen-breathing species with an adult body mass just under three times that of an Earth-human and, since Wemar's surface gravity is one point three eight standard Gs, a healthy specimen is proportionately well-muscled . . ."

If anything, Gurronsevas thought as the succession of still and moving images continued, it resembled a picture he had once seen of a rare Earth beast called a kangaroo. The differences were that the head was larger and fitted with a really ferocious set of teeth; each of the two short forelimbs terminated in six-fingered hands possessing two opposable thumbs, and the tail was more massive and tapered to a wide, flat, triangular tip which was composed of immobile osseous material enclosed by a thick, muscular sheath. The flattening at the end of the tail, Murchison explained, served a threefold purpose: as its principal natural weapon, as an emergency method of fast locomotion while hunting or being hunted, and as a means of transporting infant Wem who were too small to walk.

There was one charming picture of a pair of adults—Gurronsevas was still not sure which sex was which—dragging their tails and two of their happily squeaking offspring behind them, and a less charming sequence of them hunting. For this they began by adopting an awkward, almost ridiculous stance with their forelimbs tightly folded, their chins touching the ground, and their long legs spread so as to allow the tail to curve sharply downward and forward between the limbs so that the flat tip was at their center of balance. When the tail was straightened suddenly to full extension, it acted as a powerful third leg capable of hurling the Wem forward for a distance of five or six body lengths.

If the hunter did not land on top of its prey, kicking the creature senseless with the feet before disabling it with a deep bite through the cervical vertebrae and underlying nerve trunks, it pivoted rapidly on one leg so that the flattened edge of the tail struck its victim like a blunt, organic axe.

". . . While the tail is highly flexible where downward and forward movement is concerned," Murchison said, "it cannot be elevated above the horizontal line of the spinal column. The fine details will have to wait until we are able to make an internal scan, but you can see from the visible external structure of the dorsal and tail vertebrae and associated musculature that it's impossible for the tail to be brought close to the back without major spinal dislocation. The back and upper flanks are, therefore, the Wem's only body areas that are vulnerable to attack by natural enemies, who must also possess the element of surprise if they are not to become the victim."

There was a brief sequence showing a quadruped, with fur so black that few physical details could be seen other than its long, sharp teeth and even longer claws, leaping onto the Wem from an overhanging branch. It dug its claws deeply into the victim's cloaked back and tore at the side of its neck while the Wem used its tail to jump frantically about in an attempt to dislodge the creature so that its spear could be brought to bear. Either by accident or design, one of its near vertical jumps sent it crashing against the underside of another overhanging branch, crushing the predator's body and causing a large quantity of its own blood and internal organs to be expelled through its mouth. Both bodies dropped to the ground where, Murchison said, they terminated a few minutes later.

Gurronsevas turned his eyes towards the direct vision port before the sight made him nauseated.

Murchison went on, "The black furry creature is one of, and probably the most dangerous of, the animals hunted for food, and plainly there is room for argument regarding who are the eaters and who the eaten. But enough of the bloody melodrama. It is shown to make us more aware and cautious of the creatures, both intelligent and non-intelligent, we will be meeting down there, and to make an important anatomical point. Confirmation will have to wait on an internal scan of the Wem stomach and digestive system but, based on our external visuals we can say . . ."

For a few minutes the pathologist's language became so densely specialized that Gurronsevas could understand only the odd word. But its concluding summation, perhaps for his benefit, was clear and unambiguous.

". . . So there can be no doubt that the Wem life-form evolved as, and still remains, an omnivore," Murchison said. "There is no external evidence of it ever possessing the multiple stomach system characteristic of a ruminant herbivore, and I would say that its digestive system is unspecialized and not unlike our own. With the exception of Danalta's, that is. Add the fact that the very young Wem have been seen to eat a combination of animal and vegetable matter, the proportion of animal tissue increasing with the approach of puberty. In a sapient species this means that the carnivorous eating habit is a matter of choice rather than physiological necessity. In their past there may have been environmental or sociological factors influencing them to make this choice but, whatever the reason, in the present situation it is the wrong one. Unless the Wem can be made to change their present eating habits, their food animals will be hunted to extinction while they themselves die of starvation because they insist on being hunters. As farmers they just might survive."

Murchison paused, its features still and serious as it looked around at all of them, then it said grimly, "Somehow we must convince a planet full of meat-eaters to become vegetarians."

A long silence followed its words. The pathologist did not move and neither did Danalta, but Prilicla was being shaken by the intensity of the others' emotional radiation, and Naydrad's silvery, expressive pelt was being stirred by sudden waves and eddies as if it, too, were being blown by an unfelt wind.

Loudly, it said, "Is *that* why Gurronsevas is here?"

CHAPTER 19

Rhabwar went sub-orbital and subsonic on its approach to the north temperate zone site where, according to Williamson, there was a Wem settlement that might not be as proud and hostile as the others. Gurronsevas was being given the opportunity to view directly a large tract of Wem landscape, not because Captain Fletcher thought that they would enjoy a slow, low-level pass over a planetary surface that was new to them, but because it was considered bad practice to drag a sonic shockwave over an area where one hoped to make a good impression on the natives.

The minor scars and blemishes concealed by orbital distance and overlying clouds, showed as major lesions at *Rhabwar*'s present altitude of five thousand feet. A procession of low, wooded mountains unrolled below them, their slopes and peaks softened by greenery streaked with yellow and brown, and great, flat tracts of mottled green and brown grasslands. On another world the color variation might have been due to seasonal changes, Gurronsevas thought, but Wemar had no axial tilt.

Once they overflew a long, narrow, blackened area that parallelled the line of the prevailing winds, where a lightning strike or a careless native had started a fire that had quickly become uncontrollable in the near-desiccated vegetation. Often they passed close to the ruins of Wem cities that rose into the sky like great, grey, dried-up sores. Their streets and buildings were overgrown by sickly yellow weeds, untended, undamaged, and populated only by ghosts. He was glad when the Captain's voice interrupted his morbid imaginings.

"Control. We are estimating the Wem settlement in fifteen minutes, Doctor."

"Thank you, friend Fletcher," said Prilicla. "Please maintain the present altitude and circle the site so as to accustom them to the sight of the ship. While you are doing that, drop a two-way communicator and translator unit beside the one they destroyed. Hopefully they will consider us forgiving and persistent rather than stupid and wasteful. Land while we still have full daylight, as close as you can without inconveniencing them."

"Security, Doctor?"

"Deploy the meteorite shield to minimum distance," Prilicla replied. "Set for repulsion only—no shocks—with a visible perimeter so that they won't collide with it by accident. We will discuss individual security requirements before leaving the ship."

The Wem settlement comprised a few wooden outbuildings and a cliff-face mine of unknown depth above the floor of a deep valley that ran north to south. So steep were the valley sides that the sun shone into it for only a few hours every day, but the vegetation growing on the lower slopes and bottomland looked as healthy as any they had seen at the equator. Several small areas, which looked like gardens rather than fields, were under cultivation. There was one large ground-level entrance to the mine and three smaller openings on the cliff face, but without information on the extent of the hidden tunnel network and chambers it was impossible to estimate the number of inhabitants.

Rhabwar was incapable of making a quiet approach and, even though the upper slopes of the valley were still in sunlight, it further advertised its presence by switching on all of its external lighting so that the entire hull and wide, delta wings illuminated the mine entrance like a dazzling white triangular sun. As yet the line of emblems decorating its wings—the Red Cross of Earth, Illensa's occluded sun, the yellow leaf of Traltha, and the many other symbols representing the concept of assistance freely given throughout the Federation—meant nothing to the Wem; but hopefully that situation would soon change.

The flood of highly-amplified reassuring words pouring from the two-way communicators soft-landed before *Rhabwar*'s arrival, Gurronsevas thought, were not having any immediate effect.

"Do not feel disappointed, friend Gurronsevas," said Prilicla. "I sense feelings of curiosity from many beings, and of caution from a few, but their emotional radiation is tenuous and close to the limits of my—"

"Control," said Captain Fletcher, breaking in. "You are right, Doctor. Our sensors show a large number of Wem pushing into the mouth of the entrance tunnel. They are crowded together too tightly for an accurate estimate of sizes or numbers but we think there are at least one hundred of them. There are no indications of metal, so none of them are carrying tools, impliments or weapons. Three of them, who must be the cautious ones you mentioned, are positioned just inside the tunnel mouth and appear to be restraining the others. Orders?"

"None, friend Fletcher," said the empath. "For the present you may join us in waiting and listening."

They stood or sat or in one case hovered around the direct-vision panel facing the mine entrance, which to their unaided eyes looked empty, and listened to the prerecorded message that was going out to the Wem. The words were simple, spoken slowly and clearly so that the echoes bouncing back from the cliff-face did not distort their meaning. They were also, Gurronsevas thought after the first interminable half-hour of listening to them, unutterably boring.

"... We are friends and will not harm you," the communicator-translator was blaring. "Our vessel may seem strange and perhaps frightening to you, but our intentions are peaceful. We are here to help you, and especially to help your children, if we are able and if you allow it. We are not like the others who spoke to you. Ours is a small vessel which contains only enough food for its crew with a small reserve, so we will not risk offending you by offering food unless it is with your permission. We do not know if we can help you. But we would like to speak with you, and learn from you, so that we will know whether or not we can help.

"We are friends and will not harm you. . . ."

"Senior Physician, while we are waiting I have a question," said Gurronsevas suddenly, in an attempt to relieve both his boredom and his intense curiosity since the original remark had been made. "Earlier it was suggested that I had been appointed to the medical team as a nutritional advisor of some kind. If so, it was without my knowledge or consent. But if I am not a mere stowaway, hiding from the hospital authorities, and your earlier words to the Captain a lie aimed at concealing that fact, can you please tell me why O'Mara sent me here?"

Prilicla did not speak for a moment. Its fragile limbs and body were trembling, but Gurronsevas did not think that his own feelings of curiosity and irritation were strong or unpleasant enough to cause it. Perhaps the emotional radiation was coming from someone else or, as sometimes happened when the empath wished to avoid an emotional unpleasantness, it was preparing to tell a lie.

"Friend O'Mara radiates many and complex feelings," it said finally. "Whenever you have been mentioned I have detected feelings of approval mixed with irritation, and a desire to help you. But I am not a telepath, so the feelings were clear but the thoughts were not. If friend O'Mara intended you to join the medical team . . ."

". . . It must have been really desperate," said Naydrad suddenly, its fur rippling with excitement. "Look, they're coming out!"

The Wem were pouring out of the mine opening as if someone had turned on a faucet, running and tail-bouncing and making loud, untranslatable noises as they charged towards *Rhabwar*. Apart from the three adults who were standing to one side of the tunnel mouth, and who had presumably been responsible for holding the others back, they were all young Wem. Some of them were so small and awkward that often they fell over sideways while trying to jump with their tails. But the falls did little to impede their progress and soon they had joined their friends who were shouting, running and tail-jumping in a continuous circle just beyond the meteor shield.

Murchison laughed suddenly. "I have the feeling," it said, "that they should be waving bows and tomahawks at us."

"My own feeling," said Prilicla, "is that they are all curious and excited, and noisy as are most children in that emotional condition, and they are not a threat."

"I'm sorry," said Murchison. "That was a non-serious Earth historical reference, and not funny enough to be worth explaining. But the adults are moving closer now, two of them, anyway."

They were moving slowly and more carefully than the young Wem, and except for one who was carrying a wooden staff, their hands were empty of weapons. Two of them were approaching in a slow succession of tail-jumps with short pauses between. The third one was moving even more slowly, on its hind limbs only and using the staff to help support its weight. Murchison spoke the thoughts that were already going through Gurronsevas's mind.

"Physically they appear to be very weak," said the pathologist, "and display extreme caution in their limb and tail movements. But I have the feeling this may be due to the frailty of age rather than illness. All three are females in a state of serious debilitation and . . . The one with the staff is heading for the communicator!"

"Your feeling is accurate, friend Murchison," said Prilicla, "but your unspoken concern regarding, I suspect, the possibility of the staff being used to damage the communicator is unwarranted. The aged Wem female is radiating curiosity and minor irritation rather than anger and an urge to destroy."

"It would take more than a walking-stick," the Captain's voice broke in, "to damage that unit."

"True, friend Fletcher," said the empath. "But as soon as the

Wem reaches it, cancel the broadcast and switch to two-way communication mode. I have a feeling that it wants to talk."

"And how long has it been," said Danalta, speaking for the first time, "since one of your feelings was wrong?"

Outside the ship the crowd of young Wem were growing tired but not quiet. Instead of running and tail-jumping they had stopped to collect in small groups around the meteor screen, pushing at the resilient, near-invisible barrier or leaning against it at forty-five degree angles and shouting excitedly to each other when they did not fall over. A few of the more daring ones ran and jumped against the shield, shouting in excitement when they were bounced back. The two adults had joined them and were talking quietly together, but there were too many louder conversations going on at once for the ship's translator to separate them, and the third adult had stopped beside the communicator which immediately ceased broadcasting.

"The silence, at least, is welcome," said the Wem without any sign of hesitation. It went on, "Do you think we are all deaf? Or of retarded intelligence since the same message was repeated over and over? Don't you people know that shouting reassurances at us, loudly and continually, angers more than it reassures? From beings who must have come from the stars, I expected more intelligence. Can this stupid machine listen as well as shout? What do you want of us?"

"Sound level reduced by two-thirds," said the Captain quietly. "Go ahead, Doctor."

"Thank you," said Prilicla. It drifted closer to the communicator and tapped the transmit stud before going on, "We are sorry that the device was too noisy and that it angered you. The offense was not intended and neither was there any implication that your hearing or intelligence is defective. It was simply that we wished to be heard over a wide area.

"We want to talk with you and your friends," Prilicla continued, "and to learn from you and to help you in whatever way is possible. You are as strange to us as we will be to you when you see us.

We will answer questions about ourselves and we would like to ask questions of you. Provided there are no personal or cultural reasons for not giving the information and you are willing to give the answer to a stranger, the first question is what is your name. My name is Prilicla and I am a healer."

"That's a ridiculous name," said the Wem. "It sounds like a handful of pebbles being rattled together. I am Tawsar, the First Teacher. I leave healing and preservation to others. What is your second question?"

"Are the young Wem safe where they are," asked Prilicla, "so far from the shelter of your mine? They are in no danger from us but, now that it will soon be dark, is there a risk to them from night predators?"

Gurronsevas's first thought was that there were more important questions that Prilicla could have asked, but his second thought was that expressing an early concern for the safety of the young displayed consideration and friendliness that would reinforce its words of reassurance more than anything else it could have said.

"It is our practice," Tawsar replied, "to allow the children to escape from the mine for a few hours every day when the sun will not blight their young skins or work changes in the offspring they may one day bear. It also releases the energy that would otherwise make them unruly and noisy in class and keep them and their teachers from going to sleep. In the mine they cannot run freely or tail-jump, which is an unnatural situation for the very young. But they are in no danger from predators because all such creatures, be they large and dangerous or tiny rodents, have long since been hunted to extinction in this area. Your ship has provided a new experience for them as well as an outlet for their surplus energy. How long will your ship remain here?"

A school, thought Gurronsevas, was the ideal place to find curious and flexible minds. He could sense the medical team's growing excitement.

"As long as you allow us to stay," said Prilicla quickly. "But we would like to meet you and your friends in person instead of speaking through this device. Is that possible?"

Tawsar was silent for a long moment, then it said, "We should not waste time talking to you. Our behavior will be publicly criticized. No matter, we are curious and too old to care. But you must leave before the return of our hunters. This you must promise me."

"We promise it," said Prilicla simply, and there was no doubt in the minds of the medical team that the promise would be kept. "But there may be a problem when we show ourselves to you. Physically we differ greatly from the Wem. The young, perhaps you yourself, might find us visually horrendous and repulsive."

Tawsar made a sound that did not translate, then said, "We have not seen the creatures from the other starship, but they have given us word-pictures of themselves. They are strange, upright creatures without a balancing tail, some of them covered in fur and others with fur only on their heads. But they wanted to change our ways, so our hunters smashed their speaking devices before leaving. As for frightening the children, I doubt that you could appear more horrendous than the creatures with which their imaginations have already populated your ship.

"Upon consideration," it went on before Prilicla could reply, "it would be better if you didn't show yourselves now. The young are excited enough as it is, and if they were to see you we would have difficulty making them return to the dormitories, much less getting them to sleep. If you are to stay with us for a time, it would be more convenient for us and safer for you if we introduced you during class."

"You do not understand, Tawsar," said Prilicla carefully. "The beings who described themselves were Orligians and Earth-humans. We have five Earth-humans, they are the ones with head fur, on board, and four others who will appear even stranger to you. One is a Tralthan, a being with six legs and with a body mass at least three times greater than an adult Wem. Another is a Kelgian, who is half your size and weight, has twenty sets of walking limbs and is covered by silver, mobile fur. There is a shape-changer who can make itself appear as ferocious or friendly as the situation requires. And lastly there is a large, flying insect, myself. If the thought of meeting one of these beings distresses you, then that person will remain out of sight on the ship."

"Your shape-changer is, is . . ." began Tawsar, then went on firmly, "It is a creature out of a story told to children, to very young children. Adults are not gullible enough to believe in such things."

The empath, plainly hoping to minimize Tawsar's future embarrassment, did not reply. And on the deck below the hovering Prilicla, Danalta writhed and flowed briefly into the shape of a scaled-down, aged Wem female and said quietly, "No comment."

CHAPTER 20

Early on the following morning, when only the east-facing upper slopes of the valley were lit by the rising sun and the mine entrance was still in twilight, Tawsar presented itself beyond the shimmering curtain of the meteor shield. Several groups of twenty to thirty young Wem, each with an adult in charge, had already left the mine and were dispersing to their various places of work or learning on the valley floor and lower slopes.

It had been decided that the function of the Wem settlement fell somewhere between a teaching establishment and a safe refuge for children whose hunter parents were either absent for long periods or dead. The decision was provisional and, following the coming meeting with Tawsar, would no doubt be subject to major modification.

Remembering Tawsar's slow and obviously painful progress down to the meteor shield, it came as no surprise to Gurronsevas when Prilicla ordered out the anti-gravity litter. The equipment carried by the medical team was light and portable enough to make the vehicle redundant, but it was obvious that it was hoping that Tawsar could be persuaded to ride in comfort instead of subjecting itself to the self-inflicted pain of walking, a suffering which the empath would not be anxious to share.

Prilicla was first to exit the lock, and hovered above them as Murchison, Naydrad, Danalta and Gurronsevas followed it down the telescoping ramp to the ground and through the meteor shield, which offered no resistance to objects moving away from the ship. Gurronsevas had not been invited to accompany the medical team, but neither had he been forbidden, and he needed exercise more vigorous than was possible within the confines of the casualty deck.

Tawsar stared at them one by one without speaking as they approached and gathered around it in a semicircle which, according to Prilicla's reading of the Wem's emotional radiation, was wide enough not to cause unease and reassuring in that it left open the other's line of retreat to the mine. Prilicla's iridescent wings beat slowly in a stable hover, Naydrad's fur rippled like waves on a silver sea, Murchison smiled and Gurronsevas stood motionless. Danalta changed its shape in turn from that of a furless Kelgian to a not very complimentary copy of Pathologist Murchison before returning to a shapeless green lump topped by a single eye, ear and mouth. Finally Tawsar broke the silence.

"I see you and I still do not believe you exist," it said, its eyes on Danalta. Then it looked up at Prilicla and went on, "I do not like insects, whether they crawl or fly, but, but you are beautiful!"

"Why thank you, friend Tawsar," said Prilicla with a gentle shiver of pleasure. "You have reacted well to your first sight of off-worlders, and I have the feeling that you yourself are not afraid of us. But what of the other adults and the children?"

Tawsar made a short, untranslatable sound and said, "They were told about your strange and horrendous or puny and ridiculous appearance. They already know that your friends wanted to interfere with our customs and beliefs, and tried to tell us what we should eat, and what we should do about the Light That Rots All Things. They even asked to look inside our living bodies and do things that only a life-mate is allowed to do. Prilicla you, perhaps not you personally but your people who have come uninvited to our world, do not frighten us. They shock and repel and infuriate us. More than anything else we want them to go away quickly, but we know that it is not your wish deliberately to harm us.

"Having told you how we feel," it added, "do you still wish to call me friend?"

"Yes," said Prilicla. "But you need not call me friend until you yourself wish it."

Tawsar made a wheezing sound and said, "I do not expect to live that long. But we have much to see and many questions and answers for each other. Would you like to begin with the valley or the mine?"

"The mine is closer," said Prilicla, "and will involve less walking for you. And if you were to mount this litter, there would be no effort required at all."

"It, it doesn't rest on the ground," said Tawsar in an uncertain voice. Plainly there was a battle going on in the Wem's mind between the submission to a totally new and perhaps dangerous activity and the pain of its age-stiffened limbs. "Yet it feels solid enough and strongly supported . . ."

They had to wait for a few minutes while Tawsar talked itself into boarding the litter, then Naydrad angled the repulsion units to set the vehicle moving towards the mine entrance at the medical team's walking pace.

"I—I'm flying!" said Tawsar.

At an altitude, Gurronsevas estimated, of a few inches.

On their headsets Fletcher was reporting continuously on its observations of the widely-scattered groups of young Wem in the valley. Under the direction of a single adult, several parties were tilling the soil and gathering what seemed to be wild-growing vegetation from the lower slopes. But there were three groups of the larger children whose activities gave cause for concern because there could be no doubt that they were practicing with slingshots, crossbows and weighted nets used in conjunction with spears. The spears were blunt, crudely formed from wood, with roughened hand-grips at the middle and blunt end so that they could be used either for throwing or as two-handed stabbing weapons, and they were slightly large for the hands and muscles of the users.

"They are not playing with wooden swords and spears as many children do," the Captain insisted, "because neither they nor their instructor are treating the exercise as a game. It is much too serious. They are the oldest of the children and they might have real, metal-tipped weapons among the farming implements out there. At this range my sensors can't tell the difference. But if anything goes sour with the Tawsar contact your retreat to the ship could be cut off."

Prilicla did not reply until they were within a few minutes of reaching the mine entrance, and when it spoke Gurronsevas had the feeling that its words were aimed at reassuring the medical team as well as the Captain. It said, "The emotional radiation of the adults and children who surrounded us yesterday bore no trace of hostility, especially the concealed hostility of beings who are pretending to be friendly. Although they are decidedly not our friends, their feelings towards us are not antagonistic enough to make them want to commit acts of physical violence. Tawsar is controlling or at least trying to ignore its dislike for us, but it is feeling much more than a simple curiosity regarding strangers. I cannot be more precise, but I have the feeling that it wants something from us and, until we discover what it is, we are quite safe here.

"Besides," the empath went on, "we have friends Danalta and Gurronsevas with us. Our shape-changer can take many forms that would discourage an attack by unruly children, and the Chief Dietitian has a near-impervious skin and the body mass and muscles to do the same."

"Doctor Prilicla," said Fletcher, "this is a first contact situation so far as the medical team is concerned. One of you could do or say something that could change Tawsar's feelings about you, suddenly and drastically. So why not talk in the open where I can keep you under observation and pull you out with tractors if there is any trouble? I am worried about you going inside their mine."

At that moment the party came to a halt outside the dark

mouth of the entrance tunnel and the litter drifted gently to the ground. Tawsar looked up suddenly at Prilicla and said, "I am worried about you going into our mine."

Danalta's body twitched and it said, "In a steep valley like this one, echoes are not uncommon."

Prilicla ignored it and asked, "Why, friend Tawsar?"

The Wem looked at each one of team in turn before returning its attention to the empath. It said, "I know nothing about you people, your life habits, your feelings about strange places or people, the food you eat, nothing. Suddenly I have realized that you might not want to visit our home. The connecting tunnels are narrow and low-ceilinged, and only our places of gathering are adequately lit, and then only for a limited period each day. Even among the Wem there are those who become distressed in enclosed spaces, or at the thought of the great weight of rock that is pressing down on them.

"But you in particular," Tawsar went on, "are a free-flying creature of the air. I fear that your fragile body and wide-spreading wings are unsuited to crawling about inside a mountain."

"I am grateful for your feeling of concern, friend Tawsar," said Prilicla, "but it is unnecessary. All of us are used to working in a structure that is like a metal mountain, filled with tunnels of different sizes connecting its rooms. All are well-lit but, if yours are too dark for us, we carry our own sources of illumination. If anyone should feel distressed, it will be free to return to the outside. But I do not think that anyone will have such feelings . . ."

There was nobody better at reading feelings than Prilicla, Gurronsevas knew, but he was not as sure as the empath was about his own. He hated dark, cramped spaces but, after being named as one of the team's protectors in case of trouble, he could not act like a coward by refusing to enter the mine before first finding out what it was like inside.

". . . As for myself," Prilicla went on, "I sleep in a coccoon-like room without light. My wings and over-long limbs fold so that, if you have no objections, I will be able to ride on the litter with you.

How restricted is the space in your tunnels? Will they allow free passage for everyone here?"

"Yes," said Tawsar. It looked at Gurronsevas and added, "Just barely."

A few minutes later Naydrad guided the litter with Tawsar and Prilicla on board into the entrance, preceded by Danalta and followed by Naydrad and Murchison with Gurronsevas forming what the Captain so worryingly referred to as the rear guard and the pathologist as a mobile, organic thrombosis.

But the plug, he was pleased to discover, was a loose fit because the tunnel was wider, than he had expected and better lit so that he had no need of his image enhancer. Perhaps Wem vision was less sensitive than that of a Tralthan, for it had been apologizing in advance for the shortcomings of its technology. Prilicla and Tawsar were talking together quietly, but the constant pattering of Naydrad's many feet kept him from hearing what they were saying, and the Captain was filling the gaps in their conversation by worrying aloud.

". . . The deep sensor indications," Fletcher was saying, "are of an exhausted and long-abandoned copper mine. It could be centuries old, judging by the condition of the tunnel support structure, but shows signs of recent repair. Many of the deeper galleries have been sealed off by rock-falls, and even if the Wem don't mean you any harm, you can't talk your way out of a collapsed tunnel. Please reconsider and ask Tawsar to do the talking outside."

"No, friend Fletcher," Prilicla replied on the ship frequency. "Tawsar wants to talk inside the mine. It has strong feelings of embarrassment which suggest that it prefers our conversation to be private. It is not feeling the anxiety characteristic of impending tunnel collapse."

"Very well, Doctor," said the Captain. "Are you having any difficulty with breathing? Is anyone aware of smells that might indicate the presence of flammable gas?"

"No, friend Fletcher," said Prilicla. "The air is cool and fresh."

"You don't surprise me," said Fletcher. "Only the upper galleries are occupied and the Wem have drilled themselves a neat system of natural ventilation tunnels which require no power. They have a small electricity generator which produces enough current for lighting, powered by a subterranean river which exits at the base of the other side of the mountain. We have also detected a few hot spots that are probably cooking fires or ovens, and associated combustion byproducts, but the pollution level is not life-threatening. Be careful anyway."

"Thank you, we will," said Prilicla, and resumed its conversation with Tawsar.

They passed the openings into many side-tunnels and small, unlighted chambers, and in several places Gurronsevas' head and flanks scraped against the tunnel walls and roof, but the air that blew gently past him was cool and fresh and polluted only slightly with an odor which Murchison identified as a combination of wood smoke with trace odors of the kind associated with food preparation. A few minutes later they moved past the entrance to a kitchen.

"Friend Gurronsevas," said Prilicla, using voice amplification so that its words would carry back to him, "I feel your intense curiosity and I think I understand the reason for it, but at present it would be better for the team to stay together."

As the odor grew fainter with distance, Gurronsevas used the olfactory sense that had been sharpened by a lifetime of experience in the culinary arts in an attempt to isolate and identify the constituents of a smell that was totally beyond his previous experience. Or was it?

Carried on a fine mist of water vapor containing trace quantities of dissolved salt there was the unmistakable odor of vegetation, several different varieties, that were being boiled or stewed together. One of them had a sharp, heavy smell that reminded him of the cooked somrath plant or the Earth cabbage leaf favored by some Kelgians, but the other odors were too bland for him to make off-world comparisons. These included a faint, hot smell of what was almost certainly coarse flour baking in an oven. But the most surprising part of this Wem olfactory cocktail was the things that were not in it.

Charitably, Gurronsevas reminded himself that there were several member species of the Federation who had developed high technology and an artistically enlightened culture while remaining in a culinary wilderness.

CHAPTER 21

A few minutes later the tunnel opened into a compartment whose wall-mounted lighting fixtures failed to illuminate the high and unsupported roof while showing the rock walls and sloping, uneven floor of a large, natural cavern. Plainly it had been utilized as an extension to the mine rather than a compartment hollowed out by Wem hands.

About two hundred yards ahead there was a wall, built from large, unfinished stones bound together by cement, sealing off the mouth of the cavern. The wall was pierced by ten large window openings, three of which still retained their glass while the others looked as if they had been boarded up for a very long time. Enough daylight came through the windows to bleach the artificial lighting to a dull, yellow glow and illuminate the rows of high, bench-like Wem tables that were separated by wide aisles into groups of twenty or more.

This was the communal dining area, Gurronsevas thought, then immediately corrected himself. Facing every rectangular group of tables there was a piece of equipment whose basic design, modified to suit the size and shape of its users, was common to virtually every intelligent species in the Federation—a blackboard and easel. Ranged against the cavern walls were side tables, some of them stacked with platters and eating utensils and others with books that looked as if they were disintegrating with age. Hanging from spikes driven into the rockface were a number of large, framed wall-charts which were cracked and faded almost to illegibility.

It was a school classroom as well as a dining area.

Fletcher was seeing everything that the team was seeing through their vision pick-ups, but the Captain kept talking about it anyway because the material was probably being recorded for onward transmission to *Tremaar*.

". . . The furniture and equipment is *old*," Fletcher was saying. "You can see the corrosion stains where the original metal legs were attached, and the replacement wooden structure is not all that recent, either. The wall-frame supports are solid with rust, as well. They must be short of glass, too, otherwise they would not have boarded up the window frames in an area where daylight is available for classroom work.

"I missed seeing that wall on the cliff face," Fletcher continued, a hint of apology creeping into its tone, "because it is built from local, weathered stone that is difficult to see because it is recessed and shaded by a rock overhang. I would say that the purpose of the wall is to protect rather than confine the younger inhabitants, because the cavern mouth opens onto a sheer cliff some five hundred feet above the valley floor. But we have the wall clearly in sight now. If an emergency withdrawal becomes necessary, Danalta and Gurronsevas can easily break through the boarded-up window frames. Doctor Prilicla can fly down and the rest of you can escape using the—"

"Not on the anti-gravity litter!" Naydrad broke in, its fur spiking in agitation. "That is primarily a ground-effect vehicle. At anything over fifty feet altitude it balances like a drunken Crrelyin!"

"—Using the tractor-beam," Fletcher continued, "The ship is close enough for it to reach you and lift you down one at a time."

"Captain," said Prilicla, "the possibility of a life-threatening emergency occurring is very small. The emotional radiation of

Tawsar and the other Wem in the mine we have not yet met was not hostile, and they are the beings with authority in this establishment. Our friend is radiating a mixture of shame, embarrassment and intense curiosity. It wants something from us, possibly only information. But it does not, as your colorful but anatomically inexact Earth saying has it, want our guts for garters. Please return to translation mode or Tawsar will think we are talking about it."

Prilicla and Tawsar resumed talking, with occasional interjections from the other team members, but their conversation was becoming too medical to hold Gurronsevas's interest. He moved over to the windows to look down on *Rhabwar* shimmering inside the dome of its meteor shield, and beyond it to the valley floor and the scattered groups of young Wem who were working there. The most distant group had formed into a line and was beginning to walk back towards the mine.

The ship had not yet reported the incident. Lacking Gurronsevas's greater elevation, the watch-keeping officer would not have seen them.

He bent an eye to look behind him where Prilicla and Murchison were demonstrating the uses of the litter's handheld scanner on Naydrad and each other, but not on Danalta whose internal organs were voluntarily mobile and far too confusing for a simple first lesson in other-species anatomy. Surprisingly, for a being of its advanced age and the inflexible habits of thought which usually accompanied that condition, Tawsar was quick to grasp the idea of making a non-invasive and painless internal investigation of a living body. It stared entranced at the internal organs, the beating hearts, the lungs in their different respiration cycles and the complex skeletal structures of the Cinrusskin Senior Physician, the Earth-human Pathologist and the Kelgian Charge Nurse.

It was inevitable that Tawsar became curious and wanted to look into its own internal workings, which gave Prilicla the opening it needed to ask more personal medical questions.

". . . If you look closely at the hip and knee, here and here," the Senior Physician was saying, "you can see the layers of cartilage which separate the joints and which are supposed to form a thin, frictionless pad between them. In your case, however, the joint interfaces are no longer smooth. The bone structure has deteriorated and become uneven, and the movement of the limb, combined with the pressure of your body weight on surfaces which are no longer smooth, has torn and inflamed the cartilage and generally worsened the condition, making physical movement both restricted and painful . . ."

"Tell me something I don't know," said Tawsar.

"I will," Prilicla replied gently. "But before I do that you must be told something that you do know, that your condition is due to the aging process that is common to all species. In time, in varying lengths of time, because our life-expectancies are not the same, all of the beings you see around you will age, our physical and sometimes mental capabilities will deteriorate until eventually we will die. None of us can reverse the natural aging process, but with the proper medication and treatment the symptoms can be reduced, or their onset delayed, and the physical discomfort removed."

Tawsar did not respond for a moment, and Gurronsevas did not need to be an empath to feel the Wem's disbelief, then it said, "Your medication would poison me, or give me some foul, off-world disease. My body must remain healthy and clean, despite its infirmities. No!"

"Friend Tawsar," said Prilicla, "we would not even try to help if there was the slightest risk to yourself. You do not realize, because until now you had no way of knowing, that there are many similarities between the Wem and the off-worlders represented here. With minor differences in composition we breathe the same air and eat the same basic types of food . . ."

The Cinrusskin's pipe-stem legs and slow-beating wings began quivering, but only for a moment. It did not stop talking.

". . . Because of this, the ways that our bodies work, the processes of respiration, ingestion and waste elimination, procreation, and physical growth are all very similar. But there is one important and unique difference: we cannot catch a disease from you or from each other, or you from one of us. This is because the pathogens, the germs, which have evolved on one world are powerless to affect life-forms from another. After centuries of close and continuous contact on many worlds, this is a rule to which we have found no exception."

Prilicla bypassed the translator again and said quickly, "There was a strong emotional reaction to the mention of food. I detected the same feelings of shame, curiosity and intense hunger. Why should a native of a famine-stricken world be ashamed of feeling hungry?"

Switching back to Tawsar it went on, "We cannot promise that you will be able to run and hop like a young Wem. If we are able to treat you, there will be a marked alleviation of your discomfort. If not, no change in your condition or additional pain will be apparent. Withdrawal of the specimens we need to ensure that our medication will not harm you is also painless."

It was not just another therapeutic lie, Gurronsevas knew, because in this case the doctor was feeling everything that its patient felt. Judging from the faint tremor visible in Prilicla's limbs, it was also feeling the patient coming to a difficult decision.

"I must be damaged in the head," said Tawsar suddenly. "Very well, I agree. But don't take too long about it or I may change my mind."

The medical team gathered around the Wem who was still lying on the litter. Prilicla said, "Thank you, friend Tawsar, we will not waste time." Murchison said, "The scanner is on record," and after that the conversation became densely technical. Gurronsevas turned his back on the massively boring medical proceedings and returned to the windows.

The four most distant working or teaching parties had merged on their way back to the mine and presumably their midday meal, and the closer groups would join them so that they would all arrive at the same time. They were maintaining the slow walking pace of their teachers rather than running and hopping ahead, and he estimated their arrival time at just under an hour. *Rhabwar* would have them in sight very soon. He wondered whether their lack of haste was due to teacher discipline or disinterest in the meal awaiting them. He was increasingly curious about the kitchen smells that were drifting in from the entry tunnel.

He became suddenly aware that Prilicla was talking about him.

". . . It moving away from us means no disrespect," the empath was saying. "Because of its specialty Gurronsevas is more curious about what you put into your body than in what we are taking out and, whenever you can spare the time, it would be much more interested in investigating the Wem cooking arrangements than in—"

"It is welcome to look at our kitchen now," Tawsar broke in. "The First Cook knows of the visit by off-worlders and will be pleased to see Gurronsevas. Does it require guidance?"

"Thank you, no," said Gurronsevas. Silently, he added, "I can follow my nose."

"I shall join you in the kitchen," said Tawsar, "as soon as this strange activity is over."

He was already moving towards the exit tunnel when Prilicla switched from the translator channels to say, "Friend Gurronsevas, I was talking about you simply to give Tawsar something other than the examination to think about. But suddenly there was an emotional response of the type I detected earlier. Feelings of hunger, curiosity and intense shame or embarrassment, but much more intense. Be very careful, and observant, because I have the feeling that you could discover something important to us. Maintain voice contact at all times and please take care."

"I will be careful, Doctor," said Gurronsevas impatiently as he continued his erratic journey between the desks. Who better than himself knew how many accidents could occur in a kitchen, and how to avoid them.

Prilicla resumed its attempts to take Tawsar's mind off what Murchison and Naydrad were doing to it. Their voices sounded clearly in his earpiece.

"For the best results," the empath was saying, "we should also investigate a healthy and active young Wem, ideally one close to maturity. It would be for purposes of comparison only, not for treatment. Would this be possible?"

"Anything is possible," Tawsar replied. "Children are prone to take risks, for a dare or out of curiosity or to prove themselves better than other children. Maybe that is the reason I am subjecting myself to this experience, I was too stupid to realize that I have long since entered my second childhood."

"No, friend Tawsar," said Prilicla firmly. "There is a young and adaptable mind inside your aging body, but it is not a stupid one. There can be few others of your kind who could have faced a group of off-worlders, beings who must appear completely alien and visually horrendous to you, and help us with our investigation as you have been doing. That was and is a very brave act. But were you simply curious about us or were there other reasons for inviting us here?"

There was a long pause, then Tawsar said, "I am not a unique person. There are others here who are equally brave or stupid. Most of them are willing to meet and make whatever use of you that they can, and a few others, the majority of the absent hunters, refuse to have any part of you. As First Teacher it was my responsibility for inviting you into the mine. I was surprised that you did not need more coaxing, so perhaps you, too, are brave or stupid. And placing me under an obligation by promising to relieve the pain in my joints was unfair because I cannot repay . . ."

"Friend Tawsar," Prilicla broke in, "there is nothing to repay. But if the balancing of obligations are important to your people, you have allowed us to satisfy our medical curiosity regarding the Wem, and this would repay the debt many times over. As for your stiffening joints, the pain symptoms can be relieved easily although a cure that would allow a return to full mobility might be more difficult because the condition is advanced in your case. We might have to remove the damaged joints in their entirety and fit replacements made from metal or hardened plastic."

"*No!*"

The single word sounded so angry that it must have been accompanied by strong emotional radiation, and Gurronsevas was glad that he was not seeing Prilicla's reaction. He had moved along the tunnel and was within a few paces of the kitchen entrance by the time the empath found its voice again.

"There is nothing to fear, friend Tawsar," said the empath. "Joint replacements are done routinely, thousands every day on some worlds, and in the majority of cases the replacement is more efficient than the original. There is no pain. The operation is performed while the subject is unconscious and . . ."

"No," Tawsar broke in again, less vehemently. "That must not be done. It would render parts of my body inedible."

Gurronsevas was moving slowly into what appeared to be a service compartment adjoining the kitchen proper, which was hidden by two swinging doors that were impervious to sight but not smell. He could see long benches stacked with trays, neatly-racked eating utensils and shelves containing cooking-pots, dishes of various sizes, and cups, the majority of which were cracked or missing their handles. But as the implications of what Tawsar had said began to sink in, he came to a sudden halt.

He could only imagine how the medical team and the listening Fletcher on *Rhabwar* were reacting; like himself they must have been shocked speechless. It was the pathologist who found its voice first.

"W-We, that is, all of the intelligent species we know, bury their dead, or burn them, or dispose of them in other ways. But they do not use them as food."

"That is very stupid of you," Tawsar replied, "to waste an important natural resource like that. On Wemar we cannot afford such criminal wastage. We honor and remember our dead if their lives and deeds warrant it, but even so, a person's past life has little effect on his or her taste provided they remain healthy. We would not, of course, eat someone who was too long dead, or who had died from a disease, or whose body contained harmful substances like metal or plastic joints. If we are sure the meat will not harm us, we will eat anything. Because of my advanced age, I myself will probably be tough and stringy, but nutritious nevertheless.

"The tastiest pieces," the Wem went on, "come from the young or the newly-mature adults who die by accident or while hunting . . ."

The double doors into the main kitchen swung open suddenly to reveal the figure of a Wem wreathed in steam, and two others working some distance behind it. All three wore loosely-tied aprons of a fabric that had been washed too often for it to have retained its original color. The one nearest the door was the first to speak.

"Obviously you are one of the off-worlders," it said politely. "My name is Remrath. Please come in."

For a moment it seemed that Gurronsevas's six, massive feet were rooted to the stone floor, because he was remembering Tawsar's earliest words to him.

The First Cook will be pleased to see you.

CHAPTER 22

I've been monitoring your conversation, Doctor," said Fletcher on the ship frequency, "and I do not like what I'm hearing. About seventy young Wem and four instructors have come into sight heading for the mine entrance, and at the present rate of progress they should be there in forty-plus minutes. The other working parties have downed tools and are moving to join them, probably for lunch. Judging by what I've just heard, your people probably *are* lunch. I strongly advise you to break off contact and return to the ship at once."

"A moment, Captain," said Prilicla. "Friend Murchison, how long do you need to finish here?"

"No more than fifteen minutes," the pathologist replied. "The patient is being very cooperative and I don't feel like stopping—"

"And I share your feelings," the empath broke in. "Captain, we will complete our investigation, excuse ourselves politely and then take your advice. The revelation that the Wem are cannibals is disturbing. But please do not concern yourself; neither Tawsar nor any of the other Wem within my emotive range are radiating feelings of hostility. In fact, the opposite holds true because I feel Tawsar beginning to like us."

"Doctor," said the Captain, "when I am very hungry, as these people are all the time, I like thinking about my lunch very much. But I do not have feelings of hostility towards it."

"Friend Fletcher," Prilicla began, "you are oversimplifying . . ."

Gurronsevas had to switch to the Wem translation channel at that point because, while he was capable of looking in four directions at once, he could conduct only one conversation at a time. It appeared that there was no immediate danger from the returning work parties, and certainly not from the aged Wem left in the mine, so that he, too, had a chance to satisfy his own professional curiosity while Murchison completed its medical investigation. Besides, while he had been listening to Prilicla and Fletcher, the Wem standing before him had been speaking, and common politeness demanded that he reply.

"My apologies," he said, indicating his translator pack and telling a small diplomatic lie. "This device was not tuned to you. I heard but did not understand your earlier words. Would you oblige me by repeating them?"

"They were not of great importance," the Wem replied. "Merely an observation that I have often wished that I had four hands. They would be especially useful in this place. I am the healer and chief cook here."

"I occupy a similar position in a somewhat larger establishment. But there the functions of healing and food preparation are separate, and performed by different people. How do I address you, as doctor or . . . ?"

"My full title is verbally cumbersome and unnecessary," the Wem broke in. "It is used only during the Coming of Age ceremonies and by pupils who have misbehaved and are hoping, vainly, to avoid just chastisement. Call me Remrath."

"I am Gurronsevas," he replied, and added, "I am only a cook."

As the Galactic Federation's foremost exponent of the highly-specialized art of multi-species food preparation, Gurronsevas thought, I do not believe I said that.

"Compared with the high culinary standards said to have been achieved by our own people in the good old days," said Remrath in a voice in which anger and apology were mixed, "that is, in the centuries before the sun itself turned against us, my kitchen is primitive. To you it must appear no more than a cooking-place for savages. But if you are interested you are welcome to look around."

His reply was silenced by the voice of Fletcher speaking directly to him on the ship frequency. "Chief Dietitian, you are not trained in First Contact procedures. So far you have not said anything wrong, but please listen carefully. Do not react adversely to anything you may see or hear, no matter how repugnant it may seem to you. Try to show an interest in their equipment and processes, no matter how primitive they seem, and praise rather than criticize. Try to be agreeable, and diplomatic."

Gurronsevas did not reply. The interval between Ramrath's invitation and his answer had already stretched longer than politeness allowed.

"I am most interested," said Gurronsevas, truthfully, "and will want to ask many and possibly irritating questions. But the sounds of activity I hear, and the complex odors of food well-advanced in preparation and perhaps ready for serving, lead me to think that you are simply asking out of politeness. From long personal experience I know that, at a time like this, visitors are not welcome in the kitchen."

"That is true," said Remrath, backing through the swinging doors and holding one open while it used the other hand to beckon Gurronsevas to follow it inside. He could see that its legs and tail were too stiff in their movements to enable it to turn inside the wide entrance. It went on, "But I can see that in enclosed spaces you are more agile than I am in spite of your enormous body, and you should know enough not to get in the way at the wrong times. As you have already guessed, very soon we shall be serving the main meal of the day. Perhaps I want you to see us working under pressure when we are at our best . . ." It made a short, untranslatable sound ". . . or our worst."

He found himself in another cavern that was a continuation of the one he had just left. Facing him was a large, vertical wall of small, irregular stone blocks built around four open ovens that were burning wood or a similar form of dense, combustible vegetation. There must have been natural ventilation behind the wall because there was no smoke in the kitchen and the steam from the cooking pots that had been moved from the ovens to a long, central table, was being drawn in that direction as well. To the right of the table, which ran from the oven area almost to within a few yards of the entrance, the upper two-thirds of the rock wall was concealed by open cabinets and shelves containing cooking utensils, platters and small drinking vessels, the majority of which had been made by people whose craft had not been pottery. Although crudely made and cracked or with drinking handles missing, he noted with approval, they all appeared to be scrupulously clean.

Below the shelving there was a long trough that was supported on heavy trestles and lined with some form of ceramic filled with continually running water. A few cups and platters were visible under the surface. The wide inlet pipe at one end had no tap, so he guessed that it was fed by a natural spring rather than a storage tank, and at the other end a system of paddle-wheels fed a small generator which was, presumably, responsible for the overhead lighting.

Against the opposite wall were more shelves and open cabinets, wider spaced and more crudely built, containing what Gurronsevas guessed were the stores of Wem-edible vegetation and fuel for the ovens. Neither were in plentiful supply.

Gurronsevas followed Remrath around the kitchen, content to allow the Wem cook-healer to do all the talking, especially as the purpose of the very basic equipment was already clear and he had no need to ask questions. He was silent even when Remrath paused before a long, low cabinet positioned below the trough of running water beside the paddle-wheels and splashed by them.

There was a wide flange around the outward-facing edges of the cabinet which prevented water from seeping into its double doors, which hung open to reveal an empty interior. A simple but effective method of cooling by evaporation, he thought. Nowhere else was there anything that resembled a cold storage facility that would have indicated the presence of fresh meat.

In the light of his knowledge that the Wem were cannibals, Gurronsevas did not know whether to feel relieved or worried.

The tour of the kitchen ended with a return to the oven area where the contents of several cooking pots were simmering gently and others were on the side table, covered by thick cloths to keep them warm. Remrath said suddenly, "You have said very little, Gurronsevas, and asked no questions. Is the sight of our primitive methods of food preparation abhorrent to you?"

"To the contrary, Remrath," he replied firmly. "In essence, kitchens have been very much the same on every world I've visited, but it is the small differences that I find of greatest interest. I have many questions for you ..." He reached for a large wooden spoon that lay beside a simmering pot that had not yet been covered. ". . . and the first one is, may I be permitted to taste this? Please excuse me for a moment. My colleagues are talking to me."

It would have been truer to say, Gurronsevas thought angrily, that they were talking about him.

". . . Whether through ignorance or stupidity or both!" Captain Fletcher was saying. "Doctor Prilicla, *talk* to it! Make it see sense, dammit. You don't land on a strange planet and start sampling the local fast food outlet—"

"Friend Gurronsevas," Prilicla broke in. "Is this true? Are you about to eat Wem food?"

"No, Doctor," he replied, bypassing the translator. "I am about to taste the smallest possible portion of a Wem dish. With respect, I would remind everyone that I have a well-educated palate combined with a highly developed sense of smell, and that I would be immediately aware of it if any dish is likely to prove harmful. Since I do not intend to swallow, there is no risk of ingesting possibly toxic material. As well, in consistency the dish is something between a thin vegetable stew and a thick soup which has been boiling in a covered container for more than an hour. I am grateful for your concern, Doctor, but it is not in my nature to take stupid risks."

There was a moment's silence, then Prilicla said, "Very well, friend Gurronsevas, but if you should inadvertently swallow something, especially if it has any unusual or unpleasant effects, return to the ship at once. Be very careful."

"Thank you, Doctor," said Gurronsevas, "I most surely will."

He was about to resume speaking to Remrath when the Cinrusskin went on quickly, "You may have been too busy to listen to our conversation with Tawsar, or fully understand what you heard. The current position is that, with Tawsar's willing cooperation, we have obtained all the physiological data that we need at present and it will require further study on *Rhabwar* to help us decide what else we need. The information on the Wem social structure is meager, however, and I feel a strong reluctance from Tawsar to speak about the subject, so that further conversation is becoming increasingly difficult.

"This seems like the right time for us to break off contact without the risk of giving offense," it continued. "The imminent arrival of the working parties for their midday meal allows us to say, truthfully where everyone but Danalta is concerned, that we must return to the ship for the same purpose. Please complete your food-tasting as quickly as possible, apologize to the kitchen staff and say that you must return with us. They will assume that you, too, are due a meal. Join us as we pass the kitchen entrance in a few minutes time."

Gurronsevas was holding the long spoon a few inches above the simmering contents of the pot. As Remrath watched and listened to his untranslated words to Prilicla, he knew that it must be feeling irritated at being excluded from the conversation. Had their positions been reversed, Gurronsevas would certainly have been angry, but suddenly he found that he could not speak to either of them.

"Your emotional radiation is difficult to resolve at this range," said Prilicla, "especially with the kitchen staff adding their own emotions. Is there a problem, friend Gurronsevas?"

"No, Doctor," he replied, "not if . . . How sure are you that the Wem mean us no harm?"

"I am as sure as an empath can be about the feelings of others," Prilicla replied. "The kitchen staff are radiating curiosity and caution normal to the situation, but no hostility. Not being a telepath I cannot tell what they are actually thinking, and because of this there is a small element of doubt. Why do you ask?"

Gurronsevas was still trying to find the right words for his reply when Prilicla spoke again.

It said, "Is it because you are radiating an intense curiosity, presumably a professional curiosity, considering your present surroundings, and do not wish to leave until it is satisfied? Or is it that you feel more comfortable in a kitchen among other-species cooks than with the medics on the casualty deck of an ambulance ship?"

"Are you *sure* you are not a telepath?" asked Gurronsevas.

"I am sorry, friend Gurronsevas," said Prilicla, "I had no wish to embarrass you because your embarrassment affects me. You may remain in the kitchen, but Doctor Danalta will stay with you as a protector. It is not capable of hurting any other intelligent being, but friend Danalta can assume some truly fearsome shapes if attacked. Should your situation there become dangerous, make your way quickly to the wooden outer wall and onto the lip of the cavern mouth, where friend Fletcher will lift you to safety with a tractor-beam.

"While you are satisfying your culinary curiosity," it went on, "do you think you could widen the conversation to include general questions on the Wem social and cultural background, both past and present if possible? Do not be too obvious about it, and move away from subjects that appear to be sensitive. It may be that you will have more success with Remrath than we've had with Tawsar.

"Do not waste time replying," it ended. "I can feel Remrath's impatience growing very rapidly."

"Sorry for the interruption, Remrath," he said, doing as he had been told. "My friends, all but the one called Danalta, need to return to the ship for their own meal and this, your own eating period, seems like an opportune time. You will find Danalta an interesting being who is able to change shape at will. It can go without food for long periods, even longer than I myself can do. It is much smaller than I, a healer but not a cook, and with your permission I would like it to observe the workings of your kitchen."

Remrath, Gurronsevas suspected, knew as well as he did that there was another reason for Danalta's presence. The concept of there being safety in numbers was one shared by every thinking race.

"Your friend is welcome so long as it doesn't obstruct us," said Remrath, then pointed a bony digit at the spoon Gurronsevas was still holding above the pot. "Are you going to do something with that?"

Ignoring the sarcasm, Gurronsevas dipped the spoon into the greenish-brown, bubbling mass, stirred it briefly to feel the consistency, then raised a spoonful to his breathing orifice until he judged the temperature to be cool enough not to blister his mouth before touching it to the taste pad covering the inside of his upper lip.

"Well?" Remrath asked sharply.

Gurronsevas thought that he could detect the presence of three different forms of vegetation, but they had been so thoroughly mixed and overcooked that he could not separate the individual tastes, much less relate them to foods already known to him. No condiments, sauces, mineral or chemical flavorings were present, and not even a trace of the salt which must have been available from Wemar's seas. Plainly the food was being prepared too far in advance and the subsequent overcooking had destroyed any complementary or contrasting taste possessed by the original constituents.

"A little bland," said Gurronsevas.

Remrath made an untranslatable sound and said, "You are being much too diplomatic, off-worlder. You have tasted our staple dish, a meat and vegetable stew without the meat, and by the time it reaches table it will be scarcely warm. Bland is a polite description for this unappetizing mess, but it is not the word we or our pupils would use."

"It needs something," Gurronsevas agreed. Deliberately, he directed all four of his eyes towards the empty cold cabinet he had noticed earlier and went on, "Doubtless the meat would improve the taste, but you do not appear to have any. Is meat a part of their normal diet?"

In his head-set Prilicla said warningly, "You are in a very sensitive area, friend Gurronsevas. Remrath's emotional radiation is disturbed and angry. Tread gently."

That was a ridiculous thing to ask a physically massive Tralthan to do. Even though he knew what the empath meant, he was in the kitchen and the Wem must surely expect him to ask questions about food.

"No," said Remrath sharply. When Gurronsevas had decided that he must have given offense and it was not going to speak further, it proved him wrong by saying, "Only adults are entitled to eat meat, if and when it is available. It is forbidden to the young, but that rule is relaxed when, as is the case here, many of them are nearing maturity. The pupils who are old enough are occasionally given it in small quantities to add taste to the vegetable dishes, as a preparation for and a promise of their approaching maturity and the status they can expect as brave hunters and providers for their people.

"Our hunting party is due to return soon," Remrath ended in a quiet voice that sounded angry despite the emotion-straining process of translation. "But in recent years they have had limited success, and they will not share their meat and their mature strength with children, so they keep it all for themselves"

Plainly some kind of verbal response was needed, Gurronsevas thought worriedly, preferably a sympathetic or encouraging or innocuous one that would not increase the Wem's anger. Not knowing what to say, he tried to play safe by making a harmless and obvious statement of fact.

"You are mature," he said.

If anything Remrath became even angrier. So loudly that the two cooks at the other end of the kitchen looked up from their work, it said, "I am very mature, stranger. Too mature to take part in a hunt, or to be given the smallest share of the kill. Too mature to have my past hunts remembered with gratitude or my feelings considered. Occasionally, out of kindness or sentiment, a young and newly-mature hunter will throw me a scrap or two of meat, but those we use to add a little taste to the meals of the older children. Otherwise we eat what everyone else eats in this place—a tasteless, lukewarm vegetable mush!"

In his time Gurronsevas had heard and dealt with many complaints about food, although rarely when it had been prepared by himself, and felt able to speak without risk of giving offense.

He took a deep breath and said carefully, "I have met or know of many different kinds of creatures, intelligent beings like yourselves who have developed civilizations more advanced even than that of the Wem of many centuries past, and who eat nothing but vegetation from the time they are weaned from their mothers' milk until they die. Their meals are served hot, as are yours, or uncooked and served in a variety of different—"

"Never!" Remrath burst out. "I can believe that they eat vegetable stew until they die, because we older Wem are forced to do the same. In all probability it precipitates our dying. But it is simply a matter of filling an empty and growling stomach with tasteless organic fuel, and eating vegetation is shameful and demeaning for any adult.

"But eating raw growing things like a, like a rouglar!" it ended fiercely. "Off-worlder, you risk making me sick."

"Please excuse my ignorance," said Gurronsevas, "but what is a rouglar?"

"It used to be a large, slow-moving meat animal which ate and digested foliage all day long," Remrath replied. "A few of them are rumored to exist in the equatorial regions, but elsewhere they are extinct. They were always too slow and stupid to escape the hunters."

"With respect, you are wrong," said Gurronsevas. "Many intelligent species are herbivorous and suffer no feelings of shame because of it. Neither do they have feelings of mental or physical inadequacy among the carnivores and omnivores who eat meat only or a combination of both, as do you. Charge Nurse Naydrad, that is the one you will see with the long, silver-furred body and multiplicity of legs, eats only vegetation and is slow neither in its thoughts or movements. Differences in eating habits are not a cause for shame or pride or any other emotions except, perhaps, pleasure or displeasure over the taste, quality of the cooking or preparation of the food. They are just differences. Why do the Wem feel shame?"

Remrath did not reply. Had his question given offense, Gurronsevas wondered, or was the answer even more shameful? Rather than ask questions it might be safer to continue giving information while noting the other's reaction to it.

"Food is a fuel regardless of its type," he went on, "but the process of refueling is, or should be, a pleasurable experience. The taste can be enhanced in various ways by the addition of small quantities of substances that are animal, vegetable or edible mineral. Or a meal can be improved by using different constituents which complement or contrast with each other and make the taste more interesting. I have some small experience in this area including the preparation of . . ."

Briefly, he wondered how the subordinate kitchen staff at the Cromingan-Shesk would have reacted to such a ridiculous and uncharacteristic piece of understatement, but his listener knew nothing of multi-species cooking and would not be impressed by gratuitous displays of expertise that were completely beyond its understanding or, hopefully, its present understanding.

When he continued, Gurronsevas tried to keep the information as simple and basic as possible because this aged Wem cook, regardless of its advanced years, was the merest child in culinary matters. But as he warmed to his favorite subject and the minutes slipped past unnoticed, he grew aware that Remrath was showing signs of restlessness and possibly impatience. It was time to taper off before positive boredom set in.

"There is much more that I could tell you about food preparation," he went on, "including the fact that my efforts are wasted on a few rare and very unfortunate beings. The shape-changer Danalta is one. It eats anything, vegetation, meat, hard woods, sand, most varieties of rock, all without being able to sense any difference in taste."

He stopped suddenly with the realization that the conversations in his head-set were indicating that the medical team were boarding *Rhabwar,* the Wem students were about to reenter the mine, and Danalta had not yet arrived.

Or had it.

Standing against a poorly lit section of the wall behind the kitchen doors Gurronsevas remembered, there had been a wooden cask with the shafts of several brooms and mops projecting from the open top. Now there were two casks, identical but for a knot-hole in one of them that had the wet, transparent look of an eye—which slowly winked at him. Danalta had joined them.

Exhibitionist, thought Gurronsevas, and returned his attention to Remrath.

"We must continue this conversation at another time," the Wem said before he could speak, "because now we have much to do. Watch if you wish, but kindly stand aside and avoid hampering our movements."

Gurronsevas moved away to stand beside the cask that was not a cask. The movements that he was not supposed to hamper, he saw, were painfully slow. Remrath and its kitchen staff were ladling helpings of the vegetable stew onto deep-rimmed dishes which they placed two to a tray before adding two wide, flat spoons and two cups of drinking water taken from the entry pipe of the free-running sluice. The platters were unwarmed and some of them were still damp from washing. One by one the loaded trays with their two-place servings were carried to the outer room and placed on the big table until its entire surface was covered. While this was happening, the teachers supervising the Wem working parties and classes arrived and began adding the day's crop of vegetables to the kitchen's storage bins while their young charges moved on to the dining area.

Remrath told the newcomers that the presence of Gurronsevas would be explained later and to continue with their normal duties. The sight of them doing so was seriously elevating Gurronsevas' blood pressure.

The age-immobilized tails, the stiffness in their hands, fingers, and walking limbs and their erratic, hobbling gait meant that they could carry and balance only one small tray of two servings at a time. It also meant that the food already cooling in the outer room would be even cooler, if not stone cold, by the time it reached the dining area. But the diners were unlikely to complain about it because their impatience for a meal of cold mush would be minimal.

"I can't stand here and watch this any longer," he said with quiet vehemence to one of the casks behind him. "The organization of this kitchen is a criminal shambles, and their food delivery system is . . . Don't change or move to follow me, Danalta, unless I call for help."

He waited until Remrath was hobbling past close by, then went on in a louder voice, "I have been observing your activities closely and believe that I can be of assistance. As you have seen, I am more physically agile than you are and much faster in my movements. And I have four hands, all of which are presently idle . . ."

The Great Gurronsevas, he thought incredulously as he was carrying the first four trays along the tunnel to the dining area, waiting at table! What was happening to him?

CHAPTER 23

The conversation continued after the meal was over and the near-empty platters cleared away. Nobody, it seemed, paid the cooks the compliment of leaving clean plates. Tawsar thanked Gurronsevas for his help serving and for answering questions about himself asked by the young Wem diners. At no time did he see Tawsar touch its food, and when he mentioned this to Remrath later he was told that the First Teacher held to the old traditions and would not eat vegetation where others could witness its shame. Even though the other cooks, who had to take food to the very young children, had left them alone in the kitchen when he asked for an explanation, Remrath avoided the question.

Gurronsevas knew better than to criticize or offer suggestions about the workings of its kitchen to the cook in charge, no matter how poorly-equipped the place might be, because wars had started over less. Instead he talked about the other kitchens he had known and his criticisms were implied rather than spoken.

"We no longer ask the young to do these menial kitchen duties," Remrath said. "There was a time when those who misbehaved were given responsibility for clearing away and washing the dishes and cutlery, and for cleaning the next day's vegetables. But much crockery was broken and vegetables were improperly washed as a result, and the practice was discontinued. Reluctant helpers are not worth the trouble. Besides, it is better for the aged to remain useful rather than waste resources that seem to grow scarcer by the day. Is that a food-stain or wear on your platter? Please scrub it again."

Gurronsevas immersed the platter in the cold, running water and rubbed at it with the piece of dense, wiry moss provided for the purpose before showing it again to Remrath who was engaged in the same activity. First a waiter, he thought, and now a dishwasher!

He said, "With many of the species I have known, especially when the individual is no longer young, repeated immersion in cold water stiffens the finger joints. Is it so with you?"

"Yes," said Remrath. "And, as you must already have seen, at my age it is not only the parts bathed in cold water that suffer."

"That, too, is a common complaint on many worlds," said Gurronsevas. "But it is possible that the suffering can be relieved. I say possible because I have no knowledge of the subject myself, but Tawsar kindly submitted to a full medical examination and many metabolic tests, so we will soon know whether or not our healing can be practiced to the benefit of the Wem. But if not, on my world the young can often be made to help their elders when the right arguments are used."

Remrath washed three more platters, examined them minutely for food stains and placed them aside still dripping wet before it said, "Do you know whether Tawsar is well or ailing? Is the age-rot that grows in all our bodies, and opens the way for other flesh-poisoning diseases, working within it?"

Gurronsevas was trying to think of a suitable reply when Murchison joined in on the ship frequency. "You were correct in saying that we might not be able to alleviate a Wem arthritic condition, but there is a fair chance that we can. Tawsar is old and frail but not sick. It could live for another ten years, longer if it would eat more. For some reason these people are nearly starving themselves to death."

If the pathologist had tasted the recent Wem meal, Gurronsevas thought, the reason would be plain. To Remrath he said, "Tawsar has many years of life ahead, especially if it would eat more food."

Remrath scraped the congealed remains of a meal from a platter into a waste bin before sliding it into the washing trough. It said, "The young would help us if we asked them, but the old must do useful work while we are waiting to deliver up our bodies at the Ending, and it is work that we are allowed to do even though we are not always capable of doing it well. And we don't want to eat more food, not when it is vegetation. The subject is distasteful in every sense of the word. But I have questions for you, Gurronsevas. If they are improper, ignore them. Your work I can understand because it is not unlike my own, but what about the beings who spoke with and did things to Tawsar? Where do they come from and what do they do there?"

Gurronsevas tried to describe Sector General and the work that was done there, but his description was much too simple and far from accurate because he knew that the tremendous truth would not be believed.

"So it is a great building in the sky," said Remrath, "filled with beings who take in diseased and damaged bodies and make them clean and fresh and whole again?"

"That's as good a way as any," said Murchison, laughing softly, "of describing what we do."

"There used to be places like that on Wemar," it went on, unaware of the interruption, "but their work fell far short of that which you describe. You say that your friends on the ship come from Sector General and are willing to do this service for Tawsar and the rest of the senior staff?"

"Yes," he replied without hesitation.

"I—I am grateful," said Remrath, "but I am also uneasy about entrusting my body to strangers. Although one of them, you are known to me and . . . You, also, come from Sector General and must have knowledge that is greater than mine. I would prefer, when the time comes, that you did the work of returning my body to the freshness of youth."

"Regrettably," said Gurronsevas, pleased at the misplaced compliment, "I know nothing of these matters. My only contribution lies in the preparation, presentation and delivery of food for people there."

"Is this an important contribution?" asked Remrath. "Does it help keep them clean and fresh?"

"Yes," said Gurronsevas again. "I would say without hesitation that it is the most important one, since without it nobody would survive."

In his head-set he could hear Murchison making an untranslatable sound.

"And you want to help keep us fresh," said Remrath, lifting the last, newly-washed platter from the trough, "by making our food look nice and taste better? Impossible!"

Gurronsevas shook his hands dry because there was nothing he could see resembling a towel and said, "I would like you to allow me to try."

Without replying, Remrath turned and hobbled stiffly into the outer room to return a few minutes later with an armful of the recently arrived vegetables. It began pulling leaves off some of them and roots from others before dropping the presumably edible parts into the water before it spoke.

"You are allowed to try, stranger," it said. "But if, out of your greater knowledge and other-world experience, you cannot produce meat for us you will be wasting your time. That is our hope and the reason why I forced Tawsar to meet you in the first place. Instead of explaining our urgent need for meat, which is necessary for the survival of our species, he was ashamed and talked of other things and allowed your healers to do strange things to him.

"What do you want to do first, Gurronsevas?"

"I would like to begin," he replied, "by talking to you about the Wem . . ."

"Yes, please," said Murchison. "Apart from the physiological data, Prilicla says that you are getting more useful information from your friend in five minutes than we did from Tawsar in two hours."

". . . About what you think of yourselves and your world," he went on, ignoring yet another unexpected compliment, "as well as what you like to eat. Which objects, scenes and colors do you consider beautiful? Is the appearance of your food as important as its taste and odor? It has long been my belief that, in several important respects, a person's behavior and level of culture is reflected by the food it eats and, of course, the civilized rituals and refinements practiced while cooking, presenting and eating it . . ."

"Stranger!" Remrath broke in. "You are becoming offensive, to myself and the Wem people. Are you suggesting that we are savages?"

"Gurronsevas, be *careful,*" said Murchison urgently. "Dammit, are you trying to pick a fight?"

"That was not my intention," he said, replying to both questioners. "I know that the Wem are close to starvation, and many of the rituals of eating require a sufficiency, if not a surplus, of the preferred foods. But where I come from eating rituals can be altered, either through necessity or to relieve the boredom of an unchanging diet.

"Despite my ignorance of Wem cooking," Gurronsevas continued quickly, "I shall make suggestions on how this may be done. If these suggestions are offensive or unsuitable for any physical or psychological reason, tell me so at once without wasting time on politeness. But before you do so, let me test the foods that are available and debate the suggestion with you at length so that I as well as you will know why it is unworkable.

"To make these tests," he went on, "I need your permission to take samples, very small quantities, of the vegetation and condiments that you use here. As well, I would be grateful if you could take me out to where these plants are harvested. Seeing them in their natural state, and gathering and testing other possibly edible growths in the vicinity, might suggest alternative meals or changes in the existing menu."

"But it is meat that we need," said Remrath firmly. "Have you a suggestion for providing that?"

"Only," said Gurronsevas, suddenly impatient with the other's culinary monomania, "if you were to eat one of us."

"*Gurronsevas* . . . !" Murchison began.

"We would not eat you, Gurronsevas," said Remrath, taking the suggestion literally. "With respect, your limbs and body appear hard and tough. You might taste like the branches of a tree. The shape-changer's parts might cause indigestion by changing shape within us, and the limbs and body of the beautiful, winged creature are as fleshless as the twigs of a bush in winter. The soft being who balances on two legs and the one with the shining fur might be suitable. Are they soon to die?"

"No," said Gurronsevas.

"Then you must not offer them to us," said Remrath in a very serious voice, "The Wem believe that it is wrong to eat another intelligent being unless it dies naturally and free of disease, or its body is broken in an accident. You must not shorten another person's life out of sympathy for our hunger, no matter how desperate our present need. I am grateful for the offer, but distressed and shocked that you would behave with such a lack of feeling towards your friends. Your gift of meat is refused."

"I'm glad," said Murchison.

"So am I," said Gurronsevas, bypassing the translator, "I am tough only on the outside. But I seem to have talked myself into a corner . . ."

To Remrath, he said, "Please, there is no need for you to feel distressed or shocked because we hold the same belief. My words were ill-chosen and were a clumsy attempt at asking another question. Would the Wem accept off-planet food, provided it was palatable and we were sure that it would not harm you?"

"Off-planet meat?" Remrath asked hopefully.

"No," he said, and this time his words were well-chosen as he explained that, while it was possible to give the food the taste and consistency of different other-worldly meats, the material was not and had never been alive. The reason for this was that when different meat-eating life-forms worked together as they did at Sector General and on the ship, it was considered insensitive to eat the flesh of non-intelligent creatures who often bore a close physical resemblance to their intelligent colleagues. He ended, "The food is artificial, but you could not tell the difference."

Remrath replied with a sound that suggested disbelief. The long silence which followed was broken by it saying, "Regarding the tour of our vegetable gardens, I have duties here which allow me very little free time for walking in the valley. I have a class and I must prepare for the evening meal . . ."

Gurronsevas concealed his disappointment. He would have preferred to have Remrath as a guide and advisor on Wem plant life than to waste his own time pulling quantities of specimens—which the other would have known immediately to be toxic—and then having to wait on the results of Murchison's analyses. Politely, he said, "What are you serving this evening?"

"More of the same," said Remrath shortly. It raised one hand stiffly to point toward the outer room and went on, "But we will be able to make the necessary time, Gurronsevas, if you bring in and break up the firewood, and help me wash the vegetables."

CHAPTER 24

Remrath's movements over the rough ground of the valley floor were slower than Tawsar's had been and clearly caused it more pain, and it steadfastly refused to enter any area that was lit by the early afternoon sun. Both problems were solved by Naydrad, who joined them with the anti-gravity litter and deployed its sunscreen over the initially reluctant passenger. The Charge Nurse had been instructed to guide the litter and to leave all the conversation to Gurronsevas, and the agitated state of its fur showed what it thought of the enforced silence. Danalta, whose job as protector had been declared redundant, had rejoined Prilicla and Murchison on *Rhabwar* to help process the Wem physiological data provided by Tawsar.

The forenoon and early afternoon classes, held in the big cavern so as to keep the pupils out of the direct sunlight while taking advantage of the maximum natural illumination from the windows, had left the mine to work outdoors again, and Remrath seemed to have forgotten the time limit it had placed on the specimen-gathering exercise. Plainly it was enjoying the comfort of traveling on the litter and it was deriving even more amusement from the strange things Gurronsevas was saying and doing.

"Surely," it said during one of their stops on the higher, un-cultivated slopes, "you do not eat *flowers* on your world?"

"Sometimes," said Gurronsevas, "the stems or leaves or petals can be crushed or cooked and used to complement or contrast with the other ingredients, or arranged on the platter so as to make a meal look attractive, or simply to decorate and give a pleasing appearance and smell to the dinner table. Sometimes we eat them."

Remrath made another sound that did not translate. It had been making them for most of the afternoon.

"These berries with the brown-spotted green skin," he went on, pointing at a low-growing bush with dense, wiry foliage which he recognized as the plant he had earlier used to scrub the platters clean, "are they edible?"

"Yes, but in very small amounts," the Wem replied. "They are the running berries. Their taste is sharp now and sweet when they are fully ripened. But we do not eat them unless one of us is having difficulty with the elimination of body wastes. You, you are not going to take them, too!"

"I will take specimens of everything," said Gurronsevas, "especially from medicinal plants which can sometimes add flavor as well as health-enhancing properties to a meal. You say that the Wem use many such plants. Who is responsible for prescribing them?"

"I am," it said.

As the senior cook of the establishment, Remrath and himself had a lot in common. The Wem's knowledge and vocabulary was severely restricted, naturally, but they spoke the same language. It would be helpful to the medical team, he thought, if he was able to identify the Wem equivalent of a doctor.

"And who among you," he persisted, "deals with the more seriously ill or injured cases? Is there a special place where they are treated? And what is done for them?"

There was a long silence, during which Gurronsevas wondered whether his seemingly innocent questions had given offense, before Remrath spoke.

"Unfortunately, I am," it said. "And Gurronsevas, I do not speak of such things to off-worlders, or even to friends. Tell me more about the strange ways you serve food."

They returned to the subject that Gurronsevas knew was safe and which he considered more interesting anyway.

Initially, Remrath's interest was merely polite. Obviously it was enjoying the comfort of traveling on the litter and was anxious to prolong the experience. But once Gurronsevas was able to make it accept the idea that eating food might be something more than the simple ingesting of organic fuel, and described with enthusiasm the many other-world rituals and subtleties used in its preparation and presentation, and the large number of different courses that could be served as part of a single meal, its interest became more serious— if, at times, combined with a large measure of incredulity.

"I can believe that you consider a meal to be a work of art," Remrath said at one point, "like a beautiful wood-carving or wall-painting. Of necessity a meal is a very short-lived work of art if the artist's work is successful. But comparing the taste sensations to the pleasures of procreation is . . . surely that is an exaggeration?"

"Perhaps not," Gurronsevas replied, "if you consider that one provides a moment of intense pleasure which can be expanded and heightened by experience and controlled delays, while the other is a continuing, although admittedly a less intense pleasure, which lasts for much longer, is less subject to factors of age or physical fatigue, and is not subject to premature consummation."

"If you can do that with food," said Remrath, "you must be a very good cook."

"I am the best," said Gurronsevas simply.

Remrath made a sound which did not translate and so, for some reason, did Naydrad.

Only the topmost slopes of the valley were lit by the setting sun and the air temperature had dropped noticeably when they began their return to the mine. The young members of the working parties and classes, unsupervised, were running and hopping about in small groups on the flat area outside the entrance. This was an activity which was encouraged, Remrath explained, so as to use up their surplus energy and make them hunger for both the evening meal and sleep, because non-reparable bodily damage could occur if they were to go wandering about in the dark tunnels. Even though the waterwheels provided continuous power, except in special circumstances the mine was not lighted at night because their small remaining store of filament bulbs could not easily be replaced.

"Do you intend to work these miracles of taste for us?" said Remrath suddenly. "How will you do it when you know nothing about Wem food and have eaten barely an insect's mouthful of my stew?"

"I shall try," Gurronsevas replied. "But first the Wem samples must be tested to ensure that they will not harm me. Should they prove edible to myself as well as the Wem, only then will I try to compose something. Naturally, any meal or course that I produce must first be tested on myself. Your advice regarding taste sensations and intensities would be greatly appreciated, since my Tralthan taste sensorium will differ in certain ways from that of the Wem, but I would not serve a meal to anyone that was not first eaten in its entirety by myself."

"Even a project that is doomed to failure," said Remrath, "can be interesting to watch. Do you wish to return to the kitchen now?"

"No," said Gurronsevas sharply, unused to having his artistic ability doubted in this fashion. He went on, "The analysis and initial experimentation with the specimens may take some time. I will return tomorrow or perhaps a day or two later. With your permission, of course."

"Will you require a guide," asked Remrath, "to find your way back to my kitchen?"

"Thank you, no," he replied. "I remember the way."

No more was said until they joined the crowd of rowdy young Wem outside the mine entrance. Two of them helped Remrath off the litter, one tried to crawl through the open space between the apparently unsupported underside and the ground, then began chattering excitedly to the others about the strange, tingling sensation that the repulsion field had caused in its head and arms. Another was about to climb onto the empty litter when Remrath chased it away with threats of imminent dismemberment and other dire punishments which, considering the First Cook's physical weakness and impaired mobility, were not being taken seriously by either.

Naydrad had begun to guide the litter back toward the ship and Gurronsevas was turning to follow it when Remrath spoke again.

"Tawsar, also, would be pleased if you visited us again," it said, "to talk to the young about the other worlds and peoples and wonders you have seen. But of your work in the kitchen you must speak only to me lest some of your ideas about food cause mental distress or nausea."

He was able to control his own mental distress, caused by shock and anger that anyone would even suggest that the great Gurronsevas was capable of preparing a meal that would nauseate anyone, before he came within closer range of Prilicla's empathy.

By the time he returned to *Rhabwar*'s casualty deck, Naydrad had unloaded his samples and, fur rippling in anticipation, was busying itself at the food dispenser while Murchison and Danalta were doing incomprehensible things at the analyzer console. He looked around for Prilicla, but the pathologist answered his question before he could ask it.

"Cinrusskins are short on stamina, as you probably know," Murchison said, smiling. "It has been sleeping this past four hours and we are trying not to let our emotional radiation get too noisy. You've had a long day, Gurronsevas. Do you need food, rest, or both?"

"Neither," he replied. "I am in need of information."

"Aren't we all," said Murchison. "What exactly do you want to know?"

As precisely as possible Gurronsevas did as he was asked. It required many minutes for him to do so, and Murchison was about to reply when Prilicla flew in to join them. The Senior Physician gestured with one delicate manipulator for it to continue.

"First," the pathologist began briskly, "to deal with your questions about the testing of Wem vegetation for edibility by the FGLI classification, yourself, as well as the native DHCGs. We obtained more physiological information from Tawsar than it was aware of giving, and while we still have many questions regarding the Wem endocrinology, and the evidence we have found of a possible genetic rift in the area of the herbivore-carnivore, or perhaps herbivore-omnivore, transfer which may take place at puberty, these should become clear when we have more . . . I'm sorry, Gurronsevas, that part of the investigation is medically specialized and of no interest to you.

"What we can tell you," it went on, "is that our study of the tongue structure and analysis of the saliva indicates the presence of a taste sensorium and an oral pre-digestive system that is in most respects similar to those found in the majority of warm-blooded, oxygen-breathing life-forms, including your own. If you identify and label your specimens and give us a few hours to process them, we will be able to tell you with a fair degree of certainty which plants, or sections of plants such as roots, stems, foliage or fruit, will be edible by the Wem and yourself, and which will be toxic to a greater or lesser degree. Frequently, material which we would classify as being toxic if introduced directly into the bloodstream can be rendered harmless by the normal detoxification processes of digestion, so it is unlikely that you would poison a Wem or yourself if the food samples tested are initially kept small. The same applies to any food material for the Wem produced by *Rhabwar*'s synthesizer.

"We cannot tell you how exactly any given sample will taste," it went on. "The chemical composition will indicate whether or not the taste will be intense, but not whether it will be intensely pleasant or unpleasant to a Wem. As you more than anyone else here know, taste is a personal preference which varies between individuals of a single species, much less those with different evolutionary backgrounds."

"It seems," said Gurronsevas, "that the Wem palate will have to be reeducated."

Murchison laughed and said, "Thankfully, that isn't my problem. Is there anything else you want to know?"

"Thank you, yes," he replied, directing all of his eyes towards Prilicla. "But it is neither a medical nor a culinary matter. I would like to know how much time I have to work on the problem? The present friendly situation at the mine could change as soon as the hunting party returns. When will they arrive?"

"That knowledge will be useful to us, too," said the Senior Physician. "Friend Fletcher?"

"There is a small problem, Doctor," said the Captain's voice from the wall speaker. "*Tremaar* has been concentrating its surveillance within a circle of fifty miles radius of the mine and has seen nothing of the hunting party. Beyond that circle the surface is uneven and wooded, giving large areas of natural cover so that the observations are less than trustworthy. Other settllements are under observation, but the closest is sited on the edge of a mountain lake just over three hundred miles away. Because of the Wem aversion to sunlight, *Tremaar* thinks they may be traveling at night and resting out of sight by day. Either way, they are not carrying the type of portable equipment with a radiation signature that would reveal their presence to orbiting sensors.

"But I can put up our unmanned casualty search vehicle," Fletcher went on. "That baby will detect any sign of life even if it is close to extinction. It uses a low-level spiral search pattern and, unless the whole hunting party is dead, you will have their number, rate of travel, and estimated time of arrival within a day or so, depending on how far away they are just now."

"Do that at once, please," said Prilicla. It flew closer to him before saying, "I can feel your satisfaction, friend Gurronsevas, but we are far from satisfied with our own progress. We are a small and uniquely-equipped medical team, too small to cure the ills of an entire planet . . ."

"We are also nothing," said Naydrad, looking around from the food dispenser, "if not modest."

". . . Although we should be able to solve the problems of one small, isolated community. Our contact is not going well. Your conversations with Remrath clarified the reasons for the shame it felt as an adult over being forced to eat young food, but still Tawsar is reluctant to give information in several areas important to full understanding. Progress is being made only in the Wem kitchen on the common ground of cookery. Surely, Chief Dietitian, this must be a first in the annals of First Contact procedures."

Gurronsevas did not reply. He was pleased by both the unexpected compliment and the use of his title in conjunction with it, and he knew that the other was aware of his pleasure.

"We overheard Remrath's invitation to you," said Prilicla. "What are your plans?"

"I would like to return at the same time tomorrow," Gurronsevas replied. "By then the edible vegetation specimens will be analyzed and identified and I will know enough to make a few dietary experiments while talking to Remrath and helping in the kitchen. But there is no need for physical protection. I feel very comfortable working over there."

He did not add that he felt more at home in Remrath's steaming and smoking and altogether primitive kitchen than he did among the shining, aseptic medical technology of the casualty deck.

"I am aware of your feelings, friend Gurronsevas," said the empath gently. "But I would feel happier if Danalta accompanied you. As well as being able to assist you directly it will be available in case of a medical emergency. According to the statisticians, the kitchen is the second most likely room in which accidents are likely to occur."

"Especially," said Naydrad, "the kitchen of a bunch of cannibals."

"As you wish, Doctor," said Gurronsevas, ignoring the charge nurse. "Am I allowed to return Remrath's hospitality by inviting it here?"

"Of course," Prilicla replied, "but be careful. The same invitation was extended to Tawsar, who refused it vehemently. Its emotional radiation at the time was complex and intense and even unfriendly. Remrath might feel and react in the same fashion.

"That is why," it went on, "we must discuss the whole Wemar situation with you, the facts we know and our speculations based on them, before you speak to Remrath again. Because of their unidentified feelings of antipathy or distrust towards us, you are maintaining our most promising communications channel with the Wem. It must not be closed accidentally because we have not provided you with all the available information."

He was a cook, Gurronsevas thought, and neither a medic nor an other-species contact specialist. But now they seemed to be treating him as all three. His feelings about that were oddly pleasant and not a little fearful.

"We will continue to monitor and record your conversations in the mine or while you are with Remrath outside it," Prilicla went on reassuringly, "but we no longer think it necessary to distract you with unnecessary advice, and should there be an emergency we will react quickly; our silence will not mean that we have forgotten you. Personal security procedures will be included in your Wem briefing."

"Thank you," he said.

"Do not feel worried, friend Gurronsevas," said the empath, "either for your safety or your ability to do the job. You have done and will do well. But I find it strange that a specialist of your eminence has not complained, nor have you felt any but the most minor and temporary emotional distress about the menial work you are doing here. On Wemar they are not treating you with the respect that is your due."

"On Wemar," said Gurronsevas, "I have yet to earn their respect."

CHAPTER 25

Fletcher's low-altitude sensor vehicle discovered and sent back pictures of a party of adult Wem, forty-three in number, who were headed towards the mine but still distant by an estimated nine days' march. They were walking rather than hopping because four of them were carrying a fifth on a litter made from thin, straight branches stripped of their twigs. Two small animals of about one-fifth the body mass of the Wem were each being dragged and driven between a pair of hunters who had them double-roped at the neck. Apart from the sick or injured one on the litter, all of the Wem wore packs which sagged loosely against their backs. Plainly the hunt had not been a successful one.

It had been left to Gurronsevas's discretion whether or when to show the pictures to Remrath. The news of the arrival of the hunting party might have an unsettling effect on his steadily improving relations with Remrath. Since their trip together in the valley, the Chief Cook had never been short of words, especially, as now, when they were words of criticism.

"This is completely ridiculous and childish," said the Wem impatiently. "Gurronsevas, how often must I tell you that eating vegetation is a practice forced on us by near-starvation and not by choice. Cold or hot, raw or stewed, whatever form they take, they are still vegetables. You make them look nice on the platter, I admit, but youngsters find it easier to make designs by pushing colored stones and pieces of wood around on their desktops than by making a soggy mess with bits of raw vegetation on their platters. What is it? Surely you don't expect anyone to actually eat this stuff?"

"It is a salad," he replied patiently in an attempt to counter the other's impatience. "If you will observe it closely you will find that it is composed of small amounts of familiar Wem vegetation, diced, sliced and shredded into unfamiliar forms, covered lightly with a dressing comprised of your vrie seeds crushed and mixed with the juice of unripe moss berries to give it the necessary tang, and arranged into a visually interesting design. The crill bud can also be eaten if desired, and they will be fully opened by the time the meal is served, but their purpose is chiefly decorative as well as aroma-enhancing. I have already explained that the attraction of this dish, and of the other two dishes on the tray, lie in their visual and olfactory presentation as well as in the taste.

"Please try the salad," Gurronsevas went on. "I have eaten of all three dishes without harm to myself and, in spite of the ingredients being strange to me, I have found some of them to be quite pleasant."

That was not entirely true, he thought. During the early experimentation with Wem vegetation the pleasure had been preceded by much digestive displeasure. But, he reminded himself, a great deal of trouble had been caused throughout every world's history by people who insisted on telling too much of the truth.

"Taste them and see," he added.

"I do not understand why there have to be three separate dishes," said Remrath. "Why not mix them all together?"

The mere idea sent a small, unnoticed shiver of revulsion through Gurronsevas' massive body. He had already answered that question earlier and suspected that Remrath was simply fighting a delaying action which, as a fellow cook, it could not hope to win.

Perhaps he should answer it again, and this time leave no doubt in the other's mind about his meaning.

"Among all of the intelligent species known to me," said Gurronsevas, "the practice is to prepare and serve meals comprising a number of separate and contrasting or complementary dishes, or courses. This is because they consider eating as a pleasure of the taste sensors that can at times be subtle and long-delayed and at other times sharp and intense. The ingredients of the individual dishes are chosen to perform a similar function on a smaller scale within a single course.

"A meal can consist of many different courses," he went on enthusiastically, "five, eleven, or even more, so that the event can last for hours. With the larger and more complex meals, which often have the secondary political and psychological function of impressing the guests with their host's or its organization's or tribe's wealth, the diner is not expected to eat everything that is set before it; and great gastronomic discomfort would ensue should it try. Personally, I am not in favor of such over-large and wasteful meals, favoring as I do quality rather than quantity. Nevertheless, each and every course is meticulously prepared and served with the proper accompanying—"

"Off-worlders waste so much of their lives eating," Remrath broke in, "how did you find the time to build starships and carts that float on air and your other technical marvels?"

"We use these things without needing to understand them," Gurronsevas replied. "They are built to save time, not waste it, so that we can have more of it to enjoy the lasting pleasures of life, like eating."

Remrath's reply did not translate.

"There are other pleasures," Gurronsevas admitted, "especially those associated with procreation. But these cannot be indulged in continually, or with great frequency, without incurring severe debilitation or some other health penalty. The same applies to the exciting or dangerous activities of, say, mountain-climbing, sea-diving or flying in unpowered aircraft. The principal excitement of those occupations is that the entity concerned is pitting daring and skill against what can often become a life-threatening situation. The mental and physical coordination required for these activities deteriorates with age, but with age the ability to appreciate the pleasures of good food and drink increases with practice. And they are pleasures which can be repeatedly indulged to satiety and which, when the proper foods are ingested regularly and in the correct amounts, can significantly extend your life."

Remrath said quietly, "Eating this stuff, eating raw vegetables, will keep my body young and fresh?"

"If they are eaten from an early age and throughout maturity," Gurronsevas replied, "they will keep you younger and fresher for a much longer time. Especially if you learn to eat vegetation exclusively, as I prefer to do. Our own healers agree on this, and I have personal experience of cooking for aging beings where such was the case. But I must be truthful. Changing your eating habits would not mean that your people would live forever."

Remrath returned its attention to the tray Gurronsevas had prepared with such care, then said sourly, "If they have to eat this stuff, they would not want to."

Gurronsevas thought that he had received more professional insults since coming to Wemar than in all of his past life. He indicated the tray and returned firmly to his subject.

"As I was saying," he said, "a meal normally consists of three courses. The first, which I have already described, is a small, fresh-tasting starter designed merely to sharpen rather than blunt the appetite.

"It is followed by the main course," he continued, "which is more nutritious and varied regarding its ingredients and, as you can see, much more bulky. Here again the visual presentation is important and you will recognize most of the vegetables, although you are not used to seeing some of them in this under-cooked form. This was done so that each variety could be placed separately on the platter, which adds to the visual effect as well as allowing the vegetables to retain their individual tastes, which would otherwise be diluted or lost if they were to be mixed together in a stew. As in your stew, the principal vegetable used is the orrogne. It is, if you will excuse me saying so, a particularly bland and tasteless vegetable which I have sliced and dry-cooked, we call it roasting, after brushing on a little oil of crushed glunce berries, which you do not appear to consider a food, to avoid charring. The orrogne taste remains the same, but with the surfaces crisped and covered by a film of oil, I think you will find it more interesting to eat . . ."

"It has an interesting smell," said Remrath, inhaling loudly through its nose and bending over the tray.

". . . Especially," Gurronsevas went on, "in conjunction with the dark red jelly, which was also made from local—no, don't eat it directly with a spoon. Use your food spike, select a portion of vegetable and touch it lightly against the jelly. It is similar to Kelgian sarkun, or strong Earth mustard, and is very hot on the tongue—"

"*Hot!*" Remrath burst out, grabbing for one of the two beakers on the tray and emptying it quickly before saying, "Great Gorel, it set my whole mouth on fire! But, but what have you done to our water?"

"I may have miscalculated the level of sensitivity of the Wem palate," Gurronsevas said apologetically, "or I will need to reduce the proportion of powdered cressle root or, as with any new ingredient, the jelly may be an acquired taste. The liquids in the beakers have each been flavored with the juice of two different berries, one bitter-tasting and the other slightly sweeter and aromatic. Your names for them are unknown to me because you do not use them in the kitchen, but the healers on the ship say that they are harmless to the Wem."

Remrath did not reply. It had speared another slice of roasted orrogne on its eating spike and was touching it carefully to the jelly. Its other hand was holding the beaker close to its mouth as if in readiness to extinguish another fire.

"Your mountain spring water is cold and fresh and makes a fine liquid accompaniment to a meal," said Gurronsevas, "but by the time the water is being drunk it has become tepid and uninteresting. The flavoring is an attempt to give it an appeal that is not dependent solely on its low temperature and, hopefully, to stimulate the taste sensors to a greater appreciation of the accompanying food. On many other worlds the preferred accompaniment is wine, which is a liquid containing varying proportions of a chemical called alcohol that is produced by fermentation of certain species of vegetation. There are many different wines that can be chosen to complement and enhance the taste of the meal or the course that is being consumed, but on Wemar I have encountered problems where the production of alcohol is concerned and have been forced to give up the attempt."

There were several native plants whose fermentation would have produced alcohol, but the problem had been philosophical rather than physical. So far as the medical team knew, the use of alcohol as a beverage was unknown on Wemar and they did not want the responsibility of introducing it. Pathologist Murchison had been particularly vehement in its objections, citing the case of an early Earth-human sub-culture of the Amerindians that had been virtually destroyed through overindulgence because they had no prior experience of its mind-deadening and mood-changing effects. Prilicla had gently agreed that in their present situation the Wem had problems enough.

"The third course," Gurronsevas resumed, "we call the dessert, or the sweet. Again it is a small dish, a pleasant farewell to a stomach that is almost filled to repletion. This one is made from chopped cretto stalks, heated until the water has boiled away to leave it with the consistency of a thick, smooth, and tasteless paste, under which there are hiding a few stoned den berries, diced matto and a few other items which I will not name as yet. Please try it. It will not burn your tongue but I think it may surprise you."

"Wait," said Remrath. It had put down the beaker and was gently applying its fifth slice of orrogne to the jelly. "I haven't decided how much I dislike this one yet."

"In your own time," said Gurronsevas, and went on, "Instead

of a cold salad, the starter dish can be a hot soup. In consistency this is something between a flavored drink and a very thin stew, contains small amounts of vegetation to which are added very small quantities of your herbs and spices to vary the taste. I am still experimenting with combinations that show promising results, but I would not want you to taste the result of an unsuccessful experiment.

"You do not seem to be aware of the many edible herbs and spices growing in your valley," he continued, "the majority of which our healers have pronounced safe and even beneficial for the Wem, and myself. Regrettably, there are subtle differences in taste sensitivity and appreciation between the Wem and Tralthan species, and it is important that these differences be reconciled so that I can make further suggestions."

Remrath laid down its eating spike and dipped its spoon cautiously into the dessert. The platter containing the main course, whose portions were rather small, was more than half empty.

"You have said that the mine grows very cold at night," Gurronsevas went on, "and damp when heavy rain enters the ventilation shafts. The young Wem are not inconvenienced by this, but the teachers are. One of my suggestions is that, when your fuel reserves permit it, the teachers heat the water served with the evening meal so that they will feel warmer when they cover themselves for the night. Better still, if they were to take a thick, highly-spiced soup before retiring, one that is hot in taste as well as temperature, they would find it more comforting than shivering under their blankets until their own body heat slowly warmed them.

"For you it would be a small change in routine," he added, "but it is a popular practice among many off-world species who find that it engenders physical and mental relaxation as well as encouraging sleep."

Remrath stopped with the second spoonful of dessert halfway to its mouth and said, "It would be a small change, one of many small changes and suggestions that have led to me eating these, these outlandish mixtures of vegetation, and may lead to who knows what else. Your intention is to help us, and that is the reason why I, and to a lesser extent the other teachers, are submitting ourselves to your strange and often sickening experiments with Wem vegetation. But are you not forgetting that we, being old as well as hungry, have forced down our shame to help you, and that it is the young adults who need your help most, and that they need meat.

"Gurronsevas," it ended, "you are so enthusiastic, so forceful and so single-minded and so dismissive of objections that you act like a person who is indulging its favorite hobby."

The Great Gurronsevas a hobbyist! he thought furiously. He was too angry to speak for a moment, during which a very uncomfortable thought arose in his mind. What was the difference between a person with a hobby that claimed all of his attention and one who devoted his life to the perfection of a single, all-consuming activity?

"But you are also forgetting," Remrath went on, "that the reluctant cooperation you receive from the teachers will not be forthcoming from the taught. It may be that age has damaged our minds, or made them less resistant to argument. But if you try to make them eat this stuff, the young Wem are likely to throw your carefully prepared experimental meals against the nearest wall, or at you. What are you going to do about that?"

"Nothing," said Gurronsevas.

"Nothing?"

"About the young, nothing," Gurronsevas explained. "They will see but not be permitted to sample the new meals, which will be exclusively for adult consumption. Here again, I shall need your cooperation and that of the other teachers. You have said that Tawsar eats alone, through shame over its forced consumption of vegetation, but if it was explained that it was not doing so through choice but to assist with important food experiments being conducted by the off-worlders, that might be the excuse it needs to eat in public. When the young see all of you eating and enjoying the new meals, and I am increasingly confident that you will enjoy them, the normal curiosity of the young will take over and they will want to try them too. But still you will not permit this. They will feel increasingly aggrieved, thinking that you are being selfish in not sharing the enjoyment of the strange, off-worlder meals with them. And gradually you will relent.

"A pleasure witheld is a pleasure intensified.

"Your present kitchen staff is adequate," he went on, "for the production of stew and the very occasional meat dish. But many more, and more agile, help will be needed for the preparation, and in particular the visual presentation, of the new, three-course meals. You will select the number needed and together we will train them. As a special favor and reward for helping in the kitchen, only these selected few will be allowed to eat the new meals during training. In the manner of the young they will want to talk about their new job, perhaps even boast about it, to their less-favored friends. As a teacher, Remrath, you know how young minds think and how to influence them. It should not be long before everyone is dining like the off-worlders."

Remrath was silent for several minutes, during which it finished the dessert and renewed its cautious attack on the cooling main course. Gurronsevas cringed at the very idea of consuming a course in the wrong order of presentation, but reminded himself that culinarily the Wem were still untutored. Finally the other spoke.

"Gurronsevas," it said, "you are a cunning and devious grudlich."

Plainly the word was exclusive to the Wem language because his translator gave the word-sound without a Tralthan equivalent. Deliberately he did not ask Remrath for an exact translation. He had taken enough insults for one day.

CHAPTER 26

Supported by all the resources of *Rhabwar*'s clinical equipment and the expertise of its medical team, the culinary education of the Wem was proceeding apace. But the transfer of information was two-way and no longer restricted to cooking because the team were at last beginning to understand the full extent of the Wemar problem, and the Wem were seeing that problem from the viewpoint of the off-worlders who were trying to provide a solution to it. On both sides the learning curve had become satisfactorily steep.

Wemar had been a verdant, thickly-forested world whose dominant life-form had risen rapidly from pre-sapience to technologically advanced civilization by the traditional method of forming alliances and periodically threatening themselves with extinction through increasingly mechanistic forms of warfare. Fortunately, they had not developed nuclear fission or fusion power so that they survived with their civilization intact until they slowly learned the ways of peace and the population expanded without control. Unfortunately, they were an inward-looking culture that considered their world's resources, its animal life and its growing and fossil fuel supply to be inexhaustible.

Until too late they did not have the orbiting eyes to see what they were doing to their planet.

With every new generation the Wem population tripled, and the levels of atmospheric pollution from its power-hungry and non-nuclear manufacturing processes kept pace, until the ionization layers protecting it against the harmful parts of the solar radiation spectrum became increasingly affected. Like the majority of worlds that had no axial tilt and seasonal temperature variations, the meteorological changes were driven only by Wem's planetary rotation so that its weather systems tended to be unspectacular and predictable. As a result the pollutants found their way into the upper layers of the atmosphere to collect over the north and south poles. There the quantities of destructive material grew and spread, stripping the polar regions of their protective ionization and spreading inexorably into the upper levels of the stratosphere above the heavily populated temperate zones, and beyond.

It was a gradual process, but slowly the planetary surface from the poles to the sub-tropical latitudes adjoining the equator sickened and much of it died, as did the great herds of food animals that depended on the dying vegetation. The fish and underwater plant life occupying the on-shore shallows sickened as well, and in steadily increasing numbers so did the Wem—who starved without their meat. Worse, the sun, which had once caused plants and grasses eaten by their food animals to grow and thrive, was causing them to wither and die; and the Wem, too, were dying in great numbers from strange wasting diseases of the skin and eyes, caused by exposure to their increasingly lethal sunlight.

Gradually their technology collapsed. The steady attrition of population was accelerated by increasingly savage wars waged between the equatorial and comparatively well-fed Haves, who still had an adequate ionization layer protecting them, and the starving temperate zone Have Nots. Over the past two centuries the situation had stabilized, with the world population much diminished and the pollution it had caused removed, so that now the desperately ill planet was beginning to cure itself. The sun was beginning to reionize the upper atmosphere and renew the damaged protective layer.

In time, perhaps in four or five generations, the off-world teachers on *Tremaar* insisted, the cure would be complete. But only if the tragically few remaining Wem were able to survive, and they did not once again allow their population to grow out of control or reintroduce the old, dirty technology to support it.

"I tell you again," said Gurronsevas very seriously, "the next time the Wem try to kill themselves, you might succeed."

Remrath did not look up from the special cold desserts it was preparing for the teachers and students. Angrily, it said, "The Wem do not like being constantly reminded that we are criminally stupid. Certainly I don't."

"I feel very strongly about this situation," Gurronsevas said quickly, "so that my words were hasty and ill-considered. You are neither stupid nor a criminal, nor is any other Wem that I know of. The crime was committed by your ancestors. The problem is inherited, but it is you who must solve it."

"I know, I know," said Remrath, still without looking up. "By eating vegetables?"

"Soon," Gurronsevas replied, as he had done so often before, "there will be nothing else to eat."

Over the past few days Remrath and he had grown close, as acquaintances if not friends, so much so that he no longer allowed politeness to get in the way of truth. At first this had worried the listeners on *Rhabwar* who, as well as supplying him with the information they had been able to discover or deduce about the Wem culture, kept reminding him that he was their only effective channel of communication. But they expected him to explain to Remrath and the other teachers a situation which, not being a medic or anthropologist or even a biologist, he did not fully understand himself.

When he asked for a fuller explanation it was usually Pathologist Murchison, speaking to him in a manner identical to that of Tawsar addressing a very backward pupil, who gave the densely clinical answer. Gurronsevas knew nothing about genetic rifts, or the various other-world precedents for the Wem's apparent change from omnivore to carnivore eating habits at puberty, or the fact that on Earth tadpoles and frogs made the same changeover, and he cared less. So far as he was concerned, the legs of frogs were no more than a culinary delicacy enjoyed by some Earth-humans as well as a few other species with cultivated palates.

Unlike the Earth-human Murchison, in his youth Gurronsevas had never caught tadpoles or frogs, or kept one of them in a glass jar, because there was no equivalent of those life-forms on Traltha. But finally the pathologist had been able to make him understand the differences between the digestive systems possessed by herbivores, carnivores, and omnivores.

The large, meat-bearing herbivores were usually ruminants who had to graze continually while they were awake so that their multiple stomachs could metabolize the food which, because of its high proportion of vegetable fibre and low energy content, required a long time to digest and store. When threatened by predators, the grazers could move fast and sometimes protect themselves with horns or hooves, but they lacked the speed and stamina of the meat-eating carnivores whose food intake was more easily assimilated and available as energy.

It was only in rare environmental circumstances that a ruminant species evolved to planetary dominance or the level of intelligence that preceded civilization. If they were not hunted to extinction, they were domesticated, bred, and protected as a continuing source of food by the species which had achieved domination. And very rarely did a carnivorous species achieve the level of cooperation beyond the family unit that allowed an advanced culture to develop, and then only when they made major changes in their predatory behavior and eating habits.

Omnivorous life-forms were much more adaptable in the matter of food because they had the choice of hunting for it, gathering it or, when their ability to adapt became the stirrings of true intelligence, of herding and cultivating it. And if these intelligent omnivores were threatened with starvation because a crop had failed or their food-herds had sickened and died, they would find a way to survive even if they suffered a natural disaster on the scale of that which had overtaken Wemar.

There was a much easier way to that which the Wem hunters were now pursuing.

Gurronsevas went on, "Out of instinct or experience, the few animals that are left to hunt have learned to stay out of the sun. Large and small, they have become twilight or nocturnal creatures who shelter during daylight in deep caves and ground burrows. And because they have only each other to prey upon, they have become very dangerous indeed. Frequently, as you have told me, your hunters have to spend many dangerous hours in the sun, hampered by their protective cloaks, while digging them out or following them into deep lairs, because at night the advantage lies with their prey. It is hard, dangerous work that they do, and often your hunters become the hunted.

"A mere grower of vegetables would not attract the admiration and prestige of a brave hunter," he continued, "but the work is easier and the life-expectancy higher because vegetables don't fight back.

"Unless served with too much powdered cressle root," he added.

"Gurronsevas," said Remrath, "this is a serious matter. The Wem have always been meat-eaters."

He wished suddenly that he was back in Sector General and able to consult Chief Psychologist O'Mara or, better still, Padre Lioren, about this problem. He was pitting logic against belief, indisputable scientific fact against a situation that had become a religion; and, as so often happened with emerging cultures, science was losing the argument.

"You are right, of course," he replied. "The matter is very serious and the Wem have always, as far back as your memories and written records go, been meat-eaters. Many centuries ago, when your plains and forests were still well stocked with animal life and you could hunt them in the sunlight without fear, I think that it was not only the adults who ate meat. I think, and my thoughts are supported by the investigation of our healers on the ship, that infants, newly-weaned from their mothers' milk, were fed a thin, vegetable, meat-flavored stew because their young stomachs were unable to accept meat alone. At a very early age, however, and making allowance for their smaller physical size, they would be given meat in the same proportion as that served to the adults.

"But neither they, nor you, are necessarily carnivorous.

"Physically the Wem are not suited to be farmers," Gurronsevas went on. "Your long rear limbs and tails, your fast movements and ability to suddenly change direction, were probably evolved to escape large predators in your pre-sapient past. Until the ecological catastrophe overtook your world, meat was always plentiful and hunting and herding it was much easier than trying to grow it, so that meat-eating became a virtue of necessity. But when your meat supply diminished, and you may have difficulty accepting my words, it became a vice.

"I do not speak with certain knowledge," Gurronsevas went on quickly before Remrath could interrupt, "because I can only speculate about events that happened two or three centuries ago. But I would guess that, when the meat shortage became gradually more severe, the short period when vegetable stew was fed to young infants was increased until they reached puberty, and the restriction on eating meat was extended, probably at their own request, to those aged adults who were past their physical best. I would guess that soon afterwards only the young male hunters and female hunters, because of the increasing dangers they faced and their importance to the survival of their tribal group, were certain of having meat to eat. And in times of great shortage it might be that the hunters were expected to keep the meat they caught for themselves.

"They would not do this because of selfishness brought on by great, personal hunger," Gurronsevas added. "It would be because of a firmly held belief that the future survival of the Wem lay in feeding the food-gatherers with meat. Is this not so?"

Because the returning hunters were making slower progress than expected, there had been time for Gurronsevas to learn a little of Remrath's body language and facial expressions. The old cook was looking distressed and ashamed, emotions which could change quickly to anger, and it was not replying. In his anxiety to help the other he was pushing too hard. Something must be said quickly to lighten this conversation, he thought, or contact might be broken permanently here and now.

"If I were to ask them politely," he said, "would your hunters give me some of their meat? Just a small portion would do. I can be quite creative with a meat course."

For a moment Remrath had difficulty with its breathing, but the choking sounds subsided into the low barking that he recognized as the Wem equivalent of laughter.

"They would not!" it said. "Meat is too precious for an offworlder cooker of vegetables to risk spoiling it."

Gurronsevas remained silent, deliberately. As he had hoped, it was Remrath who now felt that it had given offense because its tone became apologetic.

"You would not spoil food deliberately," Remrath said quickly. "But you might change its taste with your sauces and spices so that they would not recognize it as meat." It hesitated, then went on, "And you are right. Unless there was a particularly successful hunt, and that has not happened since I left the hunters to become a teacher, neither the old nor the young share the meat. Sometimes, secretly, a returning hunter will spare a morsel for a teacher parent or an offspring, but I cannot remember when that last happened.

"Now meat is so scarce that even the hunters are forced to eat vegetables," it went on in a voice so quiet with shame that Gurronsevas barely heard it, "to add bulk to what would otherwise be very frugal meals. But they insist that meat is present to give them strength, and they feel privileged when the taste of meat is there. I think their hunters' pride very often brings them close to starvation and weakness rather than giving them greater strength."

That was what Gurronsevas had been trying to tell it all along, but this was not the time to be scoring argument points. Instead, he laughed and said, "Then we must go on cooking vegetables, and make the hunters envious of the taste."

Remrath did not laugh. It said, "A few days ago, before you had everyone wanting to eat your strange three-meals-in-one, that would have been a ridiculous suggestion. But now . . . Gurronsevas, vegetable novelties for the young and very old are not enough. It is meat that we need if the Wem are to survive as a race and, and, our hunters are long overdue."

In a regretful voice it added, "Need I remind you of the promise made by your First Healer that the off-worlders would leave us before the hunters returned?"

Prilicla had left it to Gurronsevas to decide when would be the best time to tell the people in the mine that their hunters could be expected soon, and this seemed to be the right moment. But with the good news there should also be a strong reminder that changes for the Wem were inevitable. He opened the satchel strapped to his side and directed an eye into it, searching for *Rhabwar*'s reconnaissance pictures.

"Allowing for the differences in size and age," he said, "the young and old Wem are healthy and active on their diet of vegetables. The healers on the ship, who have knowledge of such matters covering many worlds, say that your young adults, too, would live and thrive and proliferate on the same diet. The eating of meat is good for them, the healers agree, but it is not the only source of health and energy for them. We feel that the eating of meat has become a belief and a habit going back many generations, and that it is a habit that can be broken.

"But let us not start another argument," Gurronsevas went on quickly, "because I have good news for you. At their present rate of progress, which is slow because they are heavily loaded, your hunters will be here in the late morning of the day after tomorrow. If meat is what you want then meat you shall soon have."

Without saying how long ago the pictures had been taken he gave a simple explanation of the workings of *Rhabwar*'s casualty search vehicle and began spreading them out before Remrath. Enlarged and enhanced, they showed every detail of the five food animals struggling against their tethers, every fold in the sewn skins covering the litter that was being carried by six Wem and, because the day had been heavily overcast, the hunters had their sun cowls and cloaks tied back so that every face was clearly visible. Even to Gurronsevas the sharpness of the images was impressive.

"Maybe they are late arriving because they have five food animals and a heavily loaded litter," Gurronsevas went on enthusiastically. "You can see for yourself, so clearly that you will be able to recognize your friends. I have no idea of how much they usually bring back, but I think I know a big catch when I see one."

"You know nothing, Gurronsevas," said Remrath in a very quiet voice. "It is not a big catch. The hunters should not be walking, they should be running and tail-hopping so that the small animal carcasses in their belly-packs will not spoil before they reach us, and dragging upwards of twenty big crellan and twasacths behind them instead of five scrawny cubs. But many of their packs are empty, and they carry a Wem on a covered litter, which means that one of the hunters has been damaged and is dead or dying."

"I am sorry," said Gurronsevas. "Do you know . . . Is it a friend of yours?"

Gurronsevas knew as soon as he spoke that it was an unnecessary question. All the faces in the pictures were so clear and sharp that the other could identify the injured Wem by the simple process of elimination.

"It is Creethar, their leader," said Remrath in an even quieter voice. "A very brave and resourceful and well-loved hunter. Creethar is my last-born."

CHAPTER 27

Tawsar was reluctant but sympathetic and Remrath was adamant, which meant that it was the First Cook who won the argument. Even so, it took three hours before Rhabwar with Remrath on board was able to lift off on the kind of mission that it had been expressly designed to perform.

The situation did not bear thinking about, even for a non-medical person like himself. For an emotion-sensitive like Prilicla, he thought, it must be ghastly.

Gurronsevas knew exactly how he felt about it, and he thought that he knew how Remrath and the other people on the casualty deck were feeling. In spite of the attempts they must be making to control their feelings, they must all be emoting strongly within a few yards of Prilicla. Perhaps that was why the Senior Physician had not prefixed any of their names with "friend" for more than an hour.

The Wem were so short of meat that far-ranging hunting parties were sent out to find it, and so low in technology that there was no way that the catch could be stored for long periods unless it was brought to the mine, so the only way to transport it over long distances was to keep it alive. If the casualty was not already dead, it and its fellow hunters would try to keep it alive so that the young body meat that it must give up to its people would be fresh when it arrived home.

In spite of the continuing pain it would suffer on the journey, and of the fact that its selectively cannibalistic race knew little or nothing of the practice of curative medicine, Remrath told them that Creethar would try to stay alive until the last possible moment. As a brave and honorable Wem it was Creethar's bounden duty to do so.

Now Remrath was standing before the casualty deck's viewscreen, displaying no visible reaction as Fletcher brought *Rhabwar* down for a full emergency landing, which Gurronsevas felt sure was little more than a controlled crash, a few hundred yards from the Wem hunting party.

Prilicla was hovering unsteadily beside him. He spoke to hide his anxiety, realizing at once that no feelings could be hidden from an empath.

"When I spoke to Tawsar and Remrath," Gurronsevas said quietly, in spite of the translator bypass, "together and separately as you asked, there was disagreement. Tawsar forbade us to interfere and Remrath was anxious to help us in every way possible. So if we try to help Creethar without Tawsar's permission, our present good relations with the Wem may be jeopardized. But from what I have seen, Tawsar likes and respects its first cook and healer, and at present feels great sympathy towards it, so the risk may be a small one. Creethar is, after all, Remrath's youngest and only surviving offspring."

"You have already said these things to me," the empath replied, "and then as now your attempt at reassurance is appreciated. But as the senior medical officer of an ambulance ship I have no choice. Or is your feeling of anxiety due to something else?"

"I'm not sure," said Gurronsevas. "There seems to be a problem with communication. Against Tawsar's wishes Remrath is flying out with us to reassure the hunting party about our good intentions, so that we can bring Creethar home quickly for treatment or to die. But it doesn't seem to want that. Before it left the mine with me, you must have overheard it telling Tawsar that as the parent, it had the final say in what was to happen to the damaged First Hunter and that it wanted the off-worlders, rather than itself or another Wem, to take Creethar into the ship for as long as would be necessary.

"Nothing more was said to me directly," he went on, "and I do not have your ability to read emotional radiation. But why would a parent in this terrible situation give its offspring to us, to utterly strange beings it has known for such a short time, with so little argument? I felt sure that it was saying less, much less, than it was thinking and feeling. This worries me."

"I know your feelings, and Remrath's," said the empath. "Right now it is radiating the combination of uncertainty and grief characteristic of the expected loss of a loved one, the severity of whose injuries and chances of survival are unknown. And, almost submerged by these stronger feelings, there is a child-like wonder and excitement of its first experience of flying. It is an intelligent being with, in spite of the present near-barbaric situation on Wemar, a civilized and liberal mind who trusts us. That trust was won by you, friend Gurronsevas, and as a result we will be able to give Creethar the best treatment possible, with parental consent.

"You have no reason to worry," Prilicla ended, "but still you are worrying."

Before he could reply, the deck plating pressed gently against their feet as the gravity compensators evened out the shock of the emergency landing. Warm, outside air blew around them as the casualty deck's boarding lock swung open. Remrath climbed stiffly onto the litter and the medical team, with the exception of Pathologist Murchison who would prepare to receive the casualty following the preliminary report on its medical condition, moved down the ramp and toward the hunting party.

Remrath took charge at that point, ordering the others to remain silent while it did the talking. Unless it was present, it had insisted, any attempt the off-worlders might make to retrieve Creethar would certainly fail, probably with many casualties on both sides, if another Wem was not present to speak to them with authority. The medical team had been forced to agree. But Gurronsevas tried to put himself in the position of a Wem hunting party who were seeing a spaceship for the first time, and an off-world menagerie that was as strange as it was frightening, who were trying to take one of their number away from them.

He wondered if his friend was suffering from the overconfidence of age.

But Remrath was talking to them as if they were still its pupils, firmly, reassuringly, and with authority. First it told them that they had nothing to fear and then telling them why. It began with a brief and very simple lesson in astronomy that covered the formation of solar systems, the intelligent life-forms that some of them must contain, and the vast interstellar distances between them, and from there it went on to an equally short discussion regarding the many centuries of peaceful cooperation required to achieve the level of technology on these worlds required for travel between the stars . . .

Danalta had adopted a quadripedal shape with no fearsome natural weaponry so as not to worry any of the Wem hunters. The shape-changer moved closer to Gurronsevas and said, "When your friend offered to help us, I didn't expect anything like this."

"In spite of having a common area of interest," said Gurronsevas, "we talked about subjects other than cooking."

"Obviously," said Danalta.

They had closed to within twenty yards of Creethar's litter and the hunters were showing no sign of moving out of their way.

". . . The strange creatures around me have come in peace," Remrath was saying. "They mean us no harm and are anxious to help us. One of them . . ." it pointed at Gurronsevas, ". . . has already helped us with the provision of new food at the mine, in many strange and wonderful ways that I have not the time to describe now. The others are healers and preservers of wide experience who are also willing to help us. I have decided, as is my parental right, to allow them to practice their advanced art on our behalf. Put the litter down and remove the coverings."

In a quieter, less authoritative voice it added, "Does, does Creethar still live?"

A long silence answered it.

Prilicla moved forward to hover just above Creethar's litter. Two of the hunters raised spears and another notched an arrow to its bow, aimed, but did not draw back the string to full tension. The empath was aware of everyone's feelings, Gurronsevas told himself reassuringly, and would know if anyone really intended to attack it, hopefully in time to take evasive action. But Prilicla's hovering flight was erratic, so it was possible that the empath was as worried about its safety as he was.

"Creethar is alive," said the empath, its voice sounding loud in the silence, "but just barely. Friend Remrath, we must examine it at once, then transfer it quickly to the ship. Danalta, let us see our patient."

More spears and bows were raised, and now all of them were pointed at the shape-changer's virtually impervious hide rather than at the incredibly fragile body of Prilicla. While Danalta was carefully removing the animal skins that were draped loosely over the grounded Wem litter, Remrath created another diversion by dismounting from the team's vehicle and renewing its demand that Creethar be released to the off-worlders. The hunters crowded around the First Cook, arguing and shouting so much that they seemed to be ignoring everything that Prilicla, Danalta and Naydrad were doing and saying.

Gurronsevas tried very hard to listen to everyone, but the Wem hunters were growing louder and more excitable, and their arguments were becoming so involved that it passed beyond his comprehension. His attempts to make sense of what they were saying was further hampered by their ability to talk rapidly to each other and listen, simultaneously. He switched briefly to the ship frequency so that he could listen to the medical team without Wem interference.

Prilicla was saying, "The patient has sustained multiple fractures and lacerations to the forelimbs, chest and abdomen, with extensive contused and lacerated areas along both flanks, which suggest a rolling fall onto a hard, uneven surface, probably rocks. As you can see, there is material resembling dried soil or rock dust still adhering to the uninjured areas, indicating that the water used to irrigate the wounds was in short supply. The scanner shows damage to the rib cage but no other internal injuries. Severe crepitation and complication of the fractures has taken place during travel. There is widespread tissue wastage, suggesting a lengthy period without food and reduced water intake. When compared with the normal vital signs obtained from Tawsar, friend Creethar's are not good. It is massively debilitated, barely conscious, and its emotional radiation is characteristic of an entity who is close to termination. You are seeing what we are seeing, friend Murchison. There is no time to waste arguing with its friends and, for now, we must risk acting without their permission.

"Danalta, Naydrad," it went on briskly. "Extend the antigravity field and lift Creethar onto the litter, smoothly and with minimum disturbance to its limbs. We don't want any further complications to those fractures. Gently, that's it. Now seal the canopy, increase internal heating ten degrees and switch the atmosphere to pure oxygen. We should be back on *Rhabwar* in five minutes."

"Right," said Murchison. "Instruments for orthopedic repair and internal examination procedures are ready. However, that patient is emaciated and badly dehydrated. In addition to the trauma, it's about ready to terminate from sheer starvation. Dammit, this kind of treatment is callous, even cruel. Have the Wem never heard about the use of splints to immobilize fractures? Or do these people *care* about their injured?"

Gurronsevas knew that he had no business interrupting a medical discussion, but the pathologist's words had angered him. It was as if he was being forced to listen while a friend was being wrongly criticized. The feeling surprised him, but it was there and it was strong.

He said, "The Wem are not cruel, nor uncaring. Remrath and

I discussed this very point. It said that on Wemar the medical profession is composed only of physicians—cook-healers and herbalists, that is. There are no surgeons as we know them. Remrath thinks that there may have been such people in the old days, but the skill has long since been lost. Nowadays even a simple injury can result in death, or a long, pain-filled life of a cripple that is a burden both to the invalid and those taking care of it, as well as a drain on the food resources of its community. That being so, they do not waste food on a friend who is going to die, nor would Creethar want them to do so.

"It is Wemar that is cruel, not the Wem."

For a moment there was silence except for a soft sighing which Gurronsevas recognized as the sound Earth-humans made while exhaling through the nose, then Murchison said, "Sorry, Gurronsevas. I listened to many of your conversations with Remrath, but I must have missed that one. You are right. But it bothers me when any casualty is subjected to protracted major discomfort."

"Its discomfort will soon be eased, friend Murchison," said Prilicla gently. "Please stand by."

Suddenly the little empath rose high into the air, aided by the gravity nullifier belt set at the Cinrusskin norm of one-eighth G. Its slowly beating, iridescent wings reflected the sunlight like a great, mobile prism. Immediately, the argument around Remrath died into silence as the hunters raised their eyes to watch this strange offworlder who was literally dazzling them with its beauty, and beginning to shade their eyes with their free hands because Prilicla was moving slowly into a line between them and the sun. The altitude and position might have been chosen, Gurronsevas thought, to make the accurate use of weapons difficult. By the time the watchers realized what was happening, it was too late for them to do anything about it. Danalta, Naydrad and the litter bearing Creethar were already halfway to the ship.

As Prilicla turned to fly after them, it said reassuringly, "The emotional radiation from the hunters indicates general confusion, anger, resentment, but not, I think, of sufficient intensity to result in physical violence, and accompanied by very strong feelings of loss. There is little risk of them attacking you, friend Gurronsevas, unless you provide additional provocation. Ask Remrath if it wishes to remain with its friends or return on the ship with Creethar, and extricate yourselves as quickly as possible."

Gurronsevas spent the most unnerving fifteen minutes of his life trying to do just that. The hunters had no objection to Remrath returning to the ship, since the First Cook was too old and infirm to return on foot, but not so Gurronsevas. The off-worlder, they insisted loudly as they gathered around him to cut off his escape, must remain and travel back with them to the mine. He must do this because the creatures in the ship had taken their leader, Creethar, and Gurronsevas was a hostage against its return. They would not harm him unless he tried to escape, or unless Creethar was not returned to them.

Their voices became quieter and almost clinical in tone as they began discussing how best they might overcome the large, thick-skinned off-worlder. Spears and arrows might not be immediately disabling, they thought, so that the best procedure might be to strike heavily at the three legs on one flank with their tails. The creature's legs were short but the body appeared top-heavy, and if it could be toppled onto its side it would have difficulty regaining its feet. The skin of the underbelly appeared to be much thinner than that of the back and flanks so that a spear-thrust into that area would probably be lethal.

They were quite right, Gurronsevas thought, but he was certainly not going to tell them so. He was still trying to think of something to say when Remrath rushed to his defense.

"Listen to me," said the Wem loudly. "You had more brains when you were children. Use them. Do you want to risk an end like Creethar's, with too many of you injured and dying to be carried home? Think of the criminal waste of meat, to yourselves and your young near-adults awaiting your return. We have never seen Gurronsevas fight, because its actions towards us have always been helpful. But this creature is totally beyond your hunting experience.

It weighs twice as much as any two of you, scrawny and half-starved as you are, and I cannot imagine what it might do to you."

Gurronsevas could not imagine what he could do to them, either, so he allowed Remrath to do the talking.

"You do not need a hostage because you already have one," it continued quickly. "Gurronsevas spends all of our waking time in the mine, where it helps with the cooking, instructs and advises the kitchen staff and young trainees in the off-world methods of selecting and preparing edible vegetation, and is helpful in many other ways. We would not want it to be killed, or hurt, or even insulted in any way.

"Besides," Remrath ended, "in my professional opinion as your first cook and preserver, Gurronsevas would be totally inedible."

Surprise and pleasure at the complimentary things Remrath had just said about him kept Gurronsevas silent for a moment. The people in the mine, both young and old, had been talkative but undemonstrative, and he had thought that his presence among them was being tolerated and nothing more. He wanted to say a word of appreciation to the elderly Wem, but he was not out of trouble yet and there were other words he must speak first.

"Remrath is correct," he said loudly. "I am inedible. And Creethar, too, is inedible so far as the off-worlders on our vessel are concerned, because we do not eat meat. Remrath knows this and has given its offspring into our charge because of our greater knowledge and experience in this area. It, and all of you, have our promise that Creethar will be returned to you at the mine as soon as possible."

I am telling the truth, Gurronsevas told himself, but not all of it. *Rhabwar*'s crew and half the medical team were meat eaters, but the meals they consumed on board ship and at Sector General were a product of the food synthesizers, perfect in color, texture, and taste though they were, rather than parts from some hapless food animal—and they would certainly not eat any portion of an intelligent being. Neither did he say whether Creethar would be alive or dead when he was returned to them. He thought he knew which it would be, but the communication of that kind of bad news was better left to medics.

It suddenly occurred to him that the medical team did not know anything about their patient other than what they could see with their scanners, and information on how its injuries had been sustained might be helpful as well as allowing him to change to a less sensitive subject. The Wem were talking rapidly but quietly among themselves, and from the few words the translator picked up they seemed to be less hostile towards him now. He would risk a question.

"If it will not cause distress to you," he said, "can you tell me how Creethar received its injuries?"

Plainly the question did not cause distress because one of them, a hunter called Druuth who had replaced the injured Wem as leader, began describing the event. In complete and often harrowing detail that included the incidents and conversations leading up to and following the event as well as Creethar's own report and instructions before the First Hunter had lost consciousness, the story unfolded.

Gurronsevas formed the impression that the Wem might be talking to excuse or perhaps justify something the hunting party had or had not done.

CHAPTER 28

Soon after dawn on the thirty-third day of the worst hunt that any of them could remember, they discovered the tracks left by an adult twasach and several cubs leading from the muddy edge of a river towards a nearby hillside cave. The larger prints were not deeply impressed into the soft ground, indicating that the adult was either not fully grown or badly undernourished. But it was unlikely to be as close to starvation as its hunters, Druuth thought bleakly, which meant greater danger for the one who had to trap and kill it. Inevitably that one would be First Hunter Creethar, her mate.

In the far past, the ancient, disintegrating books at the mine told of a time when the twasachs had been tree-climbers and eaters of vegetation as well as smaller animals, but since then they had learned to attack and eat anything they could find regardless of its size, which included unwary Wem hunters. This twasach would be particularly dangerous because it was both hungry and naturally protective of its young. But the glorious prospect of trapping an entire twasach family had, in spite of Creethar's repeated warnings, made them both overeager and undercautious.

Druuth understood them well. For too long had they been catching and sharing the tiny and unsatisfying carcasses of rodents and burrowing insects, and then, to hide their shame and try to fill the noisy emptiness of their stomachs, they had left camp one by one to eat secretly the fruit and berries and roots that they had pretended not to see each other gather along the way. But suddenly they were feeling like true Hunters again, brave and proud and about to eat their fill of meat as was their right under the law.

The hillside was steep and rocky, with more sharp-edged stones carpeting the dried-up river bed at its base. There were only a few clumps of vegetation, not very securely rooted, to give a steadying grip for their hands, and the crumbling, uneven ledge leading up to the cave would bear a twasach's weight but was barely wide enough to support one Wem at a time. She followed Creethar along the narrow ledge to the cave mouth and there, clinging precariously to the slope, and with their heavy tails hanging over the ledge and threatening to overbalance them, they deployed the weighted net.

So confident of success were the other hunters that they had begun to erect a smoke-tent to dry and preserve any uneaten meat that remained, and to gather fuel for its slow-burning fires.

Working as quietly as possible, Creethar and Druuth hung the heavy net across the cave mouth, holding it in position by pushing the open mesh over convenient vegetation or wedging it loosely into rocky outcroppings. Then they took up positions on each side of the cave entrance and began shouting loudly and continuously into the dark interior.

They waited, spears ready, for a furious twasach to come charging out and into their net, but it did not come.

Between periods of shouting they tossed loose stones through the mesh and heard them clattering against the floor of the cave. But still there was no reaction except for the frightened bleating of the cubs and a low, moaning sound from the adult. The waiting hunters were growing impatient in their hunger and the words that were being shouted up to their First and Second Hunters were becoming openly disrespectful.

"Nothing is happening here," said Creethar angrily, "and I am beginning to look ridiculous. Help me lift the bottom edge of the net so that I can get under it. Be careful, or it will pull loose."

"Be careful yourself," said Druuth sharply, but too quietly for those below to hear her. "It is easy for them to criticize when their feet and tails are on solid ground. Creethar, hunger is no stranger to us on this hunt and the others we have shared. We can starve for a few more hours until the twasachs have to drink again."

Just as softly Creethar replied, "We cannot wait in this position for long. Already my legs are cramping and if I stretch or move them as I soon must, the ledge will crumble." And in the sure voice of a First Hunter he went on, "Below there! Throw some dried wood up to the ledge, and a lighted torch. If noise does not drive them out then smoke will."

Druuth lifted the net carefully and Creethar moved under it until only his tail remained outside the cave. The adult twasach was still moaning steadily and the cubs were making the soft, excited barking sound which indicated that they might be playing together. By the time the fire was set and kindled, Creethar said that his eyes were ready for a night hunt. He could see that the cave was deeper than expected and that the floor sloped upwards and angled sharply to the left so that the exact position of the animals was hidden from him, but the barking of the cubs was sounding frightened rather than playful. The billowing smoke was affecting his eyes so badly that he could see nothing, he said, and he began backing carefully out onto the ledge.

Druuth realized later that there had been a moment's warning when the moaning sounds ceased, but the beast came silently and so fast out of the smoke that its claws were tearing at Creethar's chest before he could bring up his spear.

In the open the twasach could have been swept loose and knocked unconscious with a disabling tail-blow, but in the confined space of the cave mouth Creethar could only fend it off desperately with arms that were deeply torn and bleeding while he backed carefully onto the ledge where Druuth could use her spear. But not carefully enough.

Suddenly Creethar's feet became entangled in the net. He lost balance and together the attacker and attacked tumbled backwards over the narrow ledge, and, wrapped together in netting, rolled down the rocky slope. By the time the other hunters got to them the twasach, whose body had ended up underneath that of the much heavier Wem, was dead, and Creethar was not expected to survive for long. But he did survive and while he lived, he would continue to hold authority over them because that was the law.

The dead twasach was diseased, its hunger-weakened body so covered with open, suppurating sores that it could not be safely declared edible. In spite of being severely weakened by their own hunger, the hunters had no choice but to obey when Creethar ordered them to leave the suspect carcass where it lay. A few of them wondered aloud about the internal organs which might not be affected, but their remarks were ignored.

They were also ordered to call off the hunt immediately, return to the mine and to bring all five of the cubs with them alive. It was not the first time that young twasachs had been caught by hunting parties, but previously they had been killed singly and in the open, never trapped as a complete litter in their den. For the first time in living memory, and provided the hunters and their families living in near starvation at the mine could control their hunger for a few years, there was the possibility of breeding the cubs into a food herd.

So they built a covered litter for Creethar out of branches and the skins of the smoke-tent and began the slow return to the mine. Even though Creethar was in constant pain and not always clear in his mind or speech, he spent his lucid moments talking to Druuth about the necessity of keeping all of the twasach cubs alive and trying to make them promise to continue doing so should he die before reaching the mine.

This was not strictly according to Wem law, but they did not want to argue and add in any way to the suffering of a greatly respected First Hunter, who was soon to die, or to Druuth, his mate.

Druuth insisted on being one of the litter bearers whether or not it was her turn, so as to make sure the other carriers moved as smoothly as possible over rough ground and to try to talk some of Creethar's pain away. She spoke of many things: of earlier, more successful hunts; of the strange speaking machines dropped at the mine by the off-worlders; but mostly of their first journey together from the lake settlement. Four young adults had made the long, dangerous journey in search of mates, just as the new hunters among the lake people would travel to the mine or other groups for the same purpose, because the children were sickly or damaged in their minds if the Wem mated within their own tribe. Creethar had shown his courage and strength and had claimed his right of first choice by leaving his traveling companions far behind and arriving at the lake three days before they did, and his choice had been Druuth.

But when the going was rough and Creethar's broken bones were grinding together so that she could almost hear his silent screaming in her mind, Druuth talked only about that first mating journey together, and of the things they had said and done during their long, unhurried, and wonderful return to her new home in the mine.

Creethar's deteriorating condition during the return journey was being described in such horrifying detail by Druuth that Gurronsevas was feeling a growing inner distress, and he did not have to be an empath to sense the effect of the words on Remrath, its parent. But before he could speak, the voice of Prilicla said everything that he wanted to say.

"Friend Gurronsevas," said the empath. "The information you have obtained regarding the patient's injuries and subsequent lack of treatment is helpful. But we have enough for the time being, and your friend Remrath is suffering acute emotional distress. Please sever contact with Druuth as quickly as possible and give Remrath the choice of going back in *Rhabwar* or with the hunting party, then return to the ship."

When he relayed the message, Remrath said, "Ancient in years as I am, I could probably walk faster than this starving bunch. But no, I shall return on your ship. There, there are preparations I must make."

Again Gurronsevas sensed the other's distress. In an attempt at reassurance, he said, "Please do not worry, Remrath. The off-worlders on the ship know their business and Creethar is in good hands. Would you like to watch them work?

"No!" said Remrath sharply. In a softer voice it went on, "To you it may appear that I am a weak and cowardly parent. But remember, your off-worlders have asked for this responsibility and I have passed it to them. It is very insensitive of you, Gurronsevas, to ask me to watch what they do to my offspring. This is information I prefer not to know. Please return me to the mine as quickly as possible."

During the return flight the Wem did not spare so much as a glance at the medical team who were working on Creethar, nor did it speak another word to Gurronsevas or anyone else. He tried to imagine how he would have felt if one of his children, supposing there had been any, had been seriously injured and he had been offered the chance to watch the surgeons working on it.

Perhaps Remrath was right and his remark had been most insensitive.

CHAPTER 29

Unlike Remrath, Gurronsevas could not avoid seeing or at least hearing everything that was being done. Each stage of the procedure was being relayed onto the casualty deck's large repeater screen and, since it was the first major operation on a life-form new to the Federation, the procedure was being recorded for future study, which meant that the accompanying verbal commentary was precise and detailed. Even when he directed all of his eyes away from the screen, he could not escape the word-pictures that the voices were painting.

Beyond the direct vision port the steep green slopes of the valley dimmed gradually into the monochrome of twilight and then to the near-absolute darkness that was possible only on a moonless world in a galactic sector where the star-systems were sparse, and still they worked and talked over the patient. But as the first grey hint of dawn diluted the blackness, the work slowed to a stop and the commentary went into the summation phase.

The voices were sounding increasingly concerned.

". . . You will observe," Prilicla was saying, "that the simple and complicated fractures to the leg, fore-limb, and rib cage have been reduced and immobilized where necessary, and the incised and lacerated wounds and abrasions irrigated, sutured and covered with sterile dressings. Because of the Wem physiological data furnished by Tawsar and Remrath, no difficulties were experienced during the surgical repair work. It is the minor injuries, the areas of surface laceration or abrasion associated with the fractures, which are the major cause of concern and which make the prognosis uncertain . . . "

"Translated," said Naydrad, its pointed head turning toward Gurronsevas, "it means the operation was a success but the patient will probably die."

None of the others remonstrated with it. Probably the Charge Nurse was saying only what the medical team was already thinking.

". . . While it is unnecessary to remind some of you," Prilicla went on, for the non-medical Gurronsevas's benefit, "that pathogens evolved on one world cannot affect the life-forms of another, the same cannot be said for the curative medication used by different species. We have developed a single, emergency-use specific that is effective against infections of this type found in the majority of the warm-blooded, oxygen-breathing life-forms, but there are a few species on whom the medication is lethal. Even with Sector General's facilities a lengthy investigation—two or three weeks, at minimum—would be required before it could be declared safe for use on a Wem patient. We took a small risk with the anesthetic . . . "

"We may have to take the big one, Doctor," Murchison broke in sharply. Then in a more clinical voice, it went on, "The patient is severely debilitated, initially by its injuries, then by the continuing trauma of its long journey without treatment, and now by unavoidable post-operative shock. The shock is being controlled, but the only positive measures we have been able to take are running in pure oxygen and intravenous feeding lines. At least we know enough about the Wem basic metabolism not to poison it with an IV drip.

"Whether or not to risk using Wem-untested medication is a

decision that will have to be made very soon," Murchison went on. "Thankfully it isn't mine to make. I don't have to mention the Cromsaggar Incident, because we must all be remembering it, when Lioren used untested medication and came close to committing species genocide. It isn't the fault of the Wem that they know nothing about the treatment of even the simplest injuries or infections. Seemingly, they have learned to accept the idea that a minor injury nearly always results in death or permanent disability. So they have passed responsibility for Creethar's treatment to us, the wonderful, medically advanced off-worlders. And what are we doing? We are trusting to the patient's natural resistance to fight off what should be a minor infection.

"In its present condition I doubt whether the patient has any resistance left."

"The decision is . . ." began Prilicla, then interrupted itself. "Gurronsevas, you are emoting very strongly, a combination of impatience, irritation and frustration characteristic of a person who is in disagreement but wants badly to speak. Quickly please, what is it that you want to say?"

"Pathologist Murchison is too critical of the Wem," Gurronsevas replied. "And wrong. They do treat minor, non-surgical ailments. Usually the kitchen staff double as healers, so that—"

"Are they better healers than they are cooks?" Naydrad broke in, its fur tufting with impatience.

"I am not qualified," said Gurronsevas, "to give an opinion on medical matters, but I wanted to—"

"Then why," said Murchison sharply, "are you interrupting a clinical discussion?"

"Please go on, Gurronsevas," said Prilicla, gently but very firmly. "I feel you wanting to help."

As briefly as possible he described one of his recent food experiments in the mine kitchen, where he was continually trying to find combinations of taste and consistency that would lift the vegetable meals to a level where, so far as the tradition-bound Wem were concerned, they would compete successfully with their remembered meat dishes. He had been trying every variety of root, leaf and berry that he could find, including those he found in a small and apparently little-used storage cupboard. His first attempt to incorporate them into a main dish had led to much unexplained hilarity among the kitchen staff until Remrath had told him that he was using stale materials from their medicinal herbs store.

"From the discussion that followed," he went on, "I learned that, while the Wem would not cut surgically into a living body, they use herbal remedies to treat simple medical conditions. Respiratory difficulties, problems encountered with the evacuation of body wastes, and superficial wounds are treated in this way, usually with hot poultices made from a paste of certain clays and herbs, and grasses to bind the poultice together and allow easier application to the injured area. When I asked them about your patient's injuries, Remrath said that Creethar was seriously and irreparably damaged, that parts of his body had been broken, and that treating the superficial damage would merely prolong suffering that had already gone on for far too long."

While he had been speaking, Prilicla had alighted on the bottom edge of Creethar's bed and was watching Gurronsevas, as silent and still as all the others. The patient's respirator was beginning to sound loud.

Hesitantly, he went on, "If, if I understand you correctly, Creethar's internal injuries, the fractures, have been treated and it is the surface wounds that are causing concern. That was why I mentioned—"

"Gurronsevas, I'm sorry," Murchison broke in again, "I did not think you could make any contribution, and impatience made me forget my manners. Even with the availability of these local folk-remedies whose effectiveness is still in doubt, we may not be able to cure our patient. But its chances *have* improved."

The pathologist laughed suddenly, but it was the sharp, barking sound which, Gurronsevas thought, indicated a release of tension rather than amusement. It went on, "But just look at us! We have the most technologically advanced ambulance ship in known space with, I say in all modesty, a medical team with the experience to match it, and we're back to using dark-age poultices! When Peter gets to hear about this, he will never let us live it down. Especially if the treatment works."

Feeling confused, Gurronsevas said, "I do not know the entity, Peter. Is it important?"

"You do," said Prilicla, wings beating slowly as it rose to hover above the patient. "Peter is the name used by family and friends for Pathologist Murchison's life-mate, Diagnostician Conway, a being who in the past has been no stranger to unusual medical practices. But the matter is not important to our present situation. What is important is that you speak with Remrath as quickly as possible. Ask it for supplies of its herbal medications, with information regarding their application and use. That is important, friend Gurronsevas, and very, very urgent."

Before replying, Gurronsevas turned one eye towards the direct vision port. The valley was still in darkness but the slopes of the mountains were outlined by the grey light of early dawn.

He said, "My memory for colors and shapes and smells, as well as for words of explanation, is excellent. If the matter is urgent there will be no need to talk again with Remrath. I shall leave shortly to begin gathering the necessary herbs and mosses. They are at their most effective when gathered early in the morning."

CHAPTER 30

Over the next four days Gurronsevas kept the ambulance ship
supplied with fresh herbal vegetation when required, together
with the Wem cook-healer's instructions for using it, but he continued to spend as much time as possible in the mine kitchen. His
reasons for doing so were both positive and negative.

Whenever he was present on the casualty deck, Murchison,
Danalta and Naydrad were always worrying aloud about the ethi-
cal implications of a lay person dictating a patient's course of medical treatment, and where the responsibility for treating Creethar
really lay. Nothing was said to him directly, but he did not know
how to answer the unspoken criticism and felt very disturbed by it,
even though he normally considered the opinions of other people
toward him to be of no importance. Since he had left the kitchens
of the Cromingan-Shesk, where his authority had been absolute, his
self-confidence had been under constant and successful attack. It
was not a nice feeling.

Prilicla, who could not help but know of Gurronsevas's feelings, waited until the others were either off-watch or too busy to
listen before drawing him aside so that they could speak privately.

"I understand and sympathize with your feeling of irritation and uncertainty, Chief Dietitian," said the empath, the quiet, musical trilling and clicking of its native speech barely audible above the translated voice in Gurronsevas' earpiece, "as you must try to understand those of the medical team. In spite of the things you have heard them say, they are not being critical of you so much as displaying self-irritation at their own professional inadequacy over the fact that a mere cook—my apologies, friend Gurronsevas, when they take time to think about it they will realize that you are much more than a mere cook—is able to help their patient in ways that they cannot. They can no more help their feelings than you can your own, but I shall suggest gently that they refrain from showing them to you. Until the problem of Creethar is resolved, please make allowances for them. I could not have asked this of the Chief Dietitian who joined the hospital a few months ago. You have changed, friend Gurronsevas. It is for the better."

His confused feelings were clear for the other to read, Gurronsevas knew, so he said nothing.

"For the present," Prilicla went on, "it will be more comfortable for you if you spend as much time as possible with friend Remrath in the mine."

That was not to be as easy as it first appeared. For some reason, Remrath, and to a lesser extent the rest of the kitchen staff and teachers, were acting in an increasingly unfriendly manner toward him. And Prilicla was too far away to read the subtle changes in their emotional radiation that would give him some indication of what he was saying or doing wrong.

Fortunately, the young Wem did not share the feelings of their elders and remained respectful, obedient, curious, and continually excited by speculations regarding the strange culinary marvels their off-world cook would suggest next. Even the returned hunters were sampling his offerings with decreasing reluctance, although, as staunch traditionalists, they still insisted that meat was the only proper food for an adult and that they would continue to eat it.

Considering the pitifully small amount they had brought back from their hunt—with careful rationing there would be barely enough to add a meat flavor to the standard Wem vegetable stew for a few more weeks—their personal shame must have been as great as their hunger. Gurronsevas did not openly disagree with them. He was educating ignorant palates and enticing them into trying new sensations, and generally winning their hearts and minds by a flanking attack through their stomachs. The pretense of losing the occasional battle was of no importance when he knew that he was winning the war.

But the hunters, too, were showing signs of turning against him for no reason that he could see. Unlike Remrath and the other teachers, they had never been friendly or relaxed in his presence, but they had adapted surprisingly well to having an off-worlder in their midst. Over the past few days, however, their behavior towards him had verged on the hostile. In his presence the silences of the Wem adults were lengthening to the point where an attempt to open a conversation with a simple question brought only the briefest and most reluctant of responses, delivered in a tone that should have turned the running water in the kitchen to ice. He could think of no reason for their change of behavior and it was beginning to irritate him. In the circumstances, he decided, it would be better to forget the polite niceties of a first contact situation and ask a simple, direct question.

"Remrath," he said, "why are you angry with me?"

After several minutes without a response, Gurronsevas decided that the question was being ignored. He returned his attention to the preparation of the day's alternative main meal which, in spite of being nicknamed by the Wem 'the off-world option', was one of several dishes he had devised that used only local root and leaf vegetables with an added sauce containing the barest touch of the native herb shuslish which had the effect of lighting a gentle fire on the tongue while stirring the olfactory senses with a warm expectancy. From experience he knew that his dish would be chosen by the majority of the adults and all of the young, and it would be only a few die-hard hunters who would eat the native vegetable stew with its extremely light flavoring of meat. But that was fine, Remrath had told him when they were still talking, because the remains of the hunters' kill preserved in the cold running mountain water weighed less than two pounds, and the less the demand, the longer it would last.

The dish complete, Gurronsevas stepped back to make room for the four young apprentice cooks on this shift, who moved quickly forward to begin spooning out and duplicating his presentation before moving the completed dishes to his newly introduced hot shelves to await serving. One of them—a youth called Evemth, he thought, although he still had difficulty telling near-pubescent Wem apart—had made a small rearrangement to the presentation by adding a few tiny sprigs of driss to the surface of the shuslish sauce, which would not do anything catastrophic to the overall taste but did add a certain visual attraction. The change had been made on only one platter, presumably Evemth's own.

There had been a time when he would have verbally stripped the tegument from an underling who had dared to do such a thing without permission, if only to show the miscreant that The Master was alert and quick to see the smallest of unauthorized changes. But this young Wem was displaying culinary initiative and imagination and was beginning to think and experiment for itself. Evemth, if it was Evemth, showed promise.

"I am not angry with you," said Remrath suddenly.

And black is white, thought Gurronsevas. But this was not the time to start an argument. He felt that Remrath had more to say, and remained silent.

"In a time that surprised us all by its short duration," Remrath went on, "and in spite of your horrendous appearance, we have come to feel at ease in your presence. You have gained our respect and, with one of us at least, our friendship. But we are very angry and disappointed with the preservers on your ship and, as one of the off-worlders, you must share in our anger."

"I understand," said Gurronsevas.

He knew that all of his conversations in the mine were being monitored by *Rhabwar* and *Tremaar,* but for many days they had paid him the compliment of not continually telling him what to ask or answer. There were times, as now, when he would have gladly done without both the compliment and the responsibility.

"But the preservers, like myself, want only to help the Wem. You must all know and believe that. Why are you now so angry with them? And what must I do to regain your friendship?"

In the angry, impatient voice of one who is speaking to a stupid child, Remrath said, "They are continuing to withhold Creethar from us."

Gurronsevas was relieved. It seemed that the two problems had a single solution, the speedy return of their grievously injured hunter. Choosing his words carefully, he said, "Your offspring will be returned to you as soon as possible. I am not myself a preserver so I cannot say with accuracy how long you will have to wait. I shall ask the preservers for their best estimate. Or you could visit the ship and see for yourself what is happening to Creethar and ask them any questions you wish."

"No!" said Remrath sharply, as sharply as it had done on the other occasions when a visit to Creethar was suggested. Angrily it went on, "You are most insensitive, Gurronsevas. It hurts me to say this but I, too, am beginning to suspect you, as well as the other offworlders, of gross and selfish dishonesty. I want you to prove me wrong, and until you do we shall not speak again. Go back to your ship and tell your friends to return Creethar to us without delay."

Remembering his last conversation with Prilicla, Gurronsevas set off for *Rhabwar* wondering if there was anyone anywhere who wanted his company. If it still lived, the Wem patient would talk to him and, hopefully, explain the strange behavior of Remrath and the others. Mysteries and unanswered questions were like heaps of trash littering a mind, and he liked to think that his mind was at least as well-ordered as his kitchens. He would suggest to Prilicla that he be allowed to speak to Creethar on his return.

"I was about to make the same suggestion to you, friend Gurronsevas," the empath said, surprising him. "The situation with the Wem is deteriorating more rapidly than you realize, and for no apparent reason. Did you know that they have broken contact entirely, switched off the communicators we left with them, after telling us that off-worlders were no longer welcome in the mine? Creethar is the only channel of communication left open to us; but it, too, has said repeatedly that it does not want to talk to off-worlders."

Prilicla indicated the patient's bed and flew slowly towards it. No other members of the medical team were present, Gurronsevas noted, possibly because Creethar was no longer in danger, or because it objected strongly to them being there. It was nice to have his supposition proved true.

"Clinically," Prilicla went on, "friend Creethar is doing very well. Since the application of your locally derived medication, its condition has advanced from critical to pre-convalescent. Its emotional radiation, however, is not good. There is a deep and continuing anxiety, a dread, that it is trying to conceal and control. It refuses to discuss the problem with us in spite of my attempts at reassurance . . ."

Not only was Prilicla emotion-sensitive, Gurronsevas reminded himself, the little Cinrusskin was a projective empath as well. Unless there was serious emotional distress present, it could make everyone feel better just by flying into a crowded room.

". . . During our last and very short conversation with it," said Prilicla, "it asked about its parent Remrath, the hunting party, and events at the mine. That was two days ago. Since then it has refused to speak or even listen to us, and it became extremely distressed whenever we tried to discuss the case in its presence, so much so that I switched off its translator whenever we were doing so. It is also refusing to eat. Unknown to it, we are continuing to feed it intravenously; but, psychologically and clinically, we both know that the speedy recovery of a convalescent patient is improved by the intake of solid food. In this case the patient is so gravely weakened by malnutrition that without it Creethar's termination cannot be long delayed.

"But you, friend Gurronsevas, have four distinct advantages over us," the empath continued. "It has not yet met you while conscious. You are not a medic and will therefore not feel the temptation to discuss the patient's clinical condition in its presence. You are a master cook who may be able to discover the patient's food preferences. And lastly, you have first-hand information on recent events in the mine. That is why I would like you to talk to Creethar as soon as possible."

With its iridescent wings beating slowly, the Senior Physician drifted to a halt above the patient's bed before going on. "You have been accepted as a friend by these people, much more so than any of the medical team. But do not assume, because you have grown to like and respect one of them, that they are human. They are not human, whether your yardstick is Earth-human, Cinrusskin-human, or even Tralthan-human like yourself; they are Wem-human. That difference, compounded by something we have said or done wrong, is the reason why they are no longer our friends."

"I will be careful," said Gurronsevas.

"I know you will," said Prilicla. It extended a delicate forward manipulator and briefly touched a stud on the bed console. "I will monitor and report on the patient's emotional response on a closed frequency. Its translator has been switched on. Friend Creethar's eyes are closed but it is awake and listening to us. It is better that I leave you now."

Creethar lay on the treatment bed in a position that allowed the casts enclosing its injured limbs to be suspended comfortably in a system of cross-braced slings that reminded Gurronsevas of the cordage on an old-time sailing ship. The remainder of the body and tail were immobilized by restraining straps, but he did not know whether these were to protect the patient against self-injury or the medical attendants from attack. The casts were transparent and there were no bandages, dressings, or Wem poultices visible, so that he could see that the many infected wounds that had covered the hunter's body were healed or healing. Suddenly it opened its eyes.

"Great Shavrah!" Creethar burst out, its whole body fighting the restraints. "What kind of hulking, stupid beast are *you?*"

Gurronsevas ignored the insult and responded only to the question.

"I am a Tralthan," he said reassuringly. "That is, I am a member of a species larger and perhaps more visually fearsome than the others you have met on the ship. Like them, however, I mean you no harm. Unlike them I am a cook and not a healer. But I, too, wish only to help return you to full . . ."

"A cook who isn't a healer?" Creethar broke in. Its voice was quieter and the body was beginning to relax inside the restraints. "That is strange, off-worlder. Were you incapable of completing your education?"

"My name is Gurronsevas," he said, unable to ignore the second insult in spite of Prilicla's voice in his earpiece observing that convalescent patients were notoriously argumentative. "My early training and subsequent life have been devoted to mastering the culinary arts, and I have no other interests. I am, therefore, a good cook, and that is why I have been asked to help you. Creethar, you must eat before you are returned to the mine, but you refuse ship food. If it is unpalatable to you, explain why and I shall provide an alternative."

Creethar's body moved restively but it did not speak.

"There is an adverse emotional response," said Prilicla, "a return of the feelings of fear and personal loss. I don't know why this should be, but it peaked at your mention of returning it to the mine. Please change the subject."

But the subject was supposed to be food and the necessity for making Creethar eat some, Gurronsevas thought angrily. Then, realizing that the empath was receiving his anger, he calmed himself and went on. "What did you find wrong with the ship food? Did the taste displease you?"

"No!" said Creethar with surprising vehemence. "Some of it tasted like meat, better meat than I had ever tasted before."

"Then I don't understand why you refused . . ." Gurronsevas began.

"But it was *not* meat!" the patient broke in. "It looked and tasted like meat, but it was some strange, other-world concoction from what the winged one called a synthesizer. It is not Wem food. I must not eat it lest it poison my body. You as a cook will understand the importance of meat to the adults of a species, any species. There can be no survival without it."

"As a *Tralthan* cook," said Gurronsevas firmly, "I know no such thing. The majority of my species has not eaten meat for many centuries. They do this out of preference, not because we have the stomachs of grazing animals. My home world, Traltha, and the many Traltha-seeded planets, are well-populated and thriving. You have been believing an untruth, Creethar."

The patient was silent for a moment, then it said slowly, "Your preserver friends have said this to me many times. By your standards the Wem are backward and pitifully uneducated, but we are not stupid. Neither are we small children listening to the wondrous stories told by parents to give us pleasant dreams. Do you expect a grown Wem to believe an obvious untruth because it is told to me by off-worlders?"

Gurronsevas had not been expecting a response like this from a being weakened and still recovering from serious injuries. He thought quickly, then said, "I am aware of the difference between intelligence and education, and that of the two intelligence is of vastly greater importance because it aids the acquisition of education. But there are adult Wem in the mine who are beginning to believe our stories."

"The minds of the aged," said Creethar, "too often resemble those of the very young. I do not know why you are trying to make me eat your strange, sweet-tasting meat from a machine. You are not a friend or family or even a Wem, you do not know or do not care what damage it will do to my body, and you do not have my responsibility towards my people. No matter what you tell me, I will not eat your off-world food."

Plainly Creethar had very strong feelings on the subject, too strong for logical argument to change them, and Prilicla's emotional reading was in agreement. It was time to change the approach.

He said carefully, "The last time you spoke to Doctor Prilicla, who is the beautiful one who flies, you asked about your friends at the mine. I have spoken to Remrath and many of the near adults while working in the kitchen. What would you like to know?"

Even through the translator, Creethar's tone sounded incredulous. "My mother allowed *you* in the kitchen?"

"I am a cook," said Gurronsevas.

It was without doubt the greatest understatement of his long and distinguished professional life, but the patient did not know that.

When Creethar did not respond, he began talking about his impressions of the life and people in the mine. Briefly he described the initial off-worlder contacts with the aged teachers and the Wem young, his decision to spend most of his time there and, after the passage of a few days, the increasing acceptance of his advice by Remrath.

Well did Gurronsevas know that a kitchen and its serving staff was the center for all of an establishment's gossip, scandal and current events. A table server was obvious only when he, she or it was doing something wrong, at other times remaining an inconspicuous part of the background, which meant that diners rarely felt it necessary to guard their tongues. Gurronsevas did not believe in training clumsy food-servers, so the intelligence available in the Wem kitchen was both up-to-date and accurate.

He did not always know the precise meaning, degree of scandal, or humor contained in the conversations he was relaying, but several times Creethar made untranslatable sounds and its body twitched inside the restraints, and gradually Gurronsevas was returning to the subject of food. The purpose of the conversation was, after all, to make the patient eat.

". . . Remrath has been kind enough to adopt many of my suggestions," he went on smoothly, "and they have proved popular not only with the teachers and the young but among a few of your returned hunters who say that—"

"No!" Creethar protested. "Have you given them the poison-ous off-world food from your machine?"

"I have not," said Gurronsevas reassuringly. "The ship's food dispenser is intended for crew use and it lacks the capacity to feed an entire community, so our off-world food was not offered to them. Only you have been offered it because of your gravely weak-ened and starving condition, and you have refused it.

"Your friends in the mine," he went on quickly, "are eating and, most of them have told me, enjoying the local edible vegeta-tion which was thought to be suitable only for children. They eat it because I have shown Remrath many new ways to vary the taste of your vegetable meals, and present them more attractively, and add contrasts of taste with sauces made from herbs and spices which grow all over the valley.

"For example . . ."

Creethar neither moved nor spoke while Gurronsevas, with growing enthusiasm, went on to describe the many changes he had wrought in the mine-dwellers' eating habits. The new ways he had shaped and added spices or soft berries to their coarse-ground flour before baking had met with general approval. He said that his words and Creethar's imagination were a poor substitute for the taste sen-sations he was describing. When he repeated the compliments paid to his cooking by Remrath, and even the arch-traditionalist Tawsar, there was still no response. He was fast running out of things to say.

Trying hard to control his impatience, he said, "Creethar, are you feeling hungry?"

"I am feeling hungry," Creethar replied without hesitation.

"It is feeling hungrier," Prilicla joined in, "with every word you speak."

"Then let me give you food," said Gurronsevas. "Wem, not off-worlder machine food. Surely you can find no fault with that?"

Creethar hesitated, then said, "I am unsure. The Wem food served to the young is well remembered, and it is not a pleasant memory. If you have somehow improved the taste, it may be because you have added off-world substances to it. I cannot take that risk."

In the past Gurronsevas had dealt with his share of overly fastidious diners, and the diet and natural-food fanatics had been particularly difficult, but Creethar was making some of their demands easy by comparison.

"Creethar, you must eat," he said very seriously. "I am not myself a preserver and cannot give a precise estimate, but if you begin taking food regularly you will soon be returned to your people. If you prefer Wem food to that from our machine, I can prepare the simple vegetable stew you remember as a child and, as flavoring, I shall ask Remrath for a little of the meat brought back by your hunting party. Your people are anxious to have you back, and I'm sure they wouldn't mind . . ."

"No!" said Creethar sharply, its body moving weakly against the restraints. "You must not ask my people for meat, or speak to Remrath about me. This you must promise."

"The patient," said Prilicla, "is feeling increasing distress."

I can see that for myself, Gurronsevas thought. But why was it distressed? Had it suffered undiagnosed head injuries and was no longer rational? Or was it simply behaving like a Wem?

Quickly, he said, "Very well, Creethar, I promise. But there is another possibility. Suppose I were to gather edible vegetation from your valley, and show it to you before and during every stage of its preparation and cooking. I will not promise to serve it up in the way that you remember, but I am sure that you will approve of the results. I will not even use the heating system of the food dispenser for cooking, since you might fear contamination, but will personally gather your own natural combustibles and kindle a cooking fire on the deck beside you where you can watch me at work. What do you say now, Creethar? I foresee no difficulty in meeting all of your objections."

"I am very hungry," said Creethar again.

"And you, friend Gurronsevas," said Prilicla warningly, "are being very optimistic."

CHAPTER 31

Naydrad, with the characteristic Charge Nurse's concern for the proper ordering and cleanliness of its medical empire, objected strongly to fires being lit on its aseptically clean casualty deck and wood smoke polluting the atmosphere. Pathologist Murchison said that it was bad enough to be forced back into the medical dark ages of treatment by herbs and poultices without being asked to become smoke-filled-cave dwellers. Doctor Danalta, who could adapt to any environment capable of harboring life, remained aloof but disapproving, and Senior Physician Prilicla tried to keep the peace and reduce the unpleasant emotional radiation in the area. But there were times, as now, when Gurronsevas did nothing to smooth their feelings.

"Now that Creethar has been tempted into eating regularly and in satisfactory quantities for a convalescent patient . . ." he began.

"For a convalescent glutton," said Naydrad.

". . . another and, you will be pleased to hear, non-medical idea has occurred to me," he went on. "During your last clinical discussion, which I could not help overhearing, you stated that the patient was making good progress, but that its recovery would be hastened if meat protein and certain minerals in trace quantities, all of which can be provided by our food dispenser, were added to its food intake.

"My idea is this," he continued. "Since Creethar is afraid of everything produced by the dispenser, even though it has watched us use the casualty deck outlet many times, the patient would be greatly reassured if it were to see us eating Wem food prepared by myself as well as dispenser meals. Hopefully we should be able to convince it that dispenser food will not harm it because Wem food does not harm us. You will then be able to make the required dietary change that will . . ."

Gurronsevas broke off because Naydrad's fur was standing in angry spikes all over its body, Prilicla's fragile body was trembling in the emotional gale that was sweeping the casualty deck, and Murchison, its face turning a deeper pink, was holding up both hands.

"Now just wait one *minute!*" it protested. "It was bad enough you cooking in here and choking us half to death, now you're asking us to eat your disgustingly smelly Wem meals! Next you'll want us to sing Wem songs round the campfire so that it can feel even more at home."

"With respect," said Gurronsevas in a voice that was not particularly respectful, "the temporary pollution was not life-threatening, and on one occasion the Charge Nurse told me that the odor of some of the meals was not unpleasant . . ."

"I said," Naydrad broke in, "that it killed the stink of wood smoke."

". . . You cannot know that a meal is smelly and disgusting until you have tried it," Gurronsevas continued, ignoring the interruption, "because anyone with a semblance of culinary education knows that taste and odor are complementary. I would have you know that some of the Wem vegetable sauces I have created, which I assure you are a taste well worth acquiring, are such that I shall introduce them into the Sector General menu on my return."

"Fortunately," said Danalta, "I can eat anything."

Impatiently, Gurronsevas went on, "I have never poisoned a diner in my life and I do not intend to start now. You all belong to a profession in which objectivity is a prime requirement, so why are you making purely subjective judgments now? My suggestion is that you eat one full Wem meal every day with the patient, always bearing in mind that any toying with food or other visible show of reluctance while eating it would not be reassuring to the patient. After all, it is you people who wanted the patient to eat, and now to incorporate the additional material you consider necessary. I am simply trying to tell you how this can be done."

Gurronsevas did not have to be an empath to sense that another emotional eruption was imminent from Pathologist Murchison and Charge Nurse Naydrad. But it was Senior Physician Prilicla with its firm but gentle authority who spoke first.

"I feel that a spirited exchange of views is about to occur," it said, rising and flying slowly towards the exit, "so I shall excuse myself and retire to my compartment where the resultant emotional radiation will be diluted by distance. I also have the feeling, and my feelings are never wrong, that all of you will remember the purpose of *Rhabwar* and its medical team, and recall the many strange patients and even stranger adaptations we were forced to make while treating them so that we could further that purpose. I will leave you to argue, and remember."

The argument continued, but everyone knew that Gurronsevas had already won it.

During the next four days the Wem found and destroyed the last of the communicating and listening devices left in the mine, and the few words they were able to hear before contact was lost made it plain that the off-worlders had committed a most shameful crime and were worthy only of the deepest scorn. While gathering the early morning vegetation, Gurronsevas tried to speak to a teacher in charge of one of the working parties, but the elderly Wem closed its ear flaps and the young ones had obviously been instructed to ignore him. Since all contact had been severed, the team did not know what crime they had committed or how to apologize for it.

But when Gurronsevas offered to enter the mine uninvited to ask Remrath for an explanation, Prilicla said that the Wem anger and disappointment was so strong that it could detect their feelings even on the quarter-mile distant *Rhabwar,* and it could not risk a further deterioration of the situation, if that was possible.

Creethar, it felt sure, was their only way back to full contact.

Good progress was being made with their patient. Led by Prilicla, who felt that it should set them an example, the medical team were using his Wem menu for their principal meal of the day. They had agreed not to criticize his cooking within the hearing of Creethar, and as he left the patient's side only to gather fresh vegetation every morning, he was not aware of any adverse criticism.

But when Creethar was finally enticed into eating a little dispenser food containing the required medication, and its continuing increase in body mass necessitated easing of its restraining straps, compliments of a kind were forthcoming.

"Today's meal wasn't bad, Gurronsevas," Murchison said grudgingly. "And the lutij and yant dessert could grow on me in time."

"Like a fungus," said Naydrad. But its fur remained unruffled, he noticed, so the Kelgian's disapproval could not have been extreme.

"I liked what you did with the main course," said Prilicla who, when it was unable to say anything complimentary, said nothing. "While the taste and texture were completely different, I would rate it close to my other favorite non-Cinrusskin dish, Earth-human spaghetti with cheese in tomato sauce. But I feel distended and have a need for some flying exercise outside the ship. Would one of you like to accompany me?"

It was looking only at Gurronsevas.

Prilicla did not say anything else to him until they were outside and the ship's protection screen had blinked off to let them through. With the empath hovering close to his shoulder, he walked slowly away from the mine entrance and down into the valley. Their path would pass within one hundred yards of a Wem working party, but he knew that the teacher in charge would ignore them.

"Friend Gurronsevas," the empath said suddenly, "we, but to a greater extent you, are gaining Creethar's trust, and the process would not be aided if we were to exclude it from our conversations by switching off its translator. That is why I wanted to talk to you alone.

"You must already have guessed that Creethar is ready for discharge," it went on. "Apart from one immobilized lower limb, whose cast is timed to dissolve in two weeks' time when the fractured bones have knitted fully and will support its weight, it has healed well. It should be happy, relieved and pleased at the prospect of returning to its normal life, but it is not. I am far from happy with our patient's emotional state. Something is badly wrong, and I would like to know what it is before I send Creethar back to its friends. That will be no later than two days from now because there is no clinical reason for keeping it longer."

Gurronsevas remained silent. The other was restating a problem, not asking a question.

Prilicla went on. "It may well be that returning Creethar to its people will solve all our problems. Hopefully, it will reduce their present hostility towards us, restore Remrath's personal friendship with you and enable us to resume friendly contact. But there is something about them that we do not fully understand, something that causes inexplicable emotional responses in our patient. Unless we completely understand the reasons for its unnatural feelings, sending it home could be another and even greater mistake. I cannot tell you what to say or ask, because the most general and superficial remarks about its parent Remrath, its hunter friends, and life in the mine are met with a disproportionately severe emotional reaction, which resembles that of a fearing person whose deeply held beliefs are under attack.

"I know that you are not a trained psychologist, friend Gurronsevas," Prilicla continued, "but do you think that you could spend the next two days talking to Creethar? Talk about safe generalities while listening, as we all will be, for the specific items of information which, in my own experience, many beings suffering emotional distress of this kind are secretly wanting to reveal. If, during the course of the dialogue there is anything that the team should do or refrain from doing, or an idea that might be helpful occurs to you, tell us. You will be in effective charge of the non-medical treatment.

"Creethar trusts you," Prilicla ended. "It is more likely to tell its troubles to you than to any of us. Friend Gurronsevas, will you do this for me?"

"Haven't I already been doing that," said Gurronsevas, "unofficially?"

"And now," the empath replied, "it is an official request by *Rhabwar*'s medical team leader for specialist assistance in a crucial stage of the Wem contact. This must be done because, if you are unsuccessful, the responsibility will be entirely mine. You must not blame yourself for anything that may go wrong and, in this very unusual situation, neither will the rest of the medical team. You are not an easy person to like, friend Gurronsevas. You too closely resemble some of your recent Wem dishes in that you are an acquired taste. But you have gained our respect and gratitude for your assistance with Creethar, and none of us will blame you if you fail to resolve a problem that has already baffled us. How do you feel about this, friend Gurronsevas?"

For a moment Gurronsevas was silent, then he said, "I feel complimented, encouraged, reassured, and anxious to do everything that I can possibly do to help. But, being an empath, you already know my feelings, and I think it was your intention to make me feel this way."

"You are right," said Prilicla, and gave a short trilling, untranslatable sound that might have been Cinrusskin laughter. "But I have not been tinkering with your emotional radiation. The feeling of wanting to help was already there. Now I feel you wanting to say more."

"A few suggestions, yes," said Gurronsevas. "I think you

should decide on the exact time and place of Creethar's return and inform Remrath and the others, in case there are preparations they may want to make. We know they are anxious to have Creethar back, and telling them when would be a politeness that might reduce their hostility towards us. The best time would be in the early forenoon, I think, when the working parties and teachers are returning for their midday meal. That would ensure a large number of spectators and maximum effect, but whether the effect will be good or bad I cannot say."

"Nor I," said Prilicla. Quickly it gave the time and circumstances of Creethar's discharge, then went on, "But how will you tell them, when they close their ears whenever we try to speak? Have you forgotten that problem? Because I cannot feel you worrying about it."

Gurronsevas had always tried to avoid waste, whether of time, material, or breath. Instead of answering the question he stopped, rotated his massive body slightly so as to bring his speaking mouth to bear on the Wem work-party which was less than two hundred yards away, and filled his lungs.

"This is an announcement from the preservers on the off-world ship," he said, slowly and distinctly and very loudly. "The hunter Creethar will be delivered to the mine entrance at one hour before noon on the day after tomorrow."

He could see the Wem teacher's ear flaps close at the first words, and hear the anger in its voice as it tried to make the students do the same while Gurronsevas repeated the announcement. But it was not succeeding because the young ones were hopping around their instructor in small circles and shouting excitedly to each other. He knew that the Wem adults had closed their ears to the off-worlders, but there was no way that they could stop listening to their own children.

The news about Creethar's return would be all over the mine by nightfall.

"Well done," said Prilicla, making a graceful, banking turn so that it again faced the ship. "But now you have a lot more talking to do. Let us return to our patient."

It was almost as if Creethar had become Gurronsevas's patient. They were left alone on the casualty deck for long periods while the medical team stayed in their quarters or on *Rhabwar*'s tiny dining and recreation deck. He knew that Williamson on *Tremaar* was recording everything that was said, but the other Captain's comments or criticisms were withheld so that he could talk to the patient without distractions.

He found it easy to talk to Creethar but difficult to remain on a topic which would not quickly cause it to stop talking back. Prilicla reported that its silences were invariably accompanied by severe emotional distress in which fear, anger and despair predominated. And still Gurronsevas and the listening empath could find no reason for these sudden bouts of reticence.

Talking about the Wem and their centuries-long fight for survival on a world brought close to death by the uncontrolled pollution of the distant past was a safe if not a pleasant subject, except when they disagreed about the importance of meat-eating for successful procreation. In the Old Times, Creethar said, the grasslands and forests were filled with tremendous herds of animals. The herds and teeming jungle creatures had long since vanished, but the eating of meat, even the small and infrequent morsels available after an unsuccessful hunt, had become a kind of non-spiritual religion.

In answer Gurronsevas agreed that the hunters were worthy of the meat they ate, since it was obtained after long periods of travel and hardship and great personal risk. But the growers of vegetation who stayed at home produced more food with fewer risks and none of the respect accorded the brave hunters. It was thus on Wemar now, just as it had been on countless worlds for many centuries.

Prompted by Prilicla, he told it that meat-eating in the far past had been a matter of availability, convenience and choice rather than a physiological necessity. He reminded it that as a general rule the vegetable-eating young and the very old Wem were healthier and better fed than the meat-eaters, who often starved themselves into unnecessary sickness because of their hunters' pride. The result was an angry silence that lasted for nearly an hour.

Still Creethar was not fully convinced that meat was unnecessary for sexual potency, but after a few days of eating Gurronsevas' Wem vegetable dishes its conditioning, he felt sure, was beginning to crumble.

Food was a fairly safe topic, especially the preparation and presentation of Gurronsevas's most recent Wem dishes, but when he tried to veer off the subject to talk about Creethar's hunter friends, or about Remrath or the good work that the young cook apprentices were doing in the mine, it stopped talking. Once it said angrily that the kitchen was not a suitable place nor was cooking proper work for a young Wem. When Gurronsevas asked why not, Creethar accused him of stupidity and lack of feeling.

Remrath had accused him of insensitivity, also without giving an explanation, just before Gurronsevas had been sent away from the mine. Feeling puzzled and intensely frustrated, he returned to the subject of food.

That was the one topic that he was able to discuss with complete authority. Gurronsevas could talk about food in all its multitudinous forms and flavors, and with it the weird and even more wonderful variety of beings who had been served his culinary creations. Of necessity this led into a discussion about off-worlders, their beliefs and philosophies and social practices, including the individual preferences and eating habits of the sixty-odd different species which together made up the Galactic Federation.

He was trying very hard to plant the idea in Creethar's mind that Wemar was one inhabited planet of many hundreds, while hoping that among the other intelligent species he was describing there might be one society whose behavior was similar enough to that of the Wem for the other to react, emotionally or verbally, in a manner that would enable Prilicla or himself to put a crack in this wall of Wem silence.

But Creethar's emotional and verbal responses were unchanged.

Prilicla said, "I, too, feel and share your disappointment, friend Gurronsevas. Creethar feels a deep interest and curiosity about the things you are telling it, and there is an even stronger feeling of gratitude towards you because your conversation is taking its mind off some serious personal trouble. But its despair and anger and fear are still present and have been reduced but not changed by anything you have said to it.

"The patient's strongest feeling at present is of friendship towards you," Prilicla went on. "You may not be consciously aware of it, but you have developed the same feeling towards it, just as you did following prolonged contact with its parent, Remrath. But I feel increasing weariness in both the patient and yourself. With rest a new approach to the problem may suggest itself."

"Creethar is due for discharge in less than seven hours," said Gurronsevas. "I think we have been overcautious in concealing the news of its imminent release. Now is the time to tell it. We have little to lose."

In a gentle, reproving voice Prilicla said, "I can feel your frustration, Gurronsevas, and I sympathize. But every time you even hinted at the subject of its return to the mine, there was an adverse emotional response followed by a long, angry silence. There is much to lose."

For a moment Gurronsevas was silent, then he said, "You tell me that Creethar and myself feel friendship for each other. But tell me, are we good enough friends to be able to excuse each other's bad behavior, insults or unintended hurtful words?"

Without hesitation the empath replied, "I feel your determination. You will tell Creethar the news whatever answer I give. Good luck, friend Gurronsevas."

For a moment Gurronsevas said nothing as he tried to choose words that were right and at the same time would excuse him in advance for any hurt they might cause this strange being who had become his friend, then he said, "There is much I want to say to you,

Creethar the First Hunter, and many questions I would like to ask. I have not asked them before now because, whenever I tried to do so, you grew angry and would not speak to me. Remrath will not speak to me either and, for reasons we do not understand, has forbidden the off-worlders to return to the mine. But now we have only a few hours left to talk together, and exchange questions and answers . . ."

"Be careful," said Prilicla. "Creethar's emotional radiation is changing, and not for the better."

". . . Your wounds and infections are healed and clean," he went on carefully, "and your physical condition is as good as we can make it. You will be returned to the mine before noon."

Creethar's body jerked suddenly against its restraints, something it had not done for many days, then became still. Its face turned suddenly towards Gurronsevas, but the eyes were tightly closed. What stupid piece of xenophobia or cultural conditioning, he wondered angrily, could cause such a severe reaction in a mind that he knew to be intelligent, civilized and in many ways admirable? He was not an empath, but Prilicla's next words told him only what he already knew.

"The patient is becoming seriously disturbed," said Prilicla urgently. "The feelings of friendship towards you are being negated by an upsurge of the background fear-anger-despair emotions that troubled it earlier. But it is fighting very hard to subdue those adverse feelings towards you. Can you say something that will help? Its distress is increasing."

Gurronsevas sub-vocalized a word that he had been forbidden to speak as a child and had only rarely used as an adult. The patient's reaction to what should have been good news was all wrong, and suddenly he felt both unsure of himself and angry that he was causing anguish to a friend without knowing how or why. In all other respects Creethar's thought processes and conversation were normal, but in this one respect the Wem was totally alien. Or was it the medical team, or even Gurronsevas himself who in this single respect were alien, and if so how?

He was missing something, Gurronsevas felt sure, some essential difference that was both simple and vitally important. An idea was beginning to stir in the depths of his mind, but trying to coax it out into the light seemed only to drive it deeper. He wanted to ask Prilicla for advice, but he knew that if he bypassed the translator to do so, Creethar would think that he was keeping secrets from it, and that would not be the right thing to do just now.

He did not know what to say, so he said what he felt.

"Creethar," he went on, "I feel confused, and guilty, and very, very sorry for the mental pain I am causing you. Somehow I have failed to understand you. But please believe me, it is not now and has never been my intention or that of the others on the ship to hurt you. Nevertheless we, and especially I through ignorance and insensitivity, have caused you past and present mental anguish. Is there any apology I can make, or anything else that I can say or do that will ease it?"

Creethar's body grew tense but it was not fighting the restraints. It said, "For such a fearsome creature you can be sensitive at times and grossly insensitive at others. There is something that you might do for me, Gurronsevas, but I am ashamed to speak the words. It is not the kind of favor that one ever asks of a relative or a close friend, or even a new, off-worlder friend like yourself, because it would be distressing for them."

"Ask it, friend Creethar," said Gurronsevas firmly, "and I shall do it, whatever it is."

"When, when my time comes," said Creethar in a voice that was barely audible, "will you go on talking to me about the wonders you have seen on other worlds, and stay close to me until the end?"

The brief silence that followed was broken by Prilicla, who said, "Gurronsevas, why are you feeling so *happy?*"

"Give me a few minutes to talk to it," he replied, "and Creethar and the rest of you will feel happy, too."

CHAPTER 32

The litter bearing Creethar had its sun canopy fully deployed so that the patient was hidden from sight. When Prilicla had said that it was only fitting that Gurronsevas and no one else should accompany it to the mine entrance, the only objection had come from Naydrad who was worried by the thought of an inexperienced driver being in charge of an anti-gravity vehicle.

Tawsar, the returned hunters, and all of the teachers with the exception of Remrath had been joined by the young working parties, so that the slope outside the mine entrance was covered by tightly-packed Wem bodies, except for a small area at the front of the crowd that contained three small handcarts. Slowly and silently Gurronsevas guided the litter to within a few yards of the carts, then reduced power to the anti-gravity grids. While the litter was settling to the ground he opened the canopy to reveal Creethar.

The assembled Wem were hushed and respectful as befitted the occasion, their feelings towards the off-worlders remaining hidden. Even the youngest of the children were silent as the crowd stared at the still figure of their former First Hunter whose body was clean and undamaged except for its right hind-limb, which was encased in a transparent cast. But when Creethar raised its head sud-

denly and stepped onto the ground the reaction, the sudden out-
burst of shouting and screaming, and the milling about of Wem
bodies, was beyond anything in Gurronsevas' experience. He wondered how this storm of emotional radiation was affecting Prilicla
on *Rhabwar*.

But the empath had been gently insistent that, following their
lengthy pre-discharge conversation with Creethar, there would be
no risk. The expected emotional storm, it felt, would be comprised
of shock, surprise and uncertainty, with minimum hostility. After
all, it had been Creethar's own idea to hide the facts from its own
people until the last possible moment so that its homecoming
would have the maximum effect.

Limping only slightly, Creethar moved close to the hand-carts
and stopped to look down at them. The noise from the crowd made
it difficult to think, but rather than inarticulate screaming and
shouting, the sound was changing to that of many conversations
that were being shouted only because everyone else was shouting.
And the movements within the crowd had almost ceased, but one
eye showed him a young adult who looked like Druuth disappear-
ing into the mine entrance, hopefully on the way to fetch Remrath.
The others brought him the picture of Creethar looking up from
the carts and raising its arms for silence.

"My family, friends and fellow hunters," it said slowly and
clearly when silence finally came, "you have made a serious mistake regarding the intentions and the abilities of the off-worlders
on the ship. It is the same mistake that I was making until a few
hours ago. But now you can see for yourselves that I am not a dismembered collection of dead meat ready to be loaded onto these
carts and taken to the kitchen. I am alive, and strong, and healthy.
This is because our off-world friends are not and have never been
preservers of meat.

"They are preservers of *life.*"

Creethar paused. From the crowd there came a sighing sound,
like a wind blowing gently over grass, as they all seemed to inhale
as one in surprise and wonder. But silence returned as it resumed

talking, describing all the things that had been said and done to it by the off-worlders. Only once did it stop, when its parent and its mate appeared suddenly in the mine entrance and began pushing their way to the front of the crowd. But Remrath gestured for Creethar to go on speaking and walked past it to stand beside Gurronsevas.

In a voice that carried only to him, it said, "We grievously misjudged your friends on the ship and, after all that you have done for us, you most of all. I was thinking too much like an ignorant and backward Wem, and I am sorry. You, and your preserver friends, are again welcome in our home."

"Thank you," said Gurronsevas in matching voice. "I, too, am deeply sorry, for being so stupid and insensitive, and for not listening with more care to the words you were saying to me. It was a misunderstanding."

A misunderstanding . . .

Gurronsevas cringed inwardly with shame and embarrassment at the memory of some of the things he had said to Remrath. At the time he had thought it strange and rather charming, but not important, that the arts of cooking and healing were practiced by the same person, and that among the Wem these individuals were also known as preservers. If he had been thinking properly he would have realized that in a society that had come to regard the eating of their increasingly scarce food animals as their only long-term hope of survival, meat from any source would not have been wasted. The clues had been plain for him to see. And when he had used the word "preservers" while referring to the medical team, believing that "healer" and "preserver" were synonymous so far as the Wem language was concerned, he had not been thinking at all.

If their positions had been reversed and Remrath had offered to tell Gurronsevas in detail what the off-world preservers—the beings who were thought to be responsible for cleaning and cutting away infected tissues and sectioning-up and preparing the edible body parts for the kitchen as would technicians in a slaughterhouse—were doing to his beloved offspring, physical violence rather than an angry silence and expulsion from the mine might have been the result.

The Wem had been forced to regress in many areas, but they still retained their intelligence and a civilized culture. That was why Prilicla had felt that it would be better for the contact to be renewed by their ex-patient and, as usual, the empath's feeling had been accurate and Creethar was doing fine.

". . . The off-worlders came here to tell us how we can live better lives on our sick but recovering world," Creethar was saying, "but it is only knowledge and advice they bring us. They have explained how and why the sickness came to Wemar many centuries ago, and how we can cure that sickness and keep it from returning . . ."

Knowing that the Wem had long since lost the precise language of science, Gurronsevas and Prilicla had described the ecological catastrophe that had befallen Wemar in simple words, and Creethar was doing the same. In words that they and it understood, Creethar described Wemar's centuries-past Time of Plenty and the terrible, continuous poisoning of the land, sea and air and the creatures who lived on or in them, and on which that short-lived Golden Age depended. It told of the vast quantities of noxious vapors that had been released into the air, to find their way high into the sky where they attacked and destroyed the vast shield that protected all of Wemar from the harmful parts of their sun's light.

Gradually the smallest and most delicate sea-dwellers, those on which the larger fish and in turn the Wem depended for food, perished from the polar and temperate oceans. On land the unshielded sunlight blighted or killed the vegetation that fed the small and large grazers who fed the predators and the Wem themselves. Under the two-pronged attack of starvation and the sickness of a daylight that blinded the eyes and caused uncovered parts of the body to dry and rot away, all forms of animal life were dying in their millions. Their planet was withering and its depleted population shrinking with every weak and sickly generation that was born.

But the Wem who had brought down this catastrophe upon

themselves were tough and adaptable, and so, although they had no way of knowing it at the time, was their world. The entire planetary population sickened and the technology that had housed them and harvested their food and processed their meat collapsed in ruins all around them. But a tiny proportion of them did not die, because they learned to protect themselves and their children from the deadly, invisible part of their once friendly and health-giving sunlight, and the few that remained relearned how to live in caves like their earliest ancestors. They grew crops in tiny areas of sheltered valleys, and traveled, hunted, and fished by night. The growing of vegetables and edible grains out of the direct sunlight was not a popular activity because, until the coming of the off-worlder master of cooks, Gurronsevas, it was believed implicitly that the diet of a healthy and virile adult Wem had to consist predominantly of fish or meat.

Holding stubbornly to the belief in meat-eating had been causing the remaining Wem to die, either from starvation or unnecessarily in the hunt. For the docile food animals were long gone and the few species that had adapted to become nocturnal, cave-dwelling predators had lost their docility. A similar adaptation had occurred in the sea depths where large fish attacked and ate each other or Wem fish hunters.

". . . But the monstrous reduction of population," Creethar was saying in a declamatory voice, "and the death of all transport and manufacturing technology had one beneficial effect: it enabled the ailing Wemar to begin its recovery. Over the centuries the great living creature that is our home world has dispersed and dispelled the poisons from the land and sea and partially renewed the invisible shield above us, which allows only heat and light to reach the surface. As a result, the plants are beginning to grow again and the animals and sea creatures forsake their caves and burrows and ocean depths and thrive; but for many generations we must husband our food resources by breeding animals, not hunting and eating them to extinction because of our unnecessary hunger for meat, until we have completed the work of replenishing our planet.

"But the off-worlders advise caution," Creethar continued. "Prolonged exposure to sunlight will still harm us, but not to the extent that it did in the past, and our children's children it will not harm at all. Other problems face the Wem when the surviving families and tribes join together again; we must persuade the Fat Ones at the equator to give up their simple but very dirty technology. We must do this peacefully, the off-worlders say, by using our minds rather than our spears, because there are too few Wem remaining on Wemar for violent solutions. And when we begin to redevelop our technology, they will advise us on methods of keeping it clean so that we will not poison our world again . . ."

"Your offspring," said Gurronsevas softly, "is speaking very well. I am impressed."

Remrath dismissed the compliment with an untranslatable sound, but it sounded pleased as it said, "As a youth Creethar was a teacher and a debater long before he became an adult hunter, and he will not allow anyone to forget the new wisdom you have given us. Of that you and your off-worlder friends can be sure."

"When I was telling Creethar about these matters," Gurronsevas went on, "my intention was only to take its mind off some deep worry that was troubling it. It was only early this morning that I discovered that it was worried about what it thought was its imminent death. Now it seems to understand the true meaning of what it heard better than I did. But then, I am only a cook."

"A First Cook who will change the eating habits of a world," said Remrath. It allowed time for Gurronsevas to make his own untranslatable Tralthan reaction to a compliment before going on. "Everyone assembled here, from the youngest to the oldest, came to mourn and celebrate Creethar's return to us, and to share and eat the meat of his body. Instead they are digesting the words of the off-worlders and Creethar the Hunter and Teacher."

Prilicla's voice sounded in his earpiece. It said, "This is going very well, friend Gurronsevas, as I felt it would. Even the contactors on *Tremaar* are pleased with you. Captain Williamson sends its compliments and says that it was a stroke of genius on the hospital's part to send its Chief Dietitian on the Wemar mission, and the report that it is sending to Sector General on what must be the first known instance of culinary first contact will make them very pleased with you as well. I felt I should give you the news without delay, since you may still be feeling uneasy about Colonel Skempton's reaction to your return. There is no need to worry. The Wemar success will ensure that your past misdemeanors will be forgiven and forgotten. Good, I feel your pleasure and relief."

". . . Very soon Gurronsevas and the preservers of the ship must leave," Creethar was saying. "They are fearsome beings, especially their master of cooks, who is a creature out of the most terrifying dreams of children. But even the youngest have met it and come to call it friend. The off-worlders cannot stay long with us because there will be much work awaiting them on other worlds or amid the wreckage of the great ships which travel the dark spaces between the stars, where they will be needed to heal and repair sick or damaged beings so that their lives will be preserved as was mine. They told me that the other off-worlders who follow them will not stay long among us either, because they know that the Wem are a proud and able species. They will help us gladly, but they will not allow us to become too dependent upon that help, for that could give us a sickness of the mind that would be permanently crippling. Instead they will help us to help ourselves.

"If we do this, they say, then the time taken for us to replenish our planet, rebuild our civilization and technology, and finally to visit our off-world friends among the stars, will be short indeed . . ."

"My friend," said Remrath very seriously, "we will not eat meat tonight, and I and Druuth and all of us are glad. Thank you."

Gurronsevas was uncomfortable with displays of emotion, especially his own. He looked around at the cheering crowd, and finally said, "A last-minute change of menu like that can be a real problem for the kitchen staff. Can you use another cook?"